KAIJUMAX
SEASON FOUR
SCALY IS THE NEW BLACK

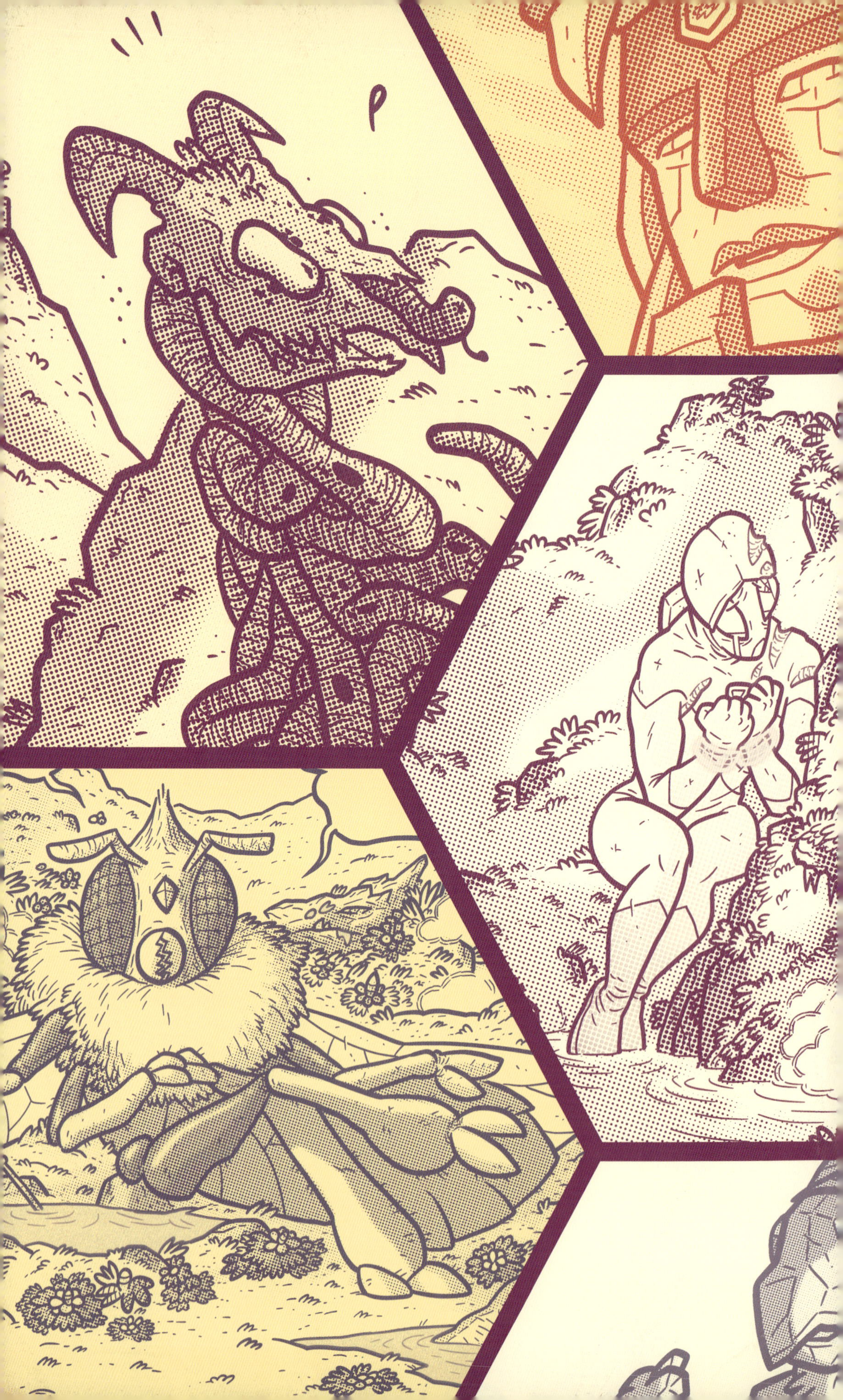

KAIJUMAX
SEASON FOUR
SCALY IS THE NEW BLACK

By Zander Cannon

Color assists by Jason Fischer

Designed by Dylan Todd
Logo by Zander Cannon

Edited by Desiree Wilson

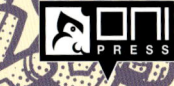

An Oni Press Publication

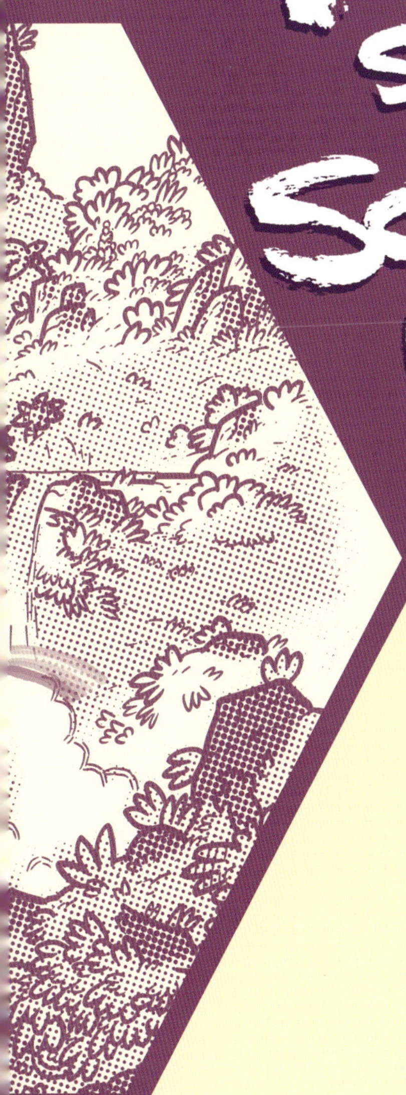

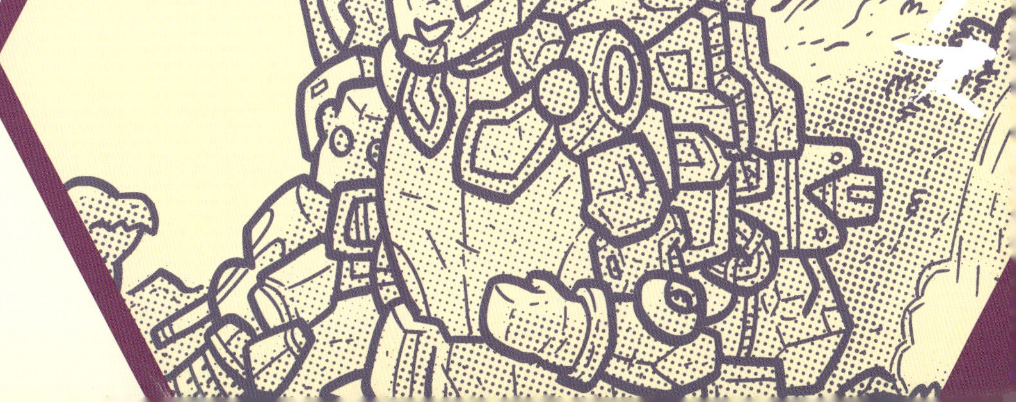

Published by Oni Press, Inc.
Joe Nozemack, founder & chief financial officer
James Lucas Jones, publisher
Sarah Gaydos, editor in chief
Charlie Chu, v.p. of creative & business development
Brad Rooks, director of operations
Melissa Meszaros, director of publicity
Margot Wood, director of sales
Sandy Tanaka, marketing design manager
Amber O'Neill, special projects manager
Troy Look, director of design & production
Kate Z. Stone, senior graphic designer
Sonja Synak, graphic designer
Angie Knowles, digital prepress lead
Robin Herrera, senior editor
Ari Yarwood, senior editor
Desiree Wilson, associate editor
Kate Light, editorial assistant
Michelle Nguyen, executive assistant
Jung Lee, logistics coordinator

onipress.com
facebook.com/onipress
twitter.com/onipress
onipress.tumblr.com
instagram.com/onipress

KAIJUMAX.COM
zandercannon.com / @zander_cannon
studiojfish.com / @studiojfish
@bigredrobot

This volume collects issues #1-6 of the Oni Press series *Kaijumax: Season Four*

First edition: September 2019

ISBN 978-1-62010-663-1
eISBN 978-1-62010-664-8

KAIJUMAX SEASON FOUR: SCALY IS THE NEW BLACK, September 2019. Published by Oni Press, Inc. 1319 SE Martin Luther King Jr. Blvd., Suite 240, Portland, OR 97214. KAIJUMAX is ™ & © 2019 Zander Cannon. All rights reserved. Oni Press logo and icon artwork created by Keith A. Wood. The events, institutions, and characters presented in this book are fictional. Any resemblance to actual persons, living or dead, is purely coincidental. No portion of this publication may be reproduced, by any means, without the express written permission of the copyright holders.

PRINTED IN CHINA.

Library of Congress Control Number: 2019932874
1 3 5 7 9 10 8 6 4 2

EPISODE

1

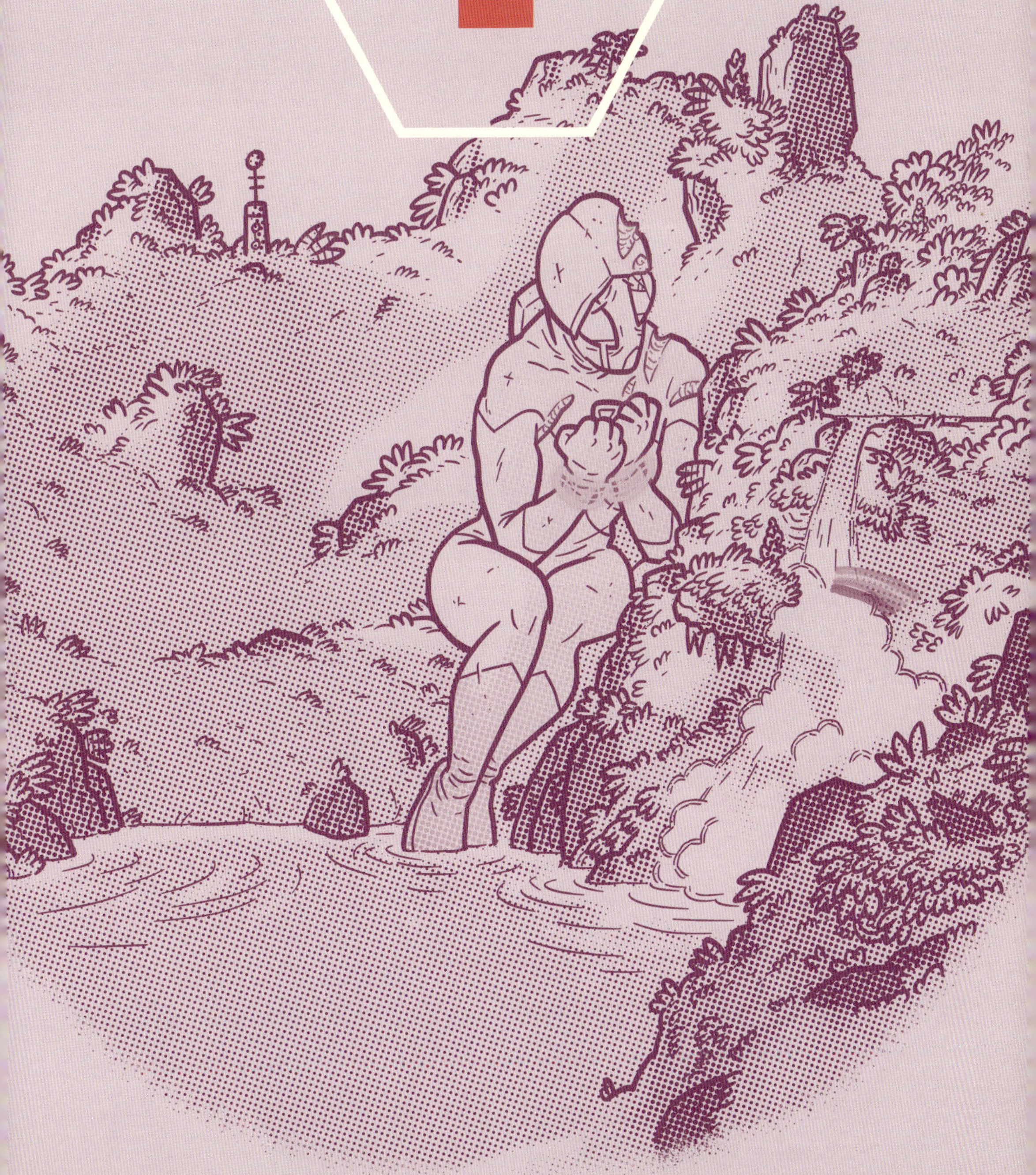

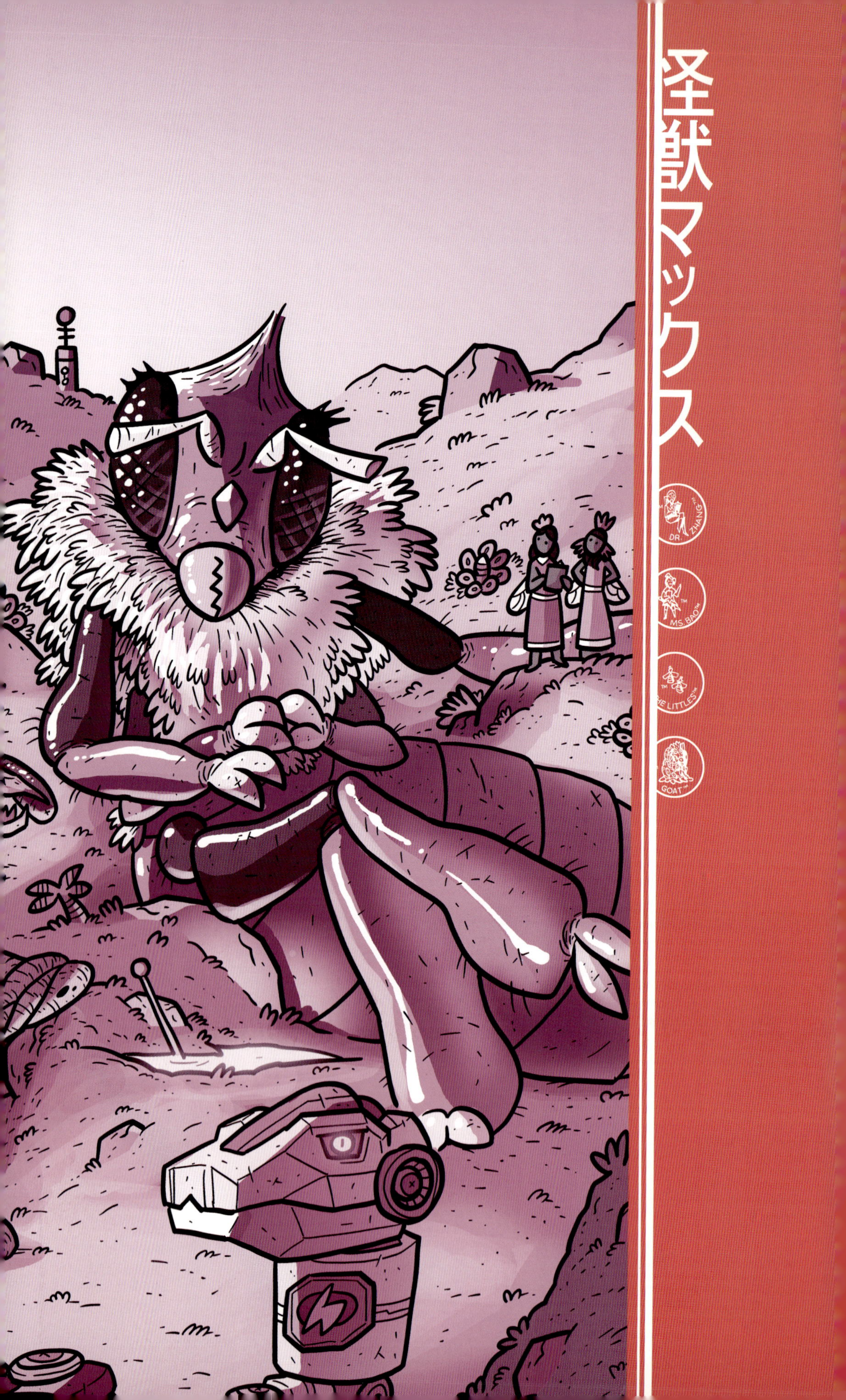

怪獣マックス
DR. ZHANG™
MS. BAO™
HE LITTLES™
GOAT™

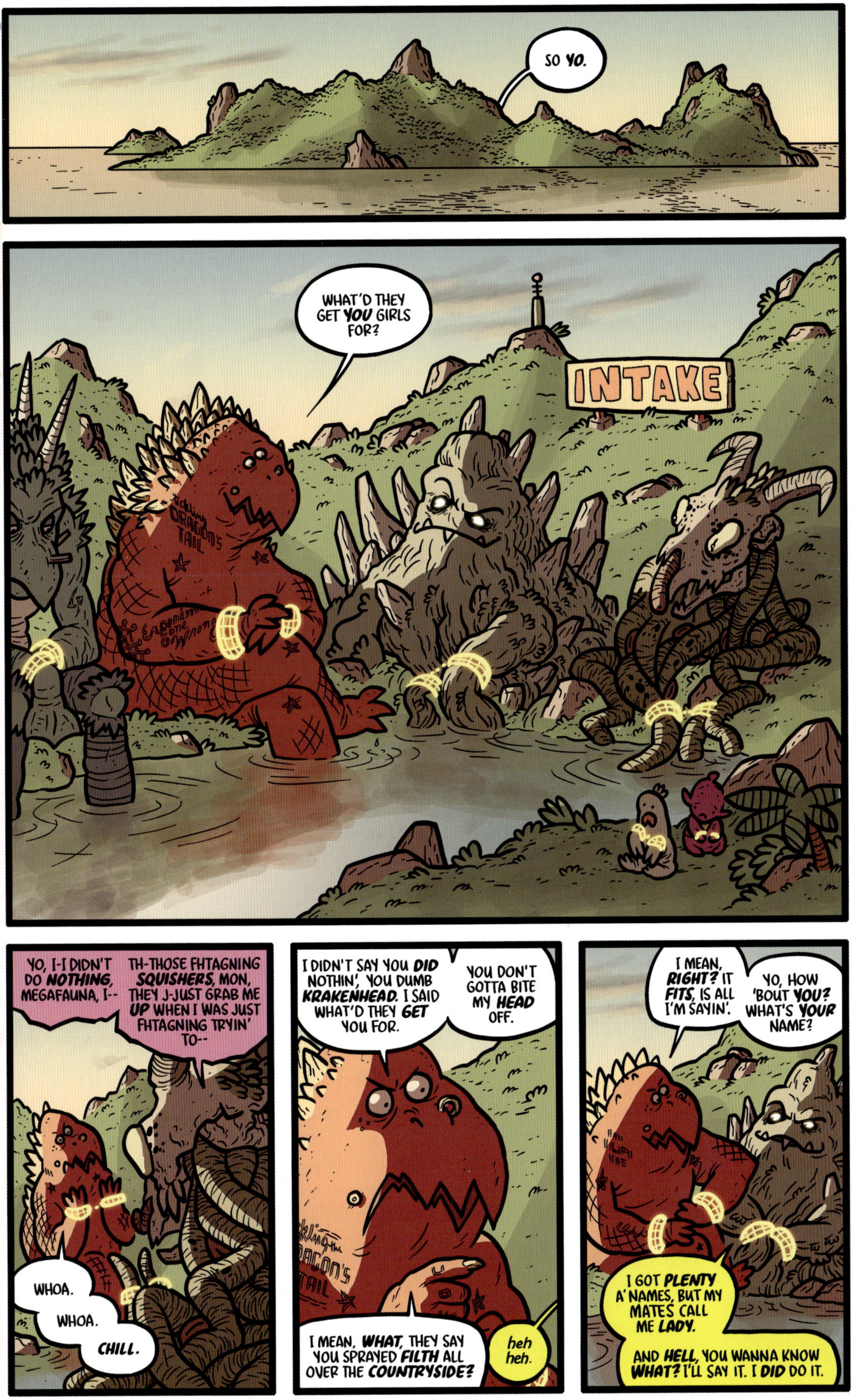
SO **YO.**
WHAT'D THEY GET **YOU** GIRLS FOR?
INTAKE
YO, I-I DIDN'T DO **NOTHING**, MEGAFAUNA, I--
TH-THOSE FHTAGNING **SQUISHERS**, MON, THEY J-JUST GRAB ME **UP** WHEN I WAS JUST FHTAGNING TRYIN' TO--
WHOA.
WHOA.
CHILL.
I DIDN'T SAY YOU **DID** NOTHIN', YOU DUMB **KRAKENHEAD.** I SAID WHAT'D THEY **GET** YOU FOR.
YOU DON'T GOTTA BITE MY **HEAD** OFF.
I MEAN, **WHAT**, THEY SAY YOU SPRAYED **FILTH** ALL OVER THE **COUNTRYSIDE?**
heh heh.
I MEAN, **RIGHT?** IT **FITS**, IS ALL I'M SAYIN'.
YO, HOW 'BOUT **YOU?** WHAT'S **YOUR** NAME?
I GOT **PLENTY** A' NAMES, BUT MY MATES CALL ME **LADY.**
AND **HELL**, YOU WANNA KNOW **WHAT?** I'LL SAY IT. I **DID** DO IT.

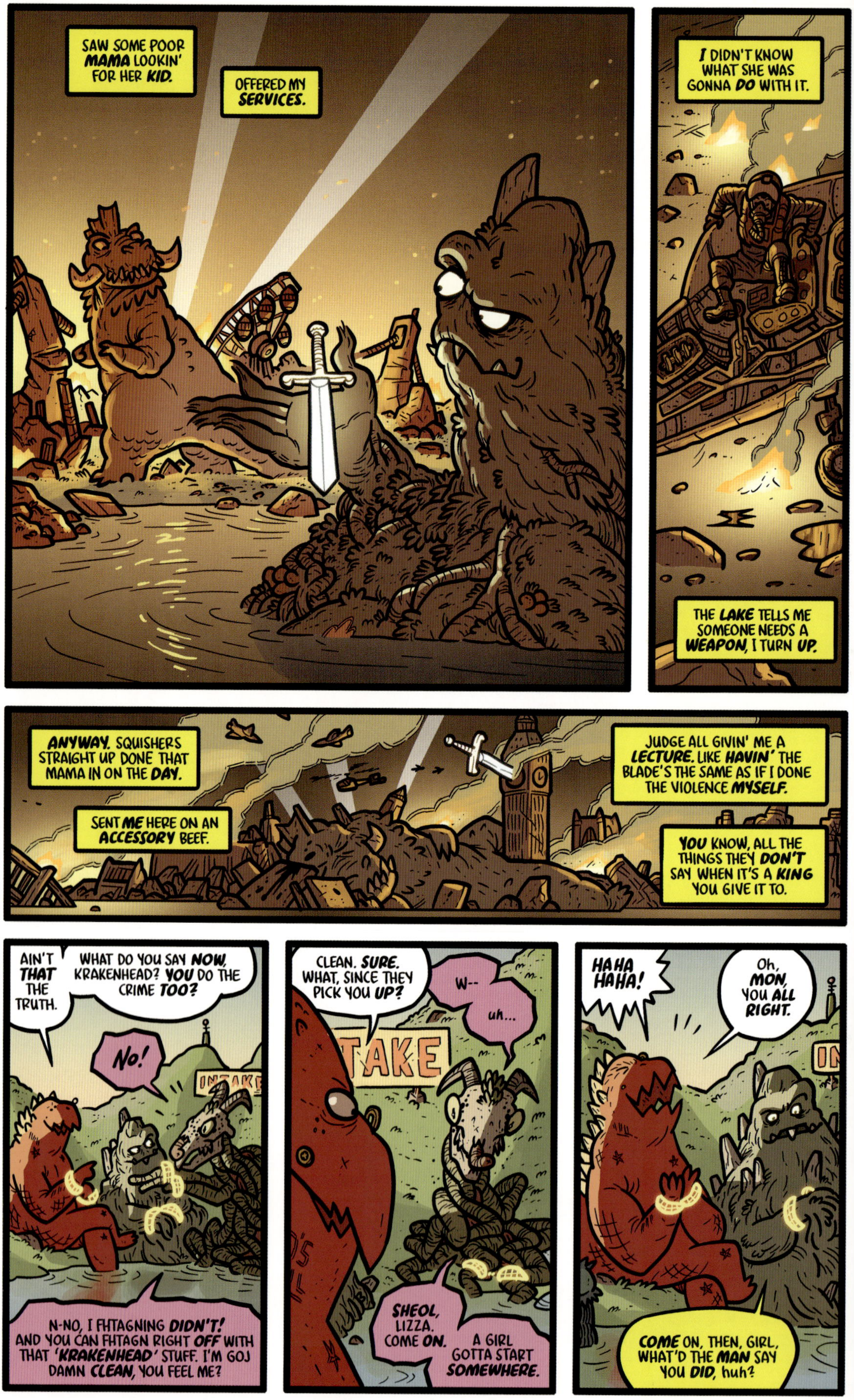
SAW SOME POOR **MAMA** LOOKIN' FOR HER **KID.**
OFFERED MY **SERVICES.**
I DIDN'T KNOW WHAT SHE WAS GONNA **DO** WITH IT.
THE **LAKE** TELLS ME SOMEONE NEEDS A **WEAPON,** I TURN **UP.**
ANYWAY. SQUISHERS STRAIGHT UP DONE THAT MAMA IN ON THE **DAY.**
SENT **ME** HERE ON AN **ACCESSORY** BEEF.
JUDGE ALL GIVIN' ME A **LECTURE.** LIKE **HAVIN'** THE BLADE'S THE SAME AS IF I DONE THE VIOLENCE **MYSELF.**
YOU KNOW, ALL THE THINGS THEY **DON'T** SAY WHEN IT'S A **KING** YOU GIVE IT TO.
AIN'T **THAT** THE TRUTH.
WHAT DO YOU SAY **NOW,** KRAKENHEAD? **YOU** DO THE CRIME **TOO?**
No!
N-NO, I FHTAGNING **DIDN'T!** AND YOU CAN FHTAGN RIGHT **OFF** WITH THAT **'KRAKENHEAD'** STUFF. I'M GOJ DAMN **CLEAN,** YOU FEEL ME?
CLEAN. **SURE.** WHAT, SINCE THEY PICK YOU **UP?**
W--
uh...
SHEOL, LIZZA. COME **ON.**
A GIRL GOTTA START **SOMEWHERE.**
HAHA HAHA!
Oh, **MON,** YOU **ALL RIGHT.**
COME ON, THEN, GIRL, WHAT'D THE **MAN** SAY YOU **DID,** huh?

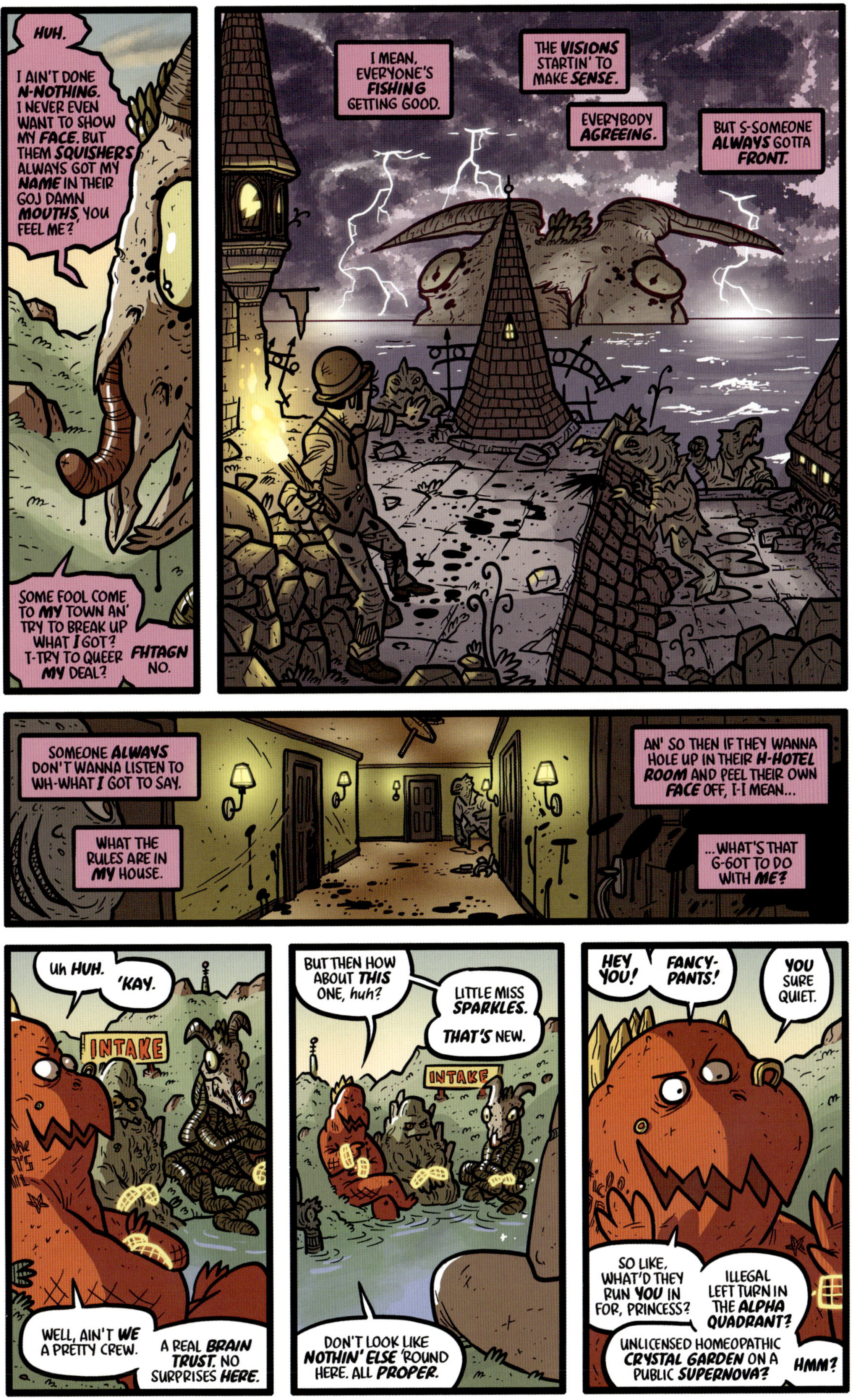
HUH.
I AIN'T DONE N-NOTHING. I NEVER EVEN WANT TO SHOW MY FACE. BUT THEM SQUISHERS ALWAYS GOT MY NAME IN THEIR GOJ DAMN MOUTHS, YOU FEEL ME?
SOME FOOL COME TO MY TOWN AN' TRY TO BREAK UP WHAT I GOT? T-TRY TO QUEER MY DEAL?
FHTAGN NO.
I MEAN, EVERYONE'S FISHING GETTING GOOD.
THE VISIONS STARTIN' TO MAKE SENSE.
EVERYBODY AGREEING.
BUT S-SOMEONE ALWAYS GOTTA FRONT.
SOMEONE ALWAYS DON'T WANNA LISTEN TO WH-WHAT I GOT TO SAY.
WHAT THE RULES ARE IN MY HOUSE.
AN' SO THEN IF THEY WANNA HOLE UP IN THEIR H-HOTEL ROOM AND PEEL THEIR OWN FACE OFF, I-I MEAN...
...WHAT'S THAT G-GOT TO DO WITH ME?
Uh HUH.
'KAY.
INTAKE
WELL, AIN'T WE A PRETTY CREW.
A REAL BRAIN TRUST. NO SURPRISES HERE.
BUT THEN HOW ABOUT THIS ONE, huh?
LITTLE MISS SPARKLES.
THAT'S NEW.
INTAKE
DON'T LOOK LIKE NOTHIN' ELSE 'ROUND HERE. ALL PROPER.
HEY YOU!
FANCY-PANTS!
YOU SURE QUIET.
SO LIKE, WHAT'D THEY RUN YOU IN FOR, PRINCESS?
ILLEGAL LEFT TURN IN THE ALPHA QUADRANT?
UNLICENSED HOMEOPATHIC CRYSTAL GARDEN ON A PUBLIC SUPERNOVA?
HMM?

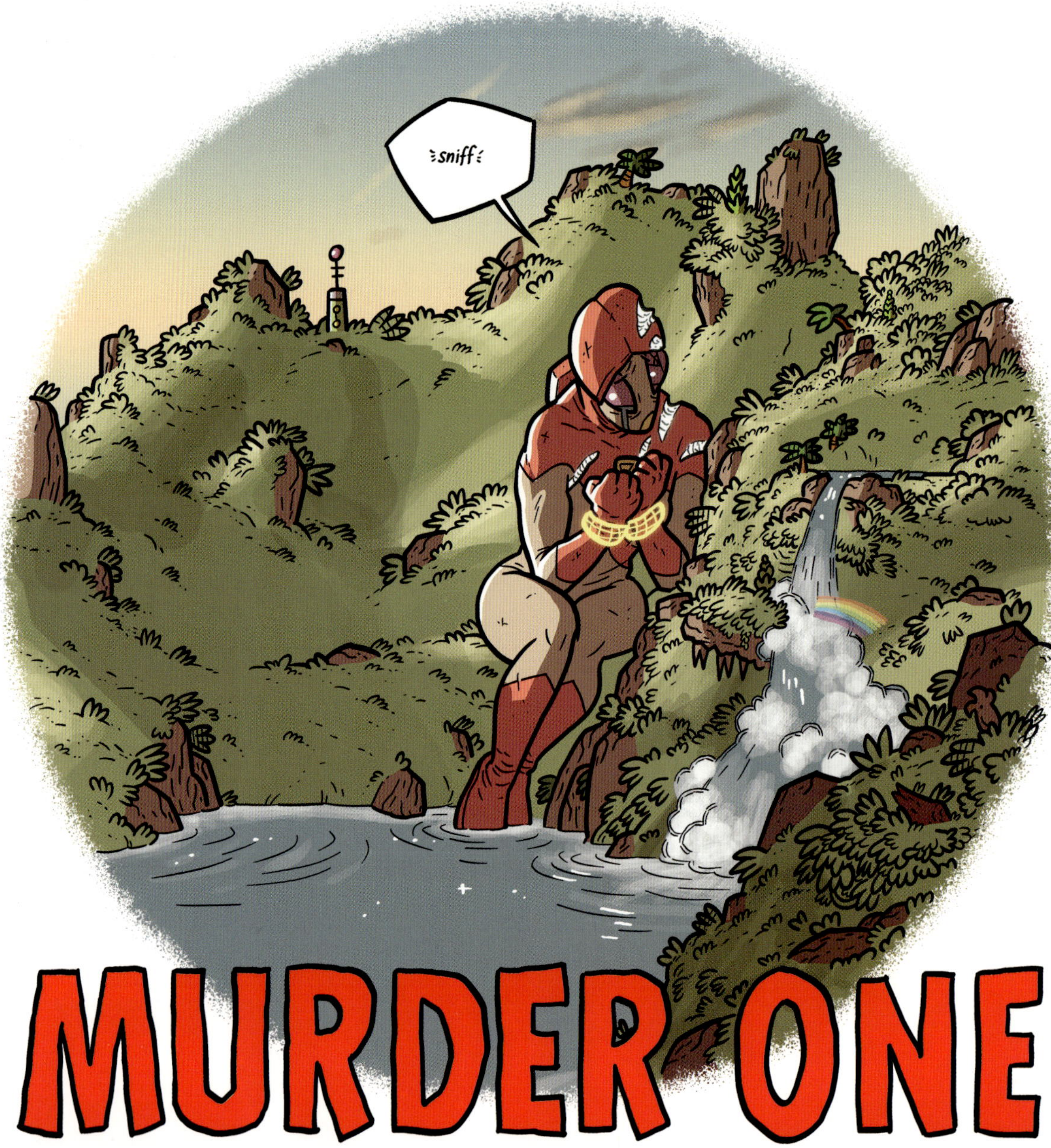
sniff

MURDER ONE

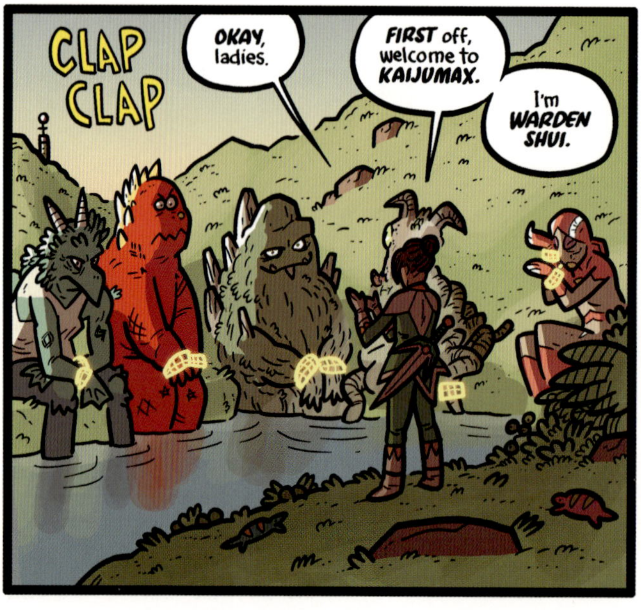
CLAP CLAP
OKAY, ladies.
FIRST off, welcome to KAIJUMAX.
I'm WARDEN SHUI.

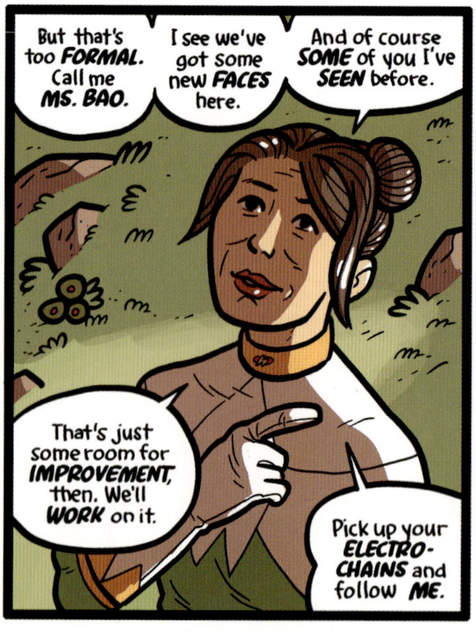
But that's too FORMAL. Call me MS. BAO.
I see we've got some new FACES here.
And of course SOME of you I've SEEN before.
That's just some room for IMPROVEMENT, then. We'll WORK on it.
Pick up your ELECTRO-CHAINS and follow ME.

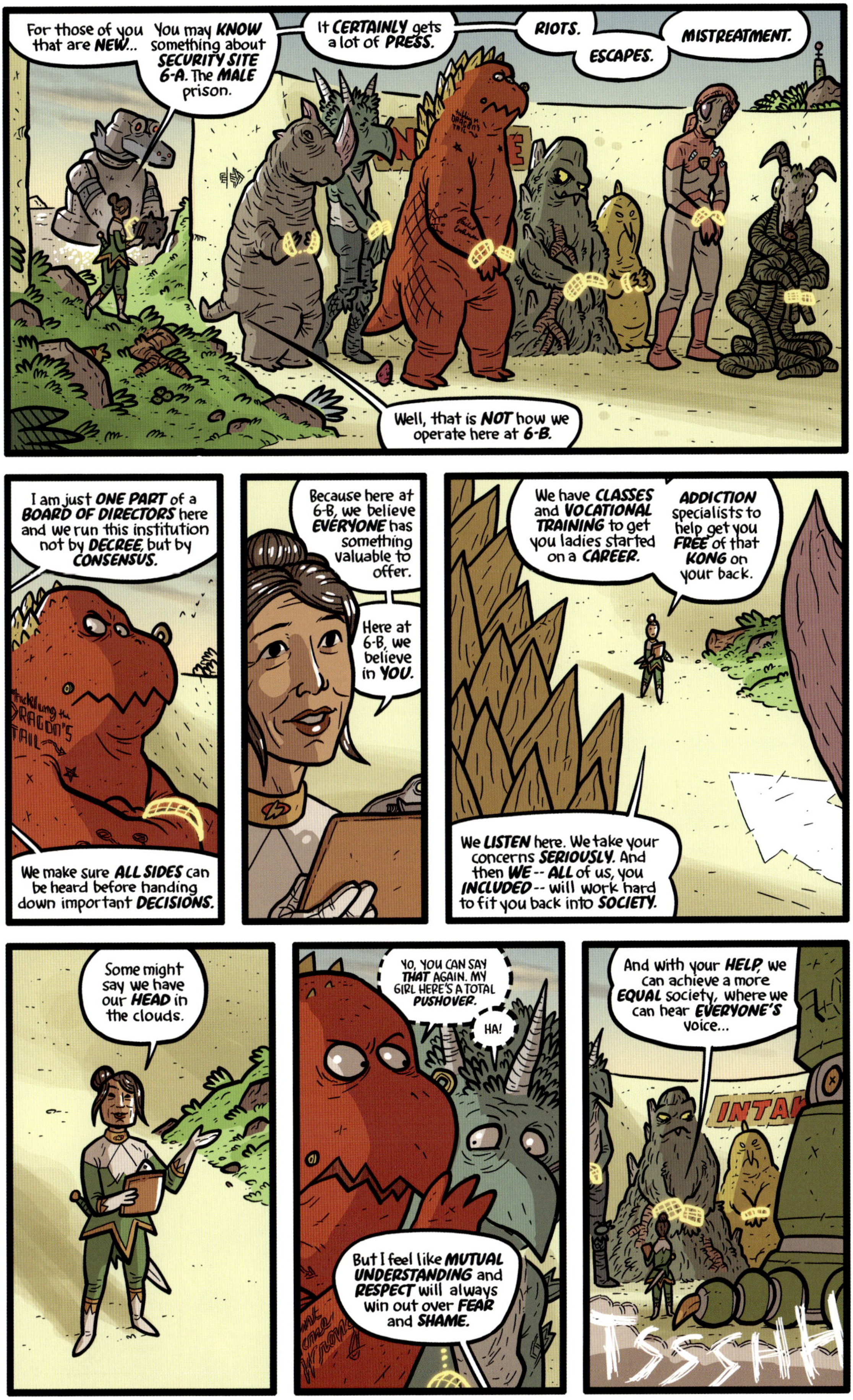
For those of you that are NEW...
You may KNOW something about SECURITY SITE 6-A. The MALE prison.
It CERTAINLY gets a lot of PRESS.
RIOTS.
ESCAPES.
MISTREATMENT.
Well, that is NOT how we operate here at 6-B.
I am just ONE PART of a BOARD OF DIRECTORS here and we run this institution not by DECREE, but by CONSENSUS.
We make sure ALL SIDES can be heard before handing down important DECISIONS.
Because here at 6-B, we believe EVERYONE has something valuable to offer.
Here at 6-B, we believe in YOU.
We have CLASSES and VOCATIONAL TRAINING to get you ladies started on a CAREER.
ADDICTION specialists to help get you FREE of that KONG on your back.
We LISTEN here. We take your concerns SERIOUSLY. And then WE -- ALL of us, you INCLUDED -- will work hard to fit you back into SOCIETY.
Some might say we have our HEAD in the clouds.
YO, YOU CAN SAY THAT AGAIN. MY GIRL HERE'S A TOTAL PUSHOVER.
HA!
But I feel like MUTUAL UNDERSTANDING and RESPECT will always win out over FEAR and SHAME.
And with your HELP, we can achieve a more EQUAL society, where we can hear EVERYONE'S voice...
INTAK
TSSSHH

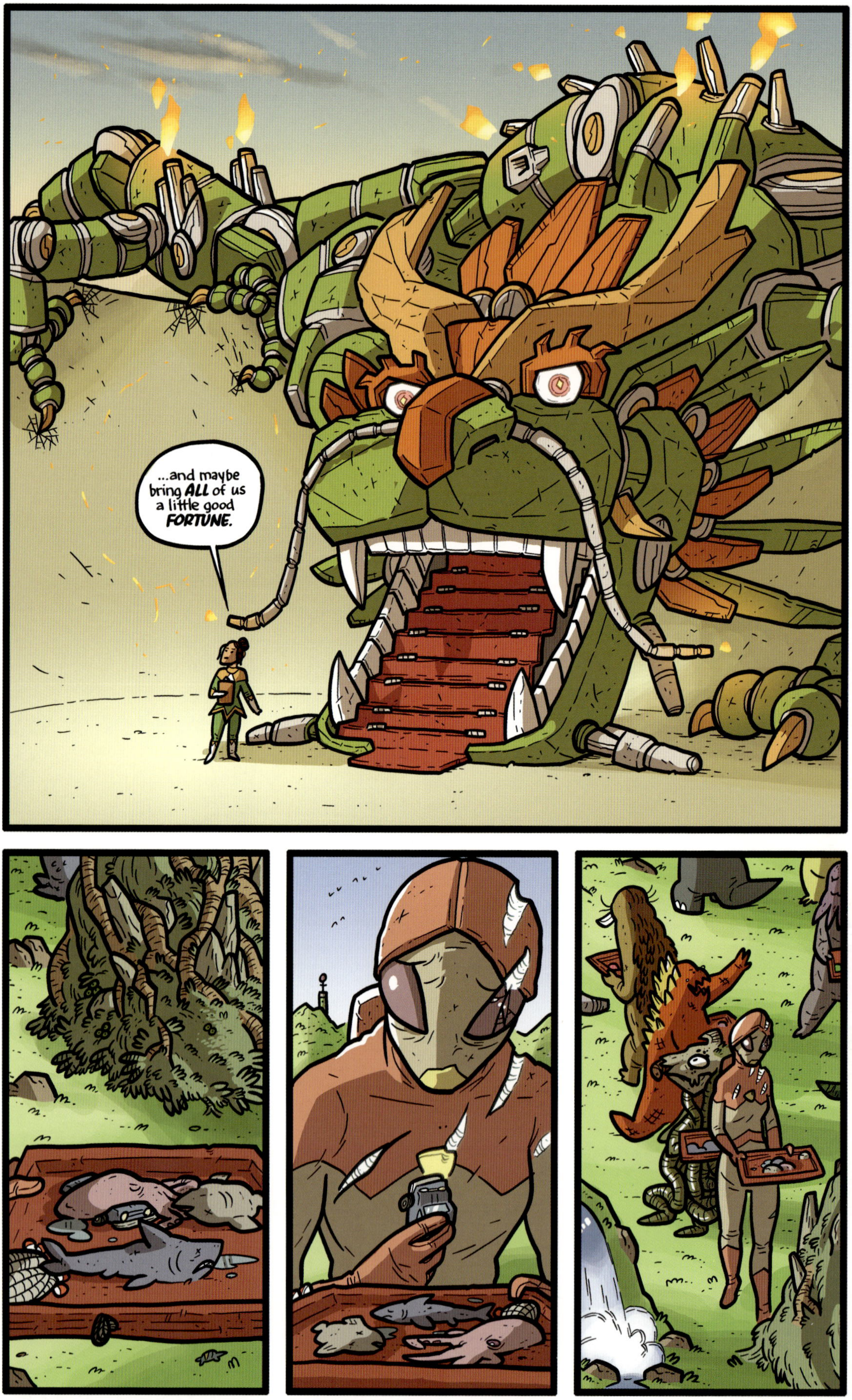
...and maybe bring ALL of us a little good FORTUNE.

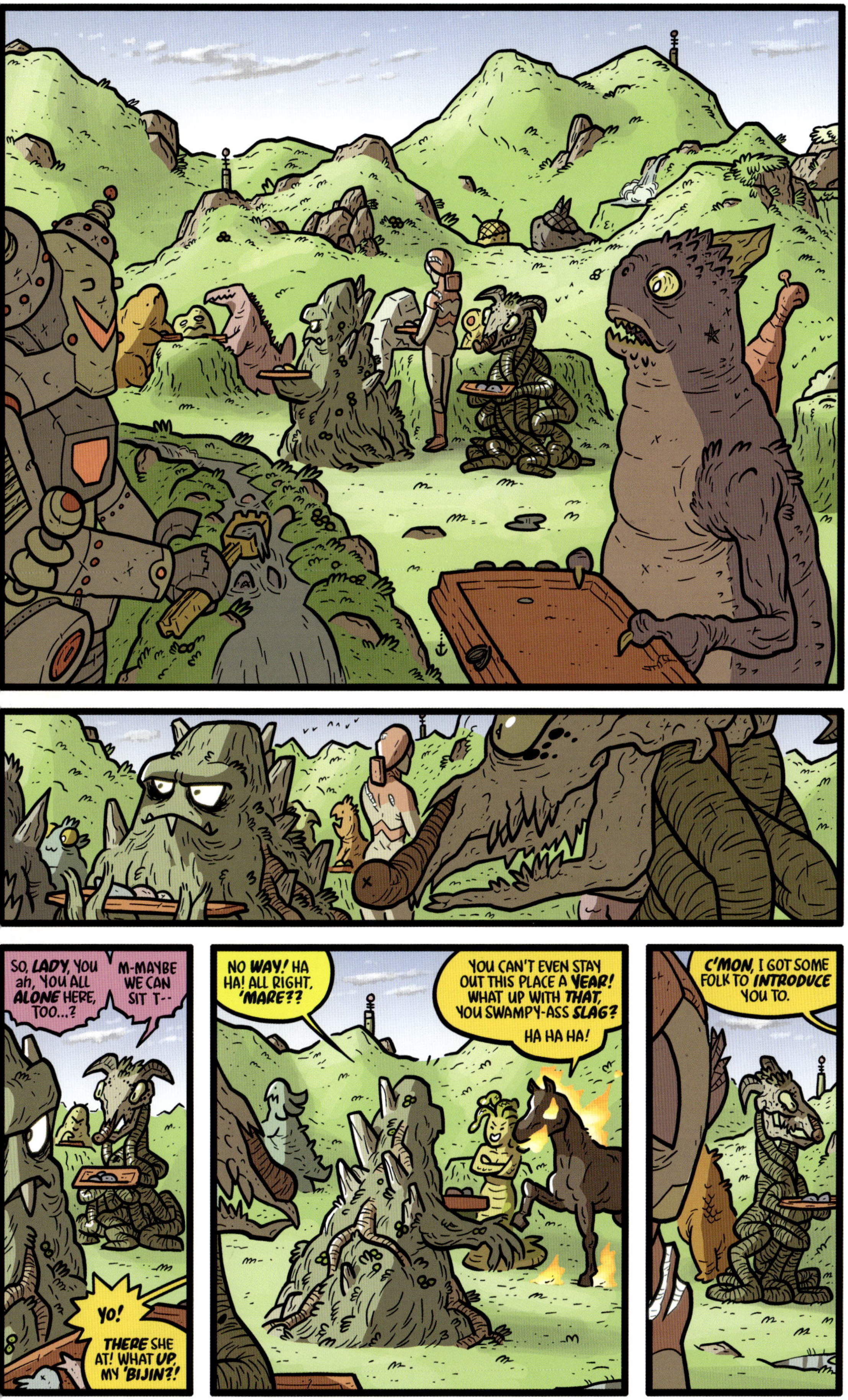
SO, LADY, YOU ah, YOU ALL ALONE HERE, TOO...?
M-MAYBE WE CAN SIT T--
YO!
THERE SHE AT! WHAT UP, MY 'BIJIN?!
NO WAY! HA HA! ALL RIGHT, 'MARE??
YOU CAN'T EVEN STAY OUT THIS PLACE A YEAR! WHAT UP WITH THAT, YOU SWAMPY-ASS SLAG?
HA HA HA!
C'MON, I GOT SOME FOLK TO INTRODUCE YOU TO.

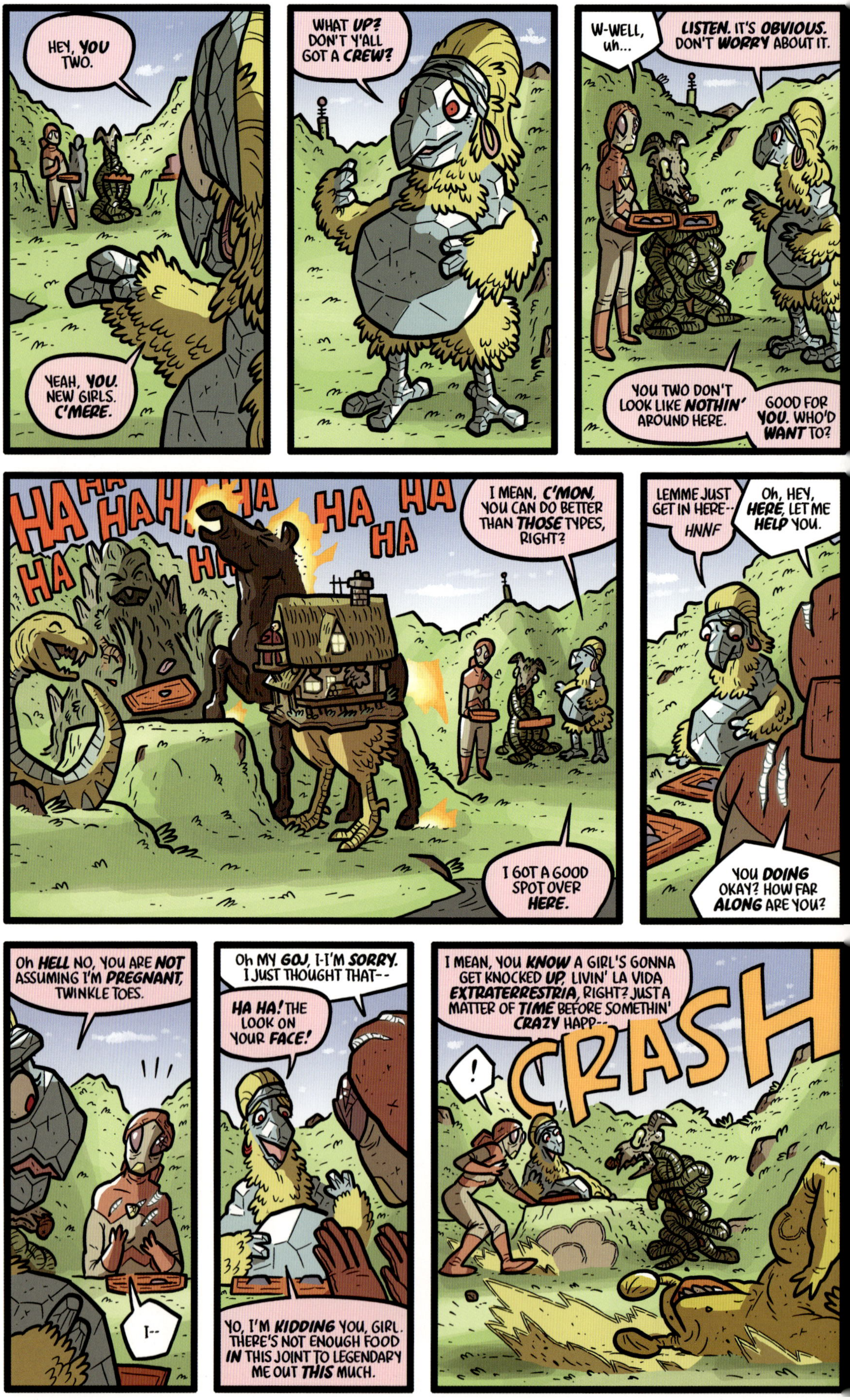
HEY, YOU TWO.
YEAH, YOU. NEW GIRLS. C'MERE.
WHAT UP? DON'T Y'ALL GOT A CREW?
W-WELL, uh...
LISTEN. IT'S OBVIOUS. DON'T WORRY ABOUT IT.
YOU TWO DON'T LOOK LIKE NOTHIN' AROUND HERE.
GOOD FOR YOU. WHO'D WANT TO?
HA HA HA HA HA HA HA HA HA HA HA
I MEAN, C'MON, YOU CAN DO BETTER THAN THOSE TYPES, RIGHT?
I GOT A GOOD SPOT OVER HERE.
LEMME JUST GET IN HERE-- HNNF
Oh, HEY, HERE, LET ME HELP YOU.
YOU DOING OKAY? HOW FAR ALONG ARE YOU?
Oh HELL NO, YOU ARE NOT ASSUMING I'M PREGNANT, TWINKLE TOES.
I--
Oh MY GOJ, I-I'M SORRY. I JUST THOUGHT THAT--
HA HA! THE LOOK ON YOUR FACE!
YO, I'M KIDDING YOU, GIRL. THERE'S NOT ENOUGH FOOD IN THIS JOINT TO LEGENDARY ME OUT THIS MUCH.
I MEAN, YOU KNOW A GIRL'S GONNA GET KNOCKED UP, LIVIN' LA VIDA EXTRATERRESTRIA, RIGHT? JUST A MATTER OF TIME BEFORE SOMETHIN' CRAZY HAPP--
!
CRASH

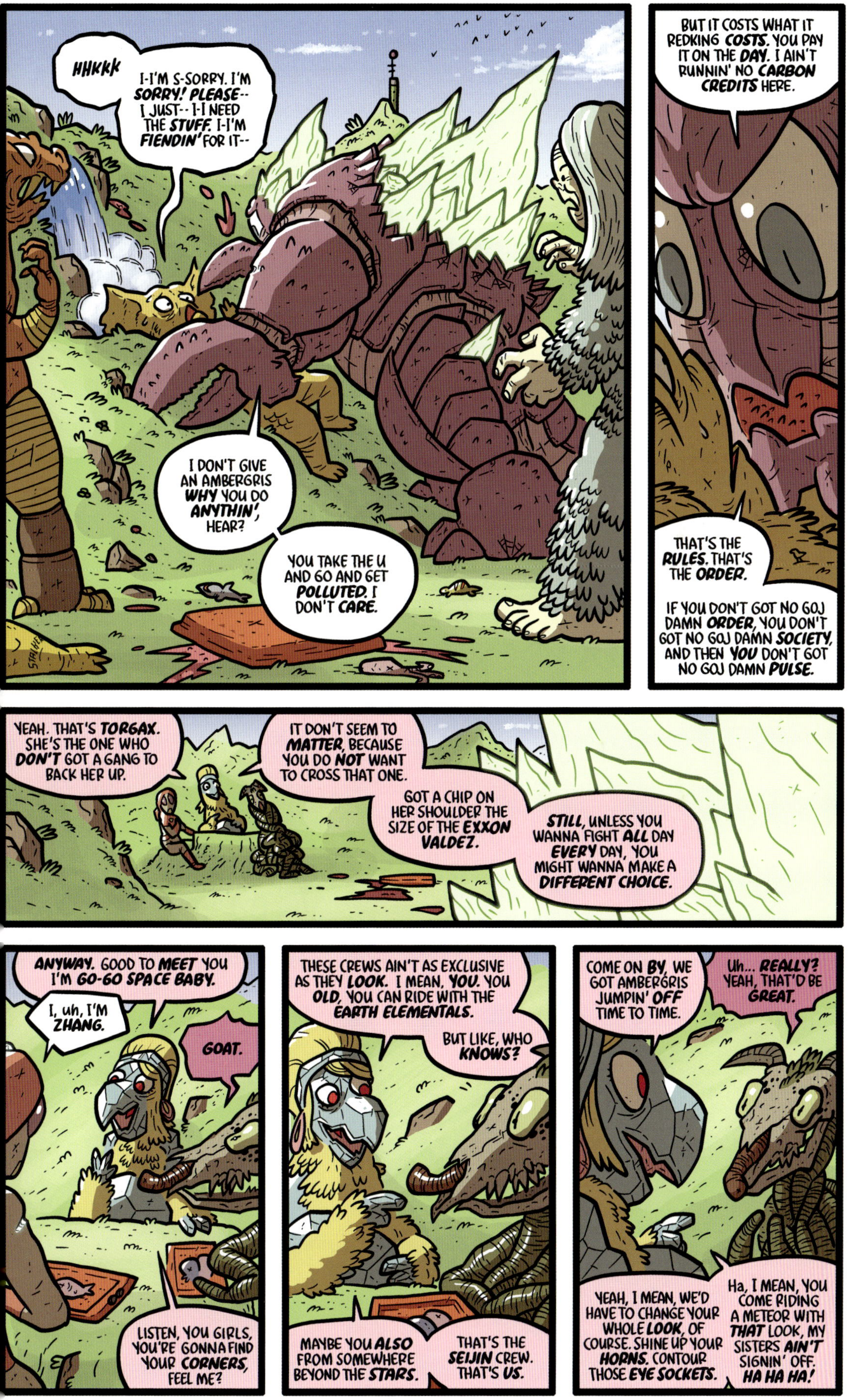
HHKKK
I-I'M S-SORRY. I'M SORRY! PLEASE-- I JUST-- I-I NEED THE STUFF. I-I'M FIENDIN' FOR IT--
I DON'T GIVE AN AMBERGRIS WHY YOU DO ANYTHIN', HEAR?
YOU TAKE THE U AND GO AND GET POLLUTED. I DON'T CARE.
BUT IT COSTS WHAT IT REDKING COSTS. YOU PAY IT ON THE DAY. I AIN'T RUNNIN' NO CARBON CREDITS HERE.
THAT'S THE RULES. THAT'S THE ORDER.
IF YOU DON'T GOT NO GOJ DAMN ORDER, YOU DON'T GOT NO GOJ DAMN SOCIETY, AND THEN YOU DON'T GOT NO GOJ DAMN PULSE.
YEAH. THAT'S TORGAX. SHE'S THE ONE WHO DON'T GOT A GANG TO BACK HER UP.
IT DON'T SEEM TO MATTER, BECAUSE YOU DO NOT WANT TO CROSS THAT ONE.
GOT A CHIP ON HER SHOULDER THE SIZE OF THE EXXON VALDEZ.
STILL, UNLESS YOU WANNA FIGHT ALL DAY EVERY DAY, YOU MIGHT WANNA MAKE A DIFFERENT CHOICE.
ANYWAY. GOOD TO MEET YOU I'M GO-GO SPACE BABY.
I, uh, I'M ZHANG.
GOAT.
LISTEN, YOU GIRLS, YOU'RE GONNA FIND YOUR CORNERS, FEEL ME?
THESE CREWS AIN'T AS EXCLUSIVE AS THEY LOOK. I MEAN, YOU. YOU OLD, YOU CAN RIDE WITH THE EARTH ELEMENTALS.
BUT LIKE, WHO KNOWS?
MAYBE YOU ALSO FROM SOMEWHERE BEYOND THE STARS.
THAT'S THE SEIJIN CREW. THAT'S US.
COME ON BY, WE GOT AMBERGRIS JUMPIN' OFF TIME TO TIME.
Uh... REALLY? YEAH, THAT'D BE GREAT.
YEAH, I MEAN, WE'D HAVE TO CHANGE YOUR WHOLE LOOK, OF COURSE. SHINE UP YOUR HORNS. CONTOUR THOSE EYE SOCKETS.
Ha, I MEAN, YOU COME RIDING A METEOR WITH THAT LOOK, MY SISTERS AIN'T SIGNIN' OFF. HA HA HA!

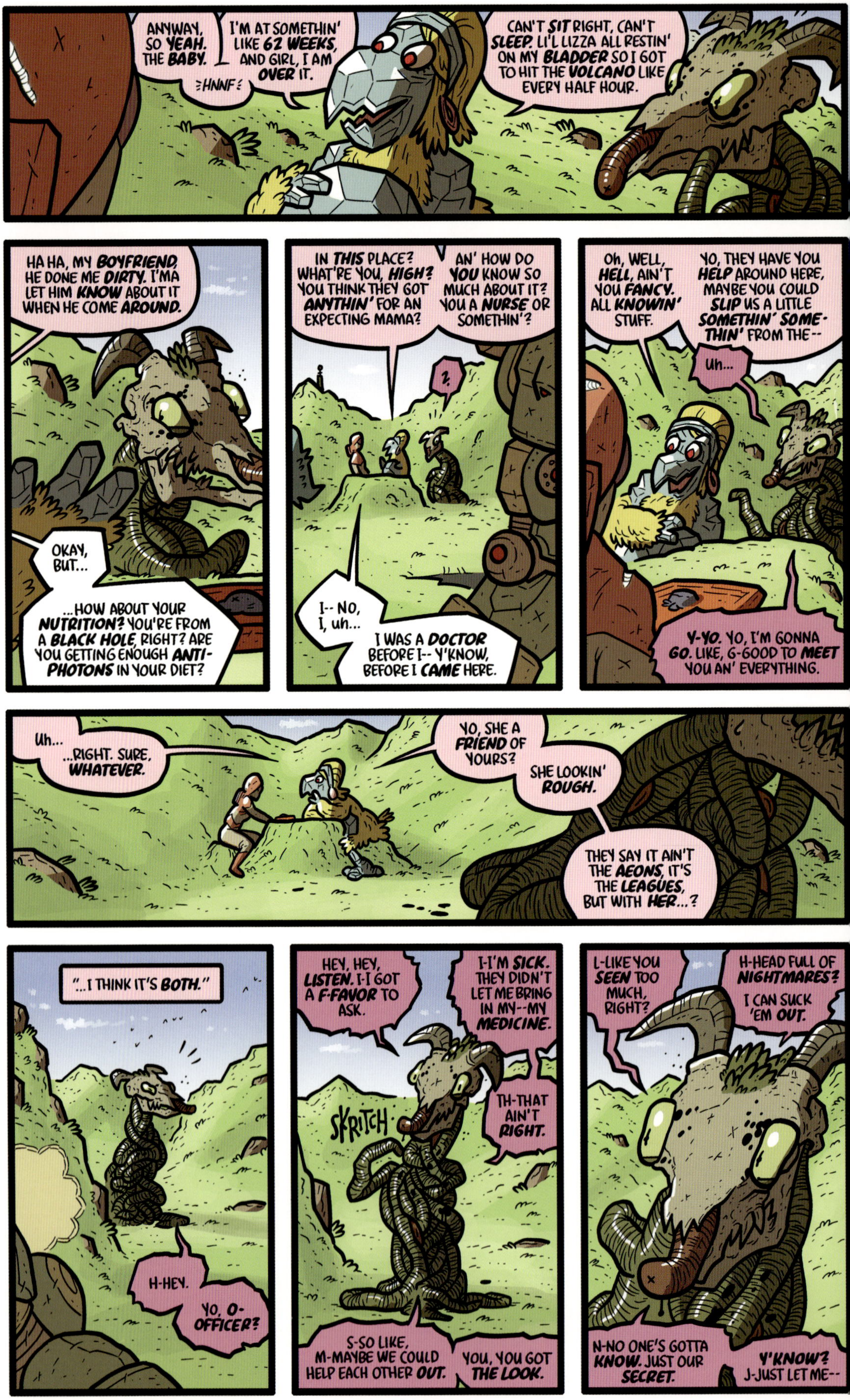
ANYWAY, SO YEAH. THE BABY.
I'M AT SOMETHIN' LIKE 62 WEEKS, AND GIRL, I AM OVER IT.
HNNF
CAN'T SIT RIGHT, CAN'T SLEEP. LI'L LIZZA ALL RESTIN' ON MY BLADDER SO I GOT TO HIT THE VOLCANO LIKE EVERY HALF HOUR.
HA HA, MY BOYFRIEND, HE DONE ME DIRTY. I'MA LET HIM KNOW ABOUT IT WHEN HE COME AROUND.
OKAY, BUT...
...HOW ABOUT YOUR NUTRITION? YOU'RE FROM A BLACK HOLE, RIGHT? ARE YOU GETTING ENOUGH ANTI-PHOTONS IN YOUR DIET?
IN THIS PLACE? WHAT'RE YOU, HIGH? YOU THINK THEY GOT ANYTHIN' FOR AN EXPECTING MAMA?
AN' HOW DO YOU KNOW SO MUCH ABOUT IT? YOU A NURSE OR SOMETHIN'?
?
I-- NO, I, uh...
I WAS A DOCTOR BEFORE I-- Y'KNOW, BEFORE I CAME HERE.
Oh, WELL, HELL, AIN'T YOU FANCY. ALL KNOWIN' STUFF.
YO, THEY HAVE YOU HELP AROUND HERE, MAYBE YOU COULD SLIP US A LITTLE SOMETHIN' SOME-THIN' FROM THE--
Uh...
Y-YO. YO, I'M GONNA GO. LIKE, G-GOOD TO MEET YOU AN' EVERYTHING.
Uh...
...RIGHT. SURE. WHATEVER.
YO, SHE A FRIEND OF YOURS?
SHE LOOKIN' ROUGH.
THEY SAY IT AIN'T THE AEONS, IT'S THE LEAGUES, BUT WITH HER...?
"...I THINK IT'S BOTH."
H-HEY.
YO, O-OFFICER?
HEY, HEY, LISTEN. I-I GOT A F-FAVOR TO ASK.
I-I'M SICK. THEY DIDN'T LET ME BRING IN MY--MY MEDICINE.
SKRITCH
TH-THAT AIN'T RIGHT.
S-SO LIKE, M-MAYBE WE COULD HELP EACH OTHER OUT.
YOU, YOU GOT THE LOOK.
L-LIKE YOU SEEN TOO MUCH, RIGHT?
H-HEAD FULL OF NIGHTMARES? I CAN SUCK 'EM OUT.
N-NO ONE'S GOTTA KNOW. JUST OUR SECRET.
Y'KNOW? J-JUST LET ME--

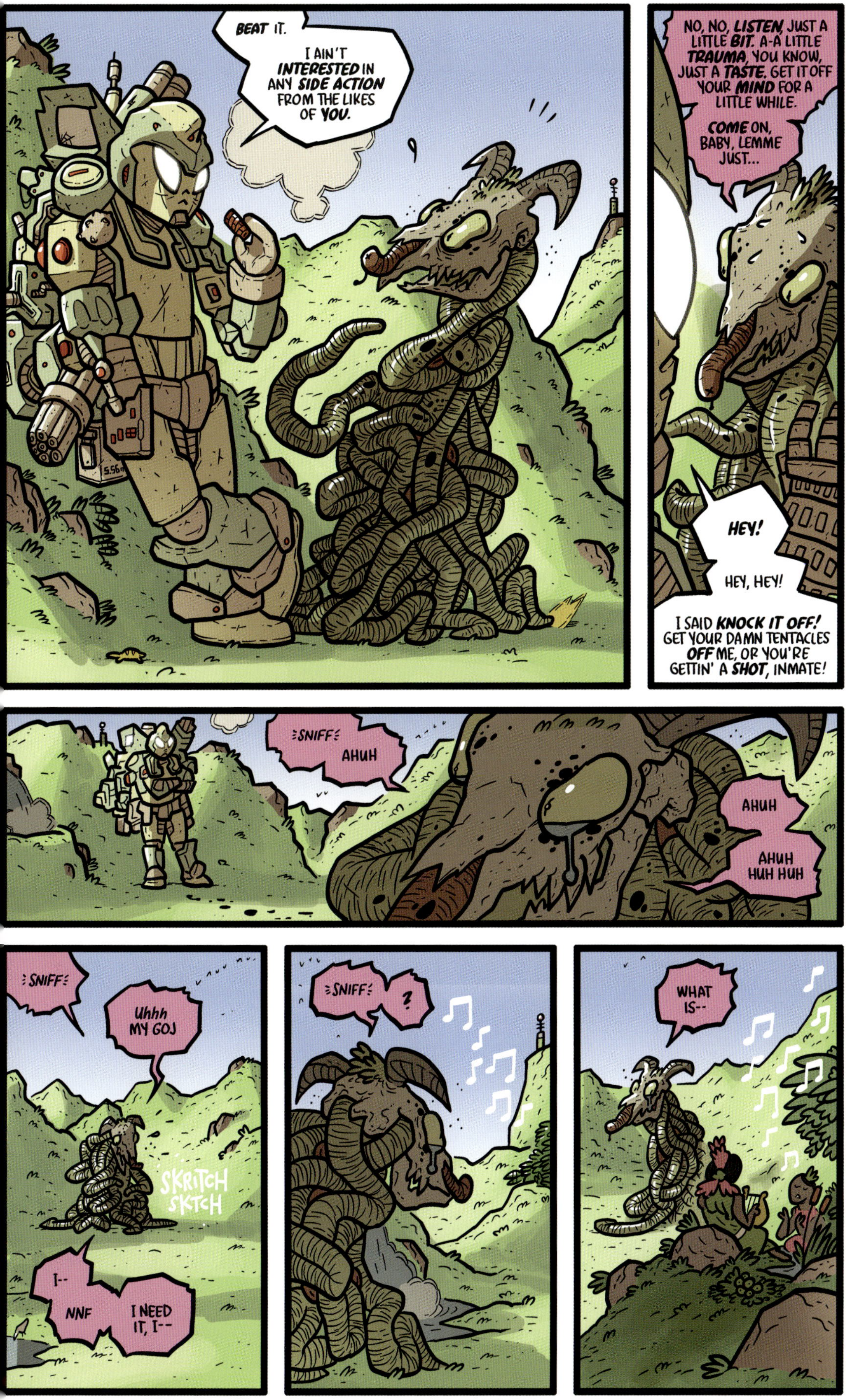
BEAT IT.
I AIN'T INTERESTED IN ANY SIDE ACTION FROM THE LIKES OF YOU.
NO, NO, LISTEN, JUST A LITTLE BIT. A-A LITTLE TRAUMA, YOU KNOW, JUST A TASTE. GET IT OFF YOUR MIND FOR A LITTLE WHILE.
COME ON, BABY, LEMME JUST...
HEY!
HEY, HEY!
I SAID KNOCK IT OFF! GET YOUR DAMN TENTACLES OFF ME, OR YOU'RE GETTIN' A SHOT, INMATE!
SNIFF
AHUH
AHUH
AHUH HUH HUH
SNIFF
Uhhh MY GOJ
SKRITCH SKTCH
I--
NNF
I NEED IT, I--
SNIFF
?
WHAT IS--

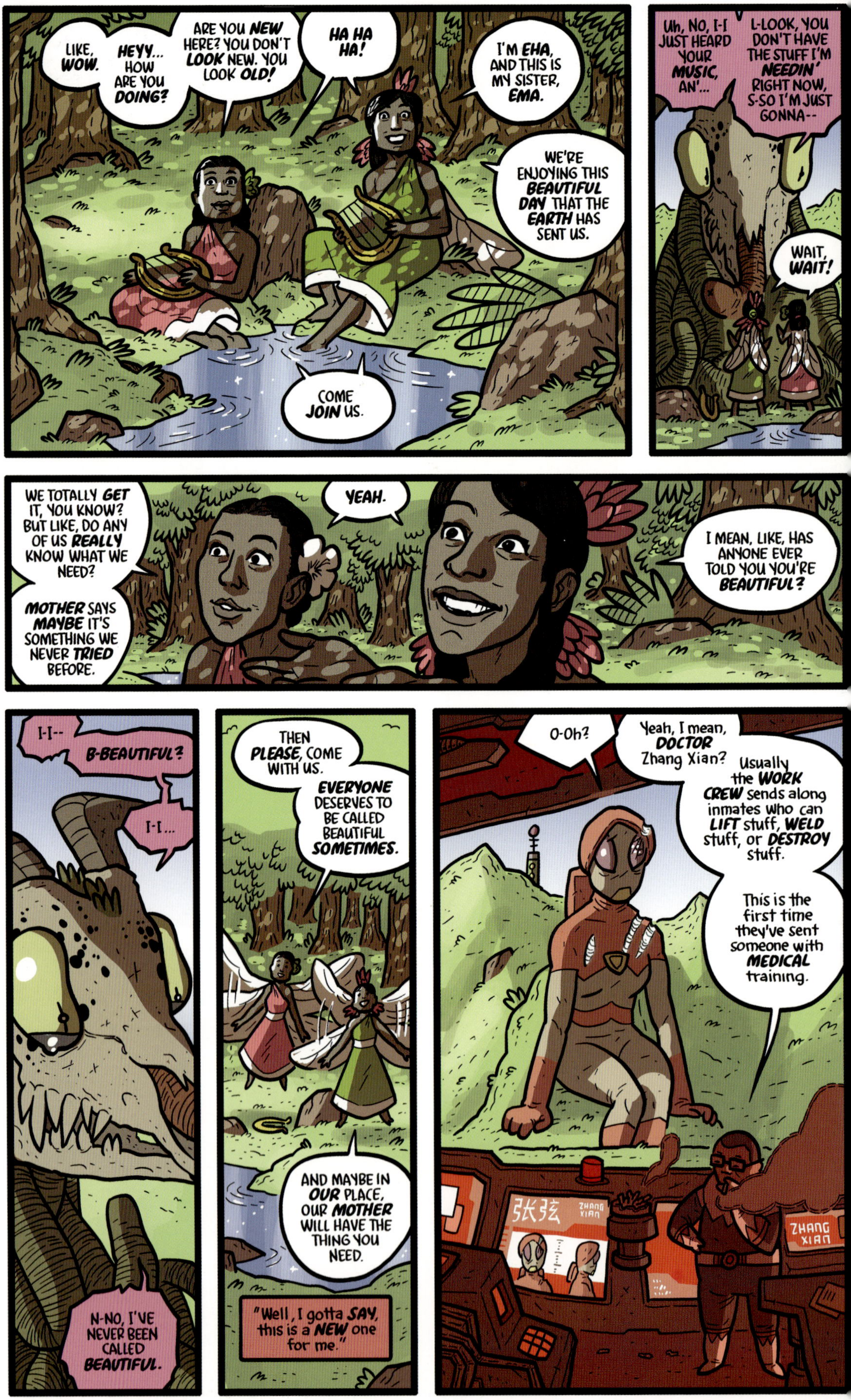
LIKE, WOW.
HEYY... HOW ARE YOU DOING?
ARE YOU NEW HERE? YOU DON'T LOOK NEW. YOU LOOK OLD!
HA HA HA!
I'M EHA, AND THIS IS MY SISTER, EMA.
WE'RE ENJOYING THIS BEAUTIFUL DAY THAT THE EARTH HAS SENT US.
COME JOIN US.
Uh, NO, I-I JUST HEARD YOUR MUSIC, AN'...
L-LOOK, YOU DON'T HAVE THE STUFF I'M NEEDIN' RIGHT NOW, S-SO I'M JUST GONNA--
WAIT, WAIT!
WE TOTALLY GET IT, YOU KNOW? BUT LIKE, DO ANY OF US REALLY KNOW WHAT WE NEED?
MOTHER SAYS MAYBE IT'S SOMETHING WE NEVER TRIED BEFORE.
YEAH.
I MEAN, LIKE, HAS ANYONE EVER TOLD YOU YOU'RE BEAUTIFUL?
I-I--
B-BEAUTIFUL?
I-I...
N-NO, I'VE NEVER BEEN CALLED BEAUTIFUL.
THEN PLEASE, COME WITH US.
EVERYONE DESERVES TO BE CALLED BEAUTIFUL SOMETIMES.
AND MAYBE IN OUR PLACE, OUR MOTHER WILL HAVE THE THING YOU NEED.
"Well, I gotta SAY, this is a NEW one for me."
O-Oh?
Yeah, I mean, DOCTOR Zhang Xian?
Usually the WORK CREW sends along inmates who can LIFT stuff, WELD stuff, or DESTROY stuff.
This is the first time they've sent someone with MEDICAL training.
张弦
ZHANG XIAN
ZHANG XIAN

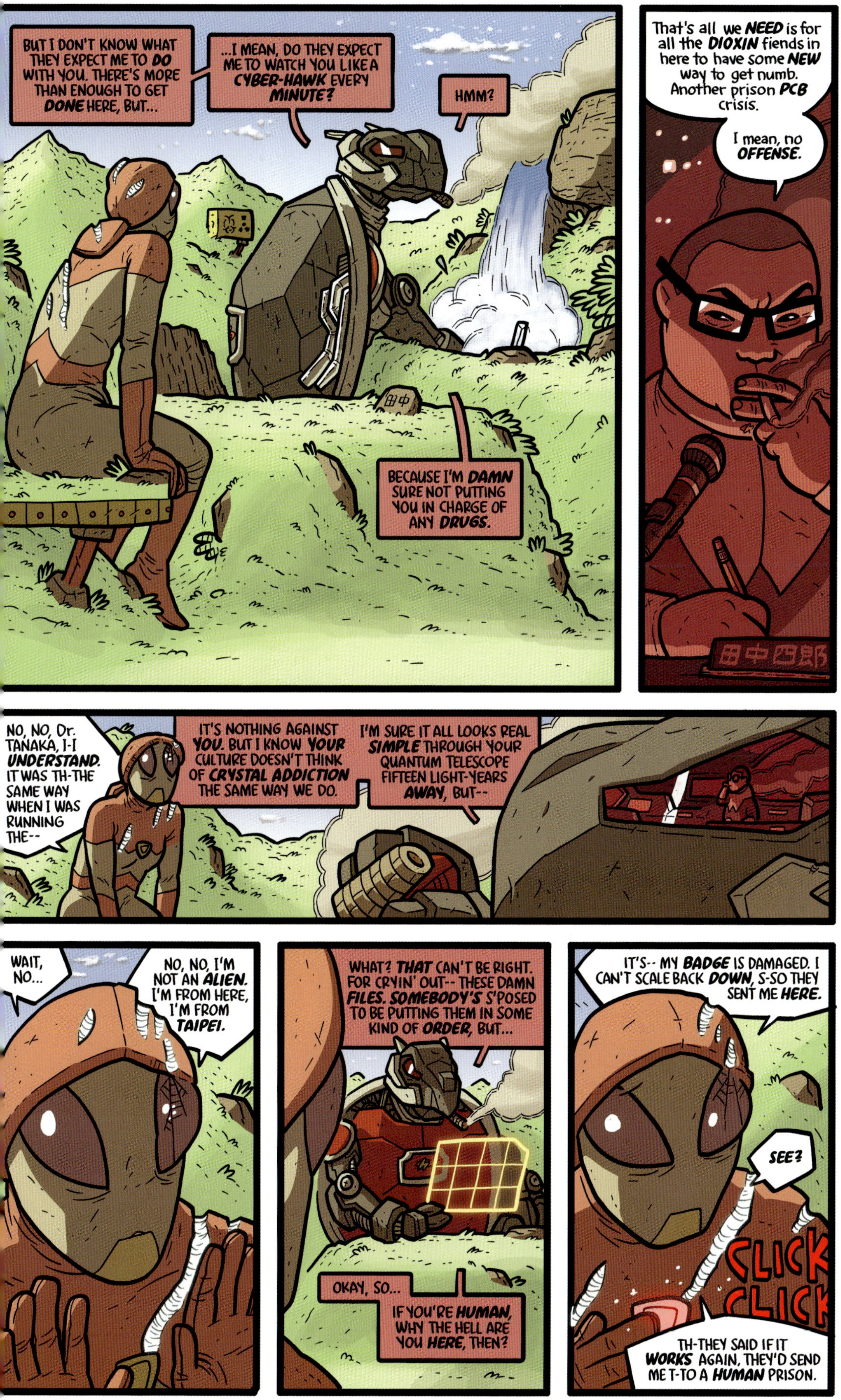
BUT I DON'T KNOW WHAT THEY EXPECT ME TO DO WITH YOU. THERE'S MORE THAN ENOUGH TO GET DONE HERE, BUT...
...I MEAN, DO THEY EXPECT ME TO WATCH YOU LIKE A CYBER-HAWK EVERY MINUTE?
HMM?
BECAUSE I'M DAMN SURE NOT PUTTING YOU IN CHARGE OF ANY DRUGS.
That's all we NEED is for all the DIOXIN fiends in here to have some NEW way to get numb. Another prison PCB crisis.
I mean, no OFFENSE.
田中四郎
NO, NO, Dr. TANAKA, I-I UNDERSTAND. IT WAS TH-THE SAME WAY WHEN I WAS RUNNING THE--
IT'S NOTHING AGAINST YOU. BUT I KNOW YOUR CULTURE DOESN'T THINK OF CRYSTAL ADDICTION THE SAME WAY WE DO.
I'M SURE IT ALL LOOKS REAL SIMPLE THROUGH YOUR QUANTUM TELESCOPE FIFTEEN LIGHT-YEARS AWAY, BUT--
WAIT, NO...
NO, NO, I'M NOT AN ALIEN. I'M FROM HERE, I'M FROM TAIPEI.
WHAT? THAT CAN'T BE RIGHT. FOR CRYIN' OUT-- THESE DAMN FILES. SOMEBODY'S S'POSED TO BE PUTTING THEM IN SOME KIND OF ORDER, BUT...
OKAY, SO...
IF YOU'RE HUMAN, WHY THE HELL ARE YOU HERE, THEN?
IT'S-- MY BADGE IS DAMAGED. I CAN'T SCALE BACK DOWN, S-SO THEY SENT ME HERE.
SEE?
CLICK CLICK
TH-THEY SAID IF IT WORKS AGAIN, THEY'D SEND ME T-TO A HUMAN PRISON.

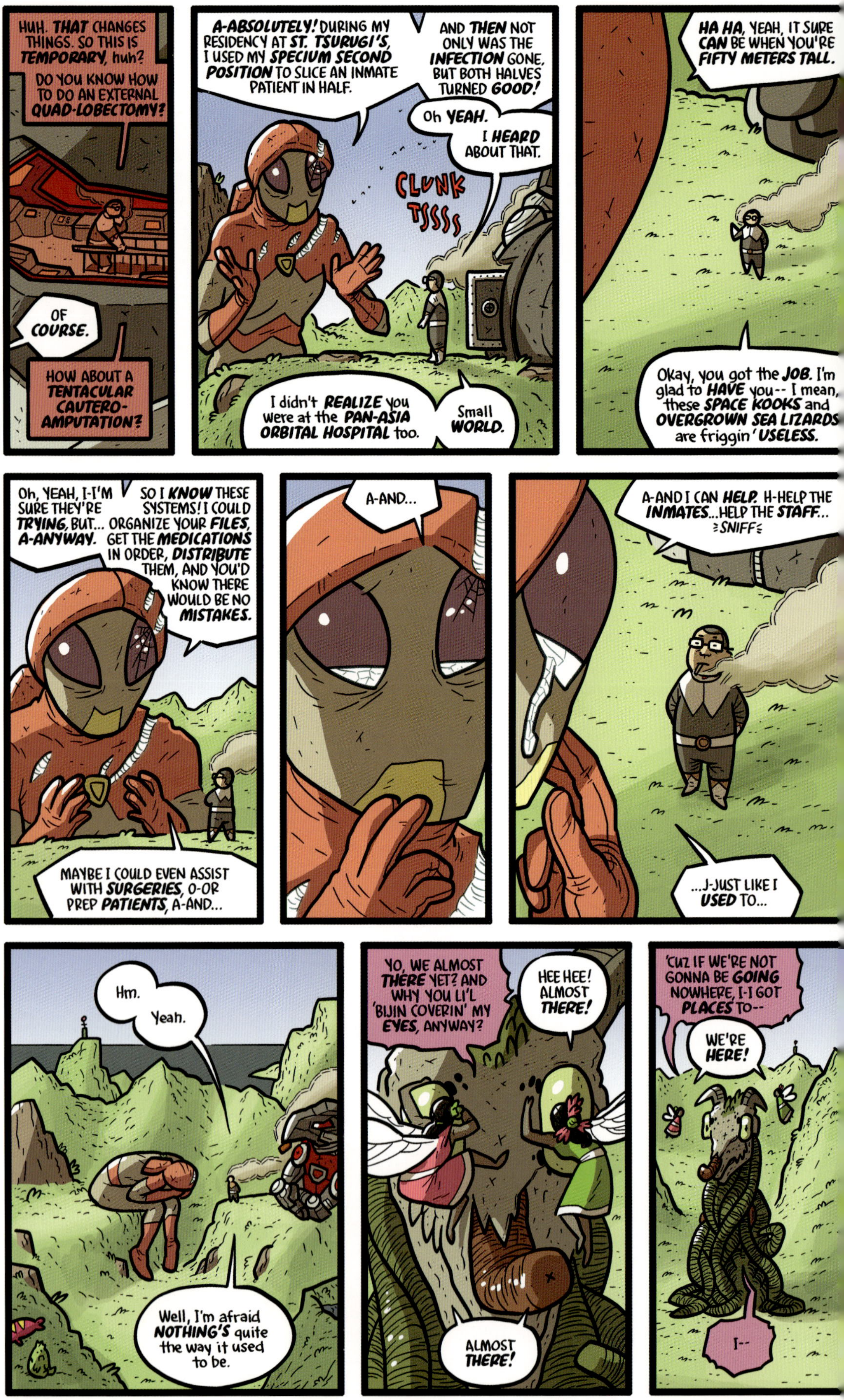

HUH. THAT CHANGES THINGS. SO THIS IS TEMPORARY, huh?
DO YOU KNOW HOW TO DO AN EXTERNAL QUAD-LOBECTOMY?
OF COURSE.
HOW ABOUT A TENTACULAR CAUTERO-AMPUTATION?
A-ABSOLUTELY! DURING MY RESIDENCY AT ST. TSURUGI'S, I USED MY SPECIUM SECOND POSITION TO SLICE AN INMATE PATIENT IN HALF.
AND THEN NOT ONLY WAS THE INFECTION GONE, BUT BOTH HALVES TURNED GOOD!
Oh YEAH.
I HEARD ABOUT THAT.
CLUNK
TSSSS
I didn't REALIZE you were at the PAN-ASIA ORBITAL HOSPITAL too.
Small WORLD.
HA HA, YEAH, IT SURE CAN BE WHEN YOU'RE FIFTY METERS TALL.
Okay, you got the JOB. I'm glad to HAVE you-- I mean, these SPACE KOOKS and OVERGROWN SEA LIZARDS are friggin' USELESS.
Oh, YEAH, I-I'M SURE THEY'RE TRYING, BUT... A-ANYWAY.
SO I KNOW THESE SYSTEMS! I COULD ORGANIZE YOUR FILES, GET THE MEDICATIONS IN ORDER, DISTRIBUTE THEM, AND YOU'D KNOW THERE WOULD BE NO MISTAKES.
MAYBE I COULD EVEN ASSIST WITH SURGERIES, O-OR PREP PATIENTS, A-AND...
A-AND...
A-AND I CAN HELP. H-HELP THE INMATES...HELP THE STAFF...
SNIFF
...J-JUST LIKE I USED TO...
Hm.
Yeah.
Well, I'm afraid NOTHING'S quite the way it used to be.
YO, WE ALMOST THERE YET? AND WHY YOU LI'L 'BIJIN COVERIN' MY EYES, ANYWAY?
HEE HEE! ALMOST THERE!
ALMOST THERE!
'CUZ IF WE'RE NOT GONNA BE GOING NOWHERE, I-I GOT PLACES TO--
WE'RE HERE!
I--

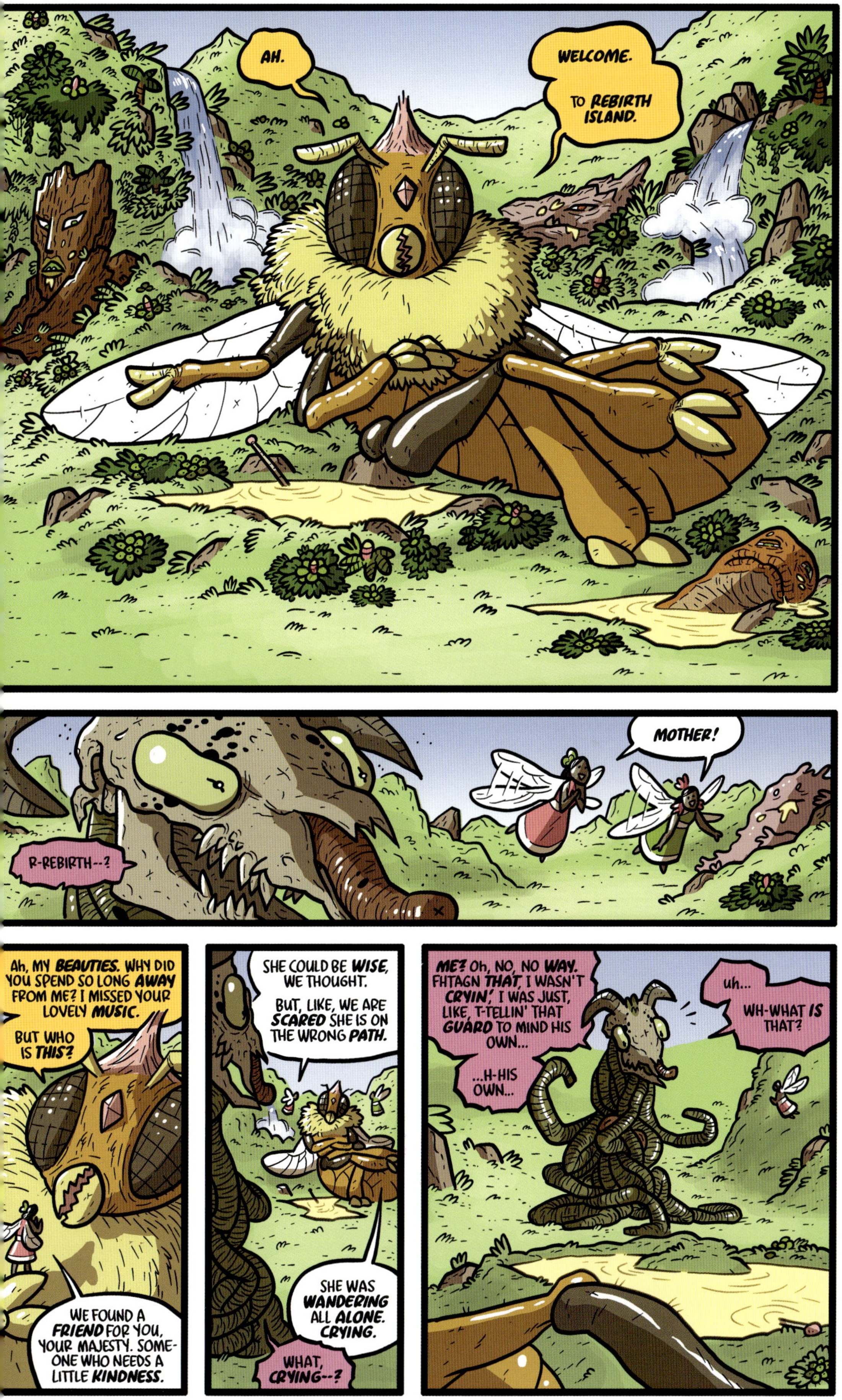
AH.
WELCOME.
TO REBIRTH ISLAND.
R-REBIRTH--?
MOTHER!
Ah, MY BEAUTIES. WHY DID YOU SPEND SO LONG AWAY FROM ME? I MISSED YOUR LOVELY MUSIC.
BUT WHO IS THIS?
WE FOUND A FRIEND FOR YOU, YOUR MAJESTY. SOME-ONE WHO NEEDS A LITTLE KINDNESS.
SHE COULD BE WISE, WE THOUGHT.
BUT, LIKE, WE ARE SCARED SHE IS ON THE WRONG PATH.
SHE WAS WANDERING ALL ALONE. CRYING.
WHAT, CRYING--?
ME? Oh, NO, NO WAY. FHTAGN THAT, I WASN'T CRYIN', I WAS JUST, LIKE, T-TELLIN' THAT GUARD TO MIND HIS OWN...
...H-HIS OWN...
uh...
WH-WHAT IS THAT?

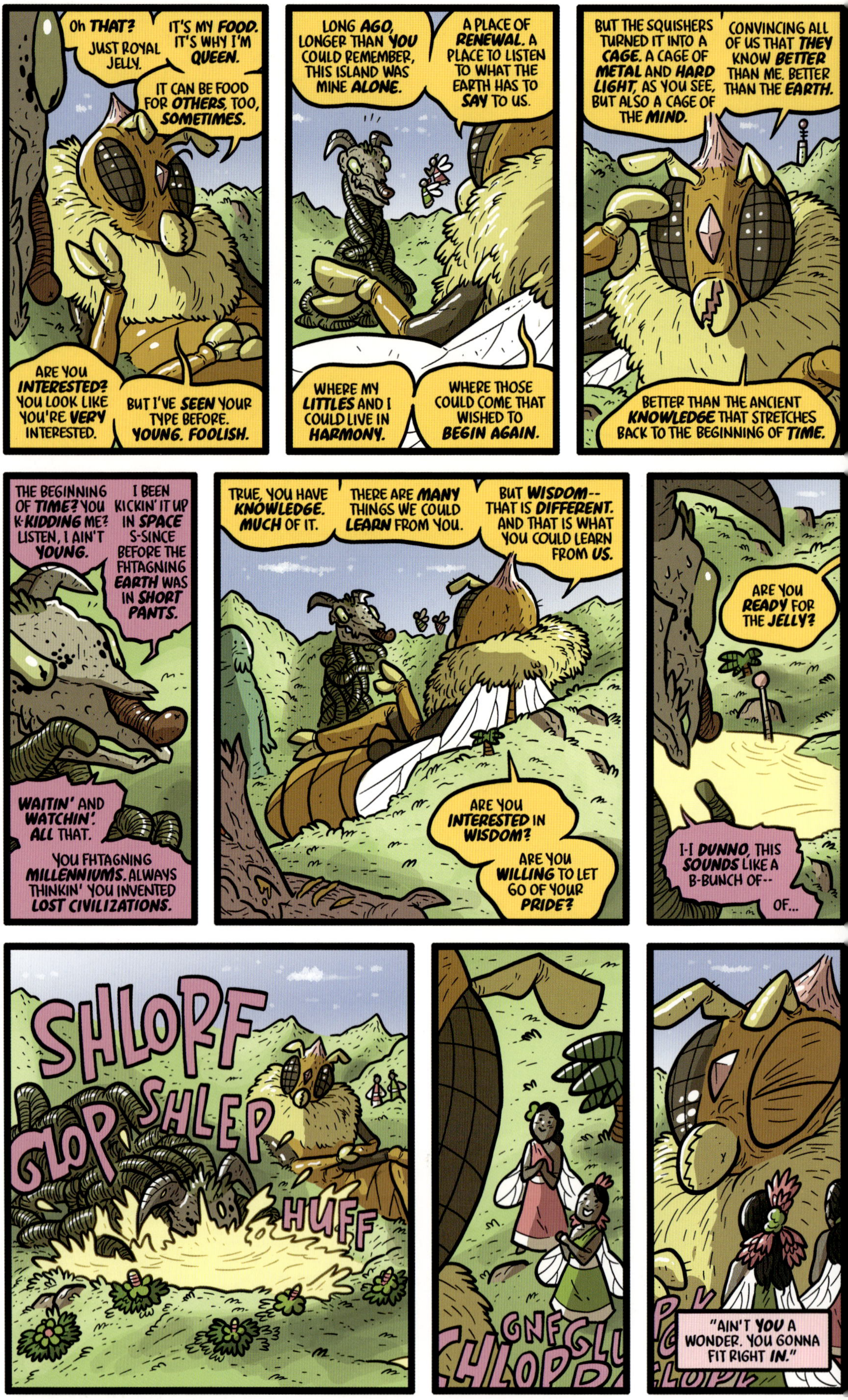
Oh THAT? JUST ROYAL JELLY.
IT'S MY FOOD. IT'S WHY I'M QUEEN.
IT CAN BE FOOD FOR OTHERS, TOO, SOMETIMES.
ARE YOU INTERESTED? YOU LOOK LIKE YOU'RE VERY INTERESTED.
BUT I'VE SEEN YOUR TYPE BEFORE. YOUNG. FOOLISH.
LONG AGO, LONGER THAN YOU COULD REMEMBER, THIS ISLAND WAS MINE ALONE.
A PLACE OF RENEWAL. A PLACE TO LISTEN TO WHAT THE EARTH HAS TO SAY TO US.
WHERE MY LITTLES AND I COULD LIVE IN HARMONY.
WHERE THOSE COULD COME THAT WISHED TO BEGIN AGAIN.
BUT THE SQUISHERS TURNED IT INTO A CAGE. A CAGE OF METAL AND HARD LIGHT, AS YOU SEE, BUT ALSO A CAGE OF THE MIND.
CONVINCING ALL OF US THAT THEY KNOW BETTER THAN ME. BETTER THAN THE EARTH.
BETTER THAN THE ANCIENT KNOWLEDGE THAT STRETCHES BACK TO THE BEGINNING OF TIME.
THE BEGINNING OF TIME? YOU K-KIDDING ME? LISTEN, I AIN'T YOUNG.
I BEEN KICKIN' IT UP IN SPACE S-SINCE BEFORE THE FHTAGNING EARTH WAS IN SHORT PANTS.
WAITIN' AND WATCHIN'. ALL THAT.
YOU FHTAGNING MILLENNIUMS. ALWAYS THINKIN' YOU INVENTED LOST CIVILIZATIONS.
TRUE, YOU HAVE KNOWLEDGE. MUCH OF IT.
THERE ARE MANY THINGS WE COULD LEARN FROM YOU.
BUT WISDOM-- THAT IS DIFFERENT. AND THAT IS WHAT YOU COULD LEARN FROM US.
ARE YOU INTERESTED IN WISDOM?
ARE YOU WILLING TO LET GO OF YOUR PRIDE?
ARE YOU READY FOR THE JELLY?
I-I DUNNO, THIS SOUNDS LIKE A B-BUNCH OF--
OF...
SHLORF
GLOP
SHLEP
HUFF
GNFGLU
"AIN'T YOU A WONDER. YOU GONNA FIT RIGHT IN."

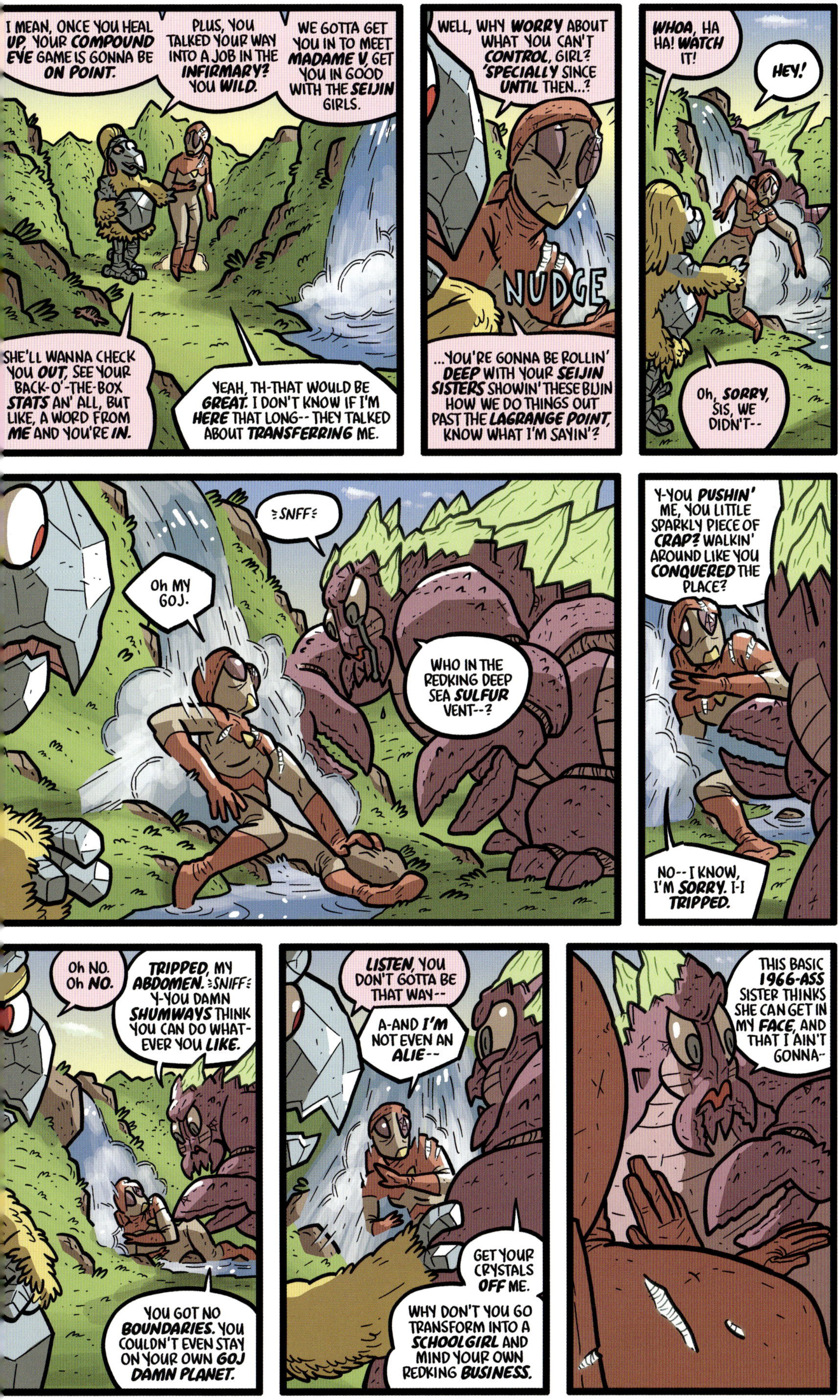
I MEAN, ONCE YOU HEAL UP, YOUR COMPOUND EYE GAME IS GONNA BE ON POINT.
PLUS, YOU TALKED YOUR WAY INTO A JOB IN THE INFIRMARY? YOU WILD.
WE GOTTA GET YOU IN TO MEET MADAME V, GET YOU IN GOOD WITH THE SEIJIN GIRLS.
SHE'LL WANNA CHECK YOU OUT, SEE YOUR BACK-O'-THE-BOX STATS AN' ALL, BUT LIKE, A WORD FROM ME AND YOU'RE IN.
YEAH, TH-THAT WOULD BE GREAT. I DON'T KNOW IF I'M HERE THAT LONG-- THEY TALKED ABOUT TRANSFERRING ME.
WELL, WHY WORRY ABOUT WHAT YOU CAN'T CONTROL, GIRL? 'SPECIALLY SINCE UNTIL THEN...?
NUDGE
...YOU'RE GONNA BE ROLLIN' DEEP WITH YOUR SEIJIN SISTERS SHOWIN' THESE BIJIN HOW WE DO THINGS OUT PAST THE LAGRANGE POINT, KNOW WHAT I'M SAYIN'?
WHOA, HA HA! WATCH IT!
HEY!
Oh, SORRY, SIS, WE DIDN'T--
SNFF
Oh MY GOJ.
WHO IN THE REDKING DEEP SEA SULFUR VENT--?
Y-YOU PUSHIN' ME, YOU LITTLE SPARKLY PIECE OF CRAP? WALKIN' AROUND LIKE YOU CONQUERED THE PLACE?
NO--I KNOW, I'M SORRY. I-I TRIPPED.
Oh NO. Oh NO.
TRIPPED, MY ABDOMEN. SNIFF Y-YOU DAMN SHUMWAYS THINK YOU CAN DO WHATEVER YOU LIKE.
YOU GOT NO BOUNDARIES. YOU COULDN'T EVEN STAY ON YOUR OWN GOJ DAMN PLANET.
LISTEN, YOU DON'T GOTTA BE THAT WAY--
A-AND I'M NOT EVEN AN ALIE--
GET YOUR CRYSTALS OFF ME.
WHY DON'T YOU GO TRANSFORM INTO A SCHOOLGIRL AND MIND YOUR OWN REDKING BUSINESS.
THIS BASIC 1966-ASS SISTER THINKS SHE CAN GET IN MY FACE, AND THAT I AIN'T GONNA-

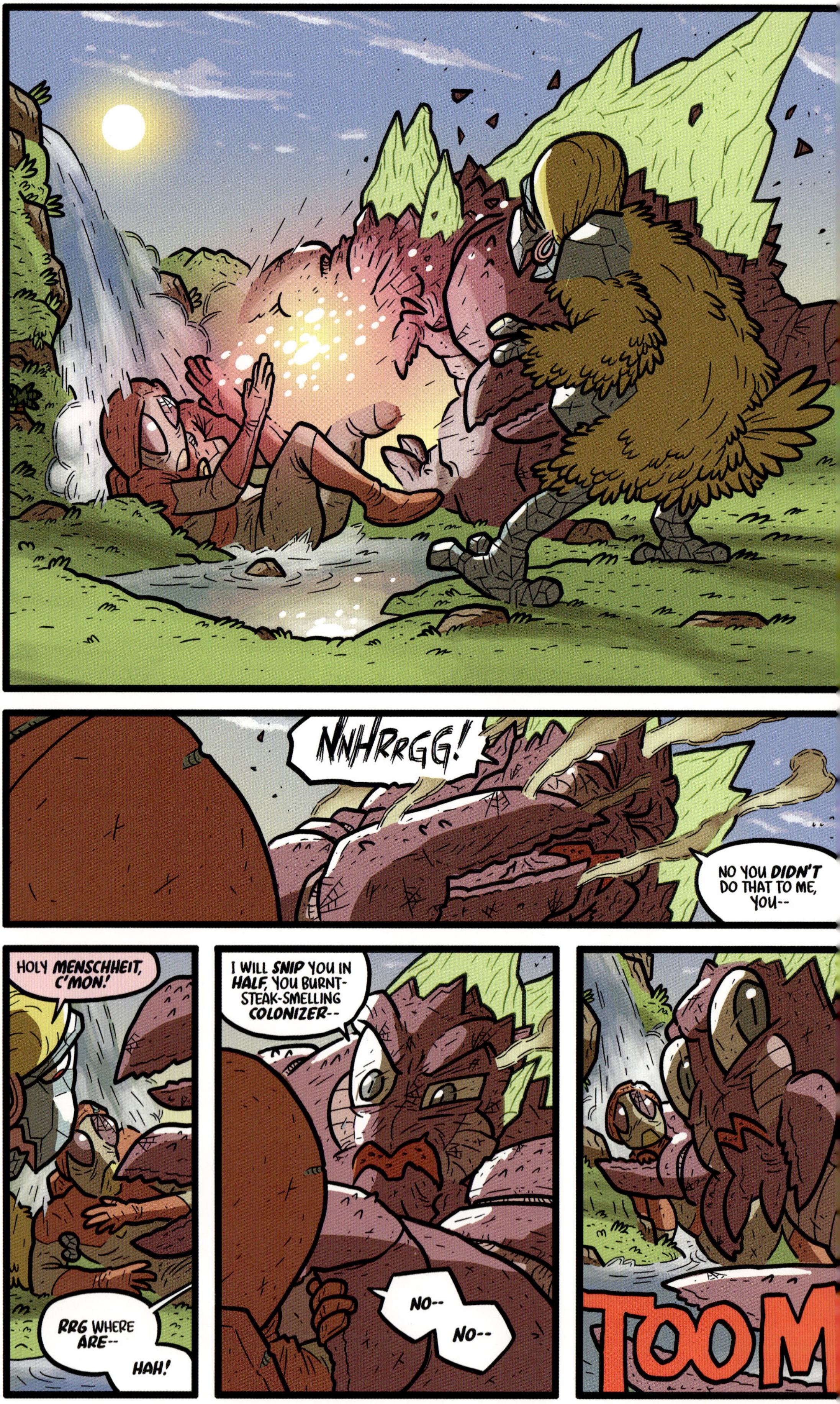
NNHRRGG!
NO YOU **DIDN'T** DO THAT TO ME, YOU--
HOLY **MENSCHHEIT,** C'MON!
RRG WHERE **ARE**--
HAH!
I WILL **SNIP** YOU IN **HALF,** YOU BURNT-STEAK-SMELLING **COLONIZER**--
NO--
NO--
TOOM

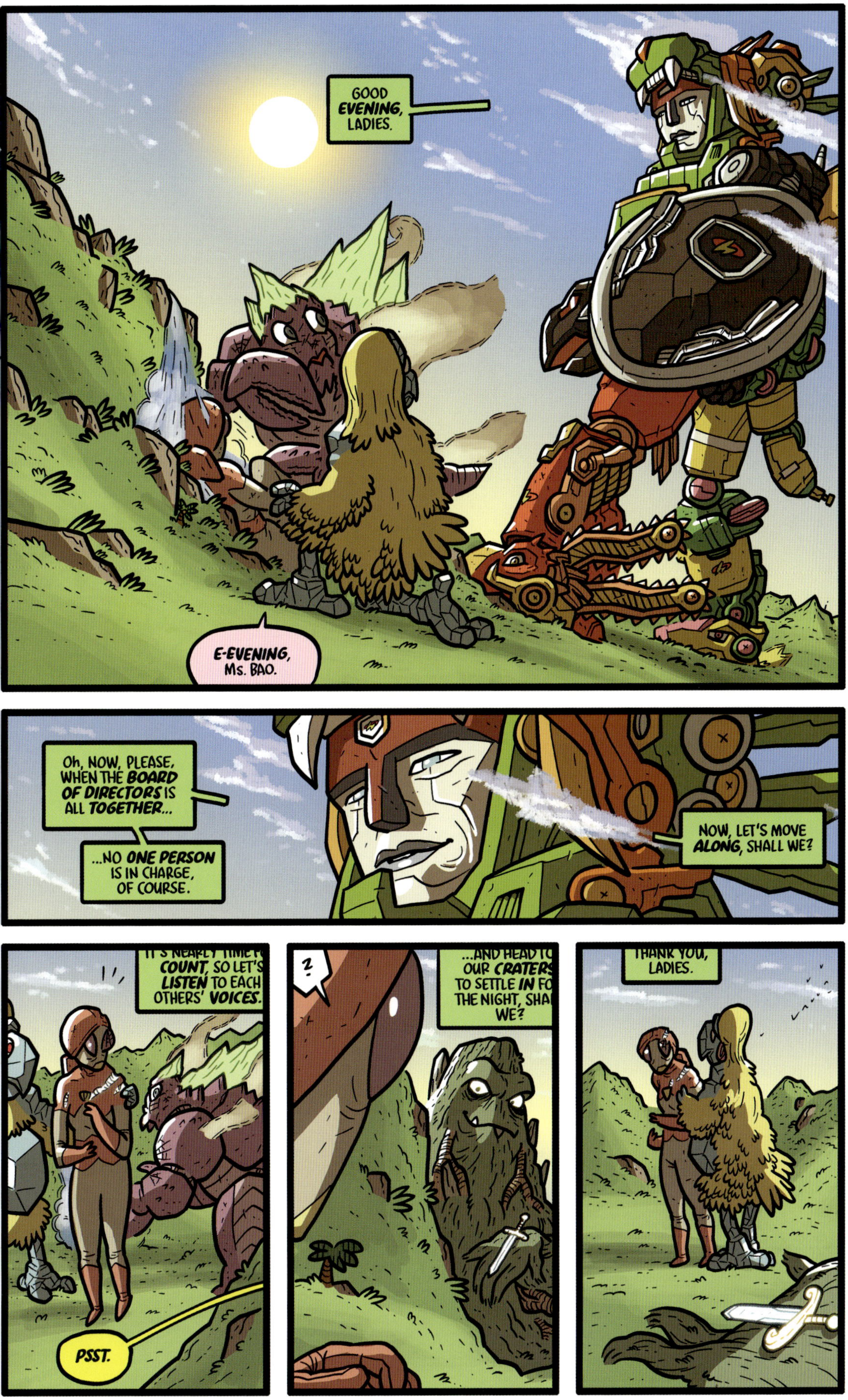
GOOD EVENING, LADIES.
E-EVENING, Ms. BAO.
Oh, NOW, PLEASE, WHEN THE BOARD OF DIRECTORS IS ALL TOGETHER...
...NO ONE PERSON IS IN CHARGE, OF COURSE.
NOW, LET'S MOVE ALONG, SHALL WE?
COUNT, SO LET'S LISTEN TO EACH OTHERS' VOICES.
PSST.
?
OUR CRATERS TO SETTLE IN FO THE NIGHT, SHA WE?
THANK YOU, LADIES.

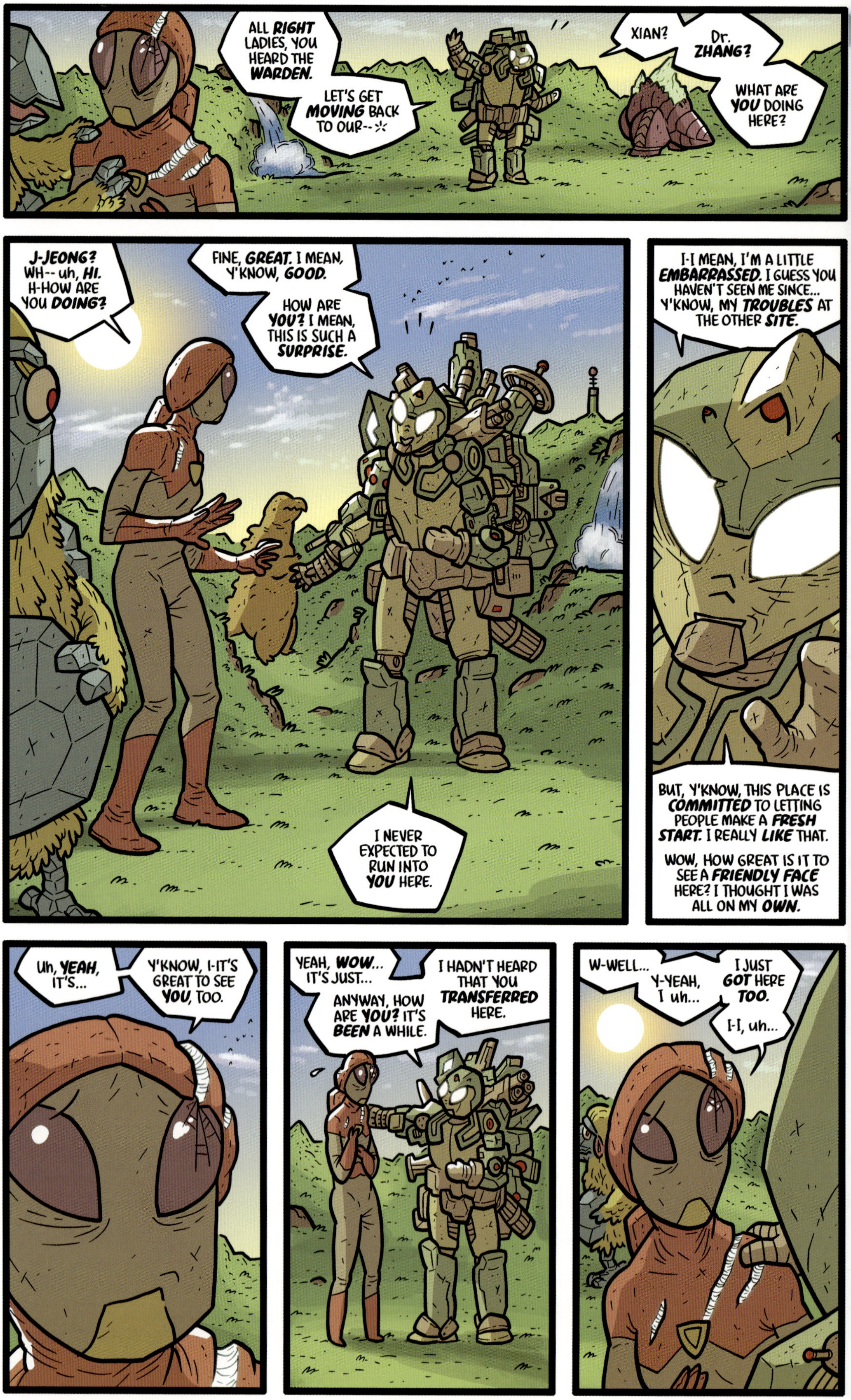
ALL RIGHT LADIES, YOU HEARD THE WARDEN.
LET'S GET MOVING BACK TO OUR--
XIAN?
Dr. ZHANG?
WHAT ARE YOU DOING HERE?
J-JEONG? WH-- uh, HI. H-HOW ARE YOU DOING?
FINE, GREAT. I MEAN, Y'KNOW, GOOD.
HOW ARE YOU? I MEAN, THIS IS SUCH A SURPRISE.
I NEVER EXPECTED TO RUN INTO YOU HERE.
I-I MEAN, I'M A LITTLE EMBARRASSED. I GUESS YOU HAVEN'T SEEN ME SINCE... Y'KNOW, MY TROUBLES AT THE OTHER SITE.
BUT, Y'KNOW, THIS PLACE IS COMMITTED TO LETTING PEOPLE MAKE A FRESH START. I REALLY LIKE THAT.
WOW, HOW GREAT IS IT TO SEE A FRIENDLY FACE HERE? I THOUGHT I WAS ALL ON MY OWN.
Uh, YEAH, IT'S...
Y'KNOW, I-IT'S GREAT TO SEE YOU, TOO.
YEAH, WOW... IT'S JUST...
ANYWAY, HOW ARE YOU? IT'S BEEN A WHILE.
I HADN'T HEARD THAT YOU TRANSFERRED HERE.
W-WELL...
Y-YEAH, I uh...
I JUST GOT HERE TOO.
I-I, uh...

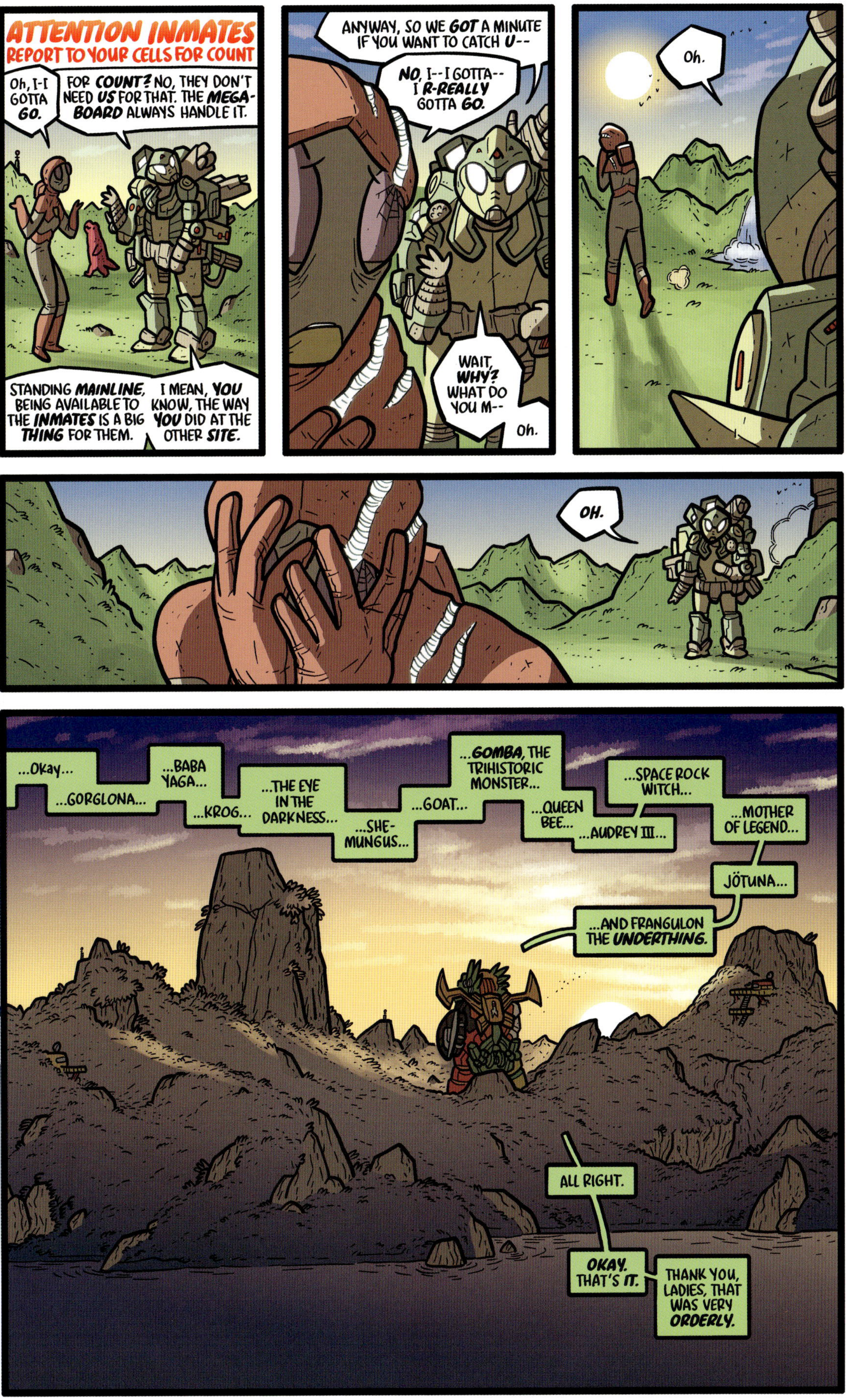
ATTENTION INMATES
REPORT TO YOUR CELLS FOR COUNT
Oh, I-I GOTTA GO.
FOR COUNT? NO, THEY DON'T NEED US FOR THAT. THE MEGA-BOARD ALWAYS HANDLE IT.
STANDING MAINLINE, BEING AVAILABLE TO THE INMATES IS A BIG THING FOR THEM.
I MEAN, YOU KNOW, THE WAY YOU DID AT THE OTHER SITE.
ANYWAY, SO WE GOT A MINUTE IF YOU WANT TO CATCH U--
NO, I--I GOTTA-- I R-REALLY GOTTA GO.
WAIT, WHY? WHAT DO YOU M--
Oh.
Oh.
OH.
...Okay...
...GORGLONA...
...BABA YAGA...
...KROG...
...THE EYE IN THE DARKNESS...
...SHE-MUNGUS...
...GOAT...
...GOMBA, THE TRIHISTORIC MONSTER...
...QUEEN BEE...
...AUDREY III...
...SPACE ROCK WITCH...
...MOTHER OF LEGEND...
JÖTUNA...
...AND FRANGULON THE UNDERTHING.
ALL RIGHT.
OKAY. THAT'S IT.
THANK YOU, LADIES, THAT WAS VERY ORDERLY.

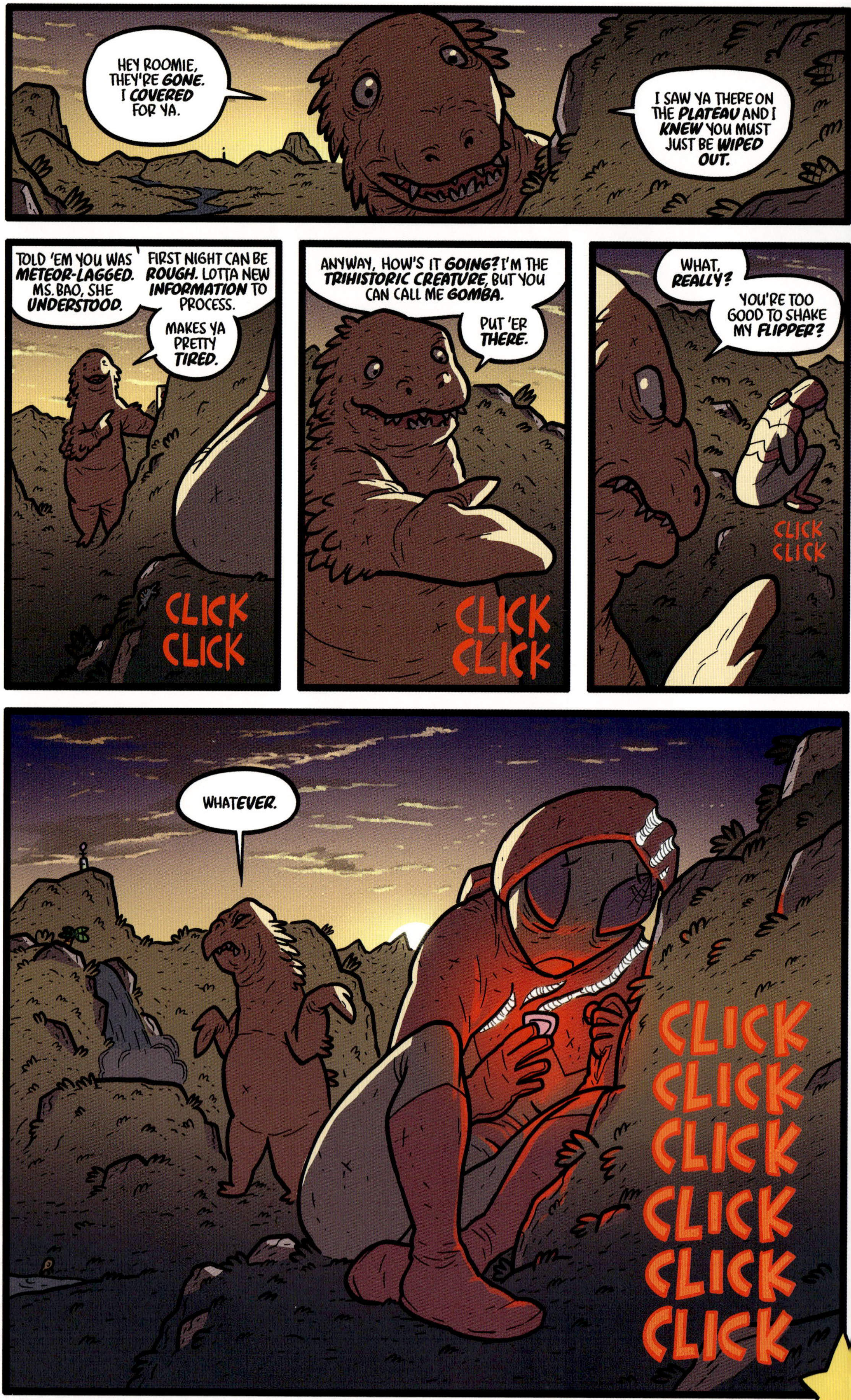
HEY ROOMIE, THEY'RE GONE. I COVERED FOR YA.
I SAW YA THERE ON THE PLATEAU AND I KNEW YOU MUST JUST BE WIPED OUT.
TOLD 'EM YOU WAS METEOR-LAGGED. MS. BAO, SHE UNDERSTOOD.
FIRST NIGHT CAN BE ROUGH. LOTTA NEW INFORMATION TO PROCESS.
MAKES YA PRETTY TIRED.
CLICK CLICK
ANYWAY, HOW'S IT GOING? I'M THE TRIHISTORIC CREATURE, BUT YOU CAN CALL ME GOMBA.
PUT 'ER THERE.
CLICK CLICK
WHAT, REALLY?
YOU'RE TOO GOOD TO SHAKE MY FLIPPER?
CLICK CLICK
WHATEVER.
CLICK CLICK CLICK CLICK CLICK CLICK

EPISODE 2

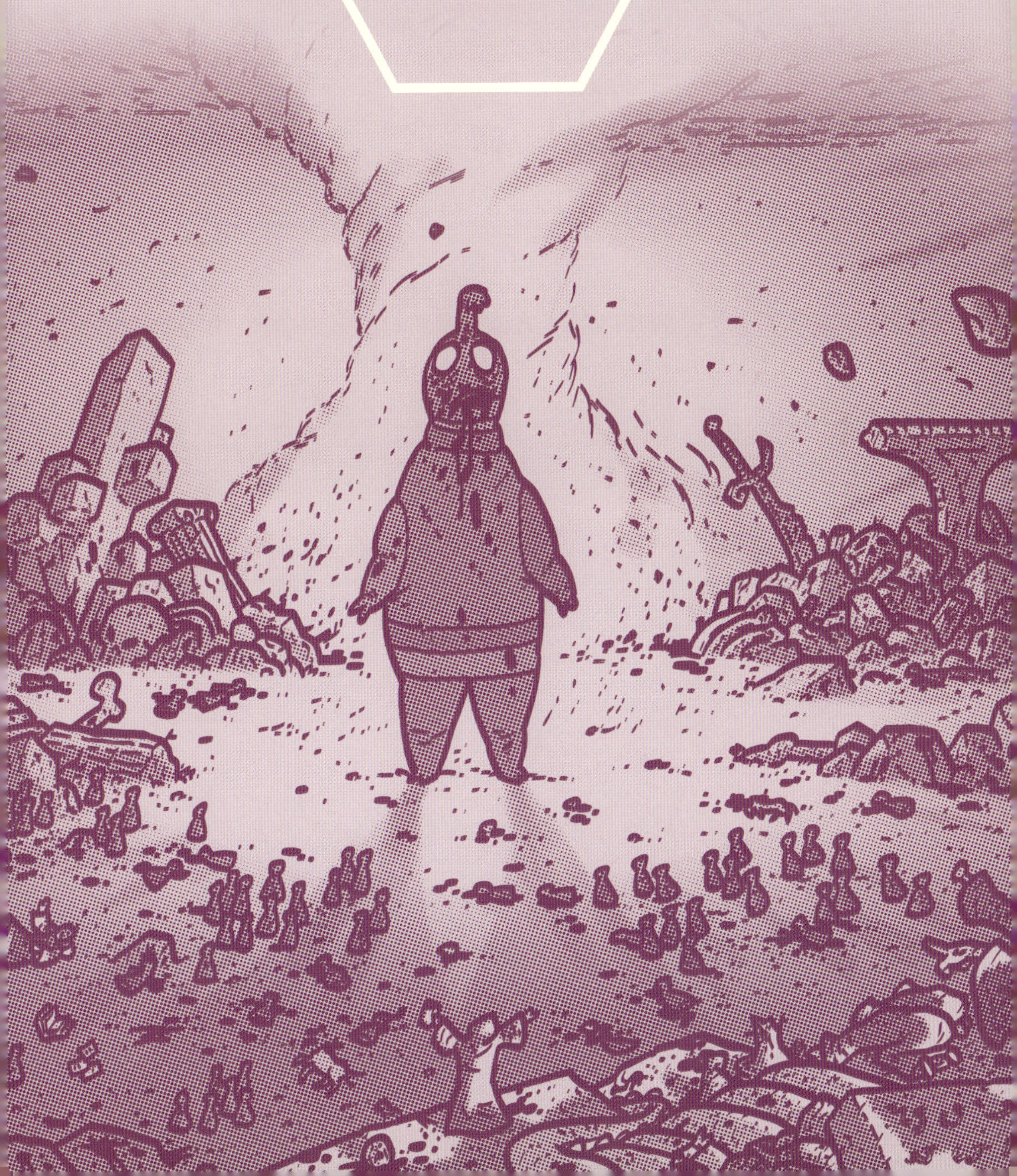

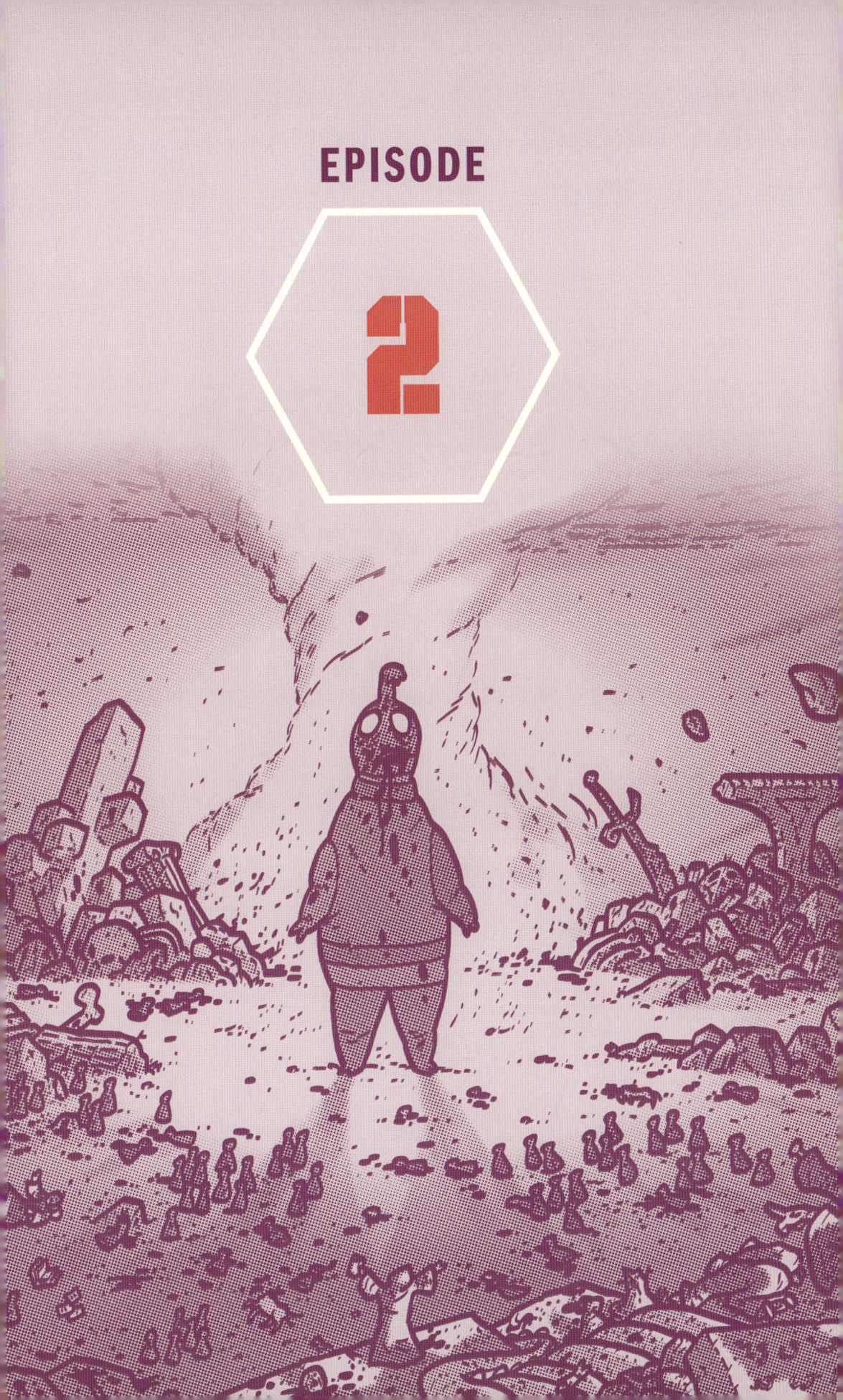

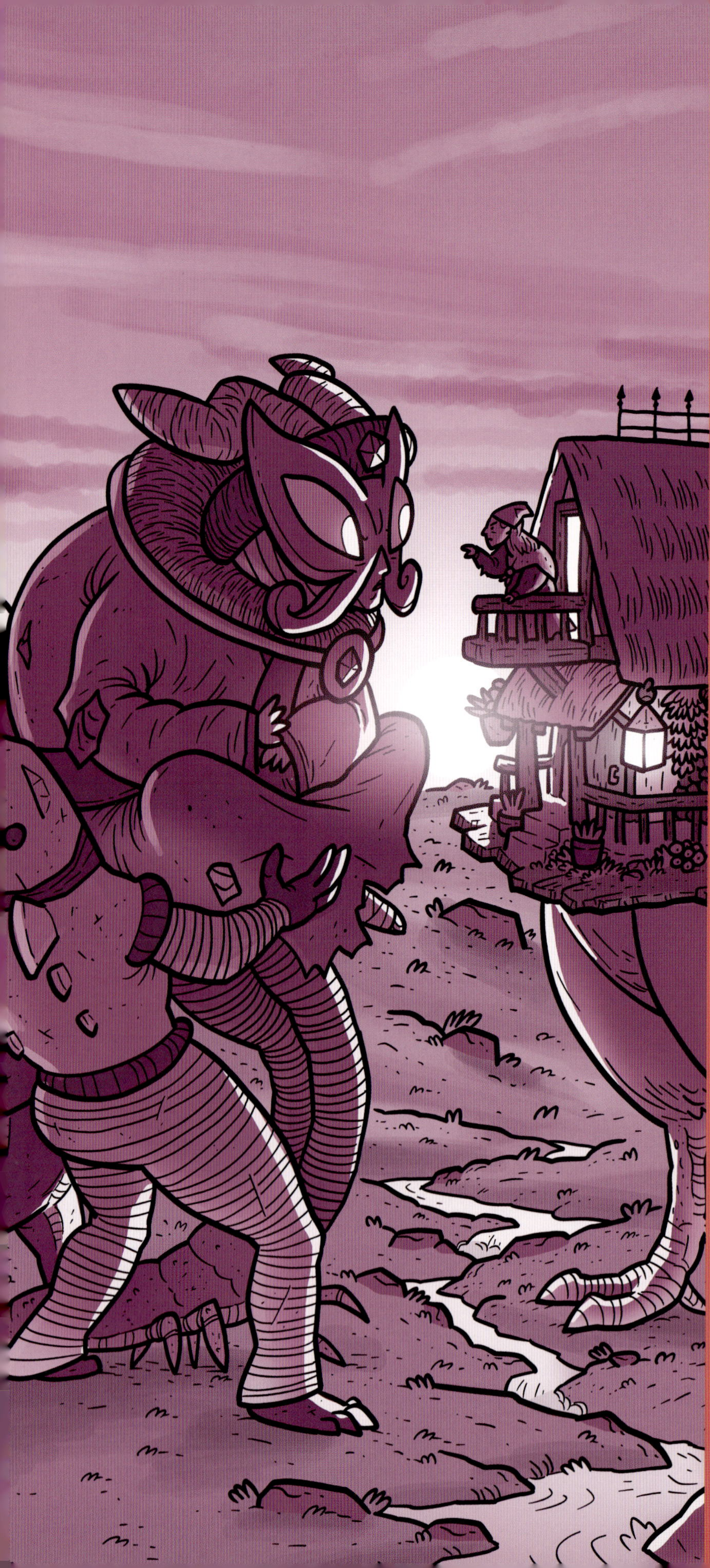

怪獣マックス

MS. BAO™
THE LITTLES™
GOAT™
WU™

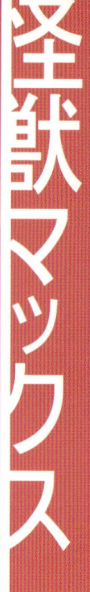

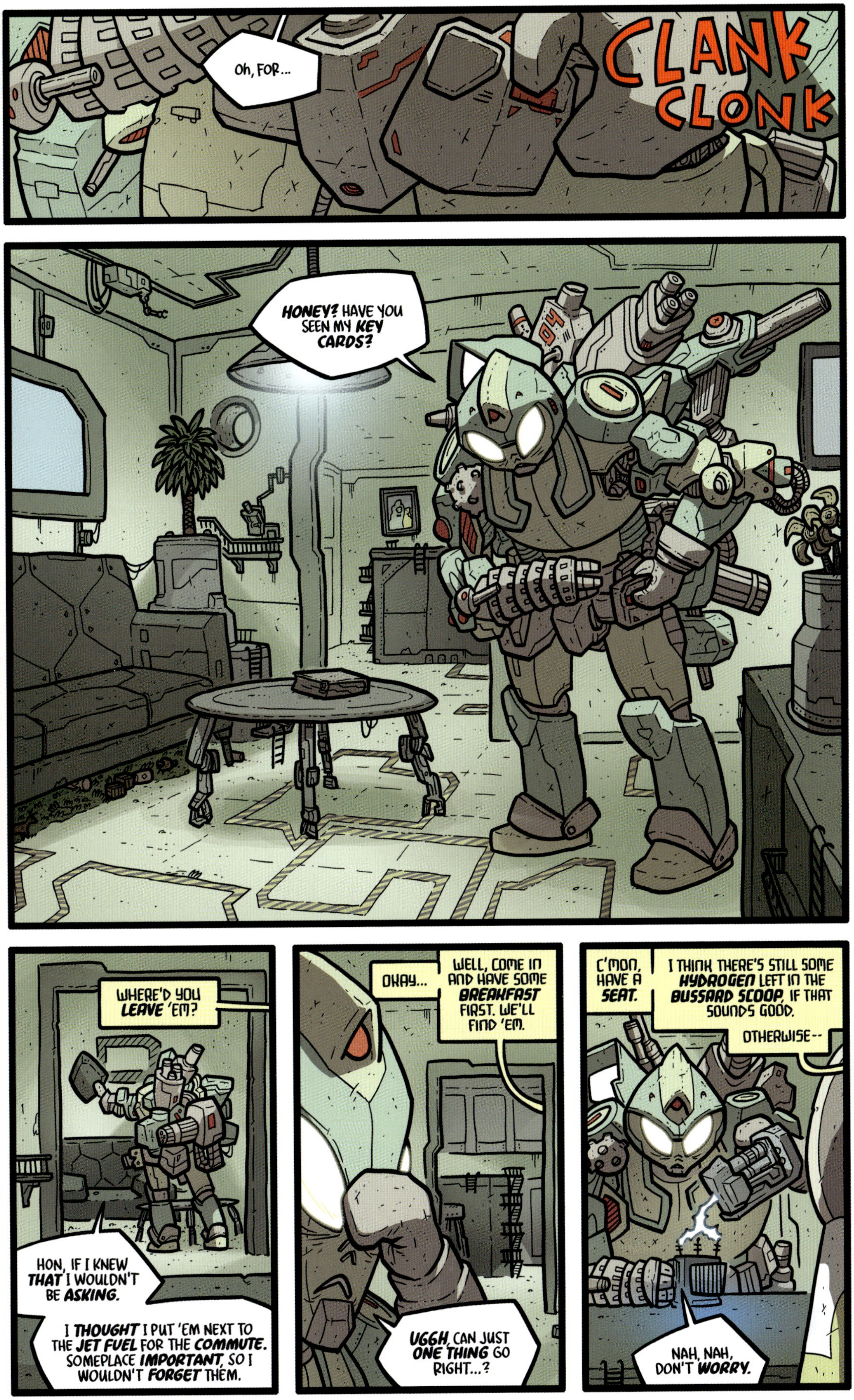
Oh, FOR...
CLANK
CLONK
HONEY? HAVE YOU SEEN MY KEY CARDS?
WHERE'D YOU LEAVE 'EM?
HON, IF I KNEW THAT I WOULDN'T BE ASKING.
I THOUGHT I PUT 'EM NEXT TO THE JET FUEL FOR THE COMMUTE. SOMEPLACE IMPORTANT, SO I WOULDN'T FORGET THEM.
OKAY...
WELL, COME IN AND HAVE SOME BREAKFAST FIRST. WE'LL FIND 'EM.
UGGH, CAN JUST ONE THING GO RIGHT...?
C'MON, HAVE A SEAT.
I THINK THERE'S STILL SOME HYDROGEN LEFT IN THE BUSSARD SCOOP, IF THAT SOUNDS GOOD.
OTHERWISE--
NAH, NAH, DON'T WORRY.

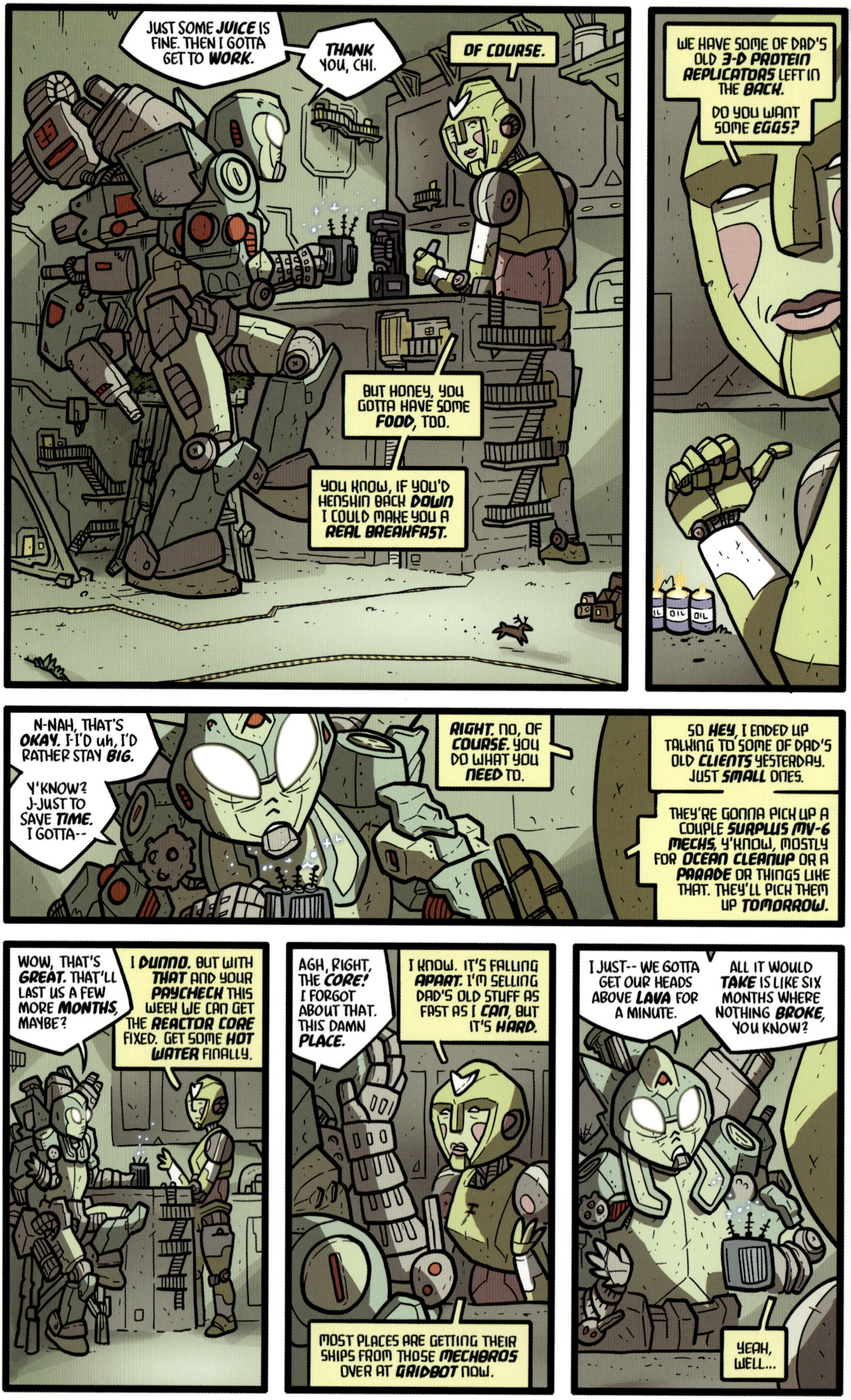
JUST SOME JUICE IS FINE. THEN I GOTTA GET TO WORK.
THANK YOU, CHI.
OF COURSE.
BUT HONEY, YOU GOTTA HAVE SOME FOOD, TOO.
YOU KNOW, IF YOU'D HENSHIN BACK DOWN I COULD MAKE YOU A REAL BREAKFAST.
WE HAVE SOME OF DAD'S OLD 3-D PROTEIN REPLICATORS LEFT IN THE BACK.
DO YOU WANT SOME EGGS?
OIL
OIL
N-NAH, THAT'S OKAY. I-I'D uh, I'D RATHER STAY BIG.
Y'KNOW? J-JUST TO SAVE TIME. I GOTTA--
RIGHT. NO, OF COURSE. YOU DO WHAT YOU NEED TO.
SO HEY, I ENDED UP TALKING TO SOME OF DAD'S OLD CLIENTS YESTERDAY. JUST SMALL ONES.
THEY'RE GONNA PICK UP A COUPLE SURPLUS MV-6 MECHS, Y'KNOW, MOSTLY FOR OCEAN CLEANUP OR A PARADE OR THINGS LIKE THAT. THEY'LL PICK THEM UP TOMORROW.
WOW, THAT'S GREAT. THAT'LL LAST US A FEW MORE MONTHS, MAYBE?
I DUNNO. BUT WITH THAT AND YOUR PAYCHECK THIS WEEK WE CAN GET THE REACTOR CORE FIXED. GET SOME HOT WATER FINALLY.
AGH, RIGHT, THE CORE! I FORGOT ABOUT THAT. THIS DAMN PLACE.
I KNOW. IT'S FALLING APART. I'M SELLING DAD'S OLD STUFF AS FAST AS I CAN, BUT IT'S HARD.
MOST PLACES ARE GETTING THEIR SHIPS FROM THOSE MECHBROS OVER AT GRIDBOT NOW.
I JUST-- WE GOTTA GET OUR HEADS ABOVE LAVA FOR A MINUTE.
ALL IT WOULD TAKE IS LIKE SIX MONTHS WHERE NOTHING BROKE, YOU KNOW?
YEAH, WELL...

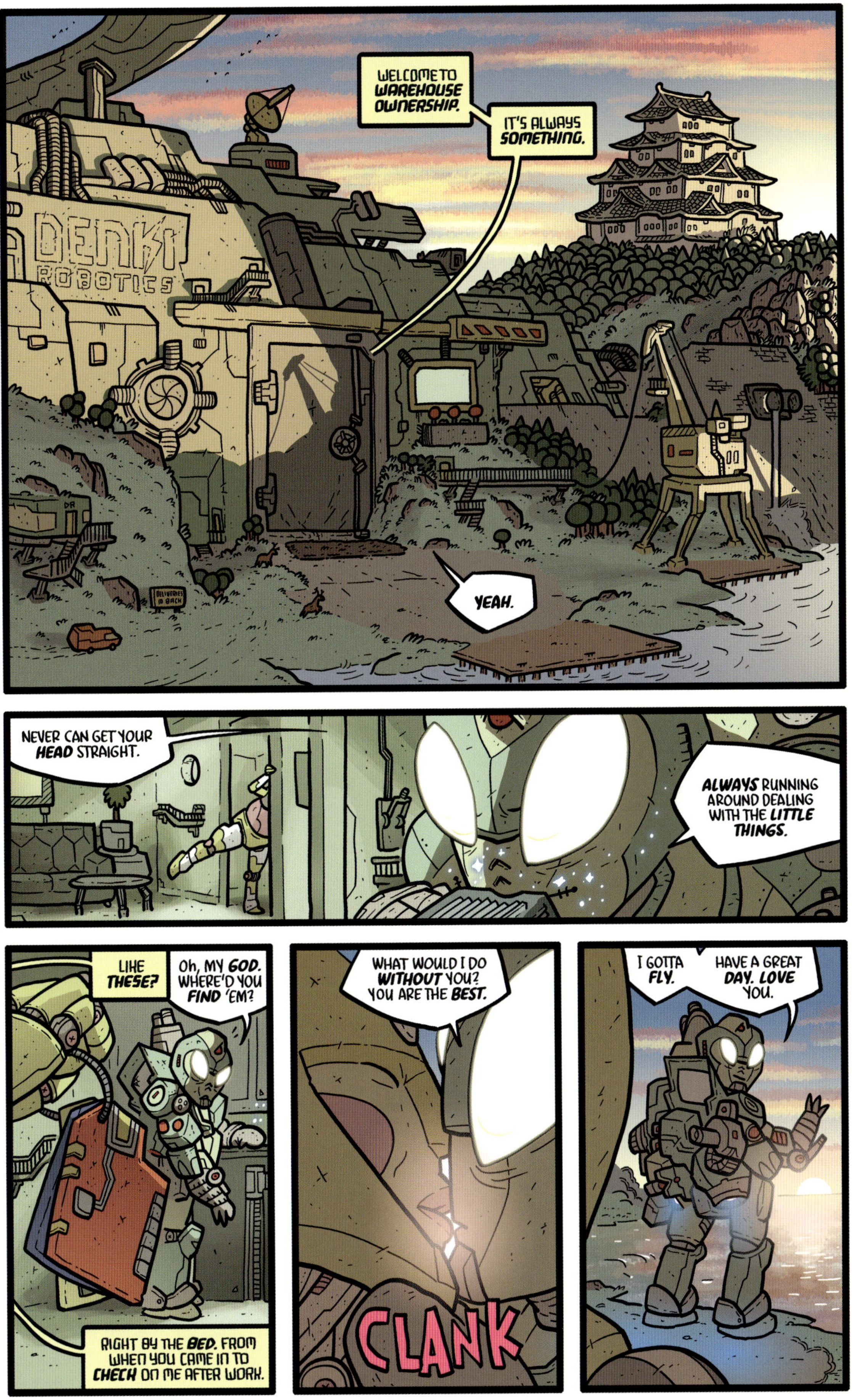
WELCOME TO WAREHOUSE OWNERSHIP.
IT'S ALWAYS SOMETHING.
DENKI ROBOTICS
YEAH.
NEVER CAN GET YOUR HEAD STRAIGHT.
ALWAYS RUNNING AROUND DEALING WITH THE LITTLE THINGS.
LIKE THESE?
Oh, MY GOD. WHERE'D YOU FIND 'EM?
RIGHT BY THE BED. FROM WHEN YOU CAME IN TO CHECK ON ME AFTER WORK.
WHAT WOULD I DO WITHOUT YOU? YOU ARE THE BEST.
CLANK
I GOTTA FLY.
HAVE A GREAT DAY. LOVE YOU.

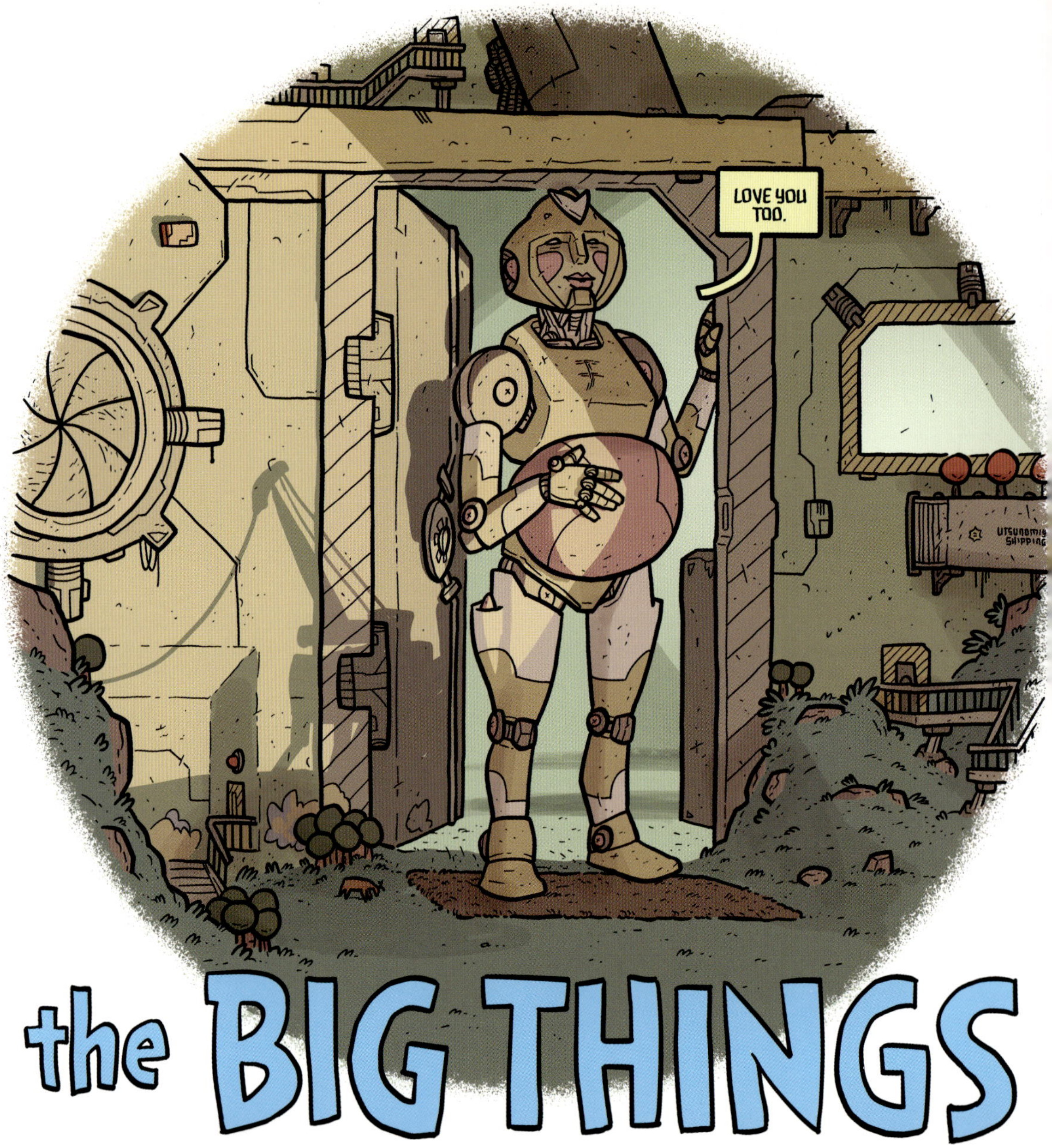
LOVE YOU TOO.
UTSUNOMIYA SHIPPING

the BIG THINGS

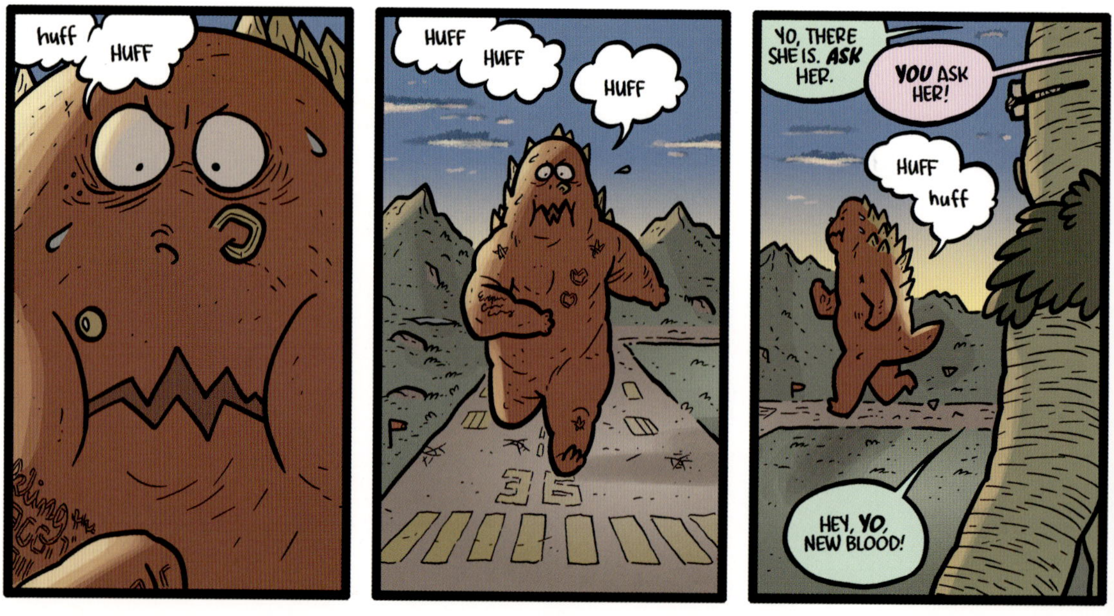
huff HUFF
HUFF HUFF
HUFF
YO, THERE SHE IS. ASK HER.
YOU ASK HER!
HUFF huff
HEY, YO, NEW BLOOD!

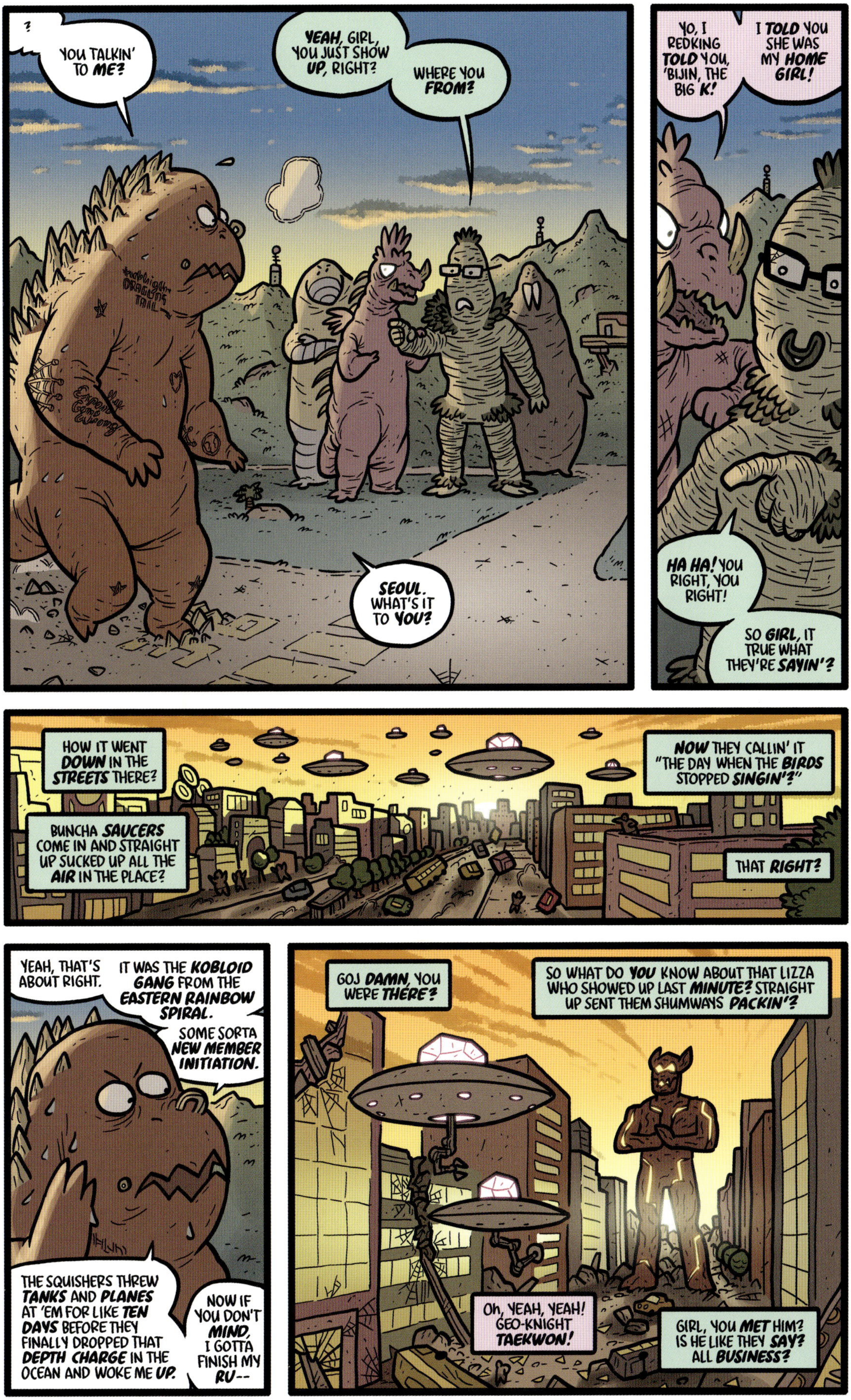
?
YOU TALKIN' TO ME?
YEAH, GIRL, YOU JUST SHOW UP, RIGHT?
WHERE YOU FROM?
SEOUL. WHAT'S IT TO YOU?
YO, I REDKING TOLD YOU, 'BIJIN, THE BIG K!
I TOLD YOU SHE WAS MY HOME GIRL!
HA HA! YOU RIGHT, YOU RIGHT!
SO GIRL, IT TRUE WHAT THEY'RE SAYIN'?
HOW IT WENT DOWN IN THE STREETS THERE?
BUNCHA SAUCERS COME IN AND STRAIGHT UP SUCKED UP ALL THE AIR IN THE PLACE?
NOW THEY CALLIN' IT "THE DAY WHEN THE BIRDS STOPPED SINGIN'?"
THAT RIGHT?
YEAH, THAT'S ABOUT RIGHT.
IT WAS THE KOBLOID GANG FROM THE EASTERN RAINBOW SPIRAL.
SOME SORTA NEW MEMBER INITIATION.
THE SQUISHERS THREW TANKS AND PLANES AT 'EM FOR LIKE TEN DAYS BEFORE THEY FINALLY DROPPED THAT DEPTH CHARGE IN THE OCEAN AND WOKE ME UP.
NOW IF YOU DON'T MIND, I GOTTA FINISH MY RU--
GOJ DAMN, YOU WERE THERE?
SO WHAT DO YOU KNOW ABOUT THAT LIZZA WHO SHOWED UP LAST MINUTE? STRAIGHT UP SENT THEM SHUMWAYS PACKIN'?
OH, YEAH, YEAH! GEO-KNIGHT TAEKWON!
GIRL, YOU MET HIM? IS HE LIKE THEY SAY? ALL BUSINESS?

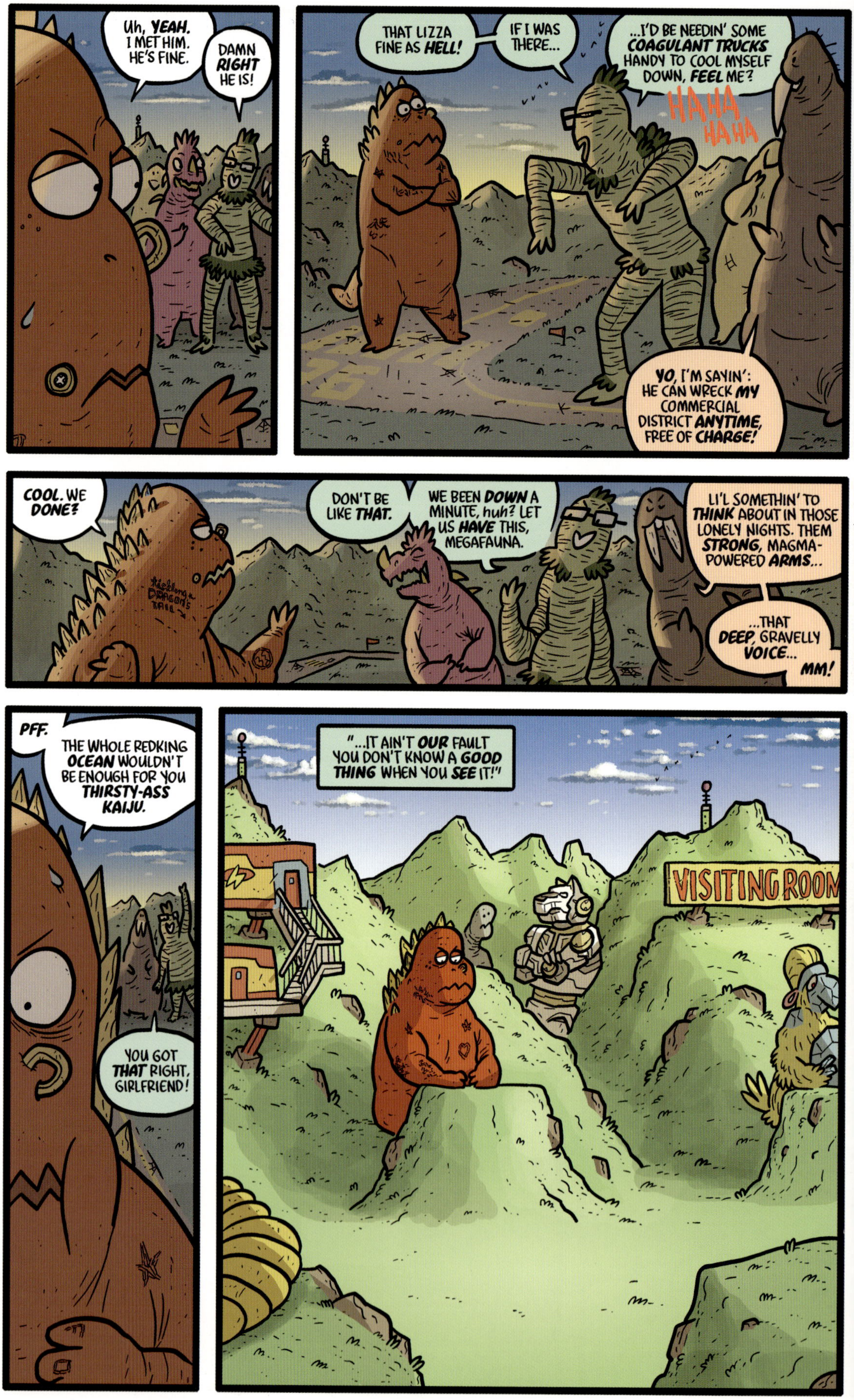

Uh, YEAH. I MET HIM. HE'S FINE.
DAMN RIGHT HE IS!
THAT LIZZA FINE AS HELL!
IF I WAS THERE...
...I'D BE NEEDIN' SOME COAGULANT TRUCKS HANDY TO COOL MYSELF DOWN, FEEL ME?
HAHA HAHA
YO, I'M SAYIN': HE CAN WRECK MY COMMERCIAL DISTRICT ANYTIME, FREE OF CHARGE!
COOL. WE DONE?
DON'T BE LIKE THAT.
WE BEEN DOWN A MINUTE, huh? LET US HAVE THIS, MEGAFAUNA.
LI'L SOMETHIN' TO THINK ABOUT IN THOSE LONELY NIGHTS. THEM STRONG, MAGMA-POWERED ARMS...
...THAT DEEP, GRAVELLY VOICE...
MM!
PFF.
THE WHOLE REDKING OCEAN WOULDN'T BE ENOUGH FOR YOU THIRSTY-ASS KAIJU.
YOU GOT THAT RIGHT, GIRLFRIEND!
"...IT AIN'T OUR FAULT YOU DON'T KNOW A GOOD THING WHEN YOU SEE IT!"
VISITING ROOM

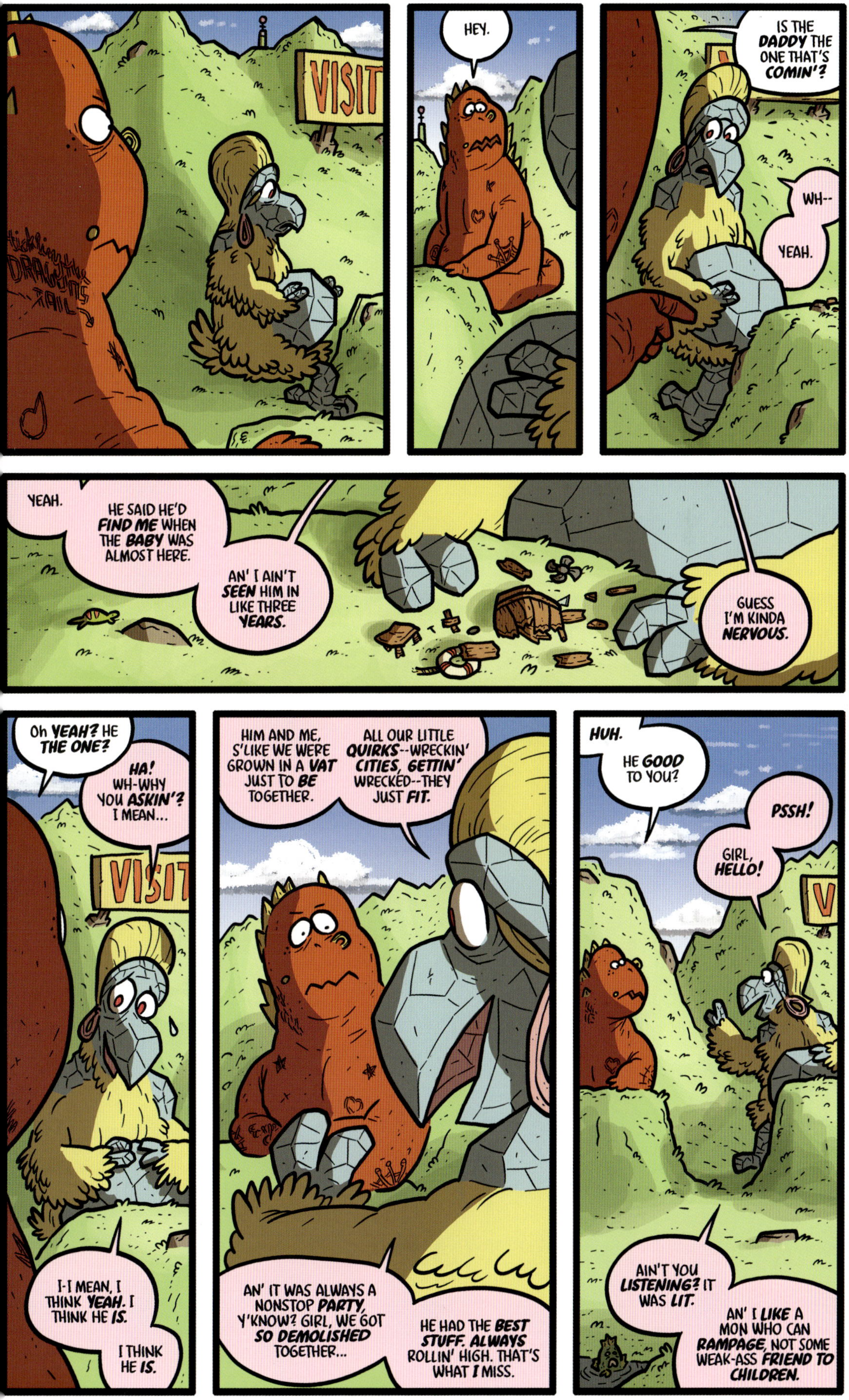

VISIT
Tickling the DRAGON'S TAIL
HEY.
IS THE **DADDY** THE ONE THAT'S **COMIN'?**
WH--
YEAH.
YEAH.
HE SAID HE'D **FIND ME** WHEN THE **BABY** WAS ALMOST HERE.
AN' I AIN'T **SEEN** HIM IN LIKE THREE **YEARS.**
GUESS I'M KINDA **NERVOUS.**
Oh **YEAH?** HE **THE ONE?**
HA! WH-WHY YOU **ASKIN'?** I MEAN...
VISIT
I-I MEAN, I THINK **YEAH.** I THINK HE **IS.**
I THINK HE **IS.**
HIM AND ME, S'LIKE WE WERE GROWN IN A **VAT** JUST TO **BE** TOGETHER.
ALL OUR LITTLE **QUIRKS**--WRECKIN' **CITIES, GETTIN'** WRECKED--THEY JUST **FIT.**
AN' IT WAS ALWAYS A NONSTOP **PARTY,** Y'KNOW? GIRL, WE GOT **SO DEMOLISHED** TOGETHER...
HE HAD THE **BEST STUFF. ALWAYS** ROLLIN' HIGH. THAT'S WHAT **I** MISS.
HUH.
HE **GOOD** TO YOU?
PSSH!
GIRL, **HELLO!**
AIN'T YOU **LISTENING?** IT WAS **LIT.**
AN' I **LIKE** A MON WHO CAN **RAMPAGE,** NOT SOME WEAK-ASS **FRIEND TO CHILDREN.**

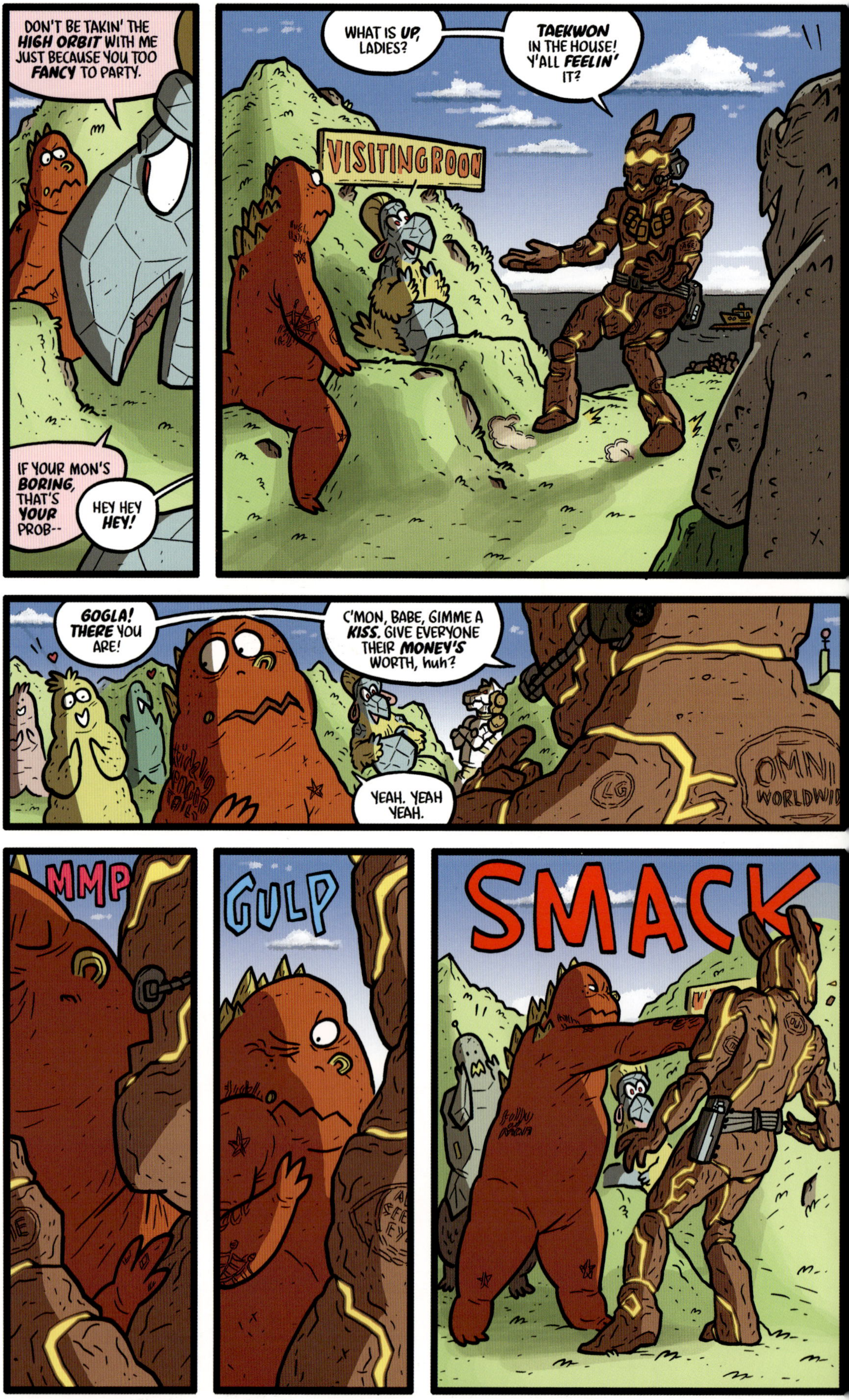
DON'T BE TAKIN' THE HIGH ORBIT WITH ME JUST BECAUSE YOU TOO FANCY TO PARTY.
IF YOUR MON'S BORING, THAT'S YOUR PROB--
HEY HEY HEY!
WHAT IS UP, LADIES?
TAEKWON IN THE HOUSE! Y'ALL FEELIN' IT?
VISITING ROOM
GOGLA! THERE YOU ARE!
C'MON, BABE, GIMME A KISS. GIVE EVERYONE THEIR MONEY'S WORTH, huh?
YEAH. YEAH YEAH.
OMNI WORLDWID
MMP
GULP
SMACK

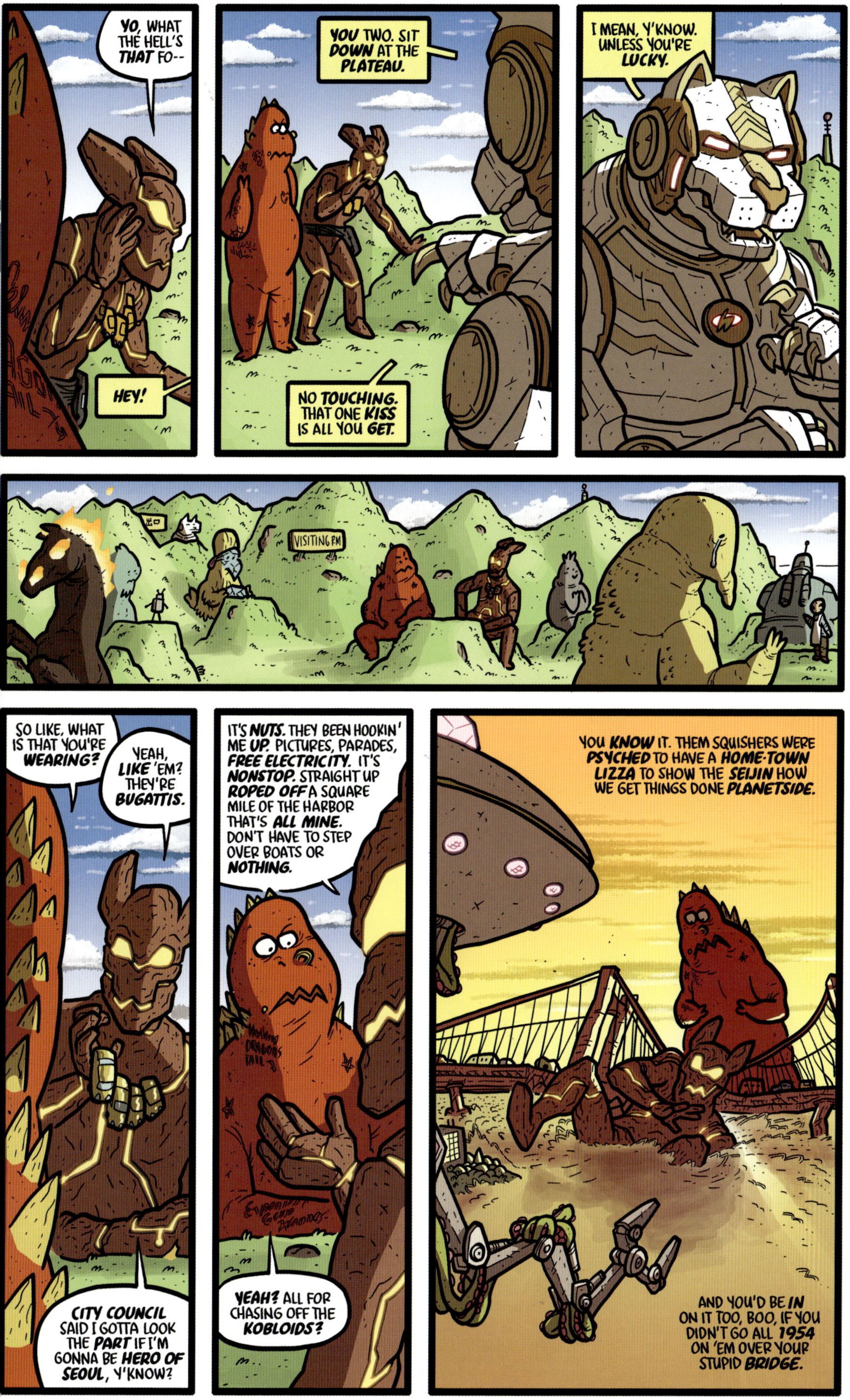

YO, WHAT THE HELL'S THAT FO--
HEY!
YOU TWO. SIT DOWN AT THE PLATEAU.
NO TOUCHING. THAT ONE KISS IS ALL YOU GET.
I MEAN, Y'KNOW. UNLESS YOU'RE LUCKY.
VISITING PM
SO LIKE, WHAT IS THAT YOU'RE WEARING?
YEAH, LIKE 'EM? THEY'RE BUGATTIS.
CITY COUNCIL SAID I GOTTA LOOK THE PART IF I'M GONNA BE HERO OF SEOUL, Y'KNOW?
IT'S NUTS. THEY BEEN HOOKIN' ME UP. PICTURES, PARADES, FREE ELECTRICITY. IT'S NONSTOP. STRAIGHT UP ROPED OFF A SQUARE MILE OF THE HARBOR THAT'S ALL MINE. DON'T HAVE TO STEP OVER BOATS OR NOTHING.
YEAH? ALL FOR CHASING OFF THE KOBLOIDS?
YOU KNOW IT. THEM SQUISHERS WERE PSYCHED TO HAVE A HOME-TOWN LIZZA TO SHOW THE SEIJIN HOW WE GET THINGS DONE PLANETSIDE.
AND YOU'D BE IN ON IT TOO, BOO, IF YOU DIDN'T GO ALL 1954 ON 'EM OVER YOUR STUPID BRIDGE.

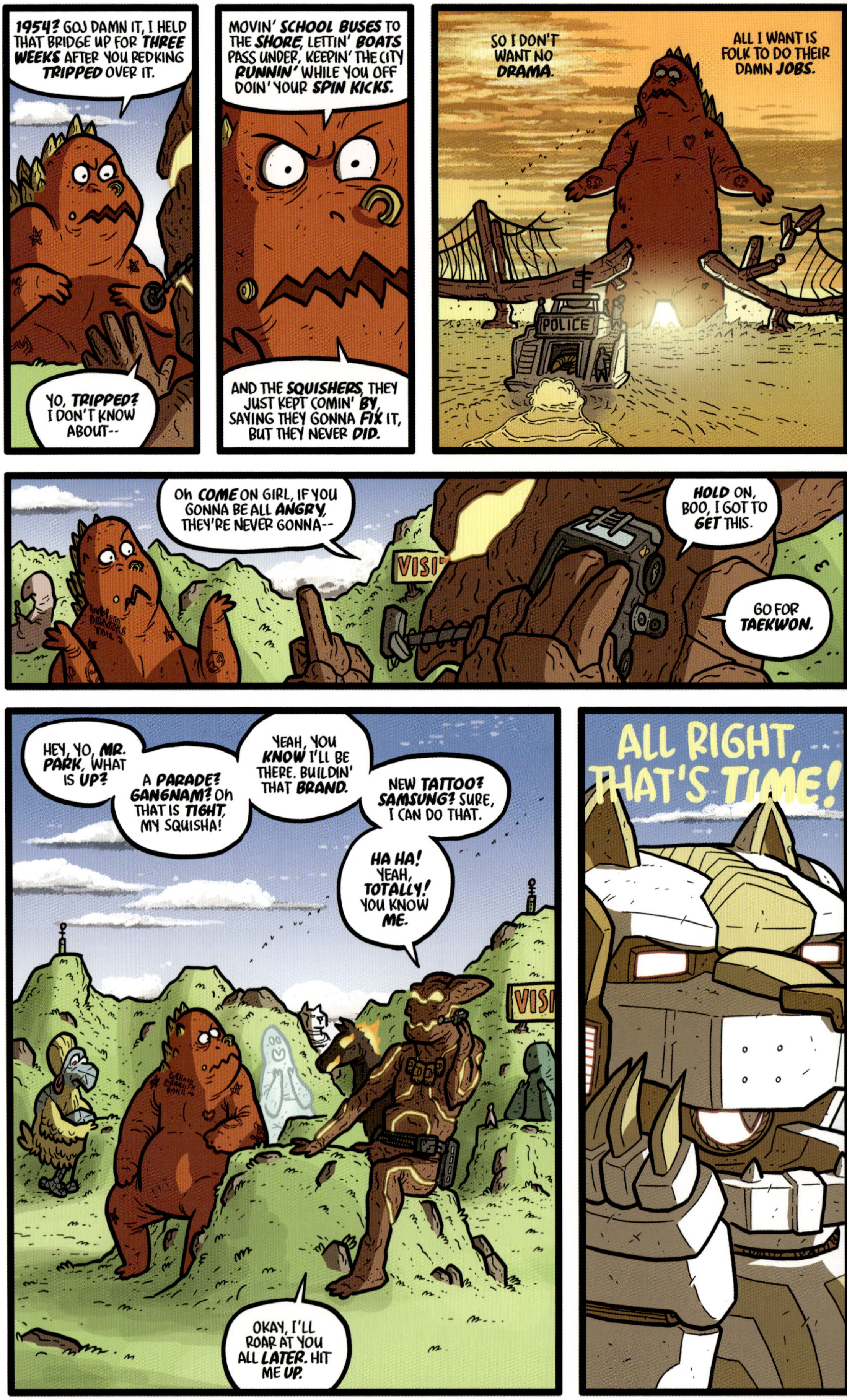
1954? GOJ DAMN IT, I HELD THAT BRIDGE UP FOR THREE WEEKS AFTER YOU REDKING TRIPPED OVER IT.
YO, TRIPPED? I DON'T KNOW ABOUT--
MOVIN' SCHOOL BUSES TO THE SHORE, LETTIN' BOATS PASS UNDER, KEEPIN' THE CITY RUNNIN' WHILE YOU OFF DOIN' YOUR SPIN KICKS.
AND THE SQUISHERS, THEY JUST KEPT COMIN' BY, SAYING THEY GONNA FIX IT, BUT THEY NEVER DID.
SO I DON'T WANT NO DRAMA.
ALL I WANT IS FOLK TO DO THEIR DAMN JOBS.
POLICE
Oh COME ON GIRL, IF YOU GONNA BE ALL ANGRY, THEY'RE NEVER GONNA--
HOLD ON, BOO, I GOT TO GET THIS.
GO FOR TAEKWON.
HEY, YO, MR. PARK, WHAT IS UP?
A PARADE? GANGNAM? Oh THAT IS TIGHT, MY SQUISHA!
YEAH, YOU KNOW I'LL BE THERE. BUILDIN' THAT BRAND.
NEW TATTOO? SAMSUNG? SURE, I CAN DO THAT.
HA HA! YEAH, TOTALLY! YOU KNOW ME.
OKAY, I'LL ROAR AT YOU ALL LATER. HIT ME UP.
ALL RIGHT, THAT'S TIME!

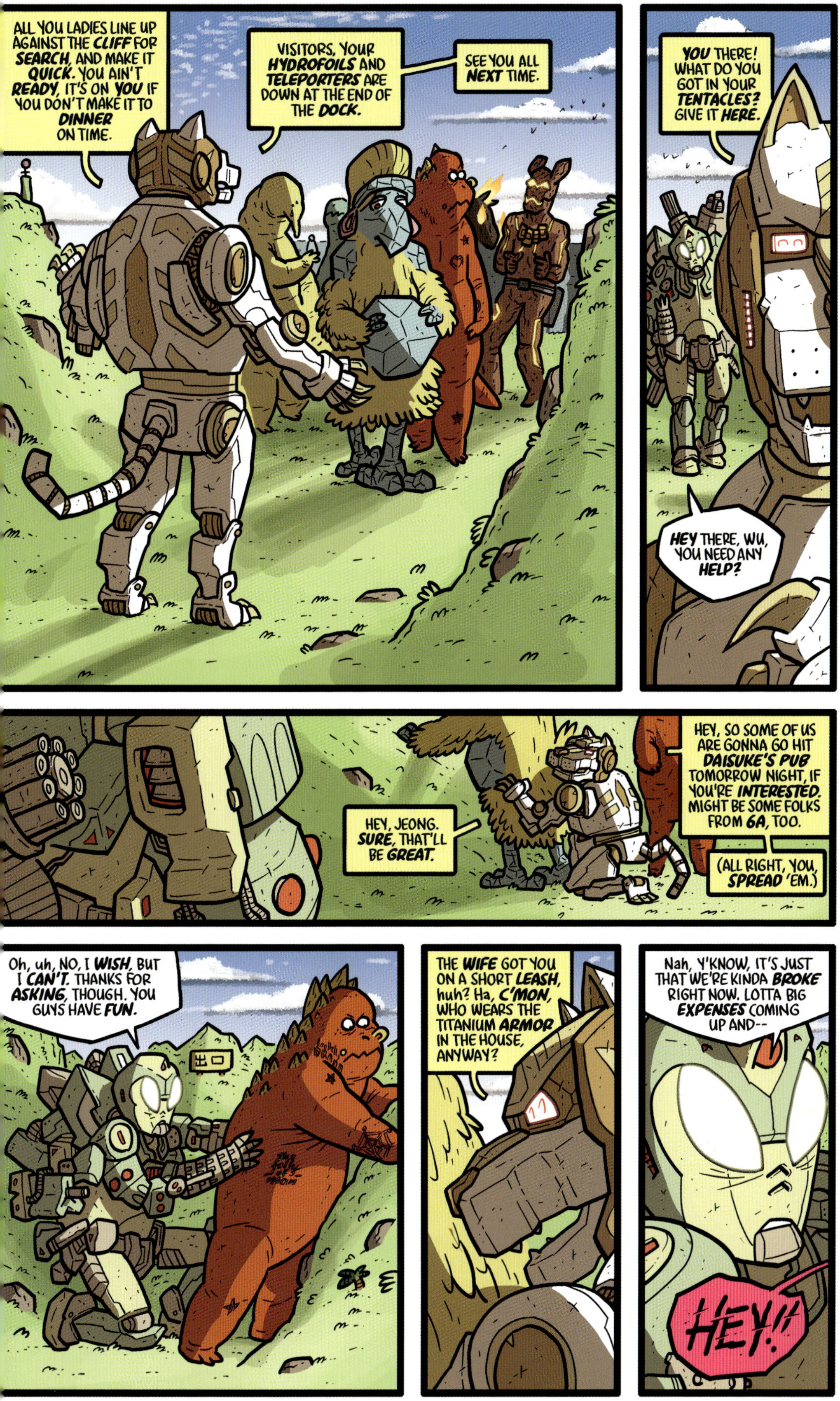
ALL YOU LADIES LINE UP AGAINST THE CLIFF FOR SEARCH, AND MAKE IT QUICK. YOU AIN'T READY, IT'S ON YOU IF YOU DON'T MAKE IT TO DINNER ON TIME.
VISITORS, YOUR HYDROFOILS AND TELEPORTERS ARE DOWN AT THE END OF THE DOCK.
SEE YOU ALL NEXT TIME.
YOU THERE! WHAT DO YOU GOT IN YOUR TENTACLES? GIVE IT HERE.
HEY THERE, WU, YOU NEED ANY HELP?
HEY, JEONG. SURE, THAT'LL BE GREAT.
HEY, SO SOME OF US ARE GONNA GO HIT DAISUKE'S PUB TOMORROW NIGHT, IF YOU'RE INTERESTED. MIGHT BE SOME FOLKS FROM 6A, TOO.
(ALL RIGHT, YOU, SPREAD 'EM.)
Oh, uh, NO, I WISH, BUT I CAN'T. THANKS FOR ASKING, THOUGH. YOU GUYS HAVE FUN.
THE WIFE GOT YOU ON A SHORT LEASH, huh? Ha, C'MON, WHO WEARS THE TITANIUM ARMOR IN THE HOUSE, ANYWAY?
Nah, Y'KNOW, IT'S JUST THAT WE'RE KINDA BROKE RIGHT NOW. LOTTA BIG EXPENSES COMING UP AND--
HEY!!

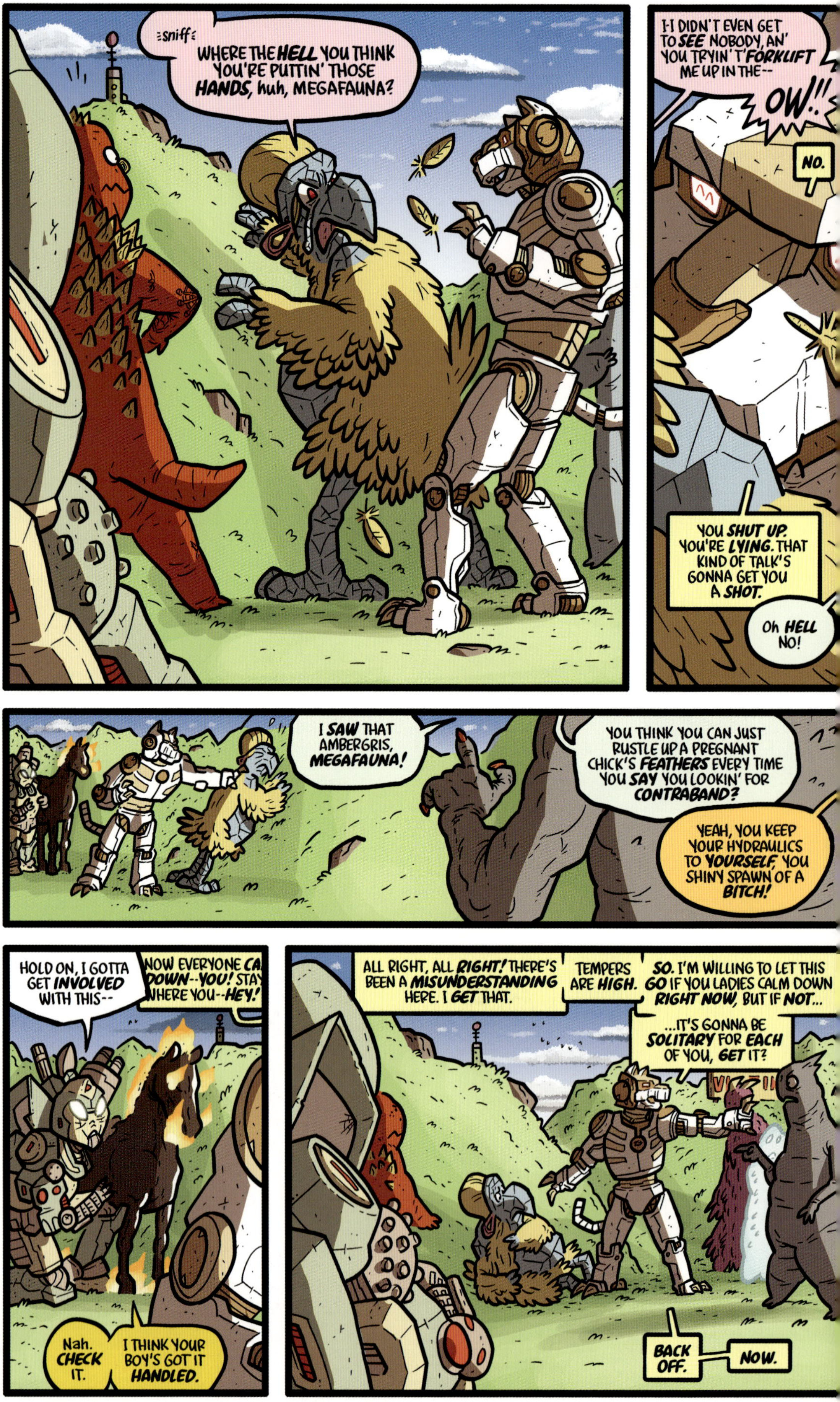

≈sniff≈
WHERE THE HELL YOU THINK YOU'RE PUTTIN' THOSE HANDS, huh, MEGAFAUNA?
I-I DIDN'T EVEN GET TO SEE NOBODY, AN' YOU TRYIN' T'FORKLIFT ME UP IN THE--
OW!!
NO.
YOU SHUT UP. YOU'RE LYING. THAT KIND OF TALK'S GONNA GET YOU A SHOT.
Oh HELL NO!
I SAW THAT AMBERGRIS, MEGAFAUNA!
YOU THINK YOU CAN JUST RUSTLE UP A PREGNANT CHICK'S FEATHERS EVERY TIME YOU SAY YOU LOOKIN' FOR CONTRABAND?
YEAH, YOU KEEP YOUR HYDRAULICS TO YOURSELF, YOU SHINY SPAWN OF A BITCH!
HOLD ON, I GOTTA GET INVOLVED WITH THIS--
NOW EVERYONE CA DOWN--YOU! STAY WHERE YOU--HEY!
Nah. CHECK IT.
I THINK YOUR BOY'S GOT IT HANDLED.
ALL RIGHT, ALL RIGHT! THERE'S BEEN A MISUNDERSTANDING HERE. I GET THAT.
TEMPERS ARE HIGH.
SO. I'M WILLING TO LET THIS GO IF YOU LADIES CALM DOWN RIGHT NOW, BUT IF NOT...
...IT'S GONNA BE SOLITARY FOR EACH OF YOU, GET IT?
BACK OFF.
NOW.

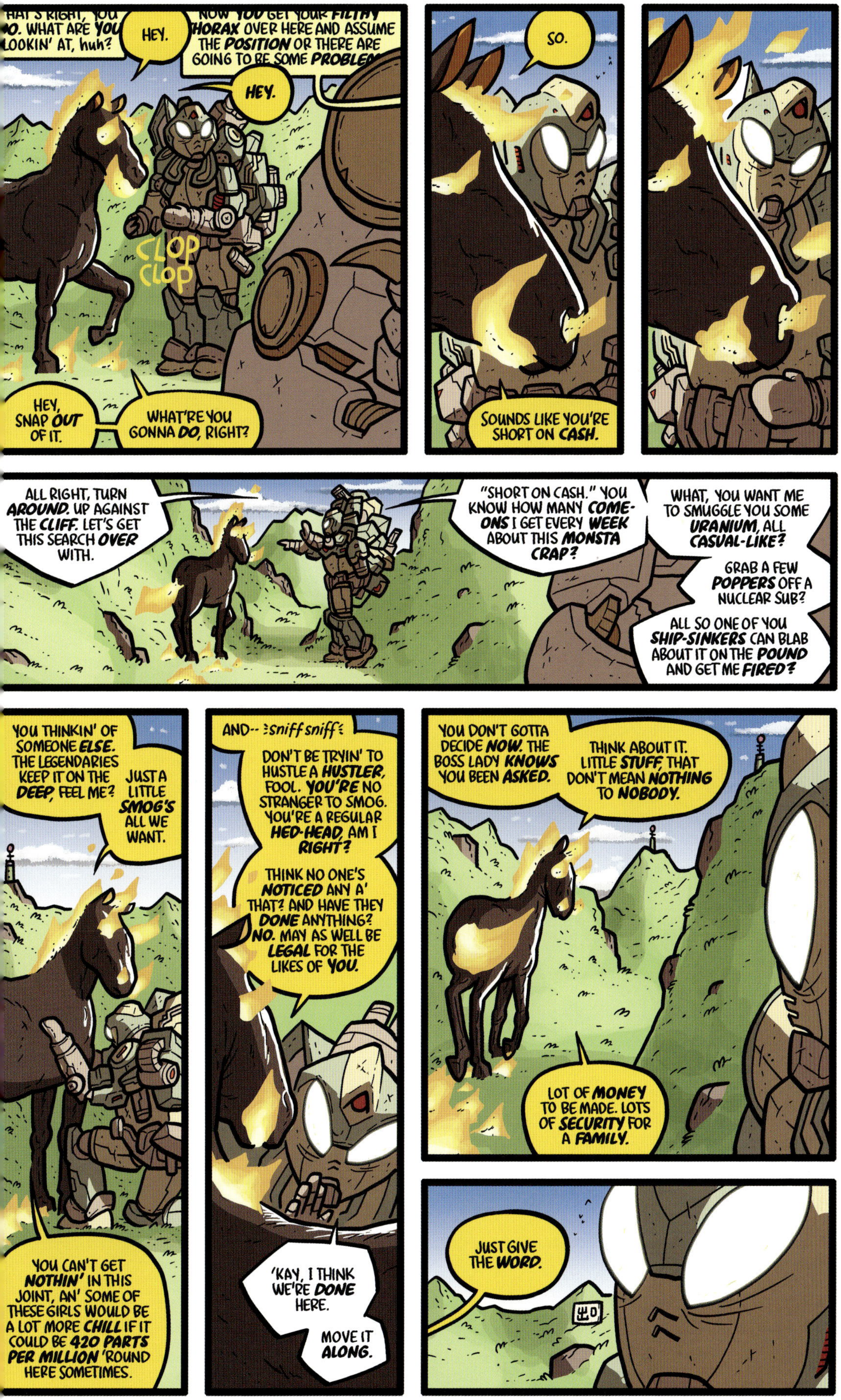
WHAT ARE YOU LOOKIN' AT, huh?
HEY.
THORAX OVER HERE AND ASSUME THE POSITION OR THERE ARE GOING TO BE SOME
HEY.
CLOP CLOP
HEY, SNAP OUT OF IT.
WHAT'RE YOU GONNA DO, RIGHT?
SO.
SOUNDS LIKE YOU'RE SHORT ON CASH.
ALL RIGHT, TURN AROUND. UP AGAINST THE CLIFF. LET'S GET THIS SEARCH OVER WITH.
"SHORT ON CASH." YOU KNOW HOW MANY COME-ONS I GET EVERY WEEK ABOUT THIS MONSTA CRAP?
WHAT, YOU WANT ME TO SMUGGLE YOU SOME URANIUM, ALL CASUAL-LIKE?
GRAB A FEW POPPERS OFF A NUCLEAR SUB?
ALL SO ONE OF YOU SHIP-SINKERS CAN BLAB ABOUT IT ON THE POUND AND GET ME FIRED?
YOU THINKIN' OF SOMEONE ELSE. THE LEGENDARIES KEEP IT ON THE DEEP, FEEL ME?
JUST A LITTLE SMOG'S ALL WE WANT.
YOU CAN'T GET NOTHIN' IN THIS JOINT, AN' SOME OF THESE GIRLS WOULD BE A LOT MORE CHILL IF IT COULD BE 420 PARTS PER MILLION 'ROUND HERE SOMETIMES.
AND-- sniff sniff
DON'T BE TRYIN' TO HUSTLE A HUSTLER, FOOL. YOU'RE NO STRANGER TO SMOG. YOU'RE A REGULAR HED-HEAD, AM I RIGHT?
THINK NO ONE'S NOTICED ANY A' THAT? AND HAVE THEY DONE ANYTHING? NO. MAY AS WELL BE LEGAL FOR THE LIKES OF YOU.
'KAY, I THINK WE'RE DONE HERE.
MOVE IT ALONG.
YOU DON'T GOTTA DECIDE NOW. THE BOSS LADY KNOWS YOU BEEN ASKED.
THINK ABOUT IT. LITTLE STUFF THAT DON'T MEAN NOTHING TO NOBODY.
LOT OF MONEY TO BE MADE. LOTS OF SECURITY FOR A FAMILY.
JUST GIVE THE WORD.

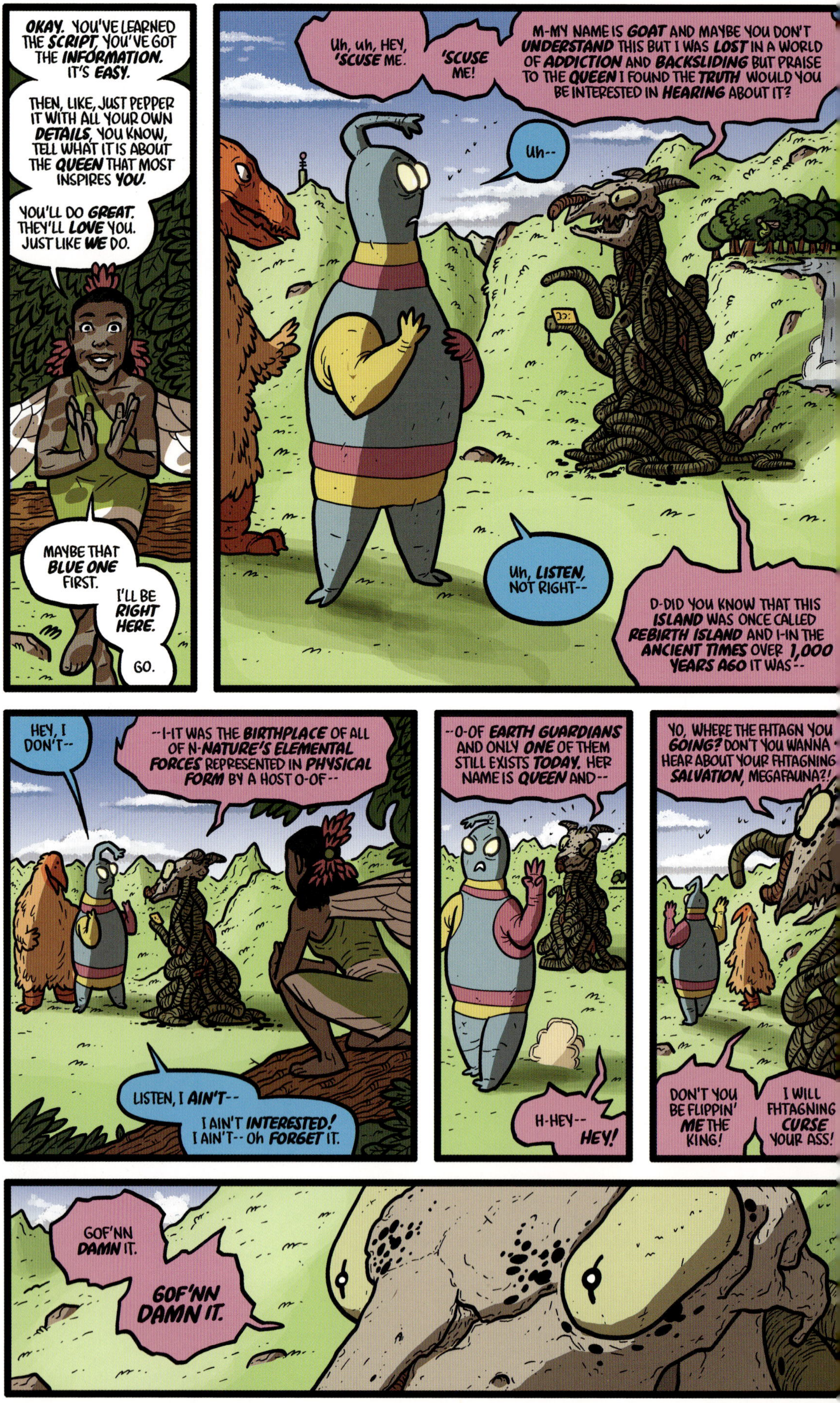
OKAY. YOU'VE LEARNED THE SCRIPT, YOU'VE GOT THE INFORMATION. IT'S EASY.
THEN, LIKE, JUST PEPPER IT WITH ALL YOUR OWN DETAILS, YOU KNOW, TELL WHAT IT IS ABOUT THE QUEEN THAT MOST INSPIRES YOU.
YOU'LL DO GREAT. THEY'LL LOVE YOU. JUST LIKE WE DO.
MAYBE THAT BLUE ONE FIRST.
I'LL BE RIGHT HERE.
GO.
Uh, uh, HEY, 'SCUSE ME.
'SCUSE ME!
M-MY NAME IS GOAT AND MAYBE YOU DON'T UNDERSTAND THIS BUT I WAS LOST IN A WORLD OF ADDICTION AND BACKSLIDING BUT PRAISE TO THE QUEEN I FOUND THE TRUTH WOULD YOU BE INTERESTED IN HEARING ABOUT IT?
Uh--
Uh, LISTEN, NOT RIGHT--
D-DID YOU KNOW THAT THIS ISLAND WAS ONCE CALLED REBIRTH ISLAND AND I-IN THE ANCIENT TIMES OVER 1,000 YEARS AGO IT WAS--
HEY, I DON'T--
--I-IT WAS THE BIRTHPLACE OF ALL OF N-NATURE'S ELEMENTAL FORCES REPRESENTED IN PHYSICAL FORM BY A HOST O-OF--
LISTEN, I AIN'T--
I AIN'T INTERESTED! I AIN'T-- Oh FORGET IT.
--O-OF EARTH GUARDIANS AND ONLY ONE OF THEM STILL EXISTS TODAY. HER NAME IS QUEEN AND--
H-HEY-- HEY!
YO, WHERE THE FHTAGN YOU GOING? DON'T YOU WANNA HEAR ABOUT YOUR FHTAGNING SALVATION, MEGAFAUNA?!
DON'T YOU BE FLIPPIN' ME THE KING!
I WILL FHTAGNING CURSE YOUR ASS!
GOF'NN DAMN IT.
GOF'NN DAMN IT.

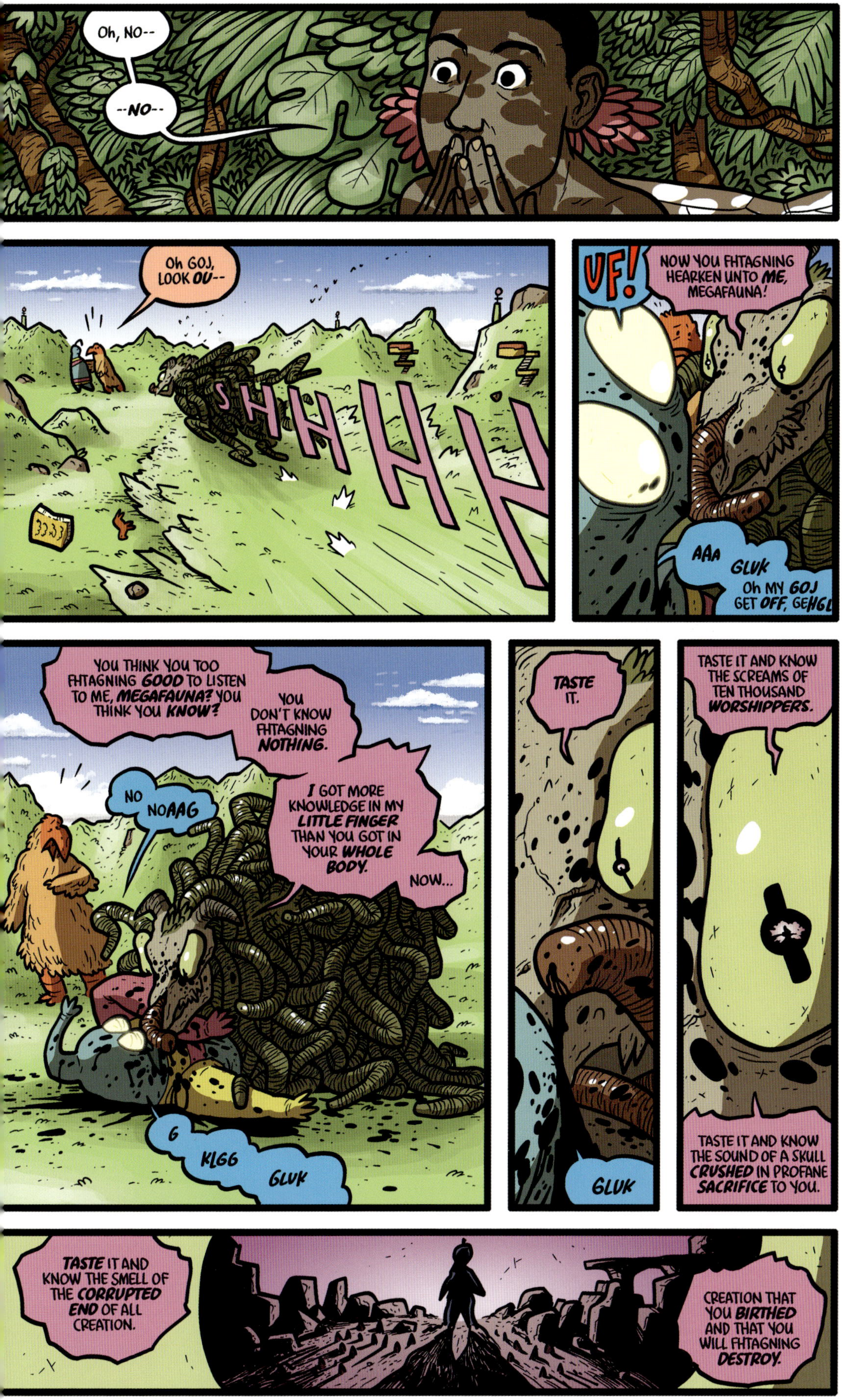

Oh, NO--
--NO--
Oh GOJ, LOOK OU--
SHHHHH
33.33
UF!
NOW YOU FHTAGNING HEARKEN UNTO ME, MEGAFAUNA!
AAA
GLUK
Oh MY GOJ GET OFF, GEHGL
YOU THINK YOU TOO FHTAGNING GOOD TO LISTEN TO ME, MEGAFAUNA? YOU THINK YOU KNOW?
YOU DON'T KNOW FHTAGNING NOTHING.
NO
NOAAG
I GOT MORE KNOWLEDGE IN MY LITTLE FINGER THAN YOU GOT IN YOUR WHOLE BODY.
NOW...
G
KLGG
GLUK
TASTE IT.
GLUK
TASTE IT AND KNOW THE SCREAMS OF TEN THOUSAND WORSHIPPERS.
TASTE IT AND KNOW THE SOUND OF A SKULL CRUSHED IN PROFANE SACRIFICE TO YOU.
TASTE IT AND KNOW THE SMELL OF THE CORRUPTED END OF ALL CREATION.
CREATION THAT YOU BIRTHED AND THAT YOU WILL FHTAGNING DESTROY.

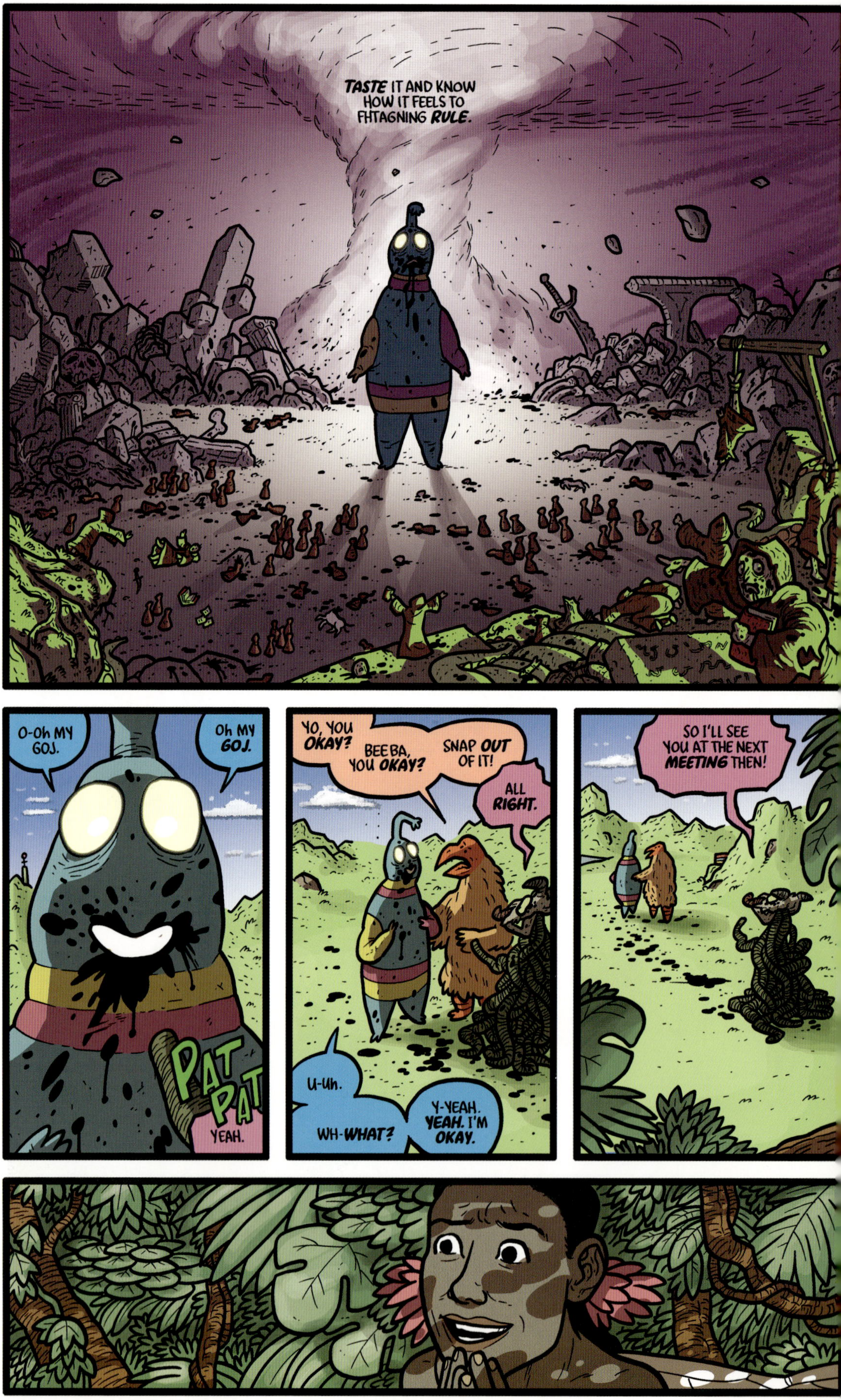

TASTE IT AND KNOW HOW IT FEELS TO FHTAGNING RULE.
O-Oh MY GOJ.
Oh MY GOJ.
PAT PAT
YEAH.
YO, YOU OKAY?
BEEBA, YOU OKAY?
SNAP OUT OF IT!
ALL RIGHT.
U-Uh.
WH-WHAT?
Y-YEAH. YEAH. I'M OKAY.
SO I'LL SEE YOU AT THE NEXT MEETING THEN!

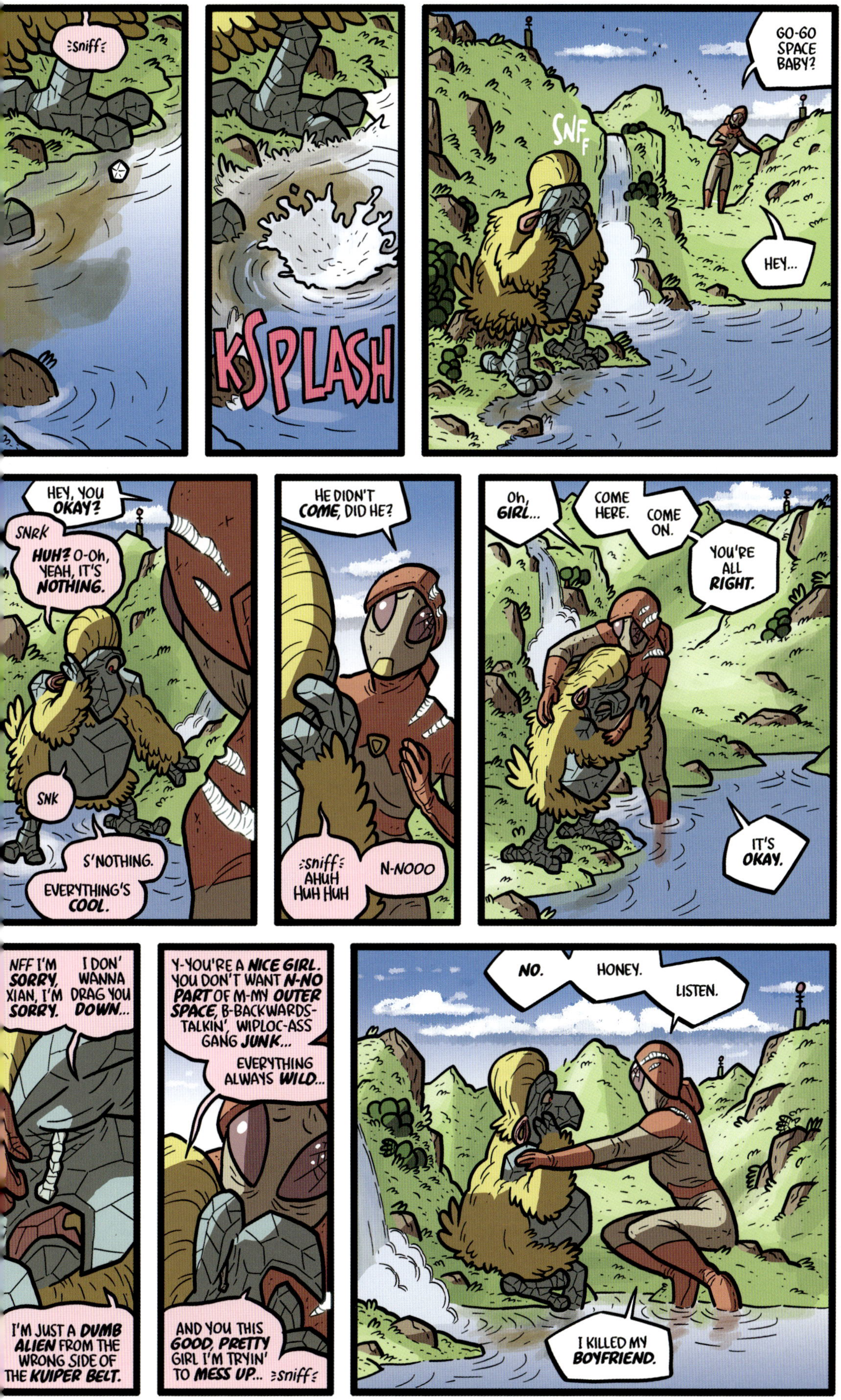

≷sniff≶
KSPLASH
SNFF
GO-GO SPACE BABY?
HEY...
HEY, YOU OKAY?
SNRK
HUH? O-Oh, YEAH, IT'S NOTHING.
SNK
S'NOTHING.
EVERYTHING'S COOL.
HE DIDN'T COME, DID HE?
≷sniff≶ AHUH HUH HUH
N-NOOO
Oh, GIRL...
COME HERE.
COME ON.
YOU'RE ALL RIGHT.
IT'S OKAY.
NFF I'M SORRY, XIAN, I'M SORRY.
I DON' WANNA DRAG YOU DOWN...
I'M JUST A DUMB ALIEN FROM THE WRONG SIDE OF THE KUIPER BELT.
Y-YOU'RE A NICE GIRL. YOU DON'T WANT N-NO PART OF M-MY OUTER SPACE, B-BACKWARDS-TALKIN' WIPLOC-ASS GANG JUNK...
EVERYTHING ALWAYS WILD...
AND YOU THIS GOOD, PRETTY GIRL I'M TRYIN' TO MESS UP... ≷sniff≶
NO.
HONEY.
LISTEN.
I KILLED MY BOYFRIEND.

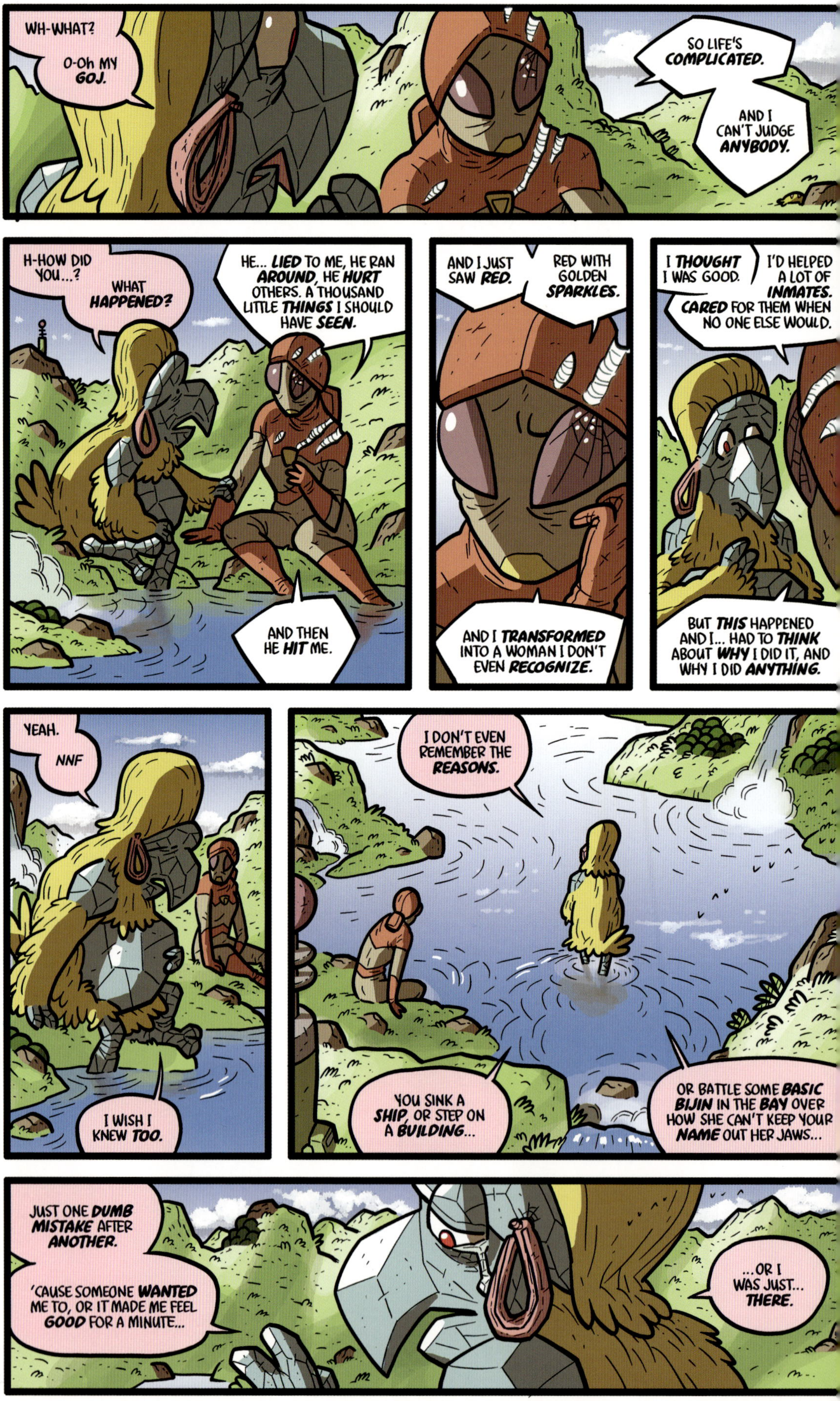

WH-WHAT?
O-OH MY GOJ.
SO LIFE'S COMPLICATED.
AND I CAN'T JUDGE ANYBODY.
H-HOW DID YOU...?
WHAT HAPPENED?
HE... LIED TO ME, HE RAN AROUND, HE HURT OTHERS. A THOUSAND LITTLE THINGS I SHOULD HAVE SEEN.
AND THEN HE HIT ME.
AND I JUST SAW RED.
RED WITH GOLDEN SPARKLES.
AND I TRANSFORMED INTO A WOMAN I DON'T EVEN RECOGNIZE.
I THOUGHT I WAS GOOD.
I'D HELPED A LOT OF INMATES. CARED FOR THEM WHEN NO ONE ELSE WOULD.
BUT THIS HAPPENED AND I... HAD TO THINK ABOUT WHY I DID IT, AND WHY I DID ANYTHING.
YEAH.
NNF
I WISH I KNEW TOO.
I DON'T EVEN REMEMBER THE REASONS.
YOU SINK A SHIP, OR STEP ON A BUILDING...
OR BATTLE SOME BASIC BIJIN IN THE BAY OVER HOW SHE CAN'T KEEP YOUR NAME OUT HER JAWS...
JUST ONE DUMB MISTAKE AFTER ANOTHER.
'CAUSE SOMEONE WANTED ME TO, OR IT MADE ME FEEL GOOD FOR A MINUTE...
...OR I WAS JUST... THERE.

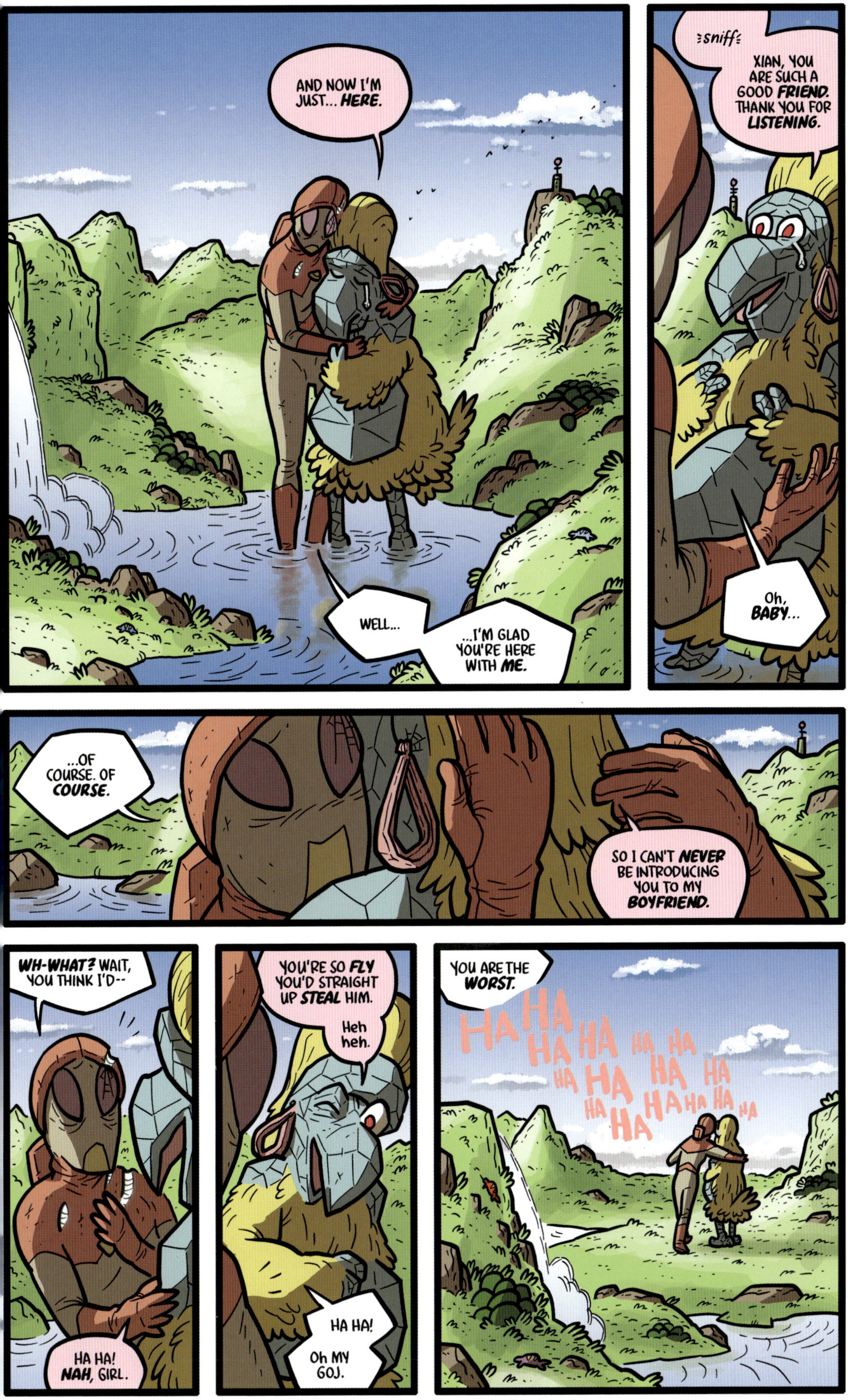
AND NOW I'M JUST... HERE.
WELL...
...I'M GLAD YOU'RE HERE WITH ME.
sniff
XIAN, YOU ARE SUCH A GOOD FRIEND. THANK YOU FOR LISTENING.
Oh, BABY...
...OF COURSE. OF COURSE.
SO I CAN'T NEVER BE INTRODUCING YOU TO MY BOYFRIEND.
WH-WHAT? WAIT, YOU THINK I'D--
HA HA! NAH, GIRL.
YOU'RE SO FLY YOU'D STRAIGHT UP STEAL HIM.
Heh heh.
HA HA!
Oh MY GOJ.
YOU ARE THE WORST.
HA HA HA HA HA HA HA HA HA HA HA HA HA HA HA HA HA

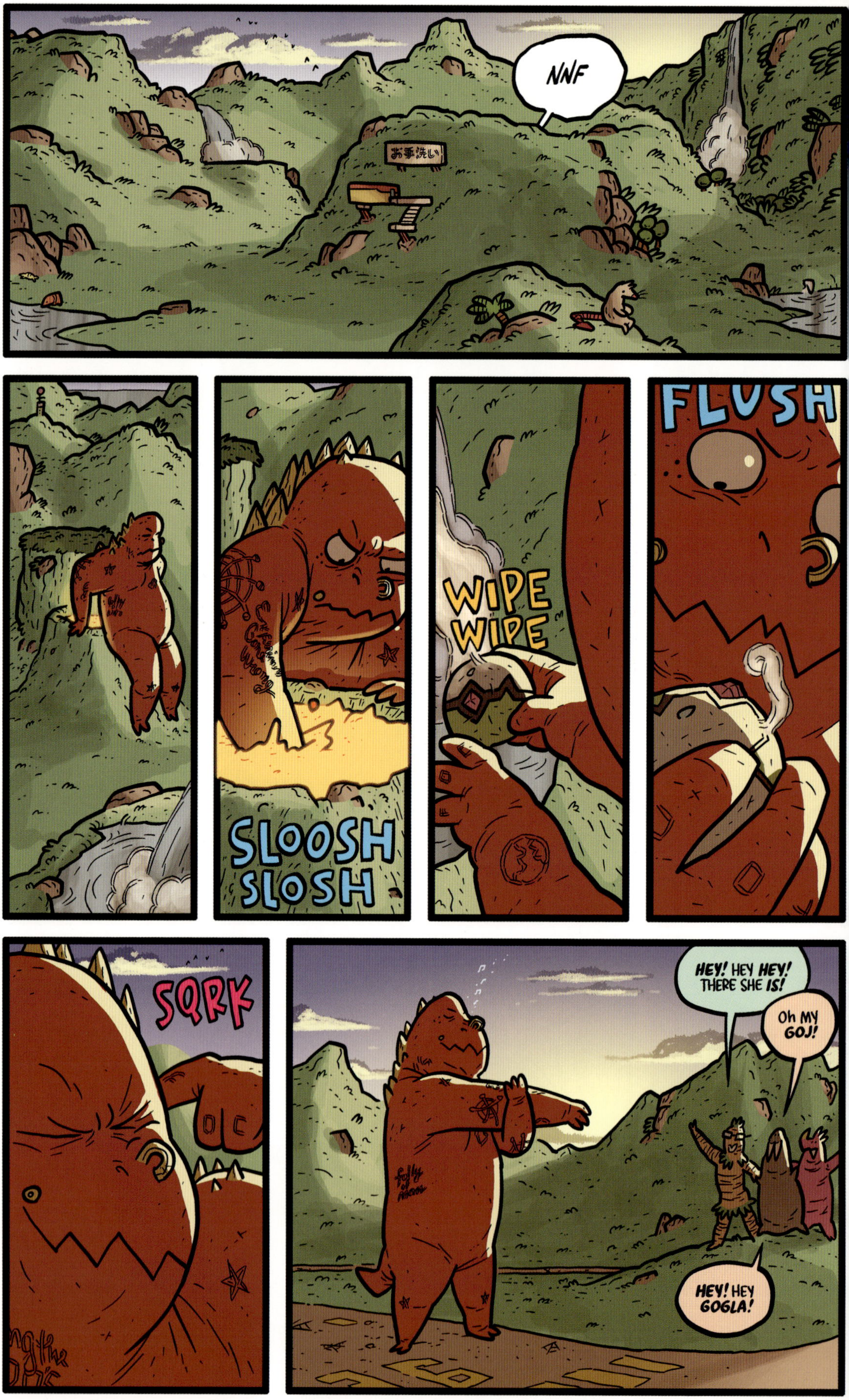
NNF
お手洗い
SLOOSH
SLOSH
WIPE
WIPE
FLUSH
SQRK
HEY! HEY HEY! THERE SHE IS!
Oh MY GOJ!
HEY! HEY GOGLA!

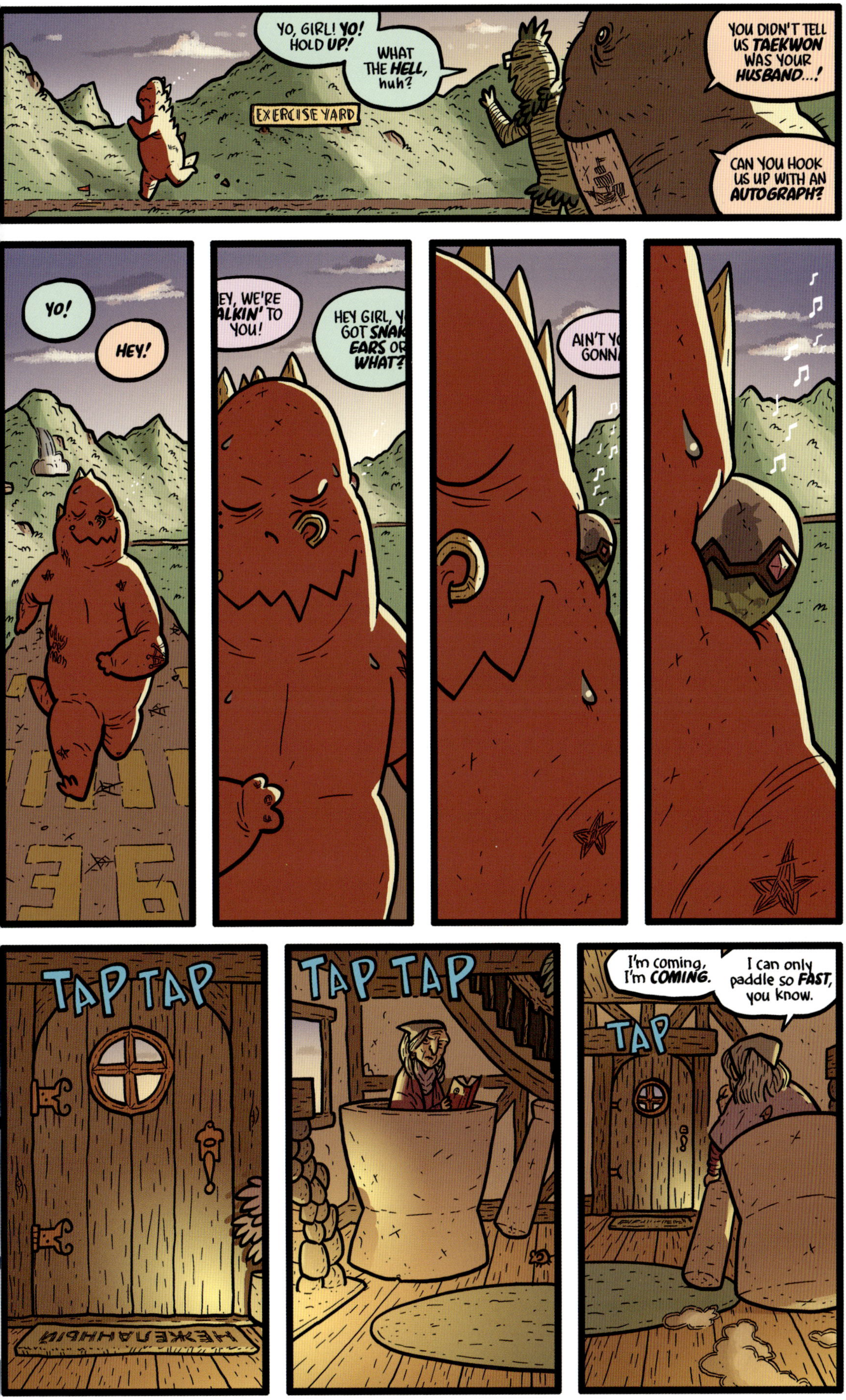

YO, GIRL! YO! HOLD UP!
WHAT THE HELL, huh?
EXERCISE YARD
YOU DIDN'T TELL US TAEKWON WAS YOUR HUSBAND...!
CAN YOU HOOK US UP WITH AN AUTOGRAPH?
YO!
HEY!
EY, WE'RE ALKIN' TO YOU!
HEY GIRL, Y GOT SNAK EARS OR WHAT?
AIN'T YO GONN
36
TAP TAP
TAP TAP
TAP
I'm coming, I'm COMING.
I can only paddle so FAST, you know.

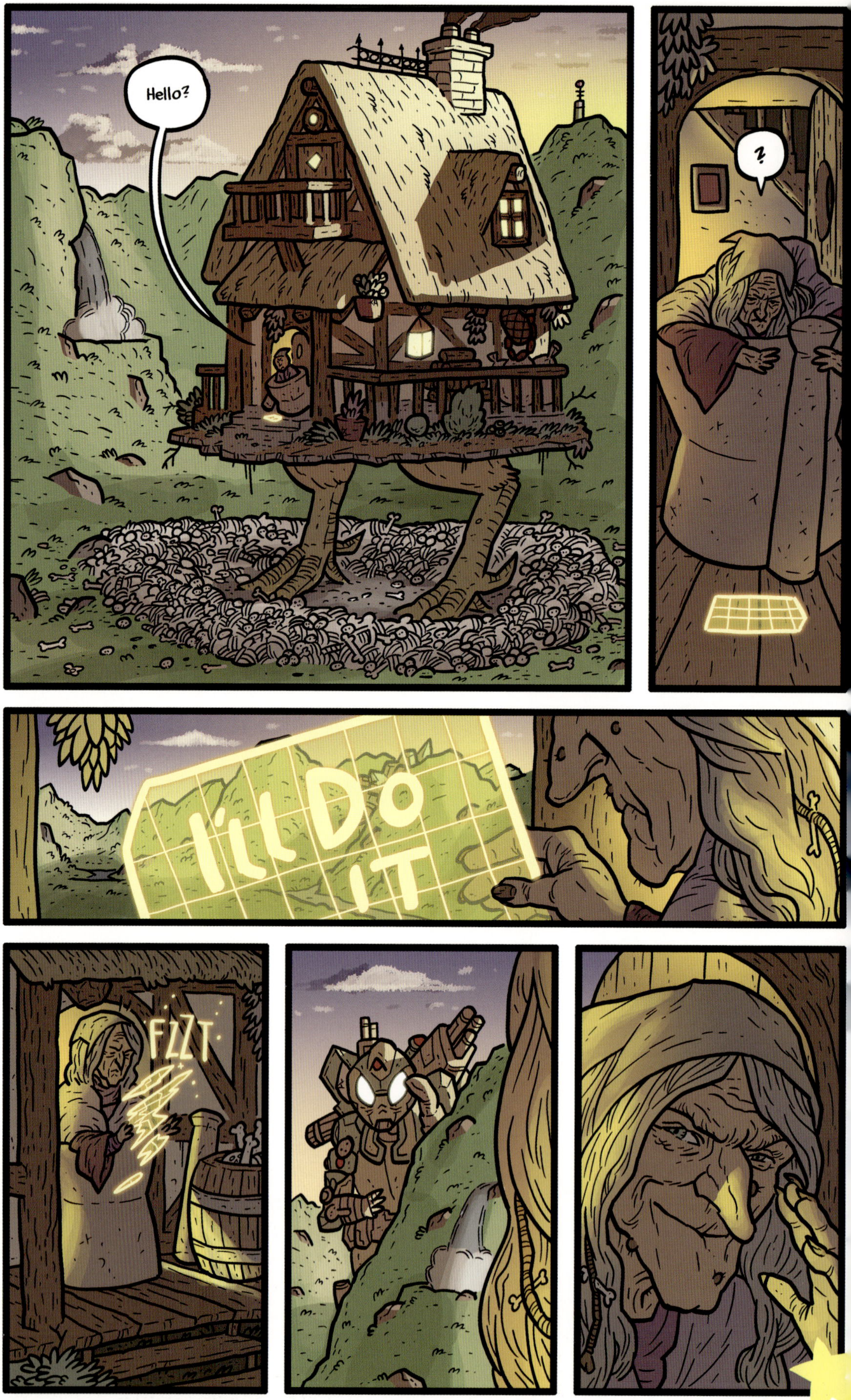
Hello?
?
I'll DO IT
FZZT

EPISODE

3

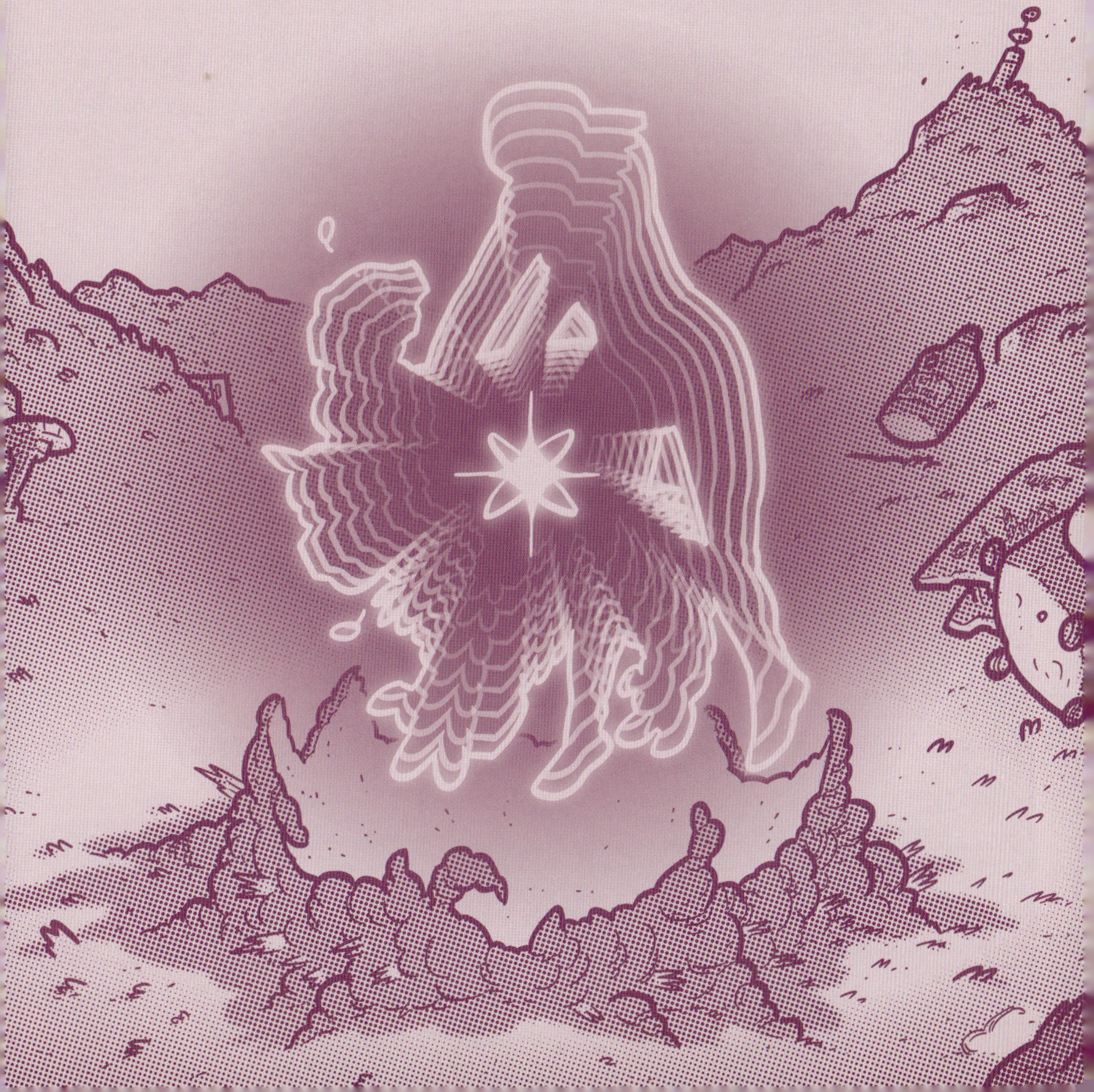

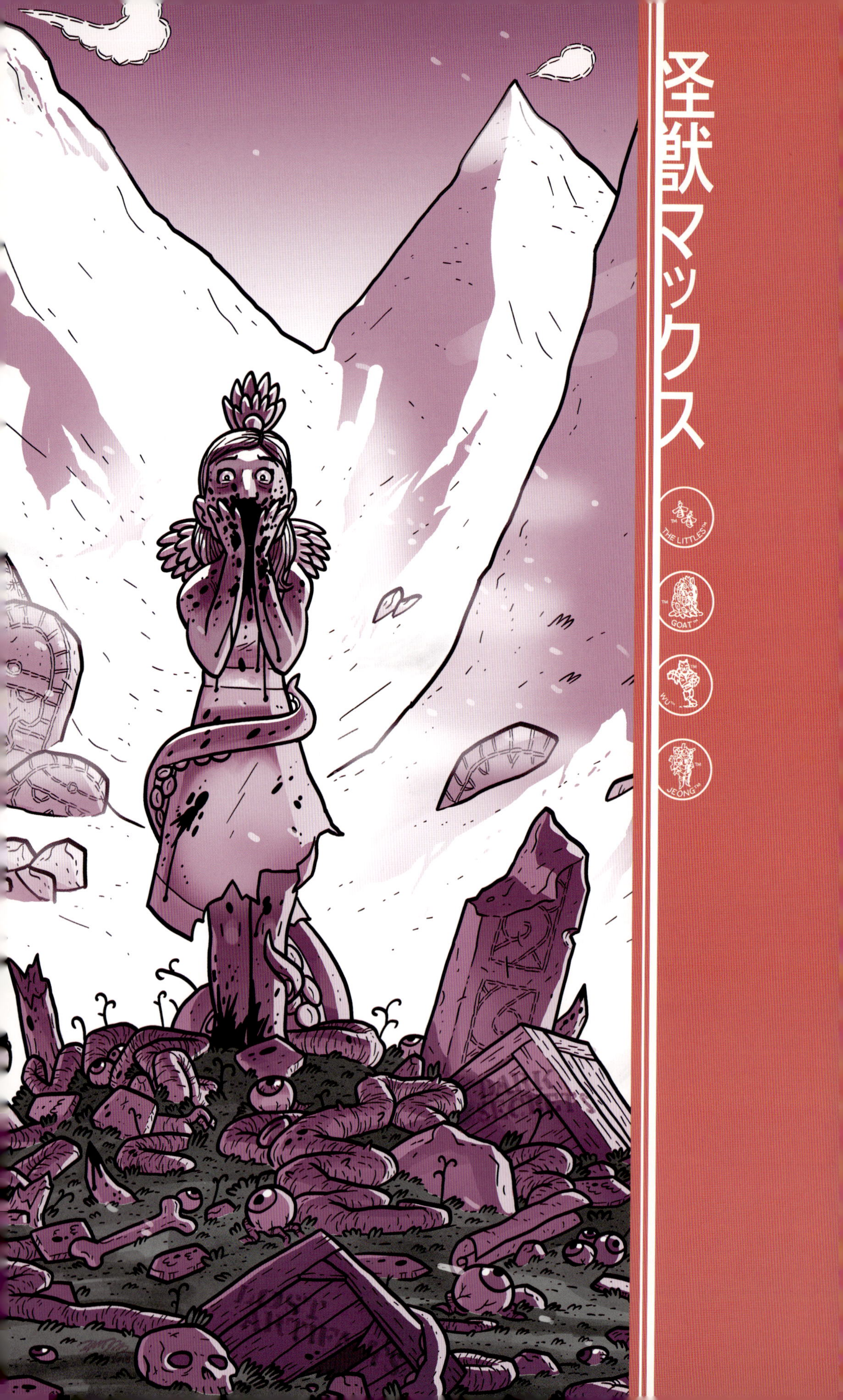
圣獣マックス
THE LITTLES™
GOAT™
WU™
JEONG™

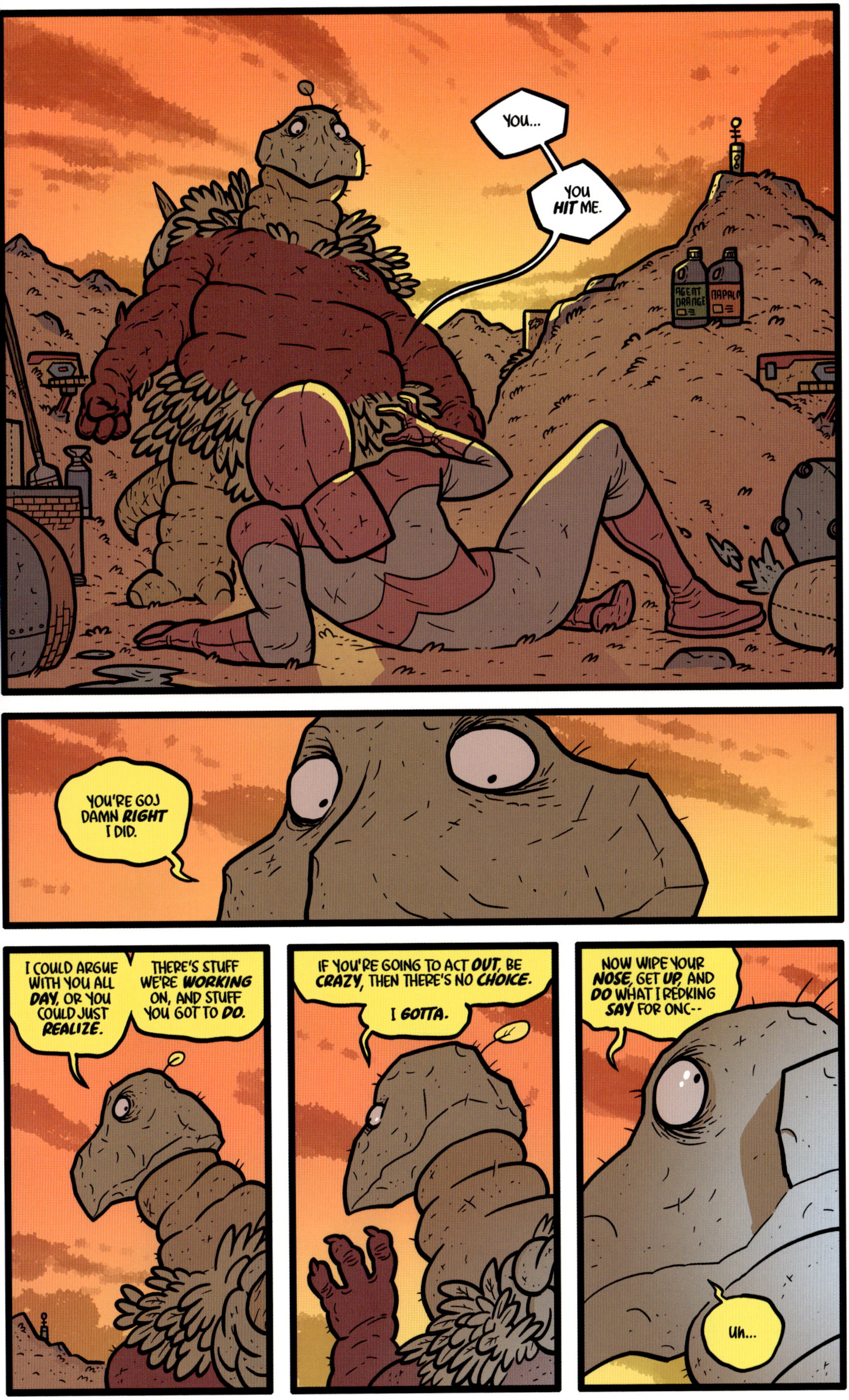
YOU...
YOU HIT ME.
AGENT ORANGE
NAPALM
YOU'RE GOJ DAMN RIGHT I DID.
I COULD ARGUE WITH YOU ALL DAY, OR YOU COULD JUST REALIZE.
THERE'S STUFF WE'RE WORKING ON, AND STUFF YOU GOT TO DO.
IF YOU'RE GOING TO ACT OUT, BE CRAZY, THEN THERE'S NO CHOICE.
I GOTTA.
NOW WIPE YOUR NOSE, GET UP, AND DO WHAT I REDKING SAY FOR ONC--
Uh...

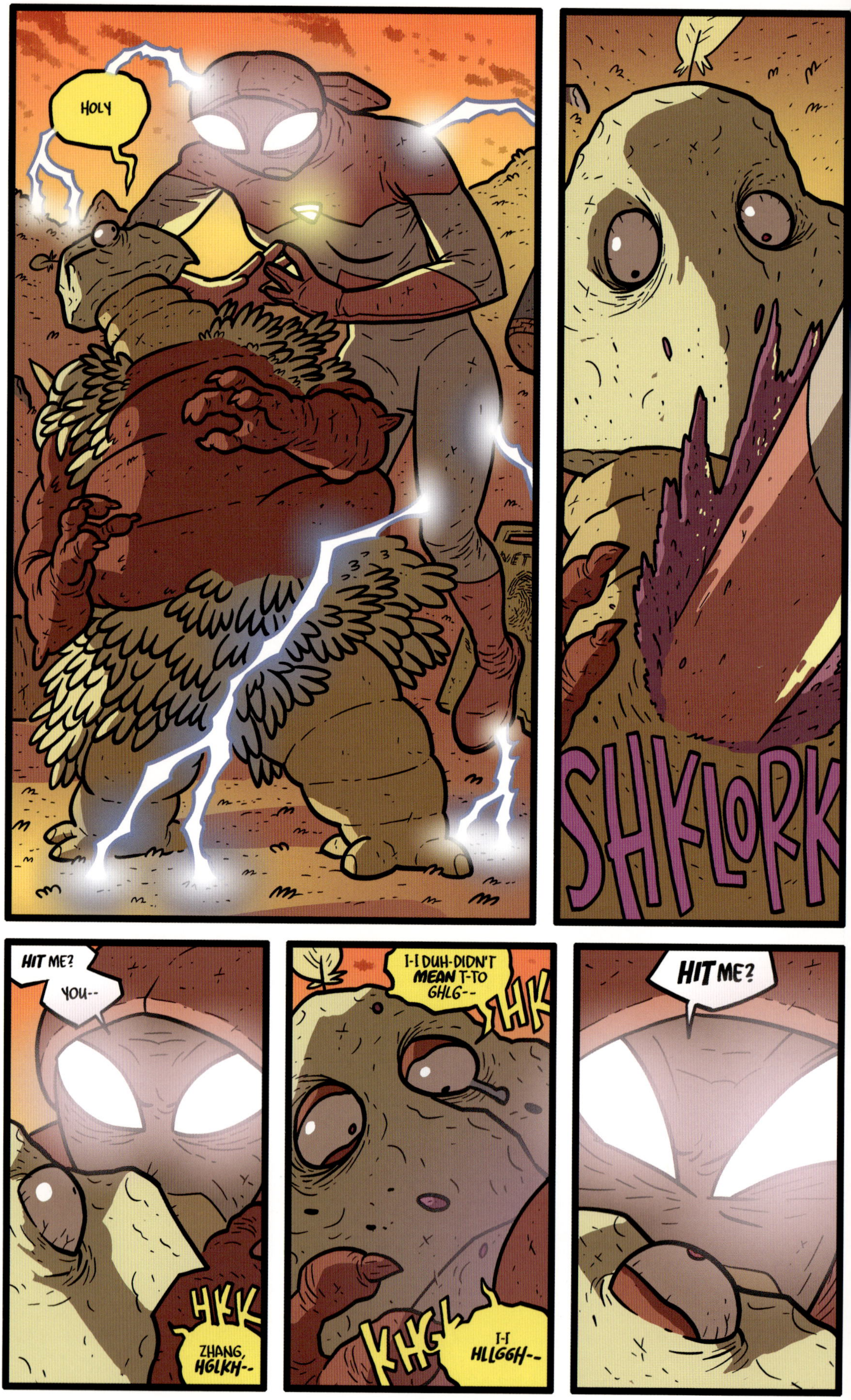
HOLY
SHKLORK
HIT ME?
YOU--
HKK
ZHANG, HGLKH--
I-I DUH-DIDN'T MEAN T-TO GHLG--
HK
KHGL
I-I HLLGGH--
HIT ME?

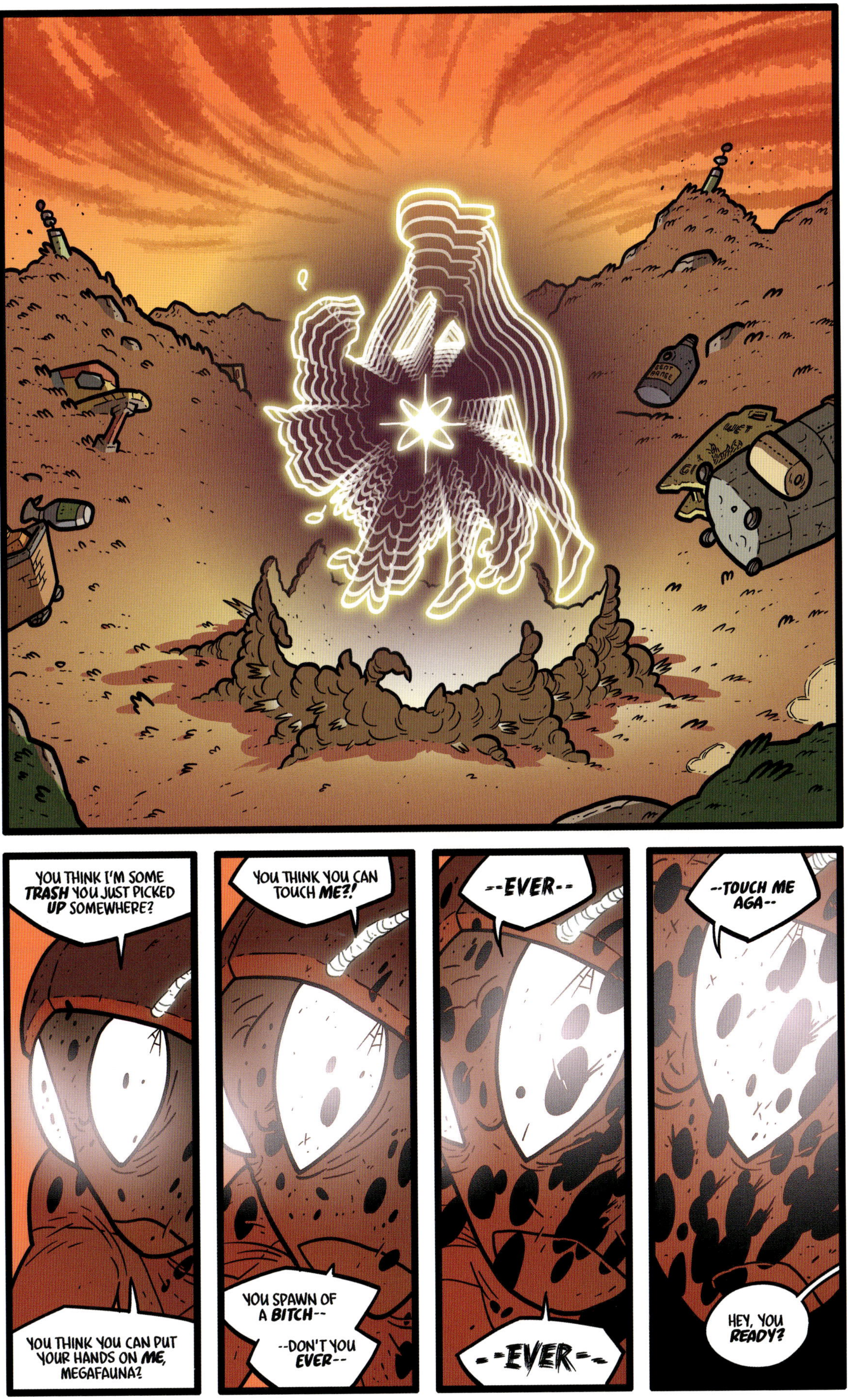
YOU THINK I'M SOME **TRASH** YOU JUST PICKED **UP** SOMEWHERE?
YOU THINK YOU CAN PUT YOUR HANDS ON **ME**, MEGAFAUNA?
YOU THINK YOU CAN TOUCH **ME?!**
YOU SPAWN OF A **BITCH**--
--DON'T YOU **EVER**--
--EVER--
--EVER--
--TOUCH ME AGA--
HEY, YOU **READY?**

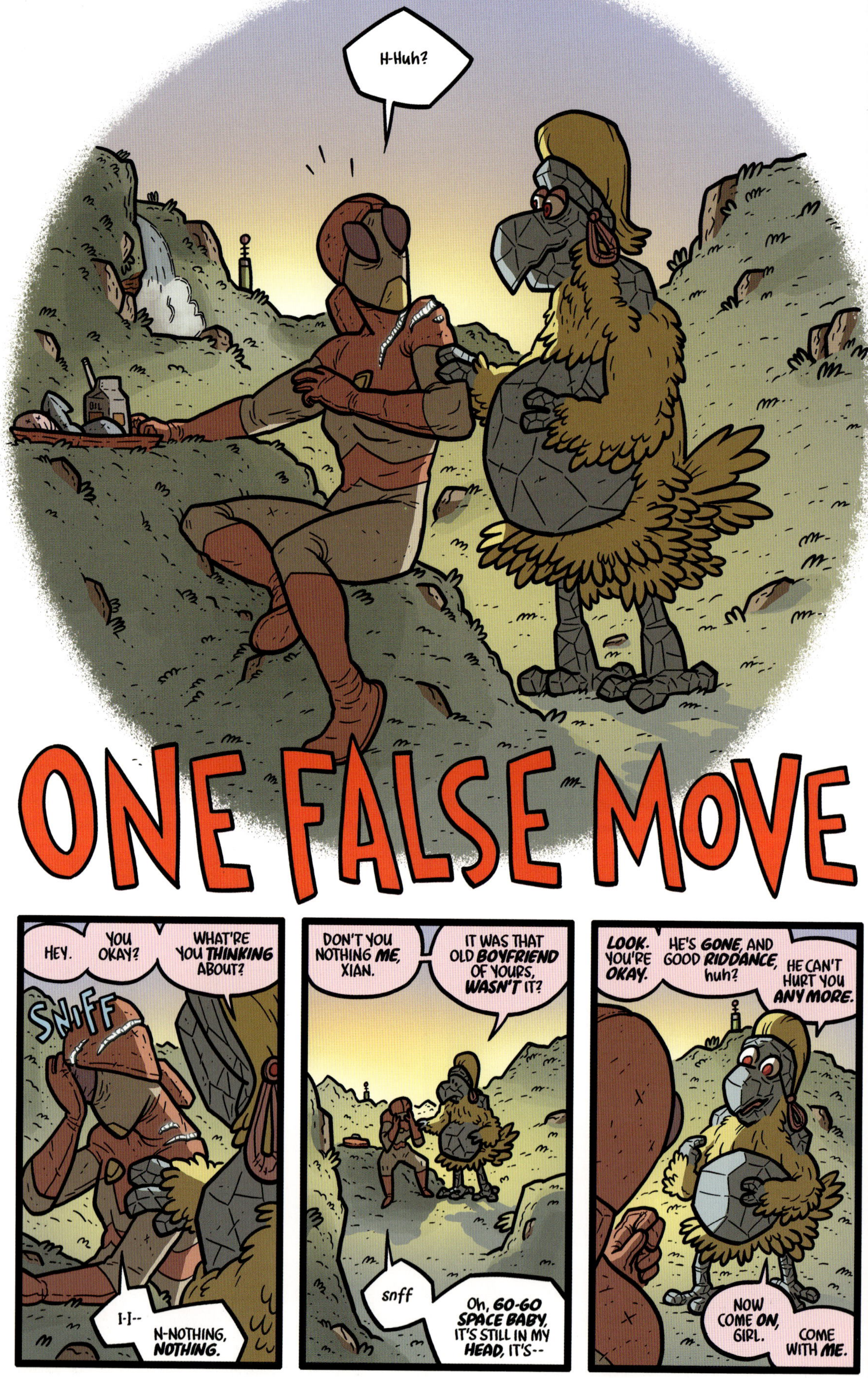
H-Huh?
ONE FALSE MOVE
HEY.
YOU OKAY?
WHAT'RE YOU THINKING ABOUT?
SNIFF
I-I--
N-NOTHING, NOTHING.
DON'T YOU NOTHING ME, XIAN.
IT WAS THAT OLD BOYFRIEND OF YOURS, WASN'T IT?
snff
Oh, GO-GO SPACE BABY, IT'S STILL IN MY HEAD, IT'S--
LOOK. YOU'RE OKAY.
HE'S GONE, AND GOOD RIDDANCE, huh?
HE CAN'T HURT YOU ANY MORE.
NOW COME ON, GIRL.
COME WITH ME.

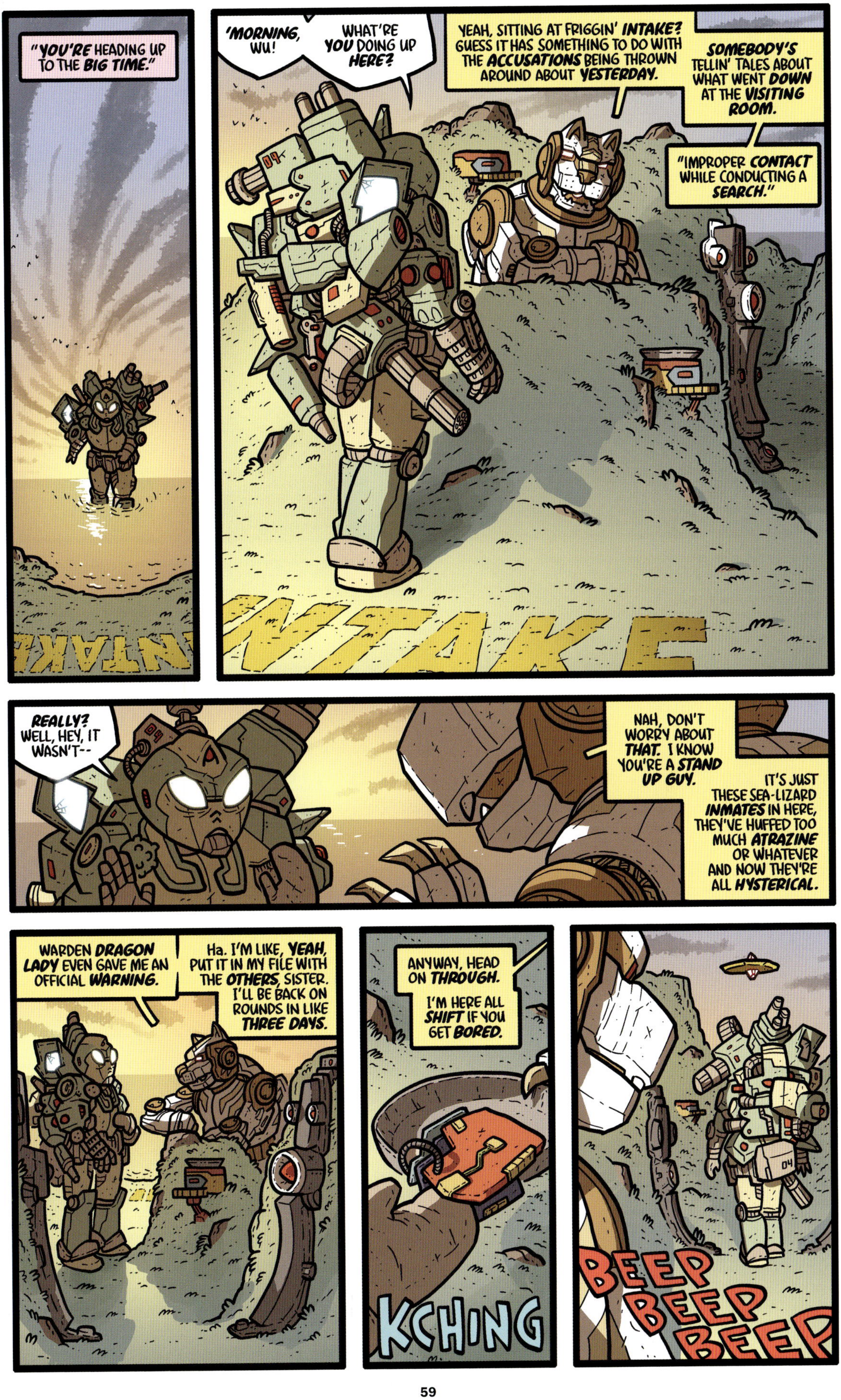
"YOU'RE HEADING UP TO THE BIG TIME."
INTAKE
'MORNING, WU!
WHAT'RE YOU DOING UP HERE?
YEAH, SITTING AT FRIGGIN' INTAKE? GUESS IT HAS SOMETHING TO DO WITH THE ACCUSATIONS BEING THROWN AROUND ABOUT YESTERDAY.
SOMEBODY'S TELLIN' TALES ABOUT WHAT WENT DOWN AT THE VISITING ROOM.
"IMPROPER CONTACT WHILE CONDUCTING A SEARCH."
INTAKE
REALLY? WELL, HEY, IT WASN'T--
NAH, DON'T WORRY ABOUT THAT. I KNOW YOU'RE A STAND UP GUY.
IT'S JUST THESE SEA-LIZARD INMATES IN HERE, THEY'VE HUFFED TOO MUCH ATRAZINE OR WHATEVER AND NOW THEY'RE ALL HYSTERICAL.
WARDEN DRAGON LADY EVEN GAVE ME AN OFFICIAL WARNING.
Ha. I'M LIKE, YEAH, PUT IT IN MY FILE WITH THE OTHERS, SISTER. I'LL BE BACK ON ROUNDS IN LIKE THREE DAYS.
ANYWAY, HEAD ON THROUGH.
I'M HERE ALL SHIFT IF YOU GET BORED.
KCHING
BEEP BEEP BEEP

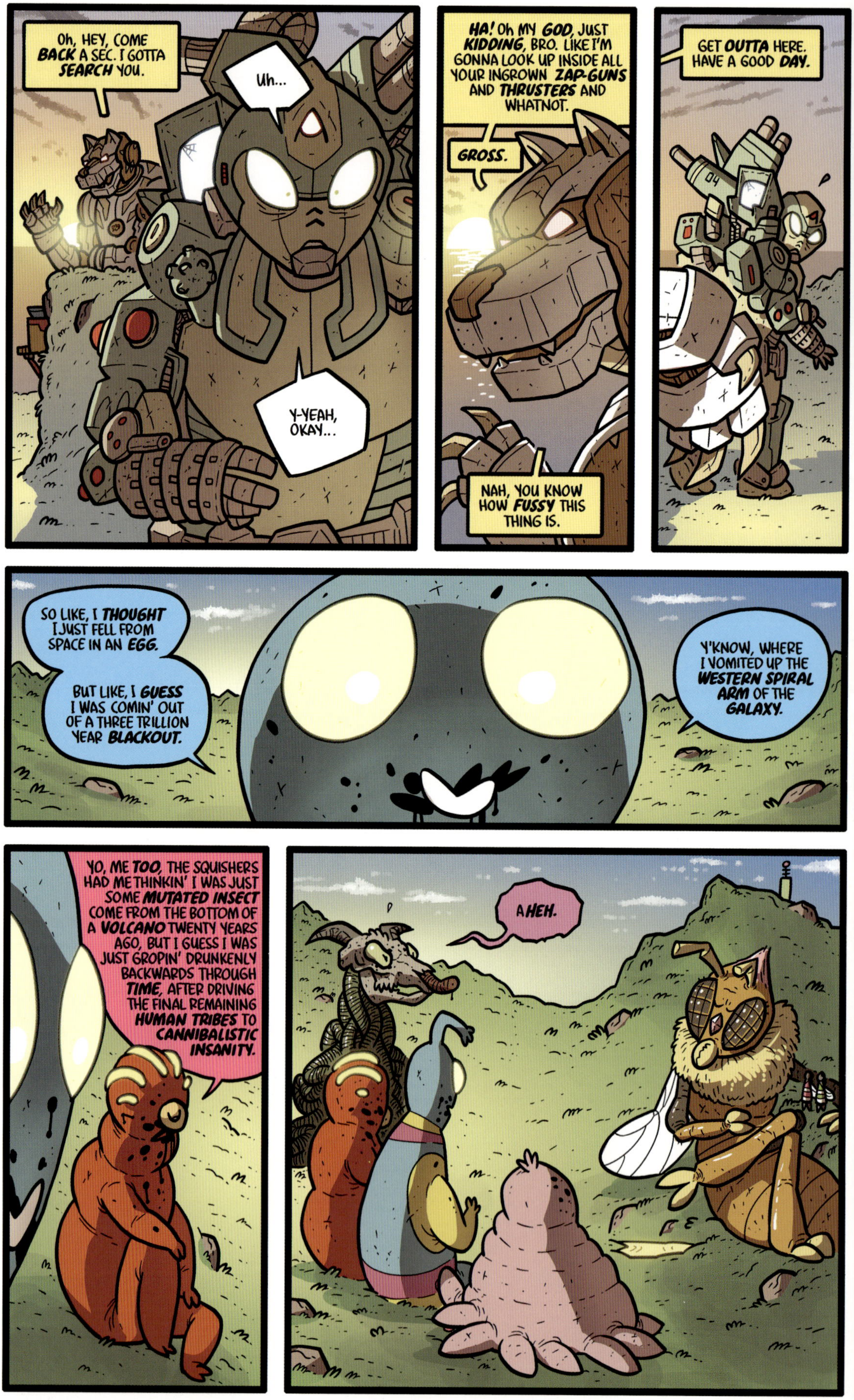
Oh, HEY, COME BACK A SEC. I GOTTA SEARCH YOU.
Uh...
Y-YEAH, OKAY...
HA! Oh MY GOD, JUST KIDDING, BRO. LIKE I'M GONNA LOOK UP INSIDE ALL YOUR INGROWN ZAP-GUNS AND THRUSTERS AND WHATNOT.
GROSS.
NAH, YOU KNOW HOW FUSSY THIS THING IS.
GET OUTTA HERE. HAVE A GOOD DAY.
SO LIKE, I THOUGHT I JUST FELL FROM SPACE IN AN EGG.
BUT LIKE, I GUESS I WAS COMIN' OUT OF A THREE TRILLION YEAR BLACKOUT.
Y'KNOW, WHERE I VOMITED UP THE WESTERN SPIRAL ARM OF THE GALAXY.
YO, ME TOO, THE SQUISHERS HAD ME THINKIN' I WAS JUST SOME MUTATED INSECT COME FROM THE BOTTOM OF A VOLCANO TWENTY YEARS AGO, BUT I GUESS I WAS JUST GROPIN' DRUNKENLY BACKWARDS THROUGH TIME, AFTER DRIVING THE FINAL REMAINING HUMAN TRIBES TO CANNIBALISTIC INSANITY.
A HEH.

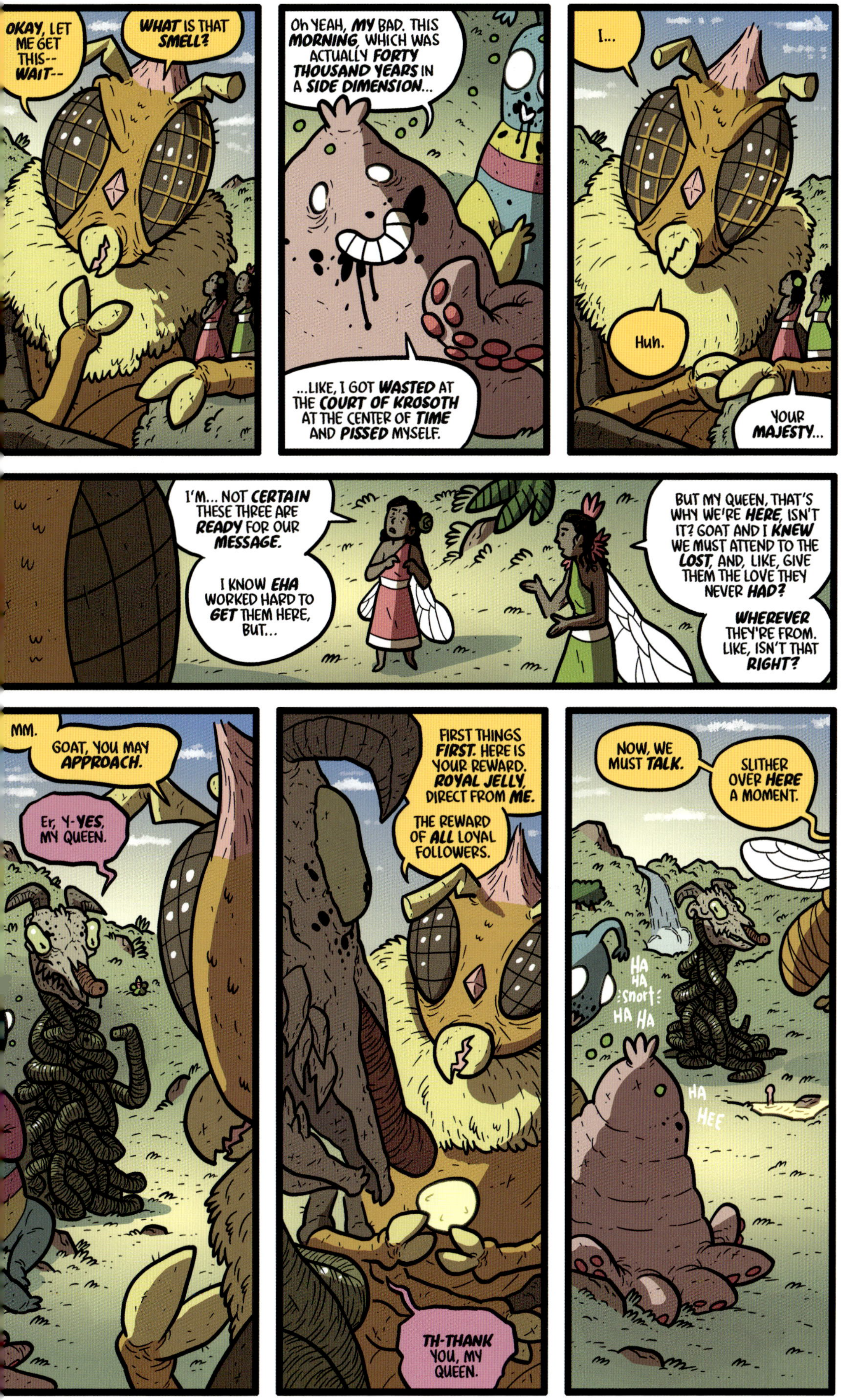

OKAY, LET ME GET THIS-- WAIT--
WHAT IS THAT SMELL?
Oh YEAH, MY BAD. THIS MORNING, WHICH WAS ACTUALLY FORTY THOUSAND YEARS IN A SIDE DIMENSION...
...LIKE, I GOT WASTED AT THE COURT OF KROSOTH AT THE CENTER OF TIME AND PISSED MYSELF.
I...
Huh.
YOUR MAJESTY...
I'M... NOT CERTAIN THESE THREE ARE READY FOR OUR MESSAGE.
I KNOW EHA WORKED HARD TO GET THEM HERE, BUT...
BUT MY QUEEN, THAT'S WHY WE'RE HERE, ISN'T IT? GOAT AND I KNEW WE MUST ATTEND TO THE LOST, AND, LIKE, GIVE THEM THE LOVE THEY NEVER HAD?
WHEREVER THEY'RE FROM. LIKE, ISN'T THAT RIGHT?
MM.
GOAT, YOU MAY APPROACH.
Er, Y-YES, MY QUEEN.
FIRST THINGS FIRST. HERE IS YOUR REWARD. ROYAL JELLY, DIRECT FROM ME.
THE REWARD OF ALL LOYAL FOLLOWERS.
TH-THANK YOU, MY QUEEN.
NOW, WE MUST TALK.
SLITHER OVER HERE A MOMENT.
HA HA snort HA HA
HA HEE

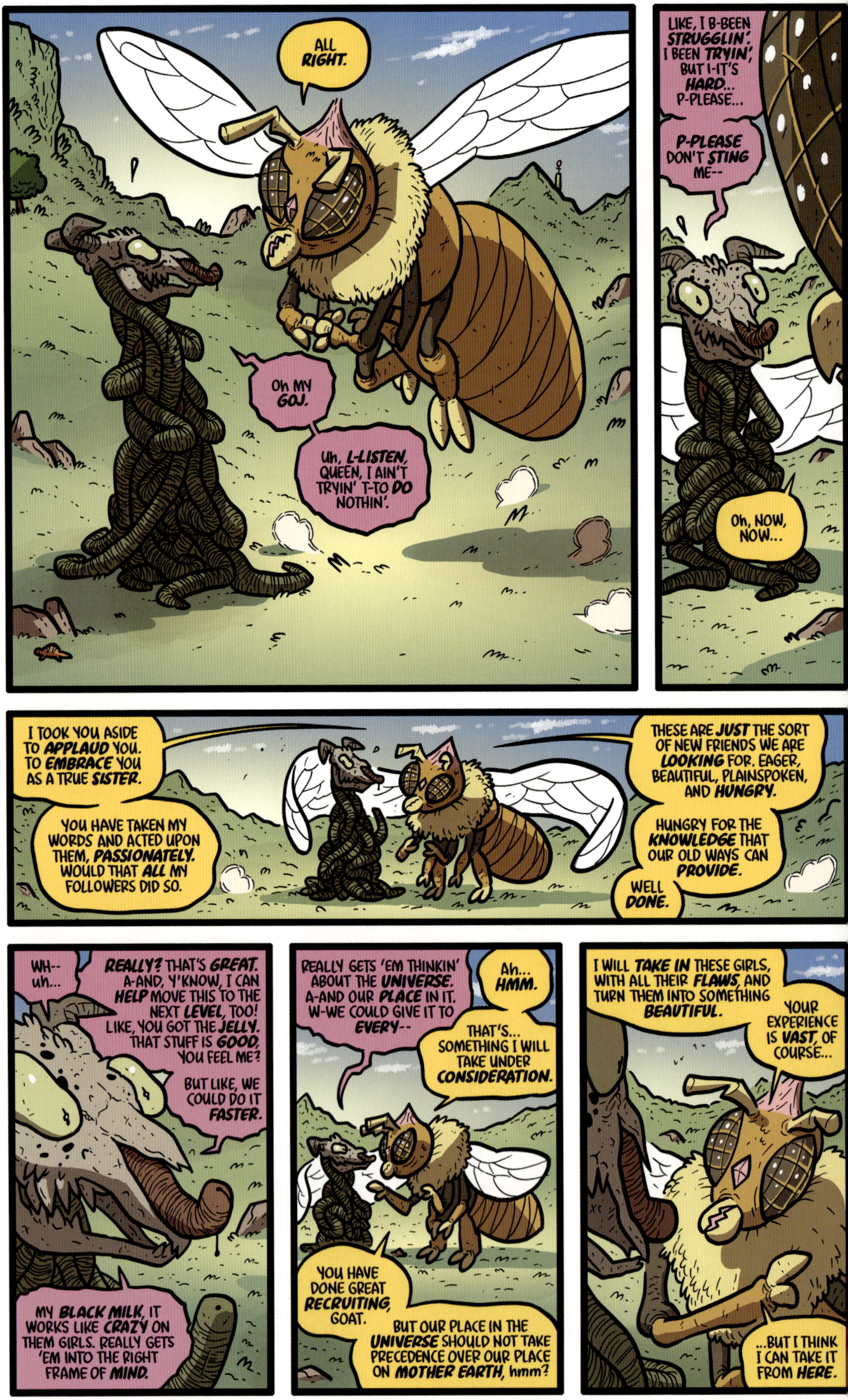
ALL RIGHT.
Oh MY GOJ.
Uh, L-LISTEN, QUEEN, I AIN'T TRYIN' T-TO DO NOTHIN'.
LIKE, I B-BEEN STRUGGLIN'. I BEEN TRYIN', BUT I-IT'S HARD... P-PLEASE...
P-PLEASE DON'T STING ME--
Oh, NOW, NOW...
I TOOK YOU ASIDE TO APPLAUD YOU. TO EMBRACE YOU AS A TRUE SISTER.
YOU HAVE TAKEN MY WORDS AND ACTED UPON THEM, PASSIONATELY. WOULD THAT ALL MY FOLLOWERS DID SO.
THESE ARE JUST THE SORT OF NEW FRIENDS WE ARE LOOKING FOR. EAGER, BEAUTIFUL, PLAINSPOKEN, AND HUNGRY.
HUNGRY FOR THE KNOWLEDGE THAT OUR OLD WAYS CAN PROVIDE.
WELL DONE.
WH-- uh...
REALLY? THAT'S GREAT. A-AND, Y'KNOW, I CAN HELP MOVE THIS TO THE NEXT LEVEL, TOO! LIKE, YOU GOT THE JELLY. THAT STUFF IS GOOD, YOU FEEL ME?
BUT LIKE, WE COULD DO IT FASTER.
MY BLACK MILK, IT WORKS LIKE CRAZY ON THEM GIRLS. REALLY GETS 'EM INTO THE RIGHT FRAME OF MIND.
REALLY GETS 'EM THINKIN' ABOUT THE UNIVERSE. A-AND OUR PLACE IN IT. W-WE COULD GIVE IT TO EVERY--
Ah... HMM.
THAT'S... SOMETHING I WILL TAKE UNDER CONSIDERATION.
YOU HAVE DONE GREAT RECRUITING, GOAT.
BUT OUR PLACE IN THE UNIVERSE SHOULD NOT TAKE PRECEDENCE OVER OUR PLACE ON MOTHER EARTH, hmm?
I WILL TAKE IN THESE GIRLS, WITH ALL THEIR FLAWS, AND TURN THEM INTO SOMETHING BEAUTIFUL.
YOUR EXPERIENCE IS VAST, OF COURSE...
...BUT I THINK I CAN TAKE IT FROM HERE.

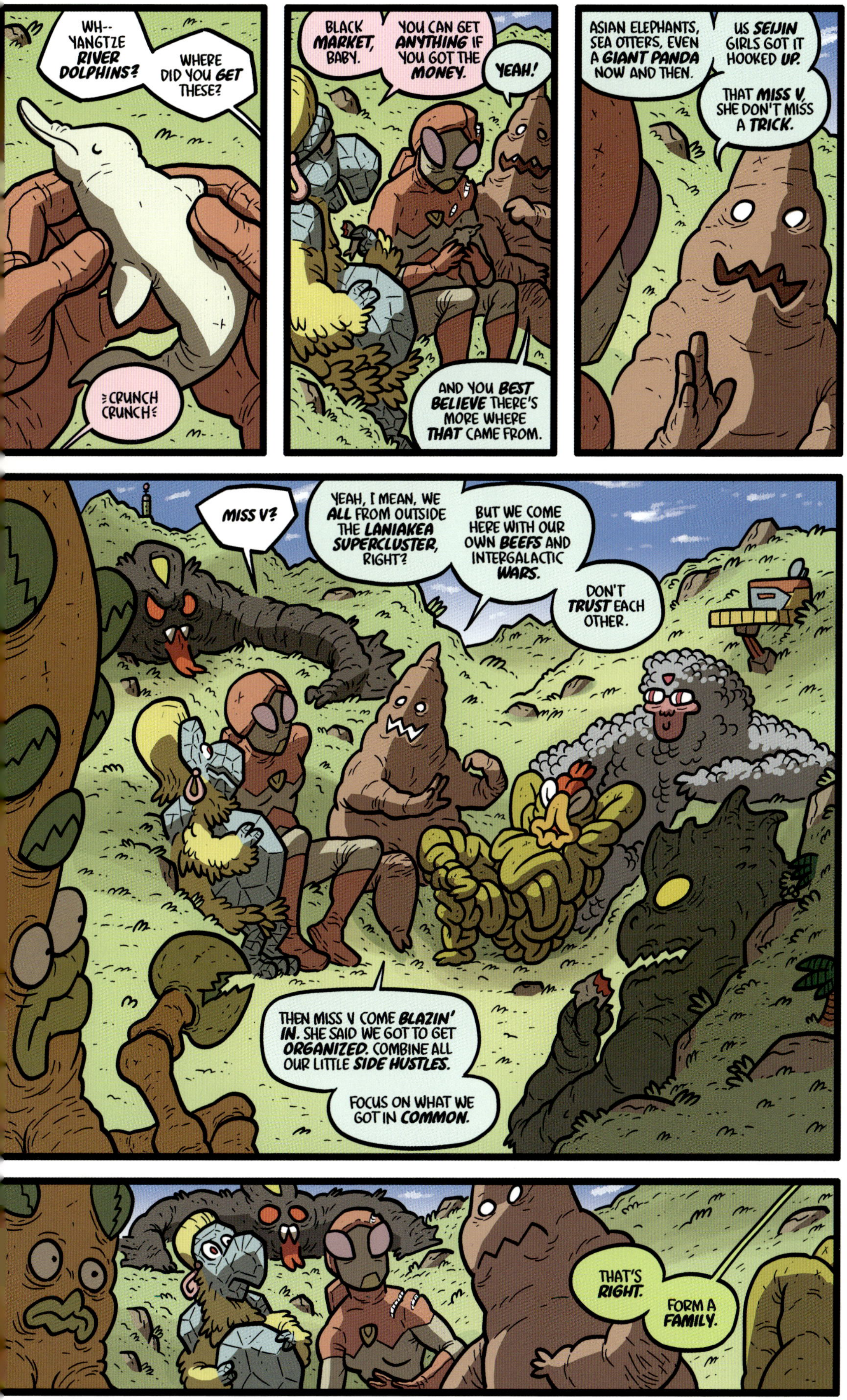
WH-- YANGTZE RIVER DOLPHINS?
WHERE DID YOU GET THESE?
≡CRUNCH CRUNCH≡
BLACK MARKET, BABY.
YOU CAN GET ANYTHING IF YOU GOT THE MONEY.
YEAH!
AND YOU BEST BELIEVE THERE'S MORE WHERE THAT CAME FROM.
ASIAN ELEPHANTS, SEA OTTERS, EVEN A GIANT PANDA NOW AND THEN.
US SEIJIN GIRLS GOT IT HOOKED UP.
THAT MISS V, SHE DON'T MISS A TRICK.
MISS V?
YEAH, I MEAN, WE ALL FROM OUTSIDE THE LANIAKEA SUPERCLUSTER, RIGHT?
BUT WE COME HERE WITH OUR OWN BEEFS AND INTERGALACTIC WARS.
DON'T TRUST EACH OTHER.
THEN MISS V COME BLAZIN' IN. SHE SAID WE GOT TO GET ORGANIZED. COMBINE ALL OUR LITTLE SIDE HUSTLES.
FOCUS ON WHAT WE GOT IN COMMON.
THAT'S RIGHT.
FORM A FAMILY.

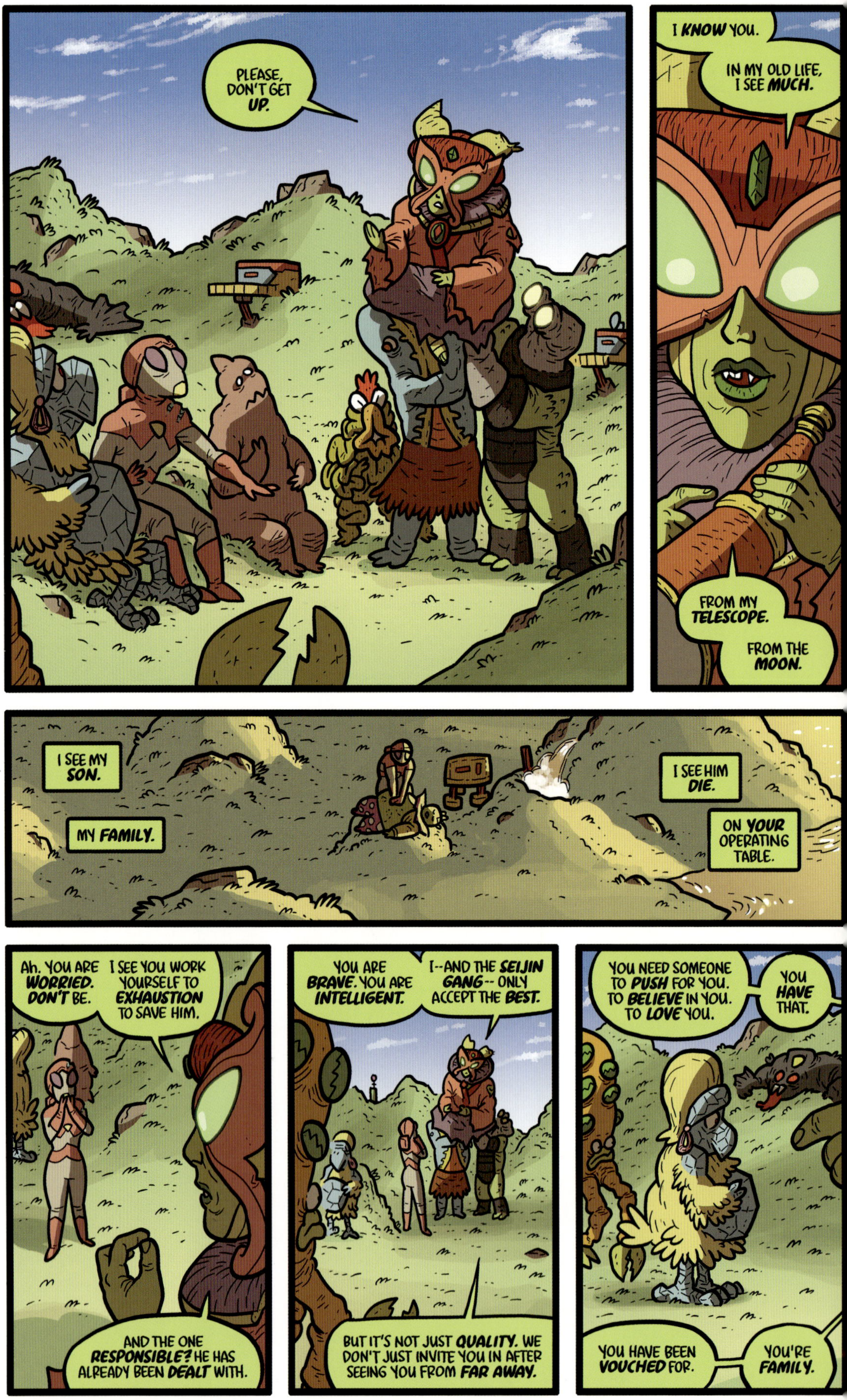
PLEASE, DON'T GET UP.
I KNOW YOU.
IN MY OLD LIFE, I SEE MUCH.
FROM MY TELESCOPE.
FROM THE MOON.
I SEE MY SON.
MY FAMILY.
I SEE HIM DIE.
ON YOUR OPERATING TABLE.
Ah. YOU ARE WORRIED. DON'T BE.
I SEE YOU WORK YOURSELF TO EXHAUSTION TO SAVE HIM.
AND THE ONE RESPONSIBLE? HE HAS ALREADY BEEN DEALT WITH.
YOU ARE BRAVE. YOU ARE INTELLIGENT.
I--AND THE SEIJIN GANG--ONLY ACCEPT THE BEST.
BUT IT'S NOT JUST QUALITY. WE DON'T JUST INVITE YOU IN AFTER SEEING YOU FROM FAR AWAY.
YOU NEED SOMEONE TO PUSH FOR YOU. TO BELIEVE IN YOU. TO LOVE YOU.
YOU HAVE THAT.
YOU HAVE BEEN VOUCHED FOR.
YOU'RE FAMILY.

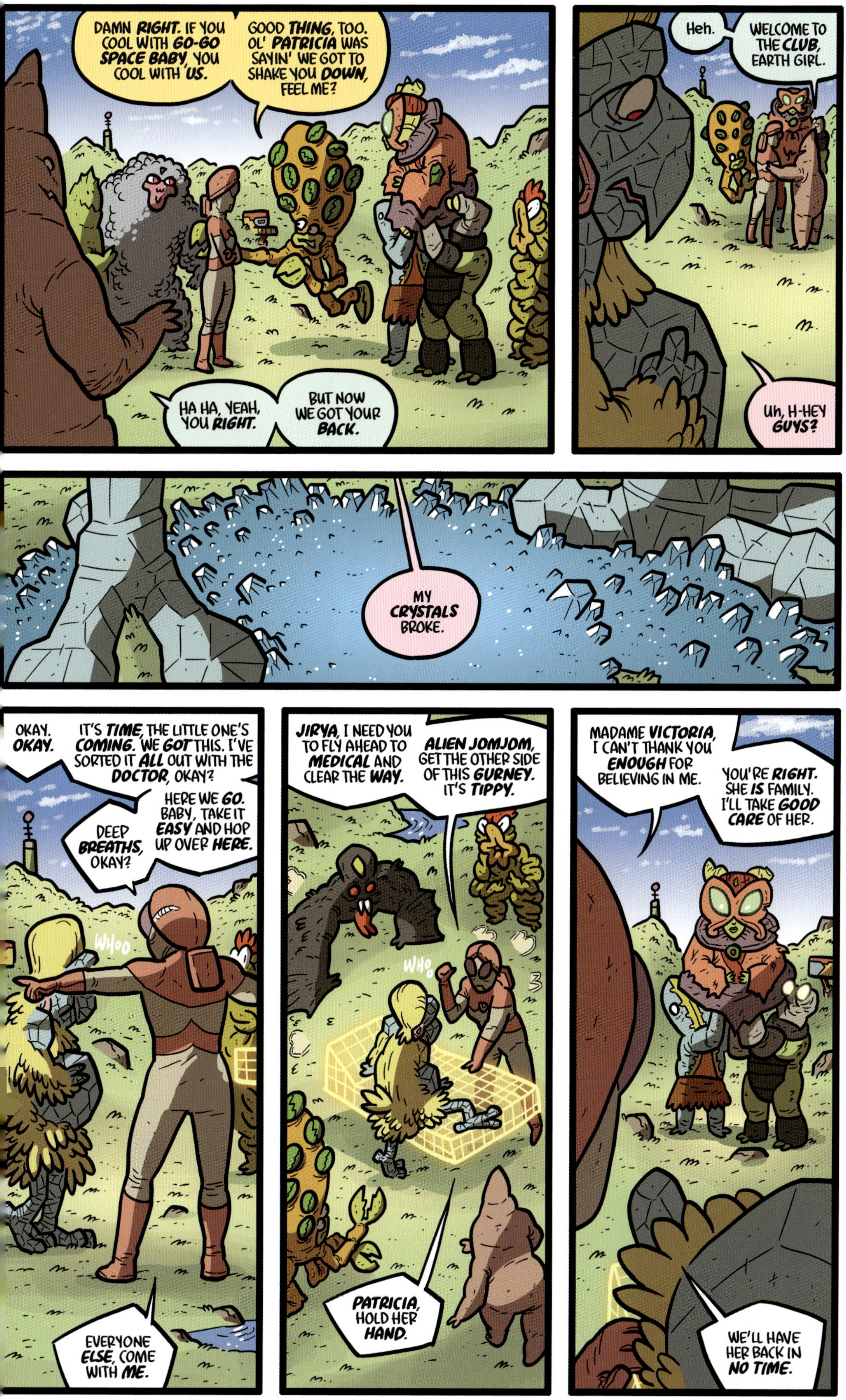

DAMN RIGHT. IF YOU COOL WITH GO-GO SPACE BABY, YOU COOL WITH US.
GOOD THING, TOO. OL' PATRICIA WAS SAYIN' WE GOT TO SHAKE YOU DOWN, FEEL ME?
HA HA, YEAH, YOU RIGHT.
BUT NOW WE GOT YOUR BACK.
Heh.
WELCOME TO THE CLUB, EARTH GIRL.
Uh, H-HEY GUYS?
MY CRYSTALS BROKE.
OKAY. OKAY.
IT'S TIME, THE LITTLE ONE'S COMING. WE GOT THIS. I'VE SORTED IT ALL OUT WITH THE DOCTOR, OKAY?
HERE WE GO. BABY, TAKE IT EASY AND HOP UP OVER HERE.
DEEP BREATHS, OKAY?
WHOO
EVERYONE ELSE, COME WITH ME.
JIRYA, I NEED YOU TO FLY AHEAD TO MEDICAL AND CLEAR THE WAY.
ALIEN JOMJOM, GET THE OTHER SIDE OF THIS GURNEY. IT'S TIPPY.
WHO
PATRICIA, HOLD HER HAND.
MADAME VICTORIA, I CAN'T THANK YOU ENOUGH FOR BELIEVING IN ME.
YOU'RE RIGHT. SHE IS FAMILY. I'LL TAKE GOOD CARE OF HER.
WE'LL HAVE HER BACK IN NO TIME.

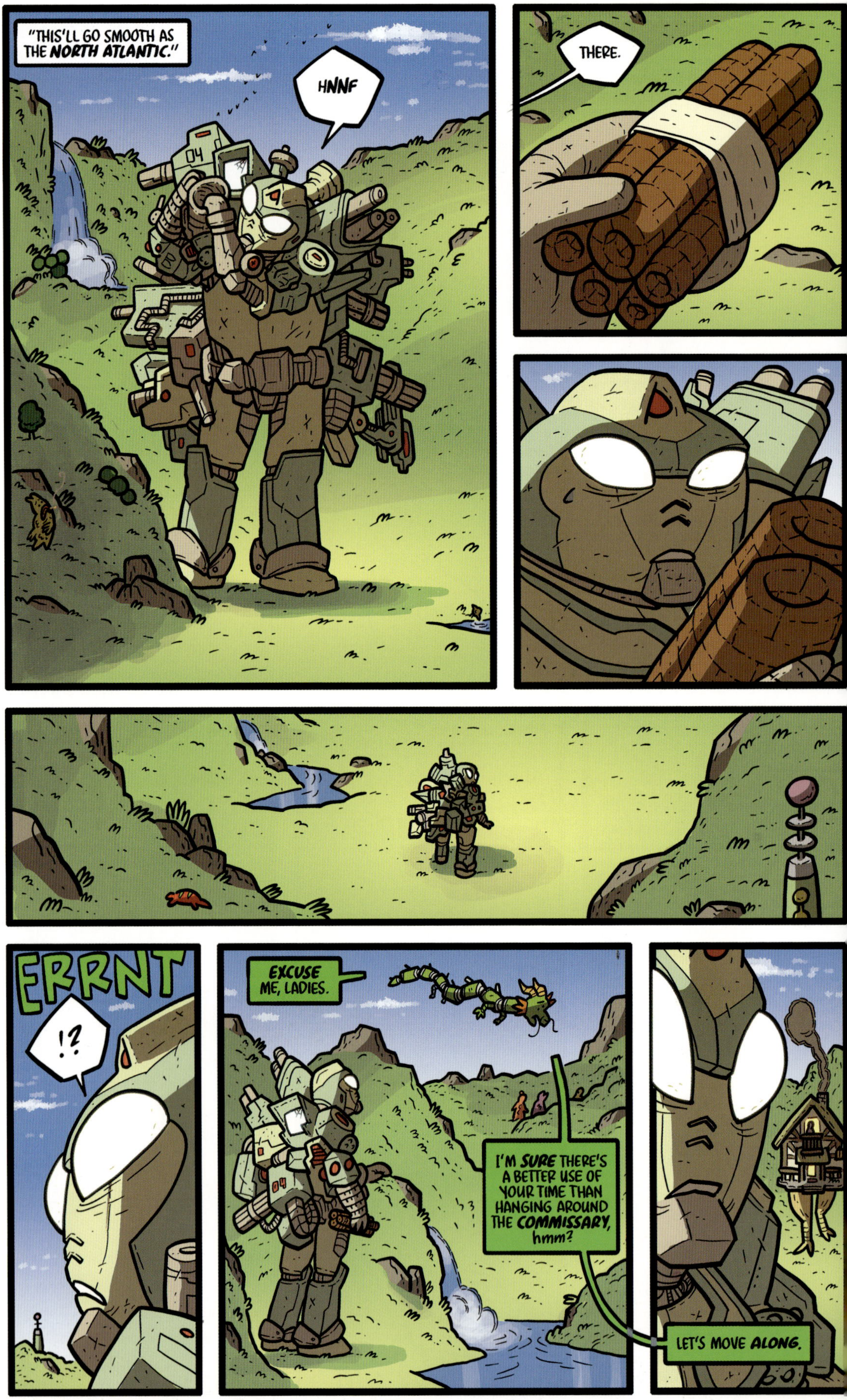
"THIS'LL GO SMOOTH AS THE NORTH ATLANTIC."
HNNF
THERE.
ERRNT
!?
EXCUSE ME, LADIES.
I'M SURE THERE'S A BETTER USE OF YOUR TIME THAN HANGING AROUND THE COMMISSARY, hmm?
LET'S MOVE ALONG.

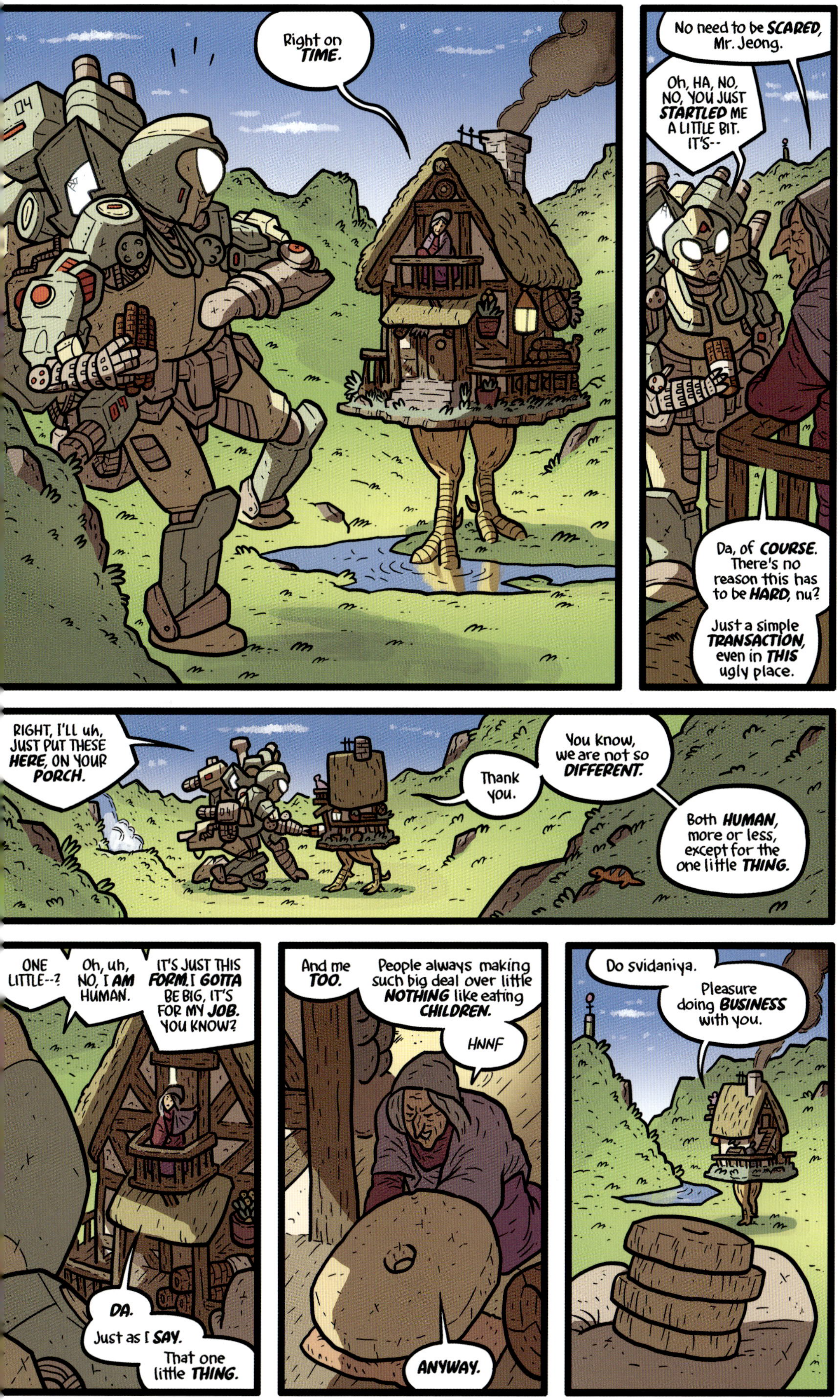
Right on TIME.
No need to be SCARED, Mr. Jeong.
Oh, HA, NO, NO, YOU JUST STARTLED ME A LITTLE BIT. IT'S--
Da, of COURSE. There's no reason this has to be HARD, nu?
Just a simple TRANSACTION, even in THIS ugly place.
RIGHT, I'LL uh, JUST PUT THESE HERE, ON YOUR PORCH.
Thank you.
You know, we are not so DIFFERENT.
Both HUMAN, more or less, except for the one little THING.
ONE LITTLE--?
Oh, uh, NO, I AM HUMAN.
IT'S JUST THIS FORM. I GOTTA BE BIG, IT'S FOR MY JOB. YOU KNOW?
DA.
Just as I SAY.
That one little THING.
And me TOO.
People always making such big deal over little NOTHING like eating CHILDREN.
HNNF
ANYWAY.
Do svidaniya.
Pleasure doing BUSINESS with you.

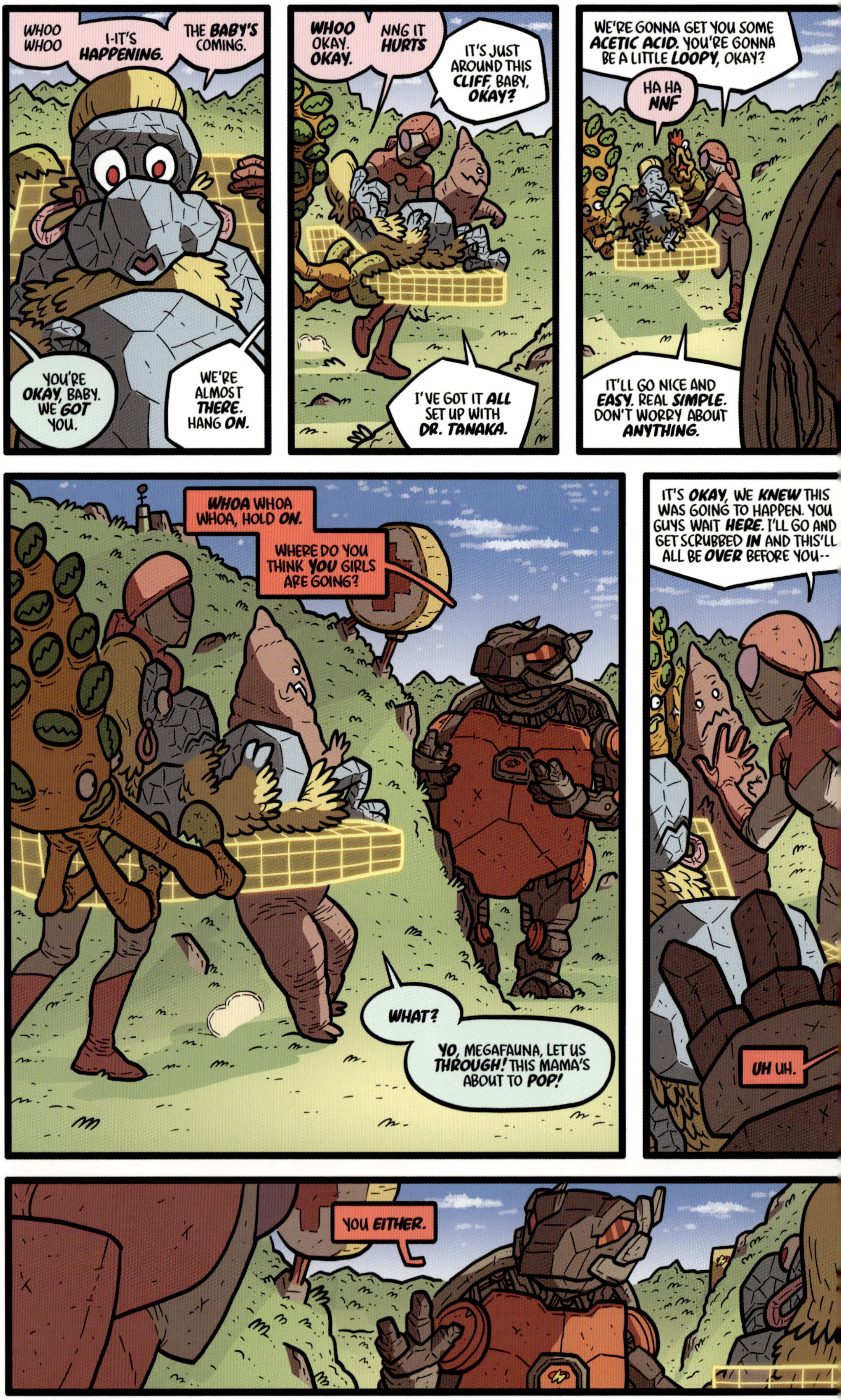
WHOO WHOO
I-IT'S HAPPENING.
THE BABY'S COMING.
YOU'RE OKAY, BABY. WE GOT YOU.
WE'RE ALMOST THERE. HANG ON.
WHOO OKAY. OKAY.
NNG IT HURTS
IT'S JUST AROUND THIS CLIFF, BABY, OKAY?
I'VE GOT IT ALL SET UP WITH DR. TANAKA.
WE'RE GONNA GET YOU SOME ACETIC ACID. YOU'RE GONNA BE A LITTLE LOOPY, OKAY?
HA HA NNF
IT'LL GO NICE AND EASY. REAL SIMPLE. DON'T WORRY ABOUT ANYTHING.
WHOA WHOA WHOA, HOLD ON.
WHERE DO YOU THINK YOU GIRLS ARE GOING?
WHAT?
YO, MEGAFAUNA, LET US THROUGH! THIS MAMA'S ABOUT TO POP!
IT'S OKAY, WE KNEW THIS WAS GOING TO HAPPEN. YOU GUYS WAIT HERE. I'LL GO AND GET SCRUBBED IN AND THIS'LL ALL BE OVER BEFORE YOU--
UH UH.
YOU EITHER.

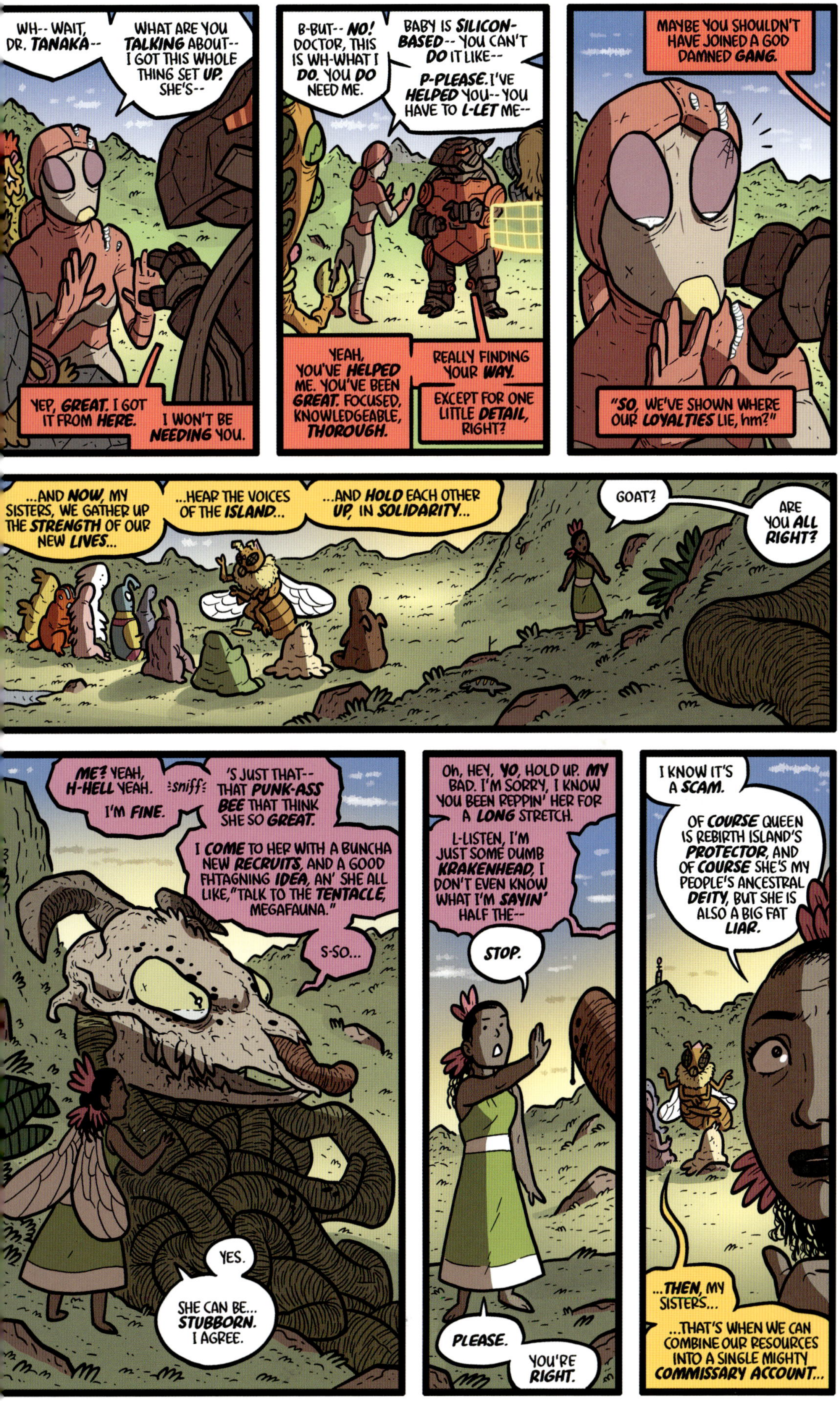
WH-- WAIT, DR. TANAKA--
WHAT ARE YOU TALKING ABOUT-- I GOT THIS WHOLE THING SET UP. SHE'S--
YEP, GREAT. I GOT IT FROM HERE.
I WON'T BE NEEDING YOU.
B-BUT-- NO! DOCTOR, THIS IS WH-WHAT I DO. YOU DO NEED ME.
BABY IS SILICON-BASED-- YOU CAN'T DO IT LIKE--
P-PLEASE. I'VE HELPED YOU-- YOU HAVE TO L-LET ME--
YEAH, YOU'VE HELPED ME. YOU'VE BEEN GREAT. FOCUSED, KNOWLEDGEABLE, THOROUGH.
REALLY FINDING YOUR WAY.
EXCEPT FOR ONE LITTLE DETAIL, RIGHT?
MAYBE YOU SHOULDN'T HAVE JOINED A GOD DAMNED GANG.
"SO, WE'VE SHOWN WHERE OUR LOYALTIES LIE, hm?"
...AND NOW, MY SISTERS, WE GATHER UP THE STRENGTH OF OUR NEW LIVES...
...HEAR THE VOICES OF THE ISLAND...
...AND HOLD EACH OTHER UP, IN SOLIDARITY...
GOAT?
ARE YOU ALL RIGHT?
ME? YEAH, H-HELL YEAH.
sniff
I'M FINE.
'S JUST THAT-- THAT PUNK-ASS BEE THAT THINK SHE SO GREAT.
I COME TO HER WITH A BUNCHA NEW RECRUITS, AND A GOOD FHTAGNING IDEA, AN' SHE ALL LIKE, "TALK TO THE TENTACLE, MEGAFAUNA."
S-SO...
YES.
SHE CAN BE... STUBBORN. I AGREE.
Oh, HEY, YO, HOLD UP. MY BAD. I'M SORRY, I KNOW YOU BEEN REPPIN' HER FOR A LONG STRETCH.
L-LISTEN, I'M JUST SOME DUMB KRAKENHEAD, I DON'T EVEN KNOW WHAT I'M SAYIN' HALF THE--
STOP.
PLEASE.
YOU'RE RIGHT.
I KNOW IT'S A SCAM.
OF COURSE QUEEN IS REBIRTH ISLAND'S PROTECTOR, AND OF COURSE SHE'S MY PEOPLE'S ANCESTRAL DEITY, BUT SHE IS ALSO A BIG FAT LIAR.
...THEN, MY SISTERS...
...THAT'S WHEN WE CAN COMBINE OUR RESOURCES INTO A SINGLE MIGHTY COMMISSARY ACCOUNT...

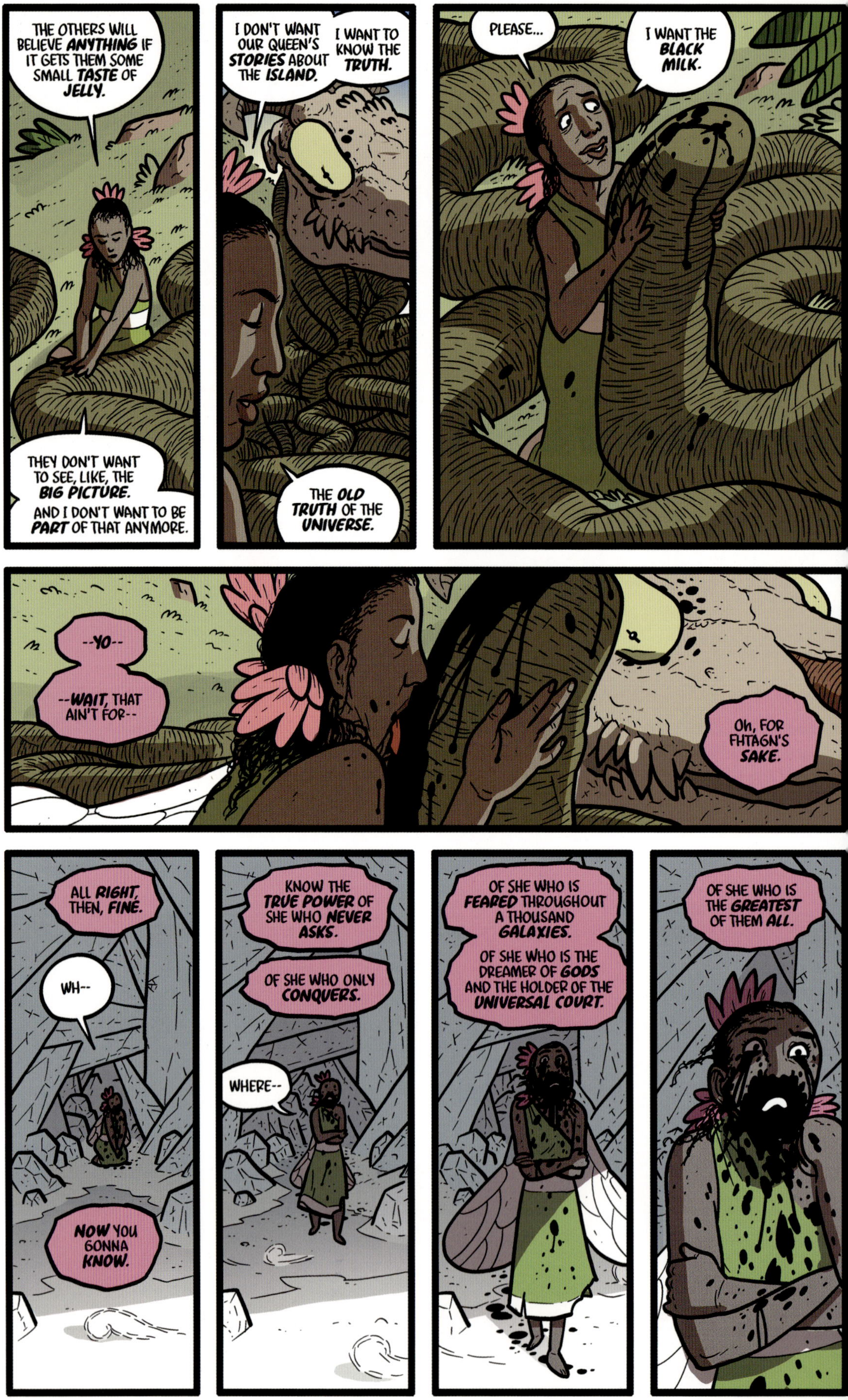
THE OTHERS WILL BELIEVE ANYTHING IF IT GETS THEM SOME SMALL TASTE OF JELLY.
THEY DON'T WANT TO SEE, LIKE, THE BIG PICTURE.
AND I DON'T WANT TO BE PART OF THAT ANYMORE.
I DON'T WANT OUR QUEEN'S STORIES ABOUT THE ISLAND.
I WANT TO KNOW THE TRUTH.
THE OLD TRUTH OF THE UNIVERSE.
PLEASE...
I WANT THE BLACK MILK.
--YO--
--WAIT, THAT AIN'T FOR--
Oh, FOR FHTAGN'S SAKE.
ALL RIGHT, THEN, FINE.
WH--
NOW YOU GONNA KNOW.
KNOW THE TRUE POWER OF SHE WHO NEVER ASKS.
OF SHE WHO ONLY CONQUERS.
WHERE--
OF SHE WHO IS FEARED THROUGHOUT A THOUSAND GALAXIES.
OF SHE WHO IS THE DREAMER OF GODS AND THE HOLDER OF THE UNIVERSAL COURT.
OF SHE WHO IS THE GREATEST OF THEM ALL.

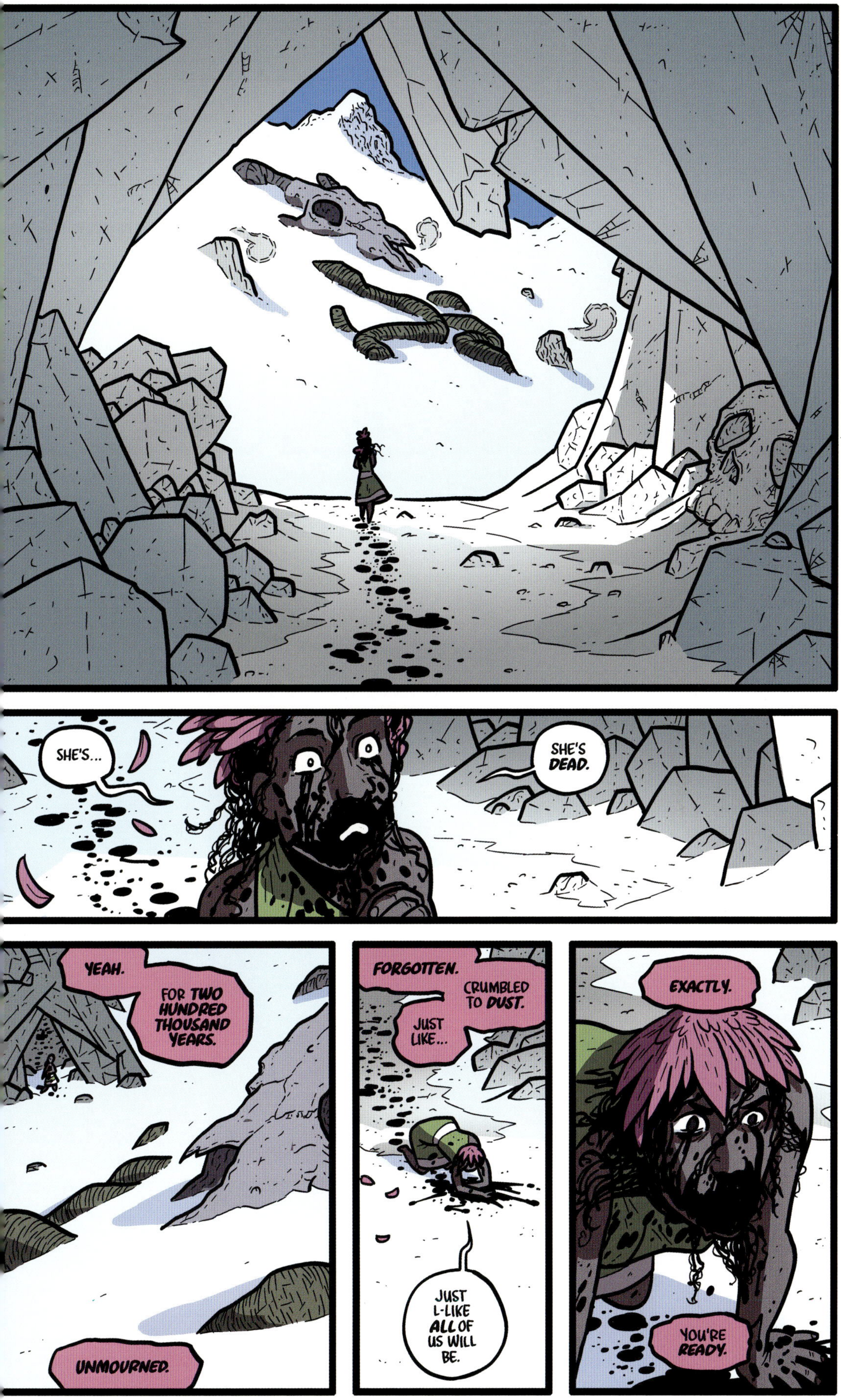

SHE'S...
SHE'S DEAD.
YEAH.
FOR TWO HUNDRED THOUSAND YEARS.
UNMOURNED.
FORGOTTEN.
CRUMBLED TO DUST.
JUST LIKE...
JUST L-LIKE ALL OF US WILL BE.
EXACTLY.
YOU'RE READY.

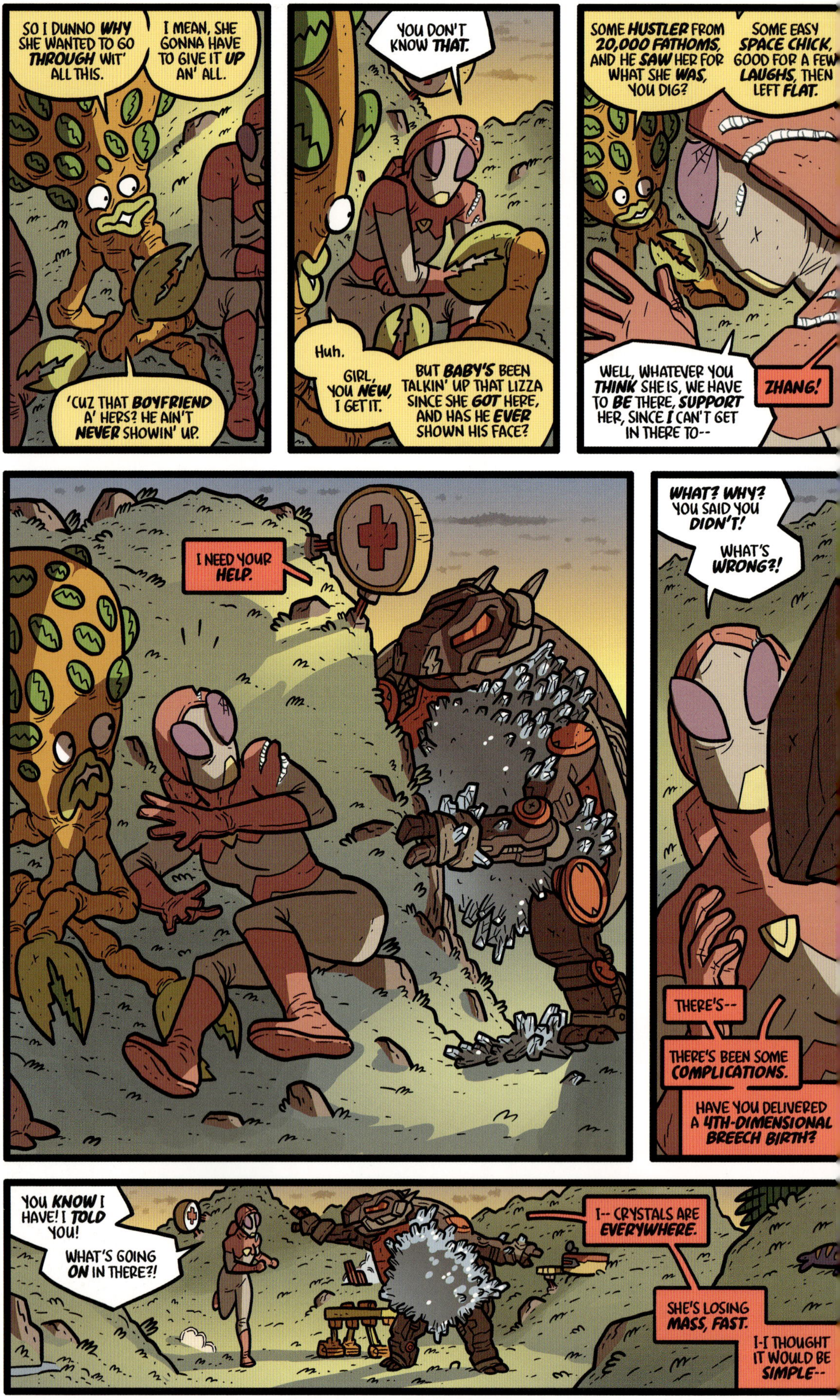
SO I DUNNO WHY SHE WANTED TO GO THROUGH WIT' ALL THIS.
I MEAN, SHE GONNA HAVE TO GIVE IT UP AN' ALL.
'CUZ THAT BOYFRIEND A' HERS? HE AIN'T NEVER SHOWIN' UP.
YOU DON'T KNOW THAT.
Huh.
GIRL, YOU NEW, I GET IT.
BUT BABY'S BEEN TALKIN' UP THAT LIZZA SINCE SHE GOT HERE, AND HAS HE EVER SHOWN HIS FACE?
SOME HUSTLER FROM 20,000 FATHOMS, AND HE SAW HER FOR WHAT SHE WAS, YOU DIG?
SOME EASY SPACE CHICK, GOOD FOR A FEW LAUGHS, THEN LEFT FLAT.
WELL, WHATEVER YOU THINK SHE IS, WE HAVE TO BE THERE, SUPPORT HER, SINCE I CAN'T GET IN THERE TO--
ZHANG!
I NEED YOUR HELP.
WHAT? WHY? YOU SAID YOU DIDN'T!
WHAT'S WRONG?!
THERE'S--
THERE'S BEEN SOME COMPLICATIONS.
HAVE YOU DELIVERED A 4TH-DIMENSIONAL BREECH BIRTH?
YOU KNOW I HAVE! I TOLD YOU!
WHAT'S GOING ON IN THERE?!
I-- CRYSTALS ARE EVERYWHERE.
SHE'S LOSING MASS, FAST.
I-I THOUGHT IT WOULD BE SIMPLE--

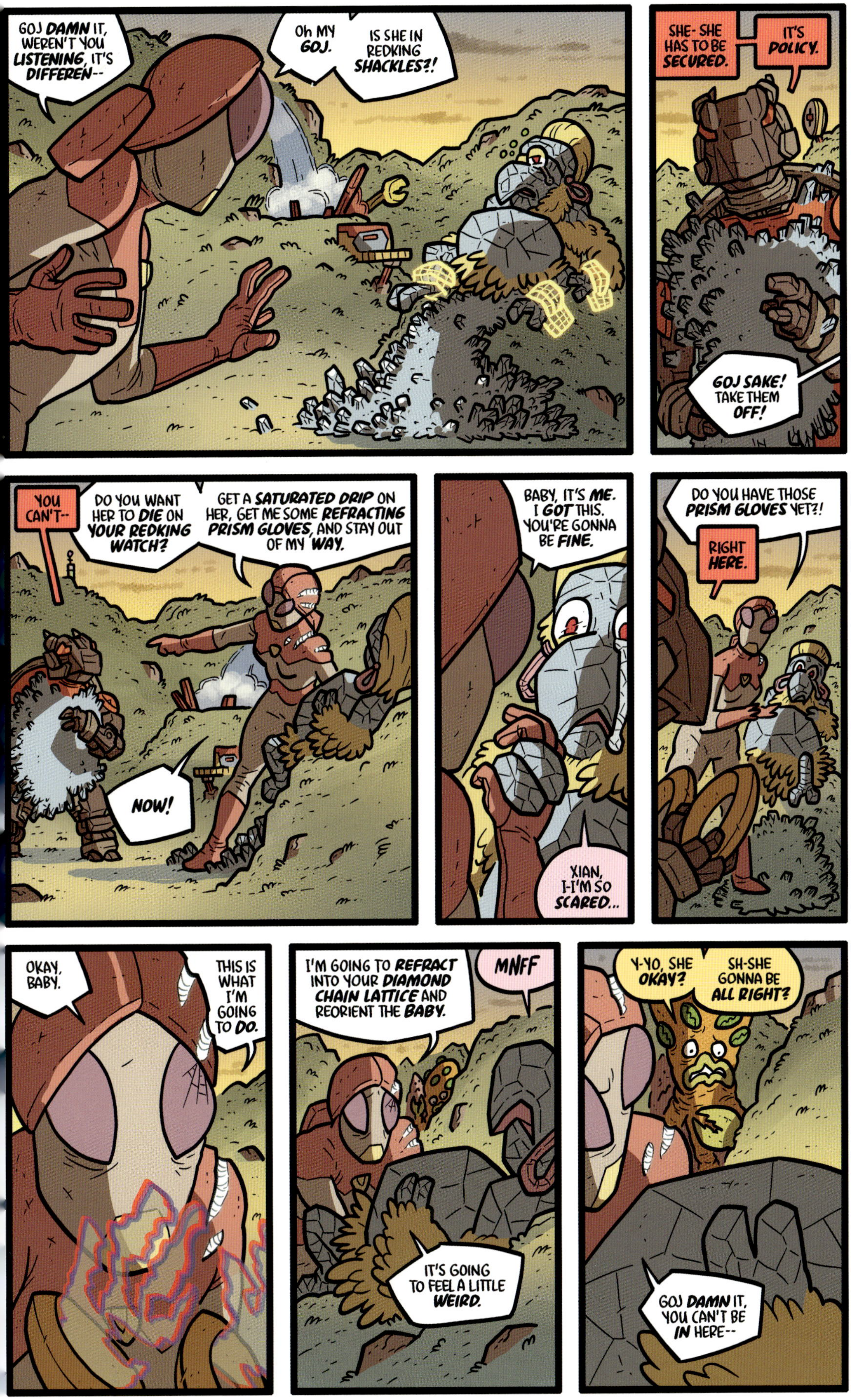
GOJ DAMN IT, WEREN'T YOU LISTENING, IT'S DIFFEREN--
Oh MY GOJ.
IS SHE IN REDKING SHACKLES?!
SHE- SHE HAS TO BE SECURED.
IT'S POLICY.
GOJ SAKE! TAKE THEM OFF!
YOU CAN'T--
DO YOU WANT HER TO DIE ON YOUR REDKING WATCH?
GET A SATURATED DRIP ON HER, GET ME SOME REFRACTING PRISM GLOVES, AND STAY OUT OF MY WAY.
NOW!
BABY, IT'S ME. I GOT THIS. YOU'RE GONNA BE FINE.
XIAN, I-I'M SO SCARED...
DO YOU HAVE THOSE PRISM GLOVES YET?!
RIGHT HERE.
OKAY, BABY.
THIS IS WHAT I'M GOING TO DO.
I'M GOING TO REFRACT INTO YOUR DIAMOND CHAIN LATTICE AND REORIENT THE BABY.
MNFF
IT'S GOING TO FEEL A LITTLE WEIRD.
Y-YO, SHE OKAY?
SH-SHE GONNA BE ALL RIGHT?
GOJ DAMN IT, YOU CAN'T BE IN HERE--

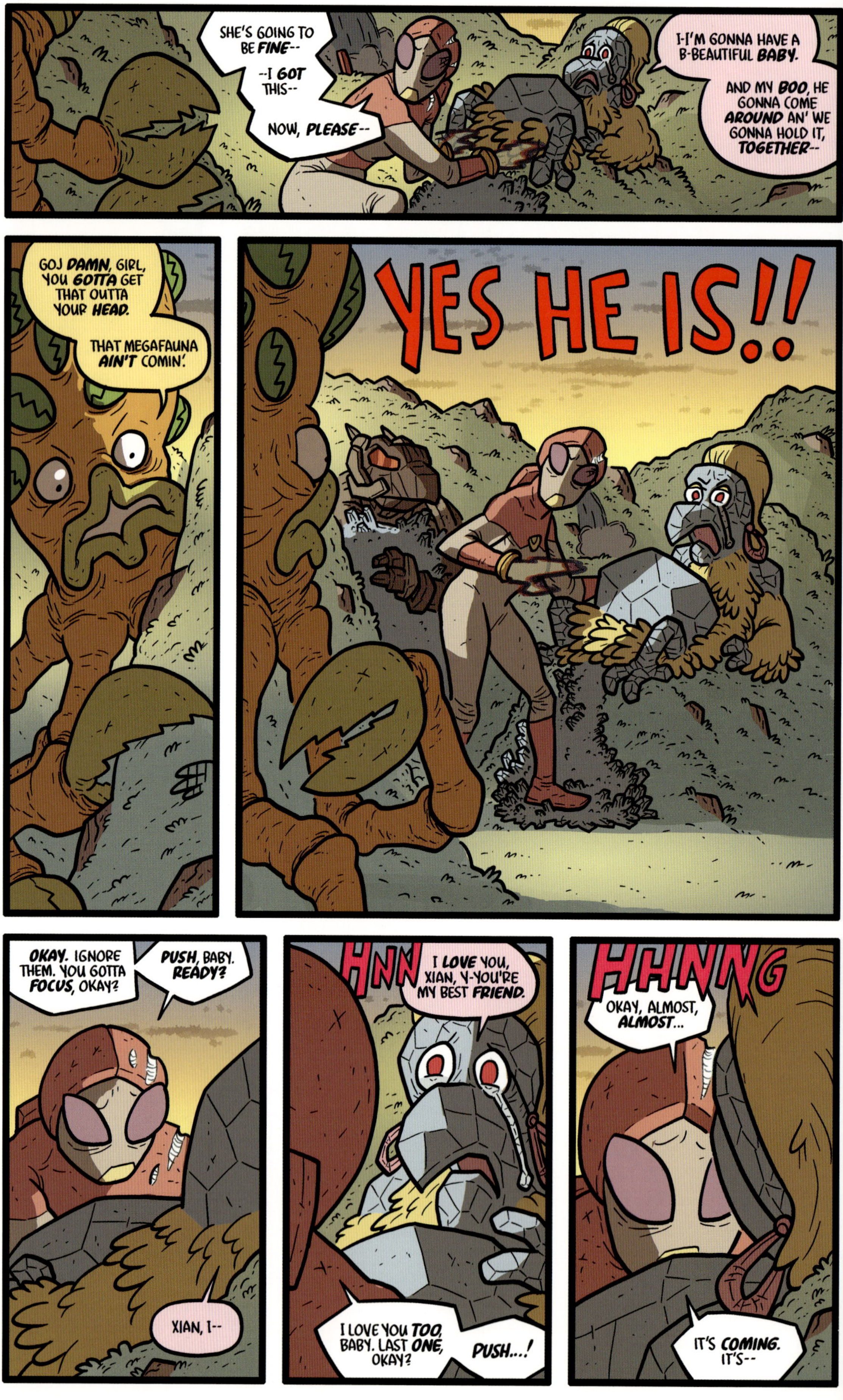

SHE'S GOING TO BE FINE--
--I GOT THIS--
NOW, PLEASE--
I-I'M GONNA HAVE A B-BEAUTIFUL BABY.
AND MY BOO, HE GONNA COME AROUND AN' WE GONNA HOLD IT, TOGETHER--
GOJ DAMN, GIRL, YOU GOTTA GET THAT OUTTA YOUR HEAD.
THAT MEGAFAUNA AIN'T COMIN'.
YES HE IS!!
OKAY. IGNORE THEM. YOU GOTTA FOCUS, OKAY?
PUSH, BABY. READY?
XIAN, I--
HNN
I LOVE YOU, XIAN, Y-YOU'RE MY BEST FRIEND.
I LOVE YOU TOO, BABY. LAST ONE, OKAY?
PUSH...!
HHNNG
OKAY, ALMOST, ALMOST...
IT'S COMING. IT'S--

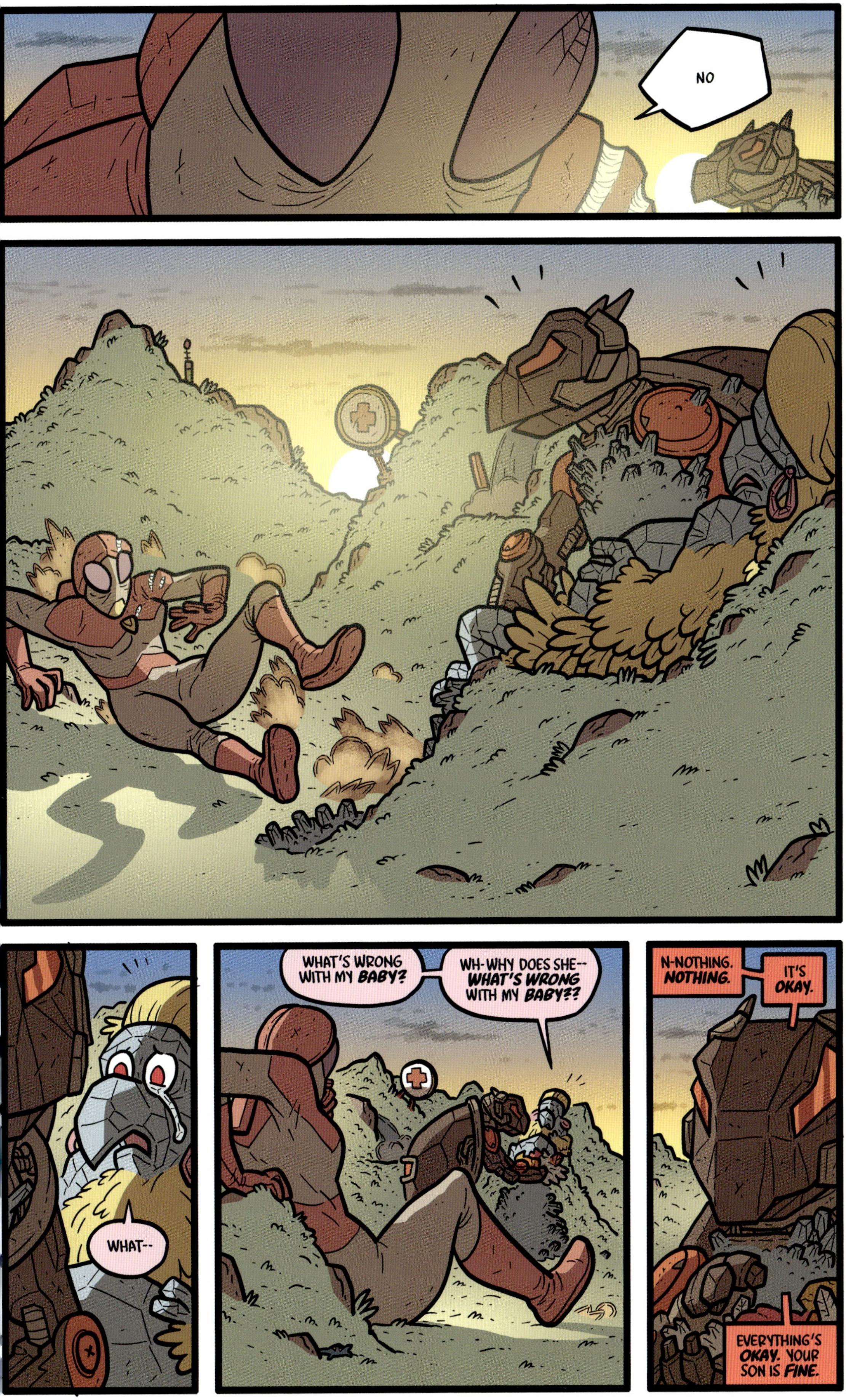
NO
WHAT--
WHAT'S WRONG WITH MY BABY?
WH-WHY DOES SHE-- WHAT'S WRONG WITH MY BABY??
N-NOTHING. NOTHING.
IT'S OKAY.
EVERYTHING'S OKAY. YOUR SON IS FINE.

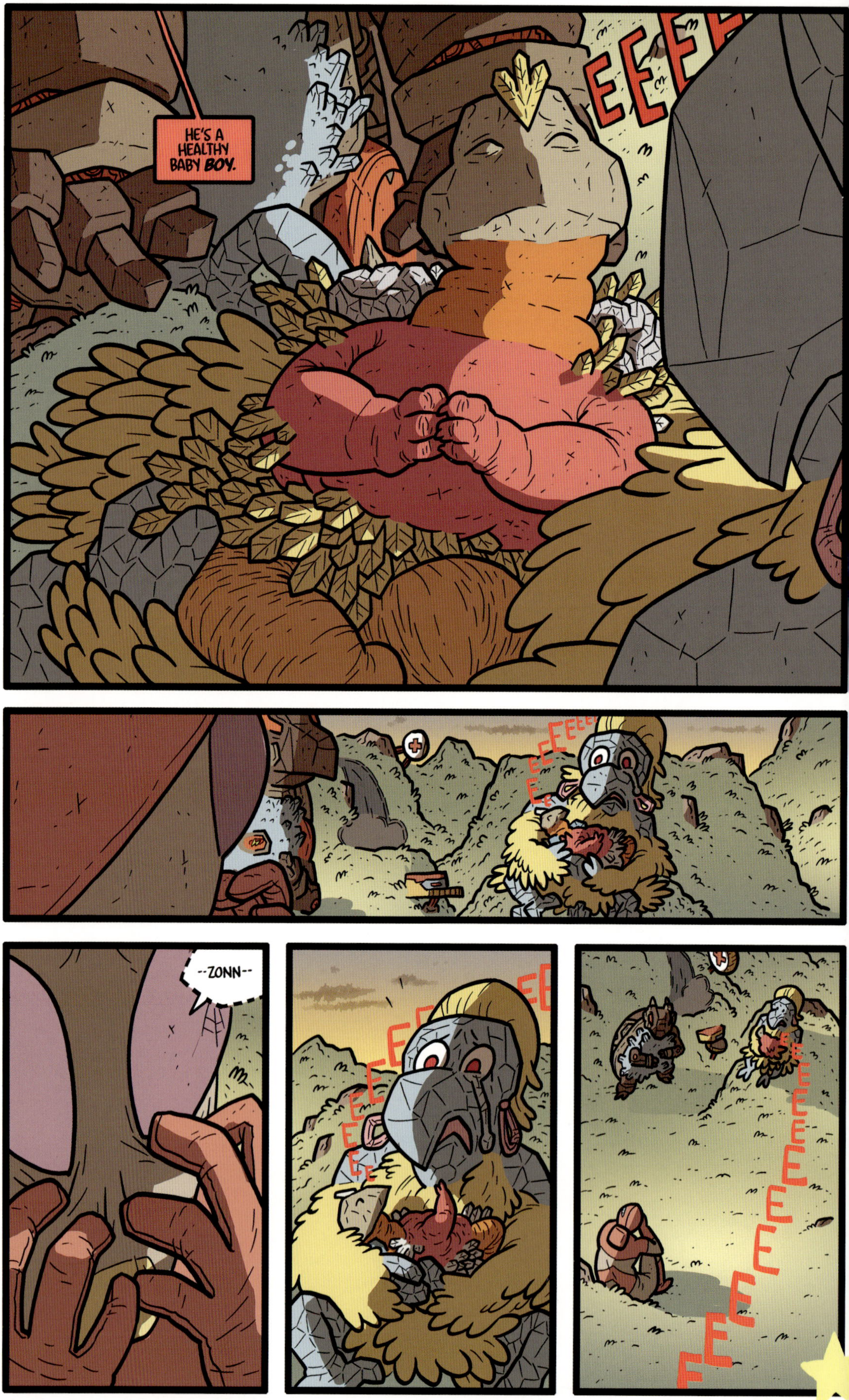
HE'S A HEALTHY BABY BOY.
EEEE
--ZONN--

EPISODE 4

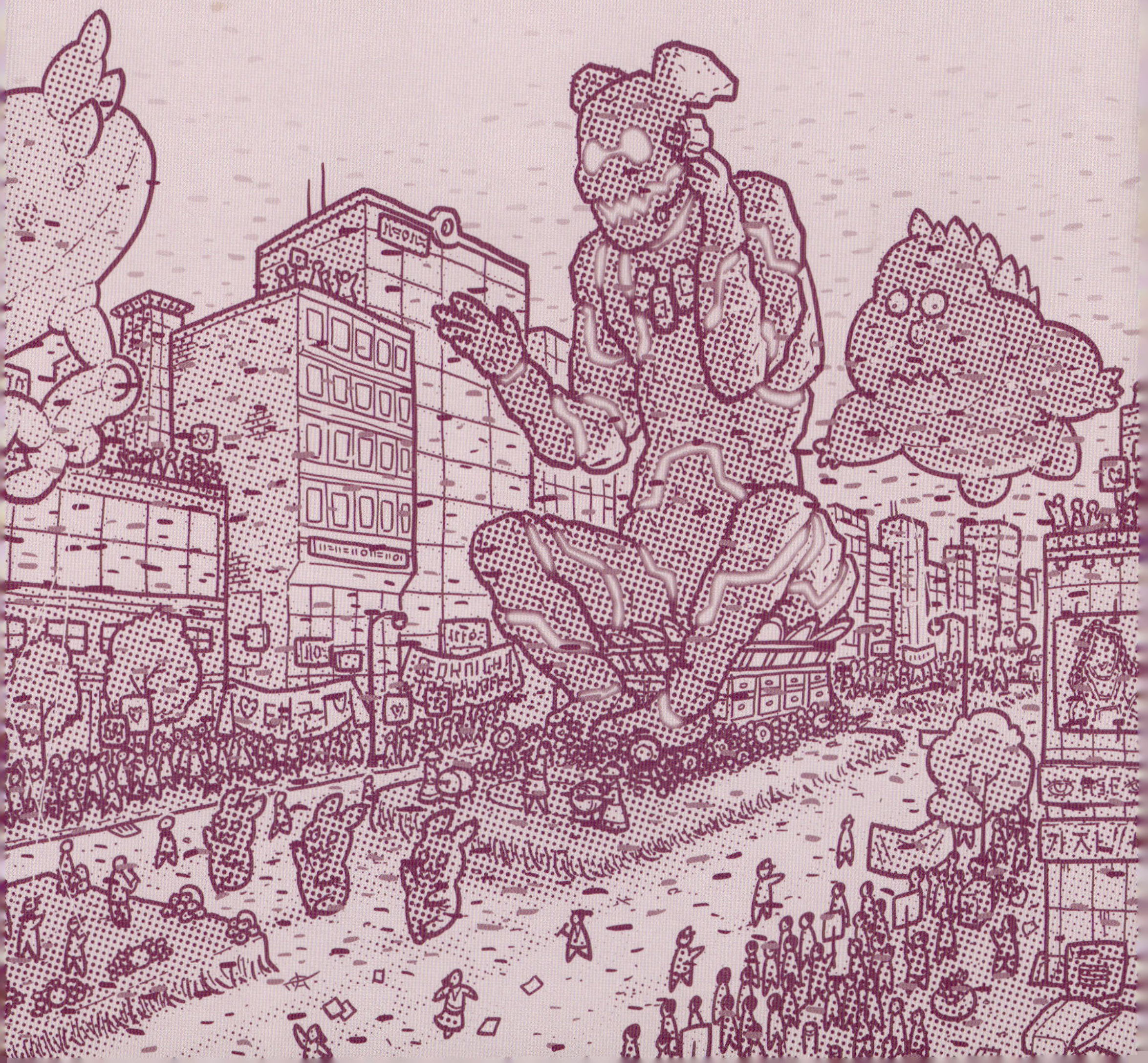

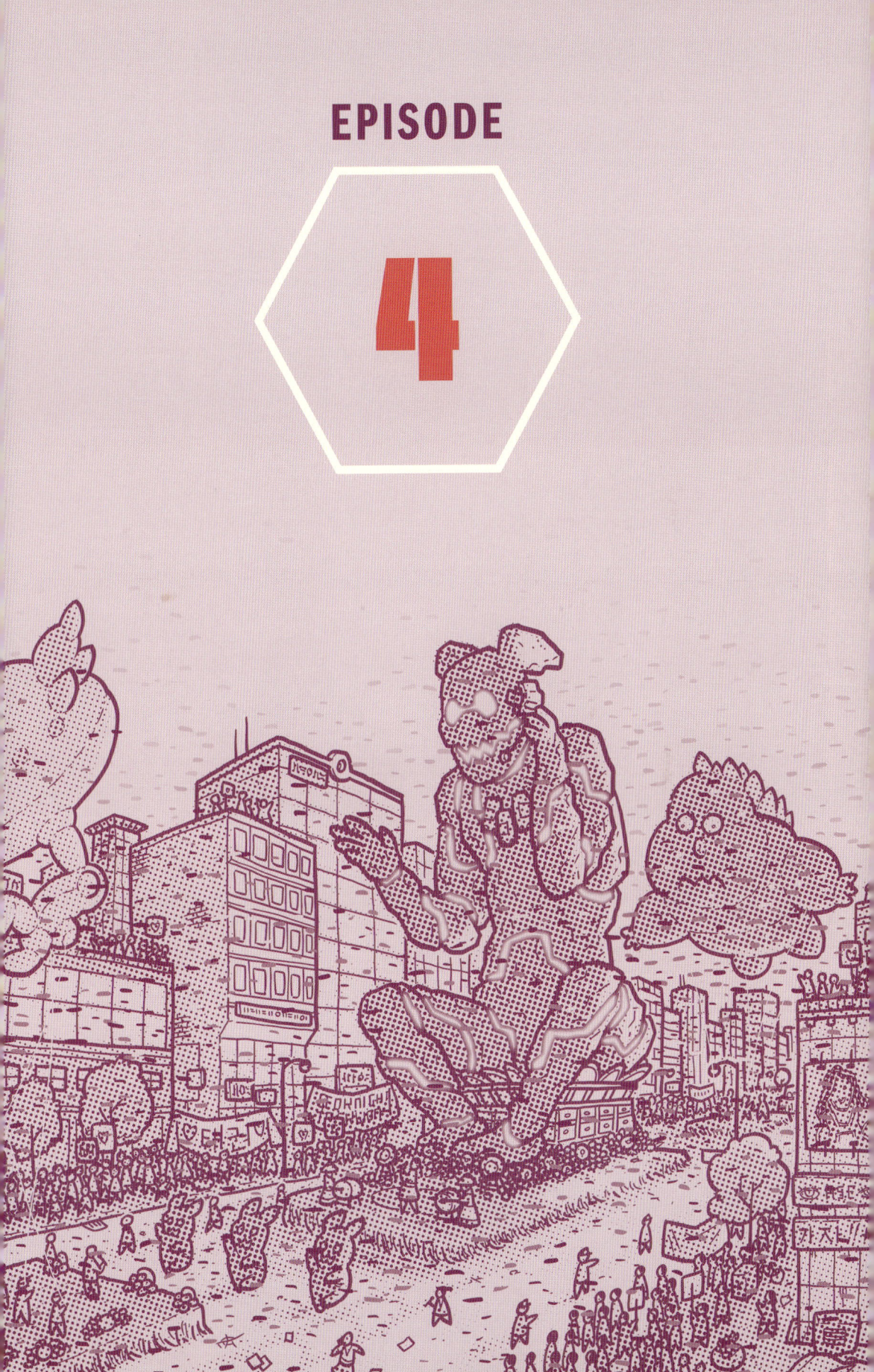

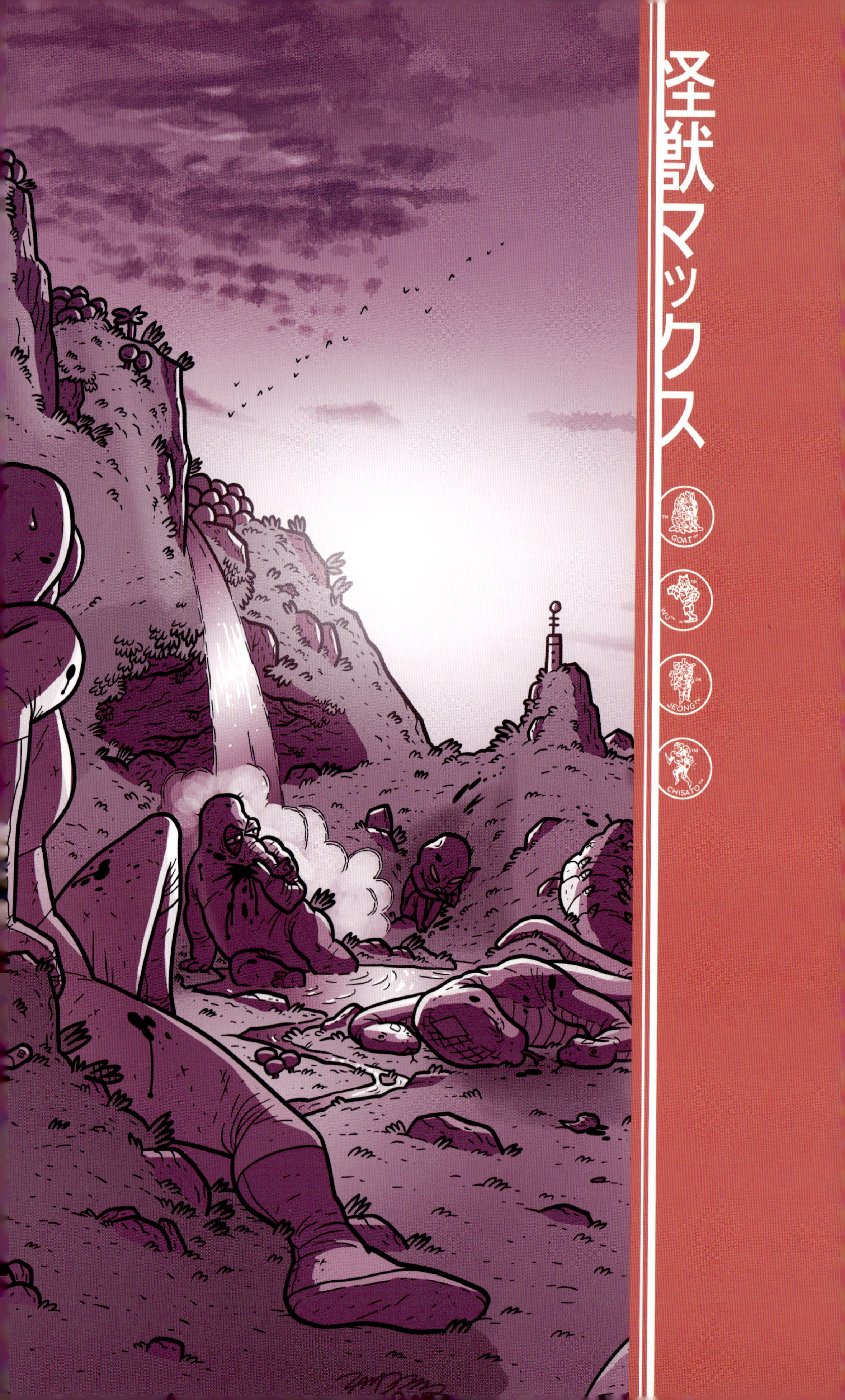
怪獣マックス
GOAT™
WU™
JEONG™
CHISATO™

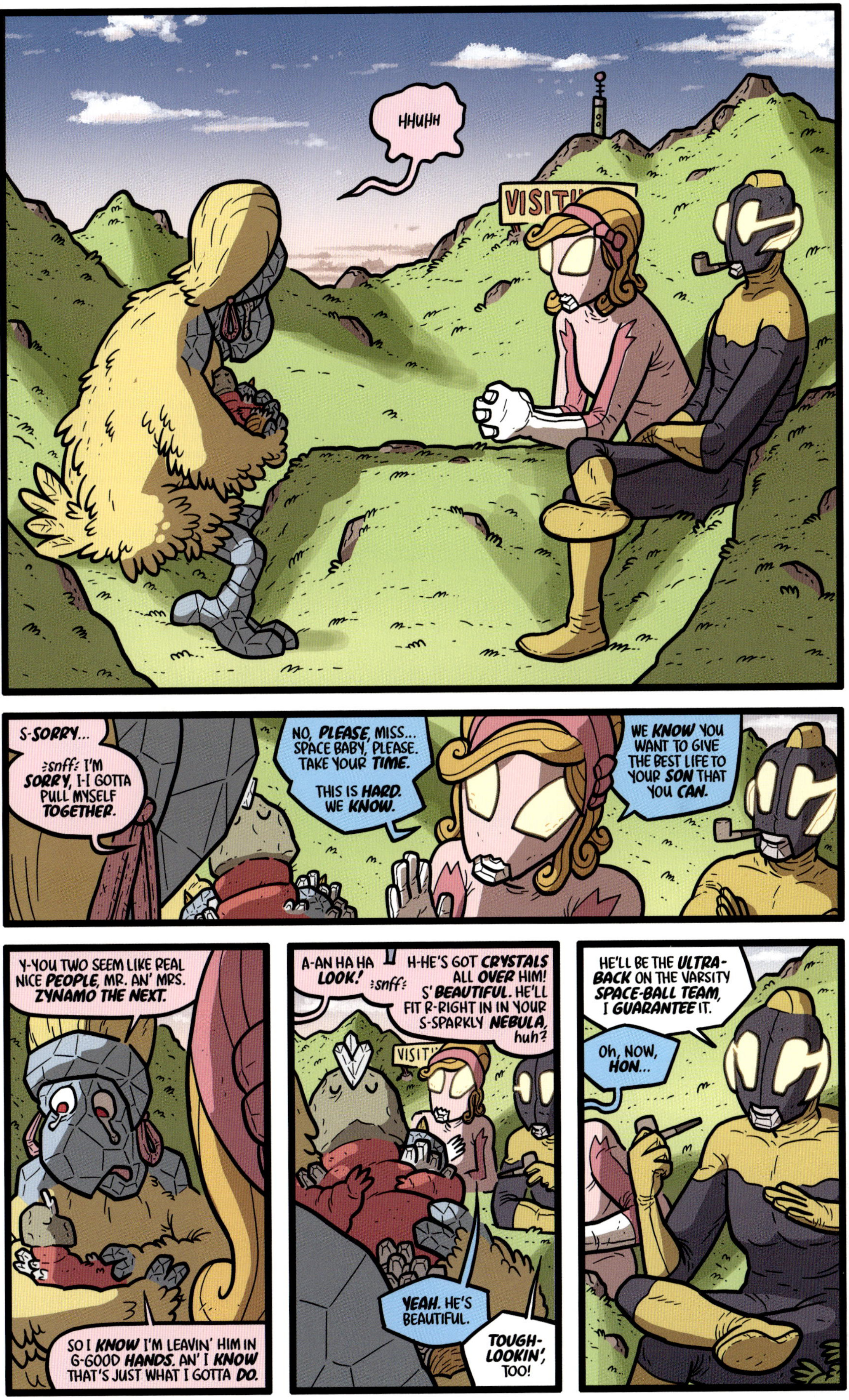
HHUHH
VISIT
S-SORRY...
snff I'M SORRY, I-I GOTTA PULL MYSELF TOGETHER.
NO, PLEASE, MISS... SPACE BABY, PLEASE. TAKE YOUR TIME.
THIS IS HARD. WE KNOW.
WE KNOW YOU WANT TO GIVE THE BEST LIFE TO YOUR SON THAT YOU CAN.
Y-YOU TWO SEEM LIKE REAL NICE PEOPLE, MR. AN' MRS. ZYNAMO THE NEXT.
SO I KNOW I'M LEAVIN' HIM IN G-GOOD HANDS. AN' I KNOW THAT'S JUST WHAT I GOTTA DO.
A-AN HA HA LOOK!
snff
H-HE'S GOT CRYSTALS ALL OVER HIM! S' BEAUTIFUL. HE'LL FIT R-RIGHT IN IN YOUR S-SPARKLY NEBULA, huh?
VISIT
YEAH. HE'S BEAUTIFUL.
TOUGH-LOOKIN', TOO!
HE'LL BE THE ULTRA-BACK ON THE VARSITY SPACE-BALL TEAM, I GUARANTEE IT.
Oh, NOW, HON...

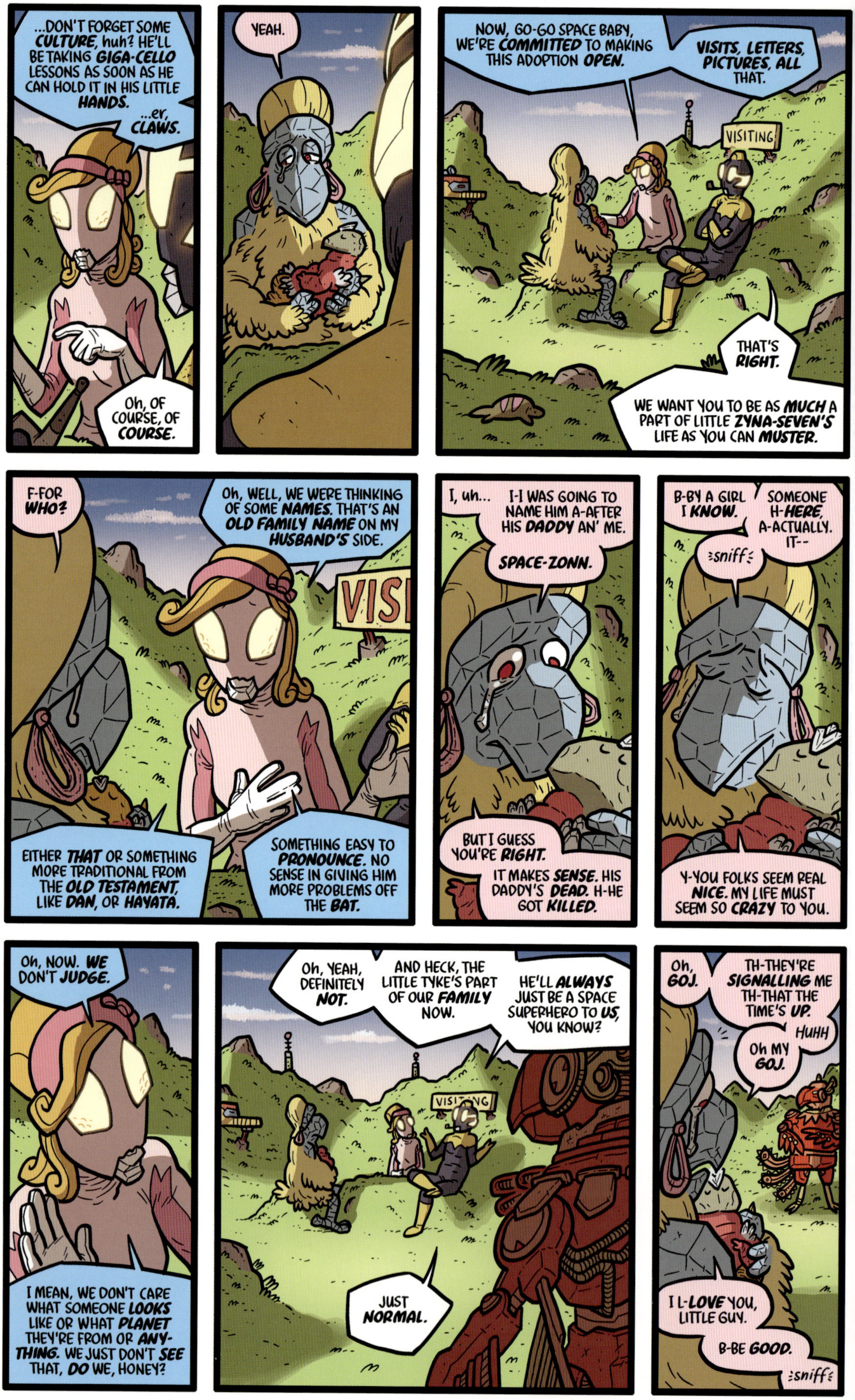
...DON'T FORGET SOME CULTURE, huh? HE'LL BE TAKING GIGA-CELLO LESSONS AS SOON AS HE CAN HOLD IT IN HIS LITTLE HANDS.
...er, CLAWS.
Oh, OF COURSE, OF COURSE.
YEAH.
NOW, GO-GO SPACE BABY, WE'RE COMMITTED TO MAKING THIS ADOPTION OPEN.
VISITS, LETTERS, PICTURES, ALL THAT.
VISITING
THAT'S RIGHT.
WE WANT YOU TO BE AS MUCH A PART OF LITTLE ZYNA-SEVEN'S LIFE AS YOU CAN MUSTER.
F-FOR WHO?
Oh, WELL, WE WERE THINKING OF SOME NAMES. THAT'S AN OLD FAMILY NAME ON MY HUSBAND'S SIDE.
VISI
EITHER THAT OR SOMETHING MORE TRADITIONAL FROM THE OLD TESTAMENT, LIKE DAN, OR HAYATA.
SOMETHING EASY TO PRONOUNCE. NO SENSE IN GIVING HIM MORE PROBLEMS OFF THE BAT.
I, uh...
I-I WAS GOING TO NAME HIM A-AFTER HIS DADDY AN' ME.
SPACE-ZONN.
BUT I GUESS YOU'RE RIGHT.
IT MAKES SENSE. HIS DADDY'S DEAD. H-HE GOT KILLED.
B-BY A GIRL I KNOW.
SOMEONE H-HERE, A-ACTUALLY. IT--
sniff
Y-YOU FOLKS SEEM REAL NICE. MY LIFE MUST SEEM SO CRAZY TO YOU.
Oh, NOW. WE DON'T JUDGE.
I MEAN, WE DON'T CARE WHAT SOMEONE LOOKS LIKE OR WHAT PLANET THEY'RE FROM OR ANY-THING. WE JUST DON'T SEE THAT, DO WE, HONEY?
Oh, YEAH, DEFINITELY NOT.
AND HECK, THE LITTLE TYKE'S PART OF OUR FAMILY NOW.
HE'LL ALWAYS JUST BE A SPACE SUPERHERO TO US, YOU KNOW?
JUST NORMAL.
Oh, GOJ.
TH-THEY'RE SIGNALLING ME TH-THAT THE TIME'S UP.
HUHH
Oh MY GOJ.
I L-LOVE YOU, LITTLE GUY.
B-BE GOOD.
sniff

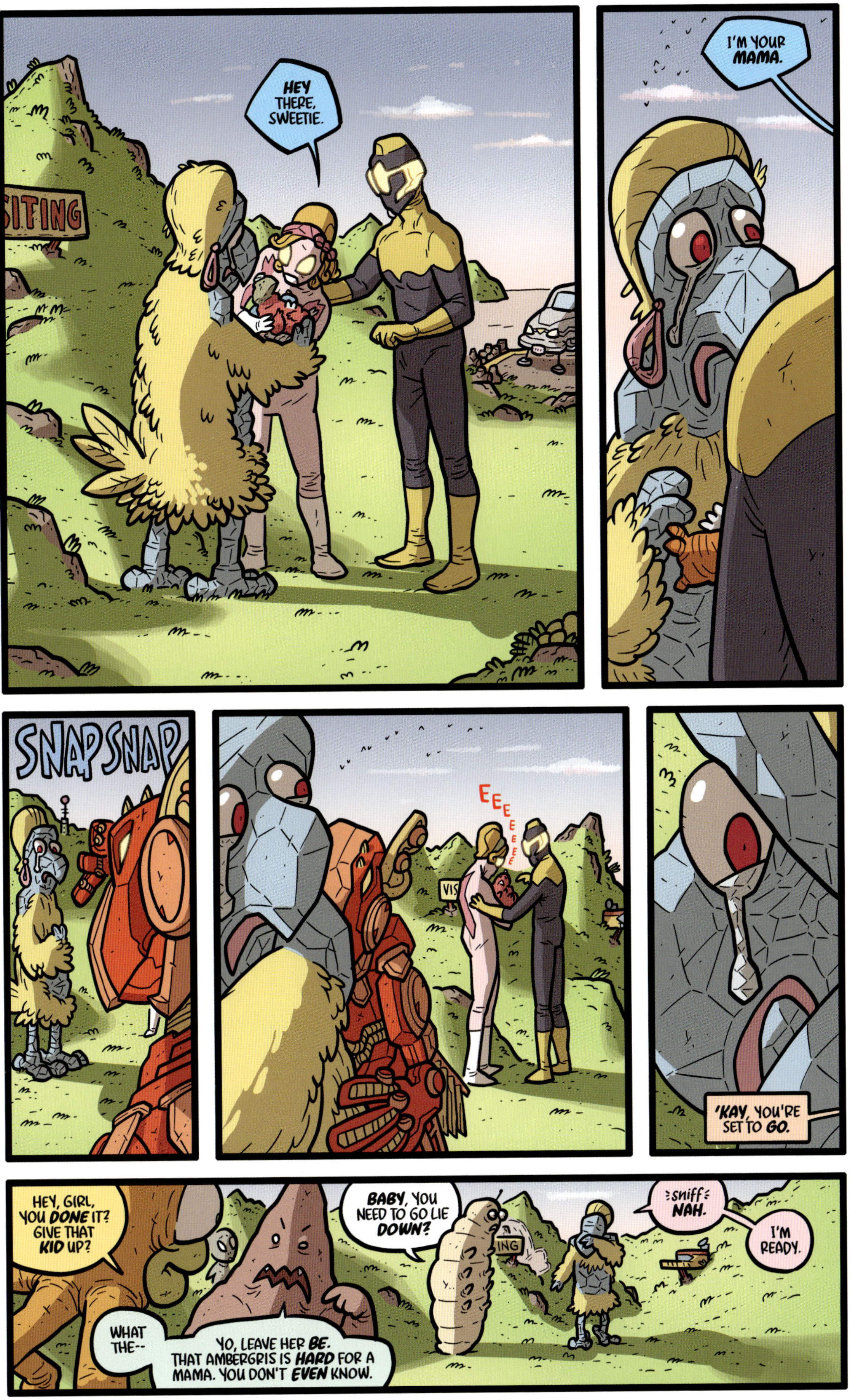

SITING
HEY THERE, SWEETIE.
I'M YOUR MAMA.
SNAP SNAP
VIS
EEEEEEE
'KAY, YOU'RE SET TO GO.
HEY, GIRL, YOU DONE IT? GIVE THAT KID UP?
WHAT THE--
YO, LEAVE HER BE. THAT AMBERGRIS IS HARD FOR A MAMA. YOU DON'T EVEN KNOW.
BABY, YOU NEED TO GO LIE DOWN?
ING
sniff NAH.
I'M READY.

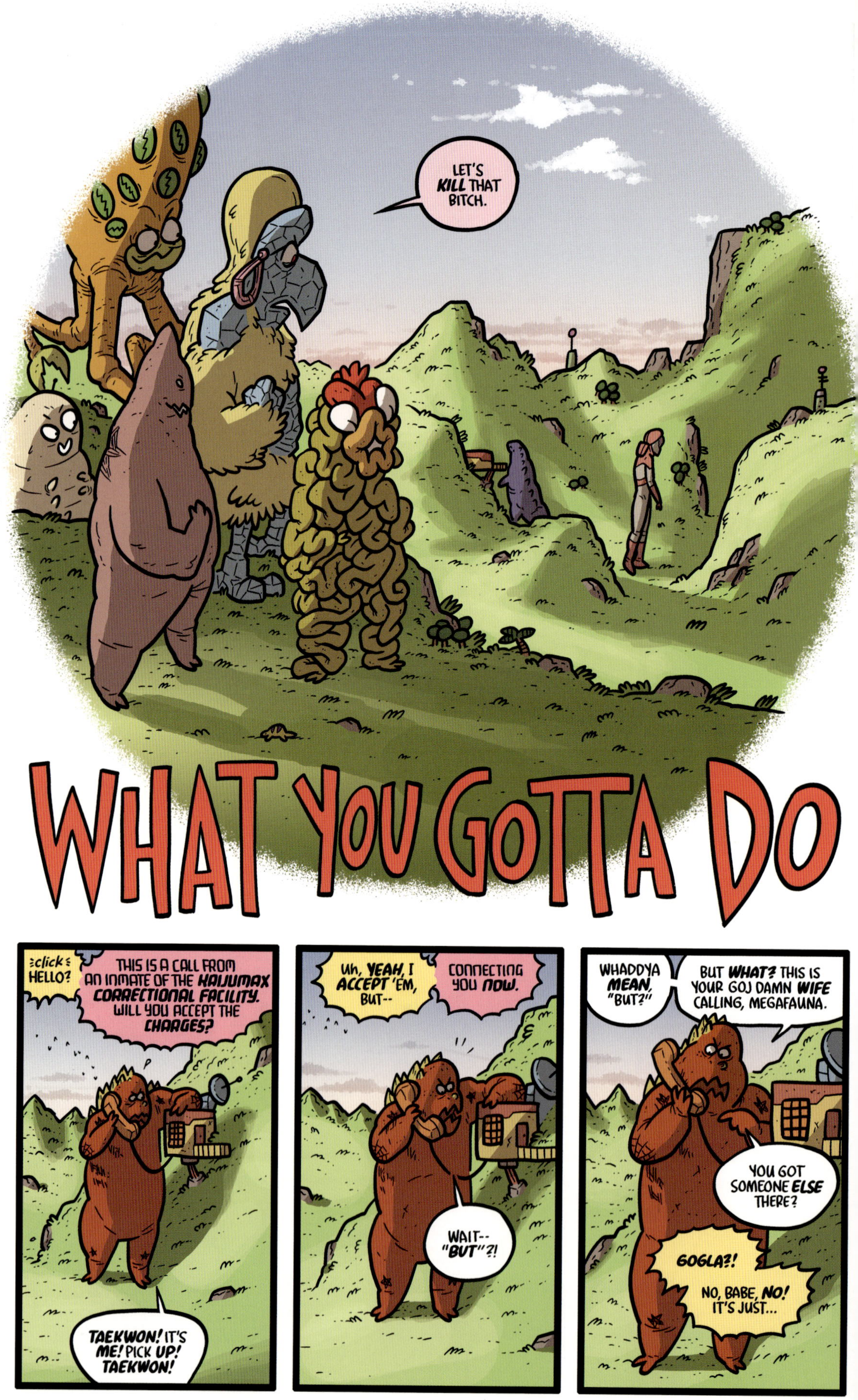
LET'S KILL THAT BITCH.
WHAT YOU GOTTA DO
click HELLO?
THIS IS A CALL FROM AN INMATE OF THE HAIJUMAX CORRECTIONAL FACILITY. WILL YOU ACCEPT THE CHARGES?
TAEKWON! IT'S ME! PICK UP! TAEKWON!
Uh, YEAH, I ACCEPT 'EM, BUT--
CONNECTING YOU NOW.
WAIT-- "BUT"?!
WHADDYA MEAN, "BUT?"
BUT WHAT? THIS IS YOUR GOJ DAMN WIFE CALLING, MEGAFAUNA.
YOU GOT SOMEONE ELSE THERE?
GOGLA?!
NO, BABE, NO! IT'S JUST...

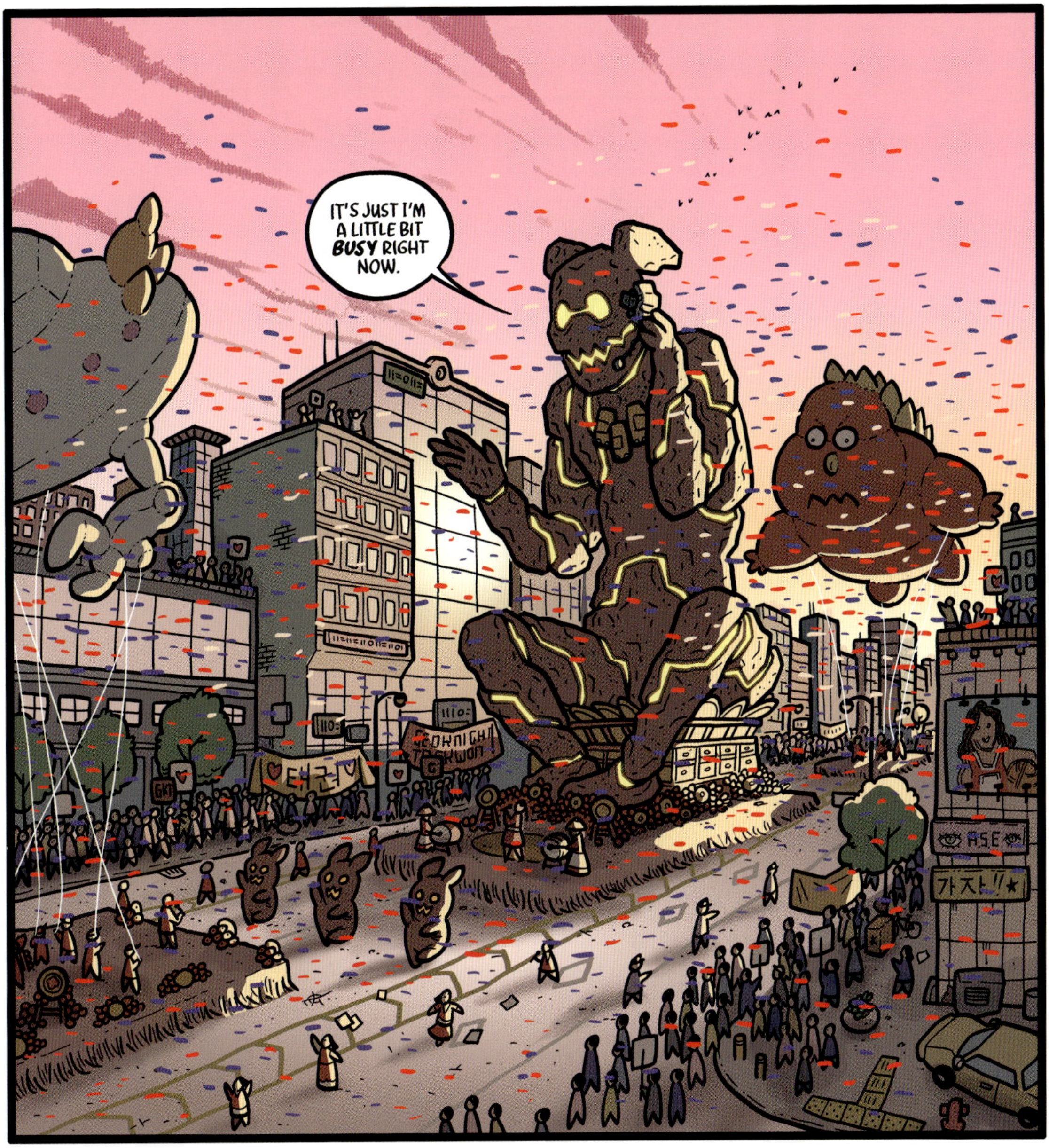
IT'S JUST I'M A LITTLE BIT **BUSY** RIGHT NOW.

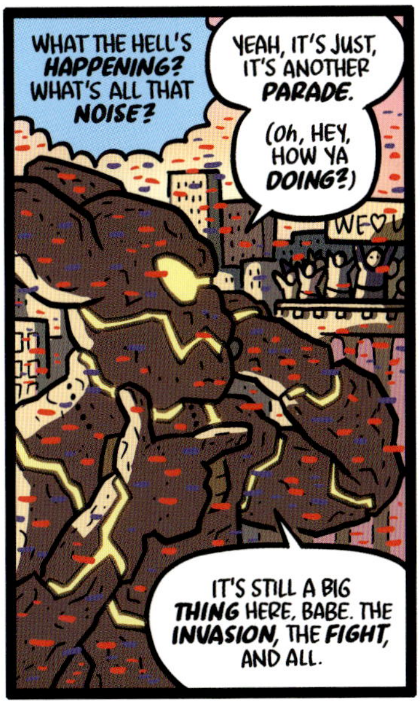
WHAT THE HELL'S **HAPPENING?** WHAT'S ALL THAT **NOISE?**
YEAH, IT'S JUST, IT'S ANOTHER **PARADE.**
(Oh, HEY, HOW YA **DOING?**)
IT'S STILL A BIG **THING** HERE, BABE. THE **INVASION**, THE **FIGHT**, AND ALL.

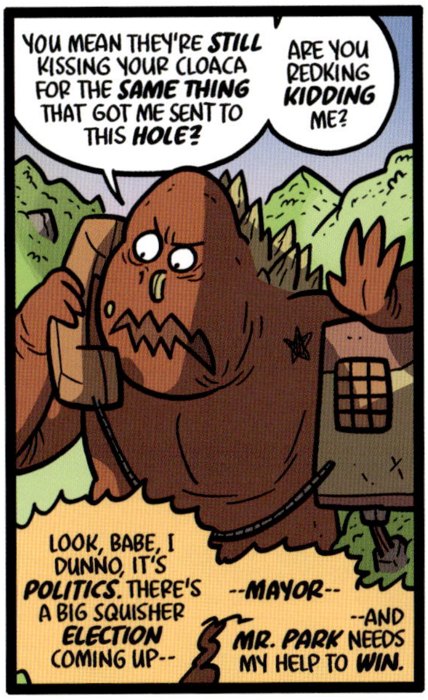
YOU MEAN THEY'RE **STILL** KISSING YOUR CLOACA FOR THE **SAME THING** THAT GOT ME SENT TO THIS **HOLE?**
ARE YOU REDKING **KIDDING** ME?
LOOK, BABE, I DUNNO, IT'S **POLITICS**. THERE'S A BIG SQUISHER **ELECTION** COMING UP--
--MAYOR--
--AND **MR. PARK** NEEDS MY HELP TO **WIN.**

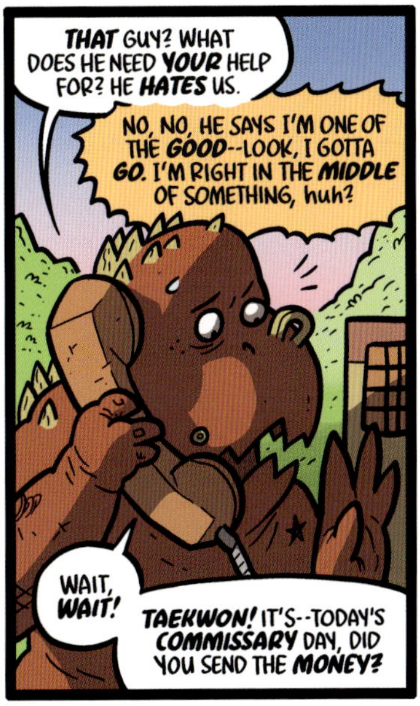
THAT GUY? WHAT DOES HE NEED **YOUR** HELP FOR? HE **HATES** US.
NO, NO, HE SAYS I'M ONE OF THE **GOOD**--LOOK, I GOTTA **GO**. I'M RIGHT IN THE **MIDDLE** OF SOMETHING, huh?
WAIT, **WAIT!**
TAEKWON! IT'S--TODAY'S **COMMISSARY** DAY, DID YOU SEND THE **MONEY?**

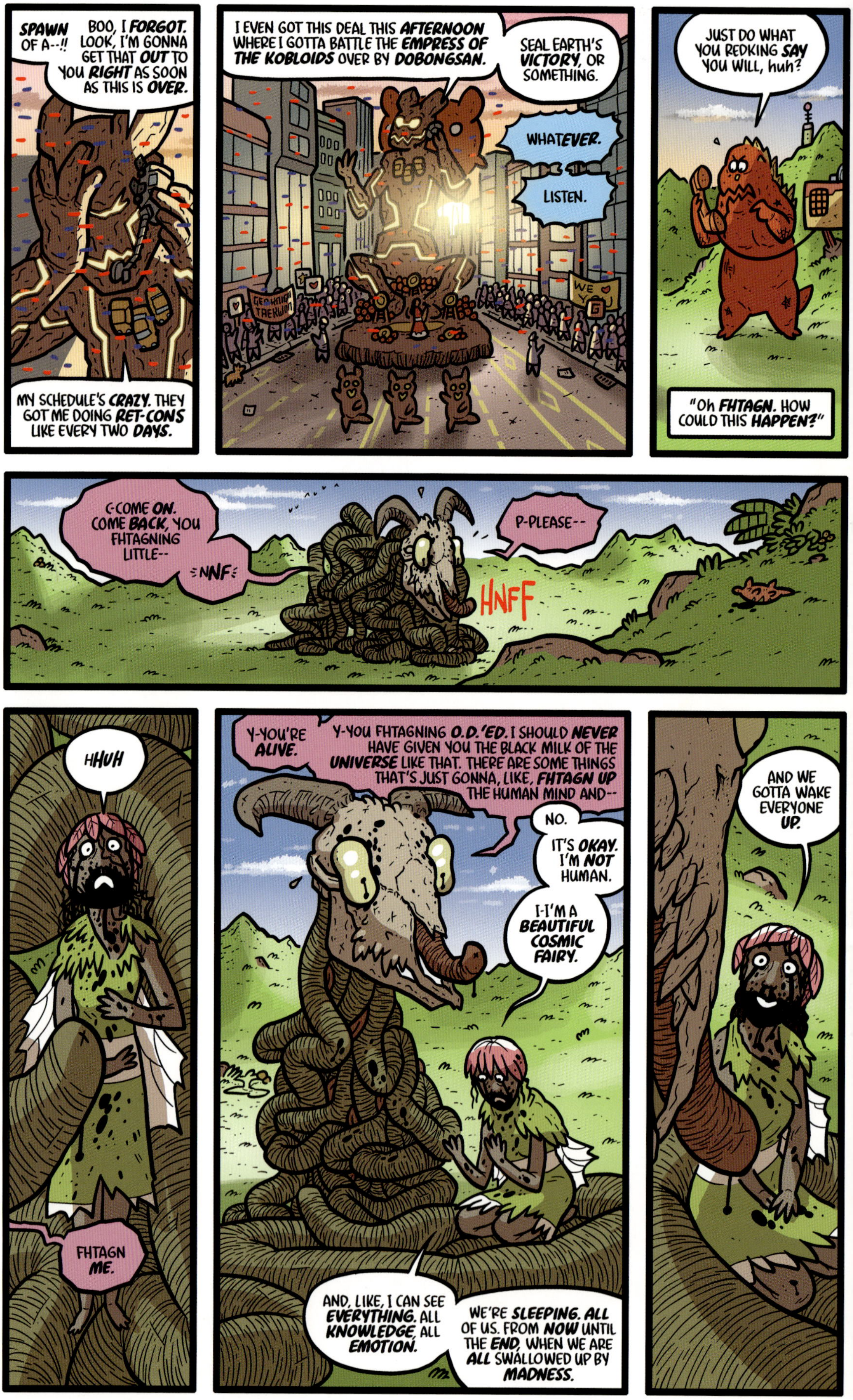
SPAWN OF A--!!
BOO, I FORGOT. LOOK, I'M GONNA GET THAT OUT TO YOU RIGHT AS SOON AS THIS IS OVER.
MY SCHEDULE'S CRAZY. THEY GOT ME DOING RET-CONS LIKE EVERY TWO DAYS.
I EVEN GOT THIS DEAL THIS AFTERNOON WHERE I GOTTA BATTLE THE EMPRESS OF THE KOBLOIDS OVER BY DOBONGSAN.
SEAL EARTH'S VICTORY, OR SOMETHING.
WHATEVER.
LISTEN.
JUST DO WHAT YOU REDKING SAY YOU WILL, huh?
"Oh FHTAGN. HOW COULD THIS HAPPEN?"
C-COME ON. COME BACK, YOU FHTAGNING LITTLE--
NNF
P-PLEASE--
HNFF
HHUH
FHTAGN ME.
Y-YOU'RE ALIVE.
Y-YOU FHTAGNING O.D.'ED. I SHOULD NEVER HAVE GIVEN YOU THE BLACK MILK OF THE UNIVERSE LIKE THAT. THERE ARE SOME THINGS THAT'S JUST GONNA, LIKE, FHTAGN UP THE HUMAN MIND AND--
NO.
IT'S OKAY. I'M NOT HUMAN.
I-I'M A BEAUTIFUL COSMIC FAIRY.
AND, LIKE, I CAN SEE EVERYTHING. ALL KNOWLEDGE, ALL EMOTION.
WE'RE SLEEPING. ALL OF US. FROM NOW UNTIL THE END, WHEN WE ARE ALL SWALLOWED UP BY MADNESS.
AND WE GOTTA WAKE EVERYONE UP.

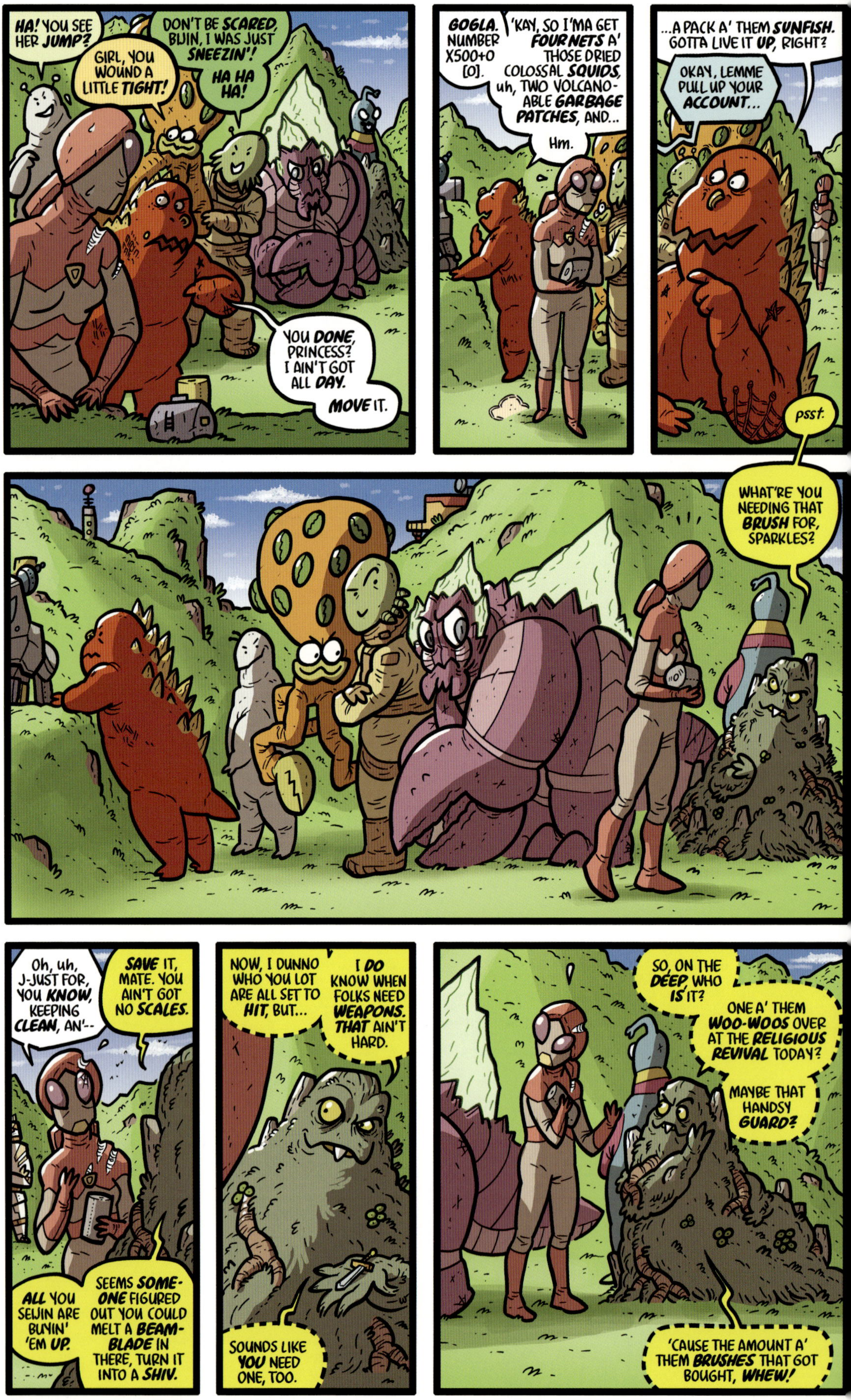
HA! YOU SEE HER JUMP?
GIRL, YOU WOUND A LITTLE TIGHT!
DON'T BE SCARED, BIJIN, I WAS JUST SNEEZIN'!
HA HA HA!
YOU DONE, PRINCESS? I AIN'T GOT ALL DAY.
MOVE IT.
GOGLA. NUMBER X500+0 [0].
'KAY, SO I'MA GET FOUR NETS A' THOSE DRIED COLOSSAL SQUIDS, uh, TWO VOLCANO-ABLE GARBAGE PATCHES, AND...
Hm.
...A PACK A' THEM SUNFISH. GOTTA LIVE IT UP, RIGHT?
OKAY, LEMME PULL UP YOUR ACCOUNT...
psst.
WHAT'RE YOU NEEDING THAT BRUSH FOR, SPARKLES?
Oh, uh, J-JUST FOR, YOU KNOW, KEEPING CLEAN, AN'--
SAVE IT, MATE. YOU AIN'T GOT NO SCALES.
ALL YOU SEIJIN ARE BUYIN' 'EM UP.
SEEMS SOME-ONE FIGURED OUT YOU COULD MELT A BEAM-BLADE IN THERE, TURN IT INTO A SHIV.
NOW, I DUNNO WHO YOU LOT ARE ALL SET TO HIT, BUT...
I DO KNOW WHEN FOLKS NEED WEAPONS. THAT AIN'T HARD.
SOUNDS LIKE YOU NEED ONE, TOO.
SO, ON THE DEEP, WHO IS IT?
ONE A' THEM WOO-WOOS OVER AT THE RELIGIOUS REVIVAL TODAY?
MAYBE THAT HANDSY GUARD?
'CAUSE THE AMOUNT A' THEM BRUSHES THAT GOT BOUGHT, WHEW!

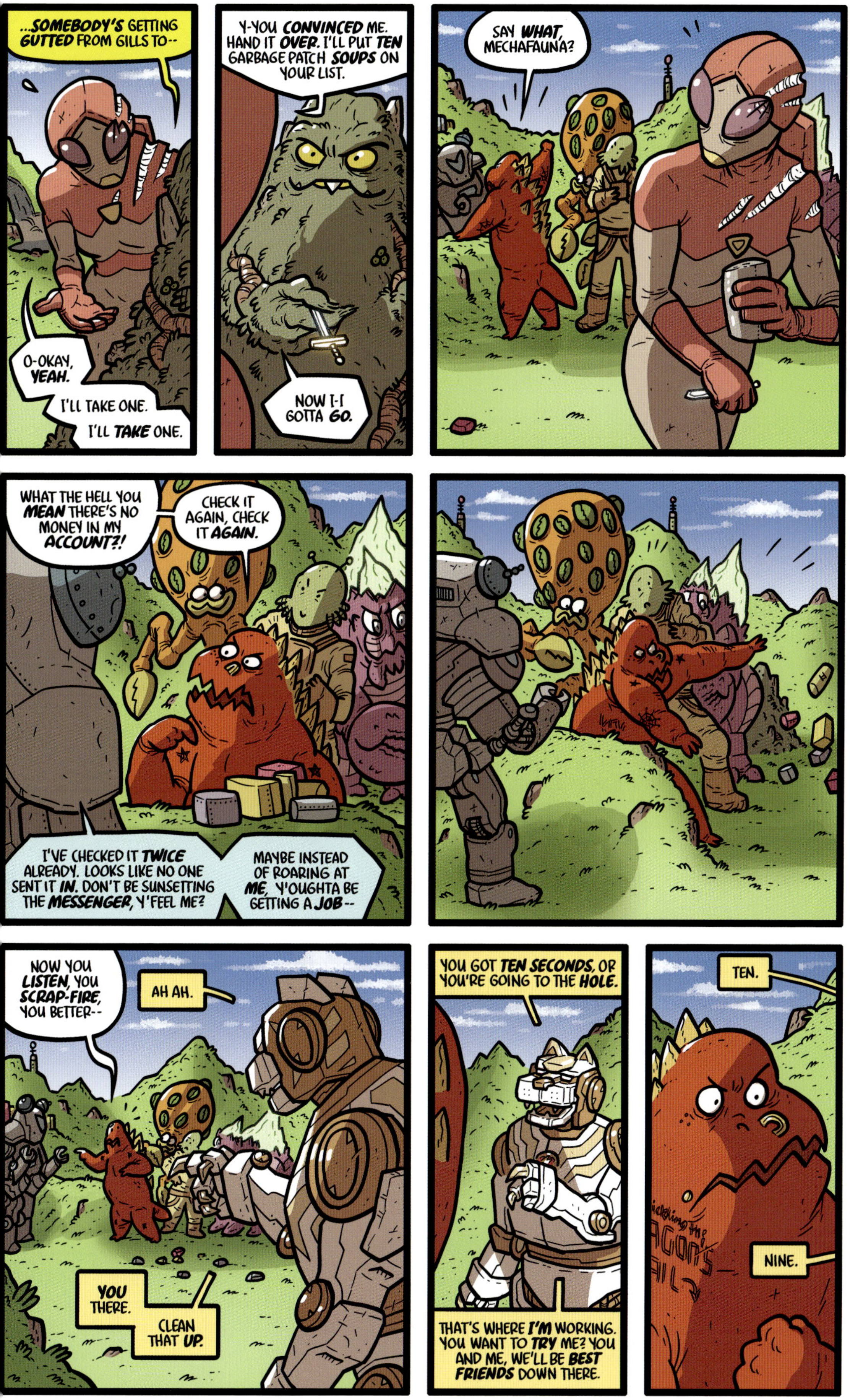
...SOMEBODY'S GETTING GUTTED FROM GILLS TO--
O-OKAY, YEAH.
I'LL TAKE ONE.
I'LL TAKE ONE.
Y-YOU CONVINCED ME. HAND IT OVER. I'LL PUT TEN GARBAGE PATCH SOUPS ON YOUR LIST.
NOW I-I GOTTA GO.
SAY WHAT, MECHAFAUNA?
WHAT THE HELL YOU MEAN THERE'S NO MONEY IN MY ACCOUNT?!
CHECK IT AGAIN, CHECK IT AGAIN.
I'VE CHECKED IT TWICE ALREADY. LOOKS LIKE NO ONE SENT IT IN. DON'T BE SUNSETTING THE MESSENGER, Y'FEEL ME?
MAYBE INSTEAD OF ROARING AT ME, Y'OUGHTA BE GETTING A JOB--
NOW YOU LISTEN, YOU SCRAP-FIRE, YOU BETTER--
AH AH.
YOU THERE.
CLEAN THAT UP.
YOU GOT TEN SECONDS, OR YOU'RE GOING TO THE HOLE.
THAT'S WHERE I'M WORKING. YOU WANT TO TRY ME? YOU AND ME, WE'LL BE BEST FRIENDS DOWN THERE.
TEN.
NINE.

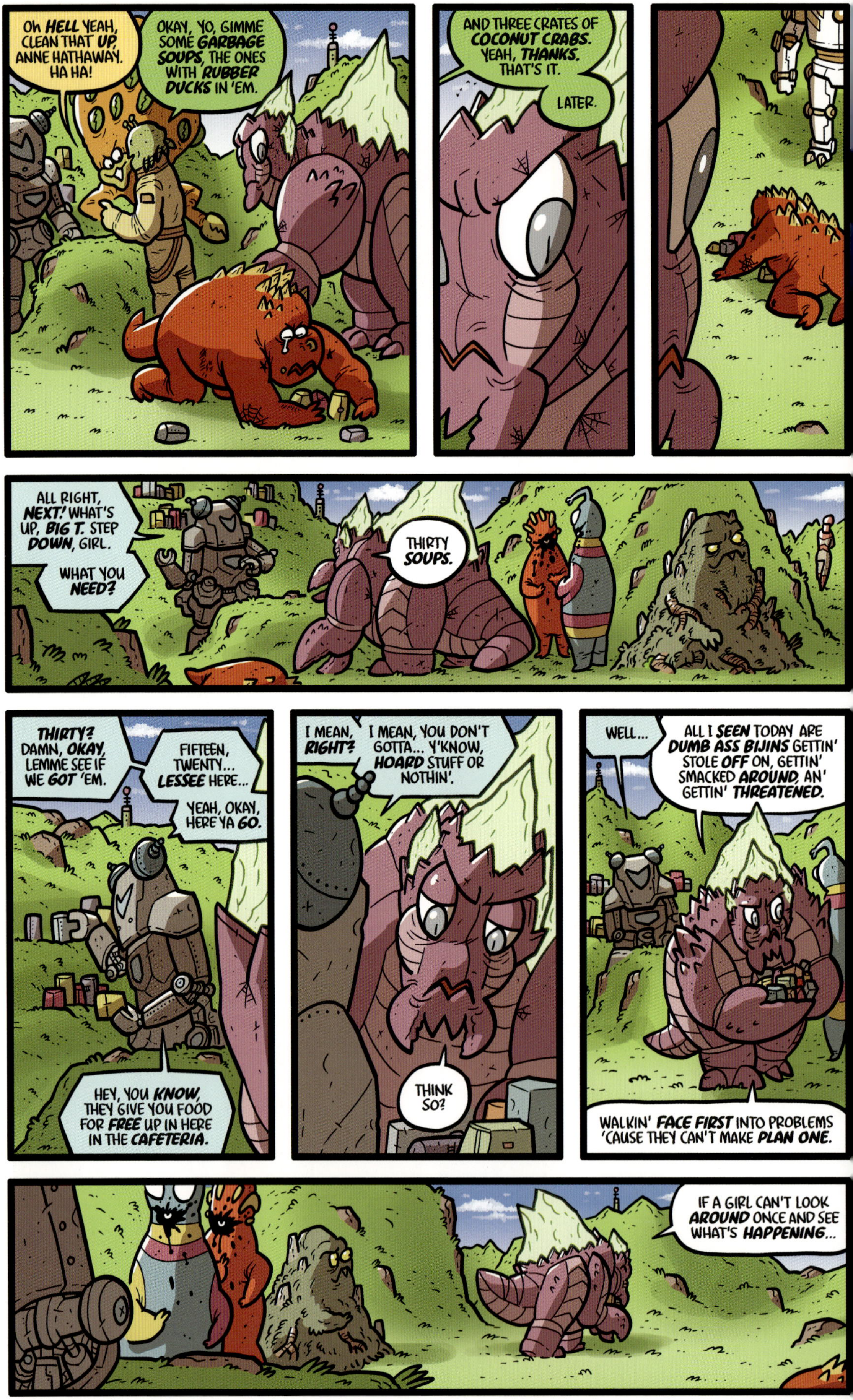
Oh HELL YEAH, CLEAN THAT UP, ANNE HATHAWAY. HA HA!
OKAY, YO, GIMME SOME GARBAGE SOUPS, THE ONES WITH RUBBER DUCKS IN 'EM.
AND THREE CRATES OF COCONUT CRABS. YEAH, THANKS. THAT'S IT.
LATER.
ALL RIGHT, NEXT! WHAT'S UP, BIG T. STEP DOWN, GIRL.
WHAT YOU NEED?
THIRTY SOUPS.
THIRTY? DAMN, OKAY, LEMME SEE IF WE GOT 'EM.
FIFTEEN, TWENTY... LESSEE HERE...
YEAH, OKAY, HERE YA GO.
HEY, YOU KNOW, THEY GIVE YOU FOOD FOR FREE UP IN HERE IN THE CAFETERIA.
I MEAN, RIGHT?
I MEAN, YOU DON'T GOTTA... Y'KNOW, HOARD STUFF OR NOTHIN'.
THINK SO?
WELL...
ALL I SEEN TODAY ARE DUMB ASS BIJINS GETTIN' STOLE OFF ON, GETTIN' SMACKED AROUND, AN' GETTIN' THREATENED.
WALKIN' FACE FIRST INTO PROBLEMS 'CAUSE THEY CAN'T MAKE PLAN ONE.
IF A GIRL CAN'T LOOK AROUND ONCE AND SEE WHAT'S HAPPENING...

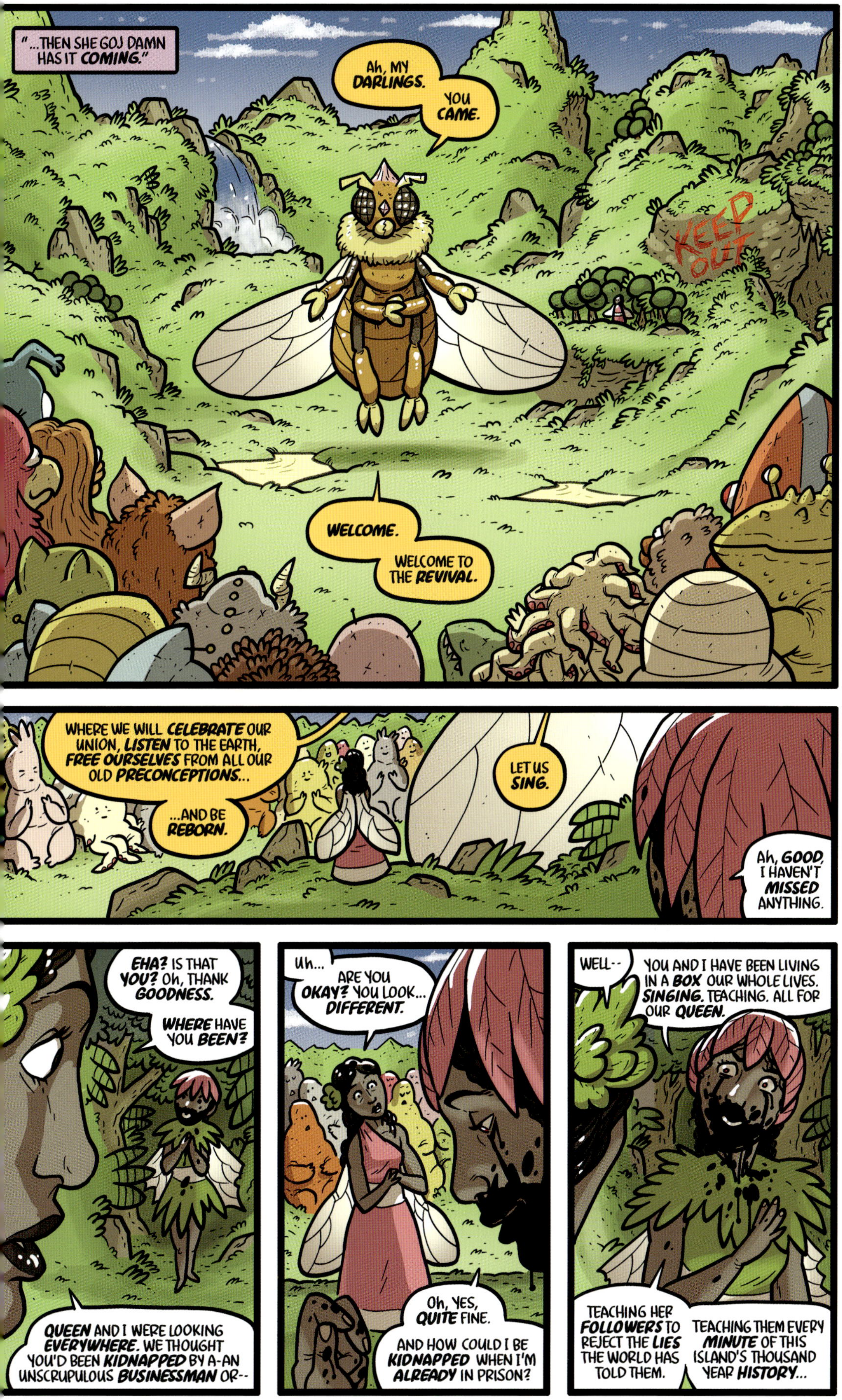
"...THEN SHE GOJ DAMN HAS IT COMING."
Ah, MY DARLINGS.
YOU CAME.
KEEP OUT
WELCOME.
WELCOME TO THE REVIVAL.
WHERE WE WILL CELEBRATE OUR UNION, LISTEN TO THE EARTH, FREE OURSELVES FROM ALL OUR OLD PRECONCEPTIONS...
...AND BE REBORN.
LET US SING.
Ah, GOOD, I HAVEN'T MISSED ANYTHING.
EHA? IS THAT YOU? Oh, THANK GOODNESS.
WHERE HAVE YOU BEEN?
QUEEN AND I WERE LOOKING EVERYWHERE. WE THOUGHT YOU'D BEEN KIDNAPPED BY A-AN UNSCRUPULOUS BUSINESSMAN OR--
Uh...
ARE YOU OKAY? YOU LOOK... DIFFERENT.
Oh, YES, QUITE FINE.
AND HOW COULD I BE KIDNAPPED WHEN I'M ALREADY IN PRISON?
WELL--
YOU AND I HAVE BEEN LIVING IN A BOX OUR WHOLE LIVES. SINGING. TEACHING. ALL FOR OUR QUEEN.
TEACHING HER FOLLOWERS TO REJECT THE LIES THE WORLD HAS TOLD THEM.
TEACHING THEM EVERY MINUTE OF THIS ISLAND'S THOUSAND YEAR HISTORY...

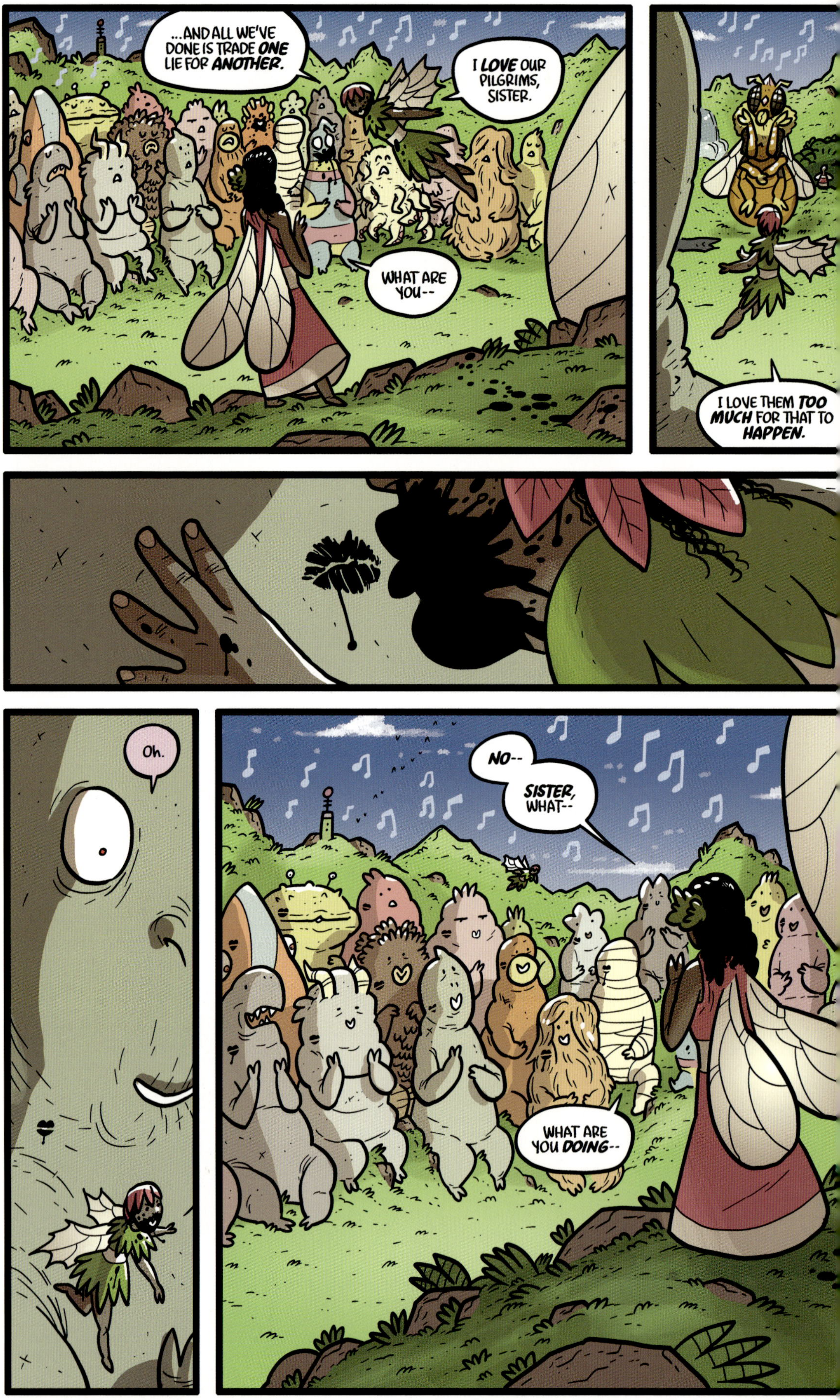
...AND ALL WE'VE DONE IS TRADE ONE LIE FOR ANOTHER.
I LOVE OUR PILGRIMS, SISTER.
WHAT ARE YOU--
I LOVE THEM TOO MUCH FOR THAT TO HAPPEN.
Oh.
NO--
SISTER, WHAT--
WHAT ARE YOU DOING--

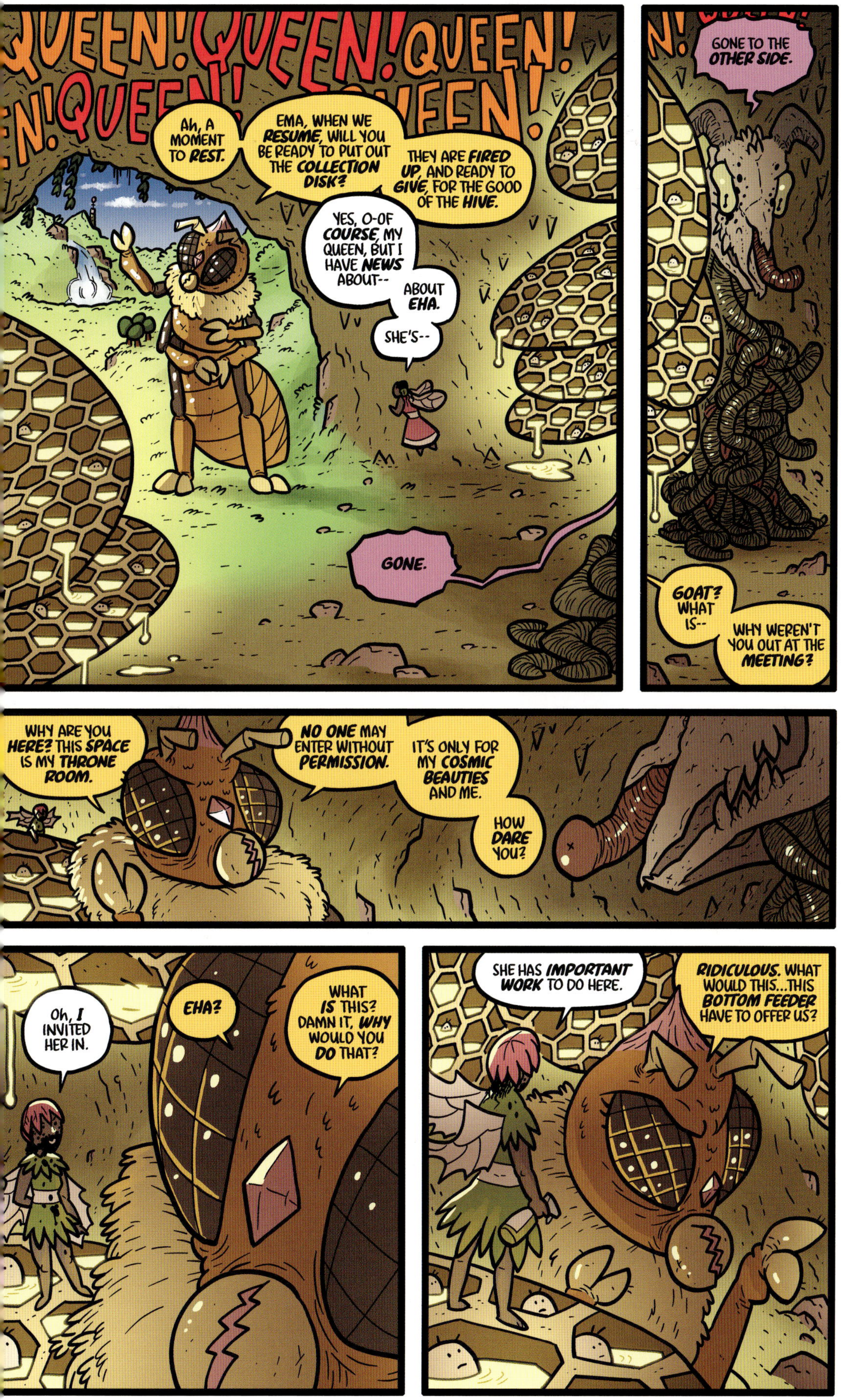
QUEEN! QUEEN! QUEEN!
Ah, A MOMENT TO REST.
EMA, WHEN WE RESUME, WILL YOU BE READY TO PUT OUT THE COLLECTION DISK?
THEY ARE FIRED UP, AND READY TO GIVE, FOR THE GOOD OF THE HIVE.
YES, O-OF COURSE, MY QUEEN, BUT I HAVE NEWS ABOUT--
ABOUT EHA.
SHE'S--
GONE.
GONE TO THE OTHER SIDE.
GOAT? WHAT IS--
WHY WEREN'T YOU OUT AT THE MEETING?
WHY ARE YOU HERE? THIS SPACE IS MY THRONE ROOM.
NO ONE MAY ENTER WITHOUT PERMISSION.
IT'S ONLY FOR MY COSMIC BEAUTIES AND ME.
HOW DARE YOU?
Oh, I INVITED HER IN.
EHA?
WHAT IS THIS? DAMN IT, WHY WOULD YOU DO THAT?
SHE HAS IMPORTANT WORK TO DO HERE.
RIDICULOUS. WHAT WOULD THIS...THIS BOTTOM FEEDER HAVE TO OFFER US?

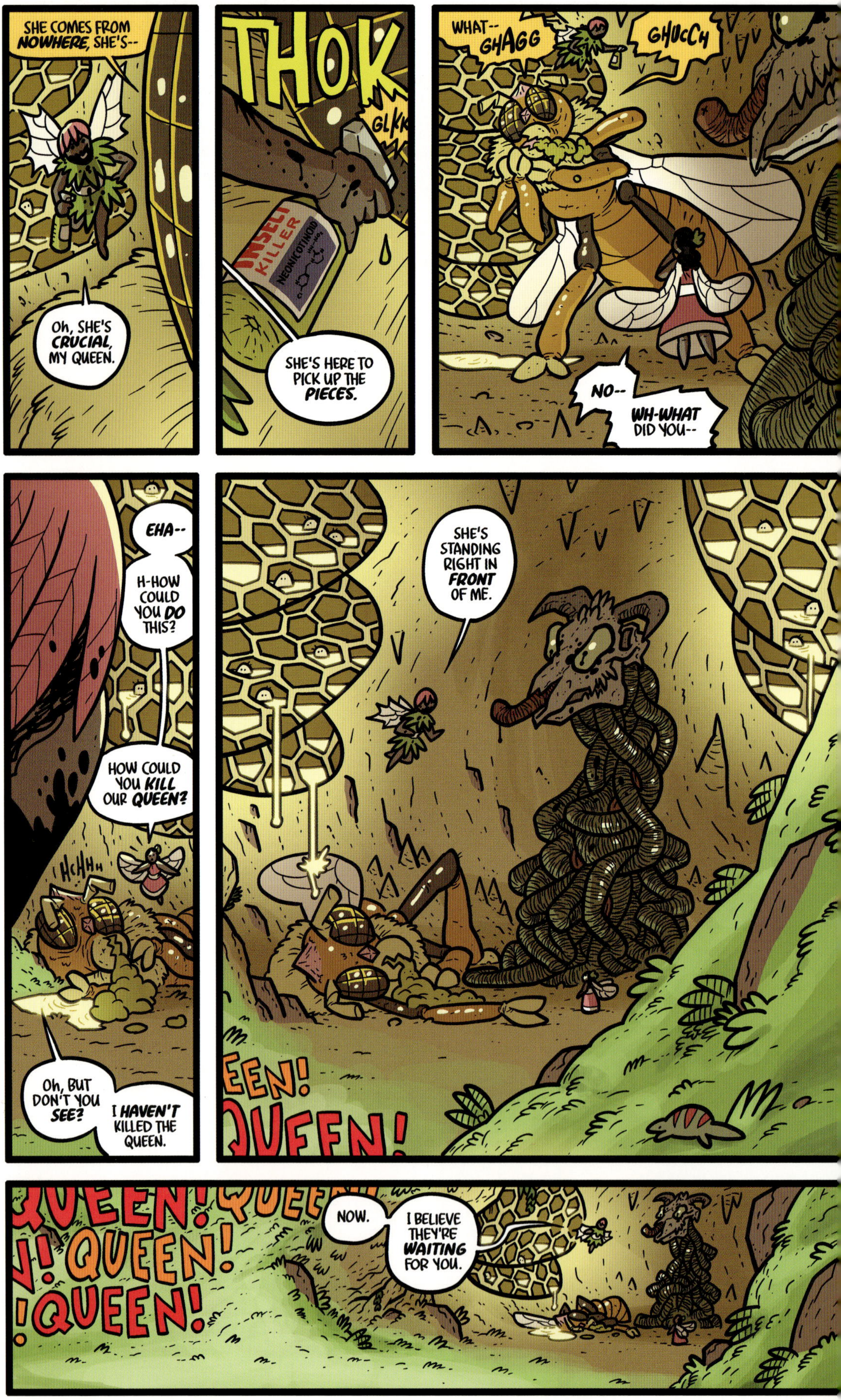

SHE COMES FROM **NOWHERE**, SHE'S--
Oh, SHE'S **CRUCIAL**, MY QUEEN.
THOK
GLKK
KILLER
NEONICOTINOID
SHE'S HERE TO PICK UP THE **PIECES.**
WHAT--
GHAGG
GHUCCH
NO--
WH-WHAT DID YOU--
EHA--
H-HOW COULD YOU **DO** THIS?
HOW COULD YOU **KILL** OUR **QUEEN?**
HCHHH
Oh, BUT DON'T YOU **SEE?**
I **HAVEN'T** KILLED THE QUEEN.
SHE'S STANDING RIGHT IN **FRONT** OF ME.
EEN!
QUEEN!
QUEEN!
QUEEN!
QUEEN!
NOW.
I BELIEVE THEY'RE **WAITING** FOR YOU.

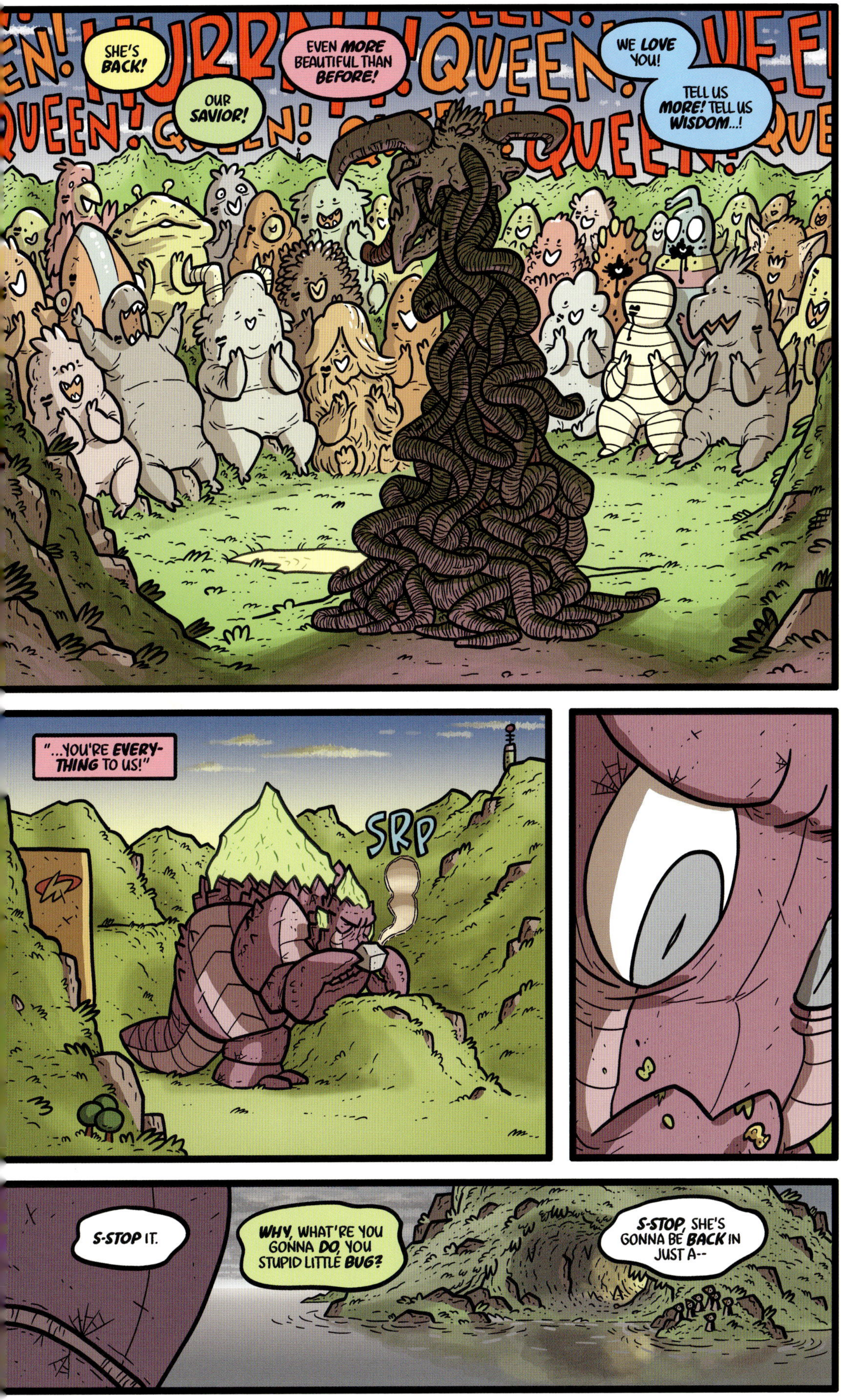
QUEEN!
SHE'S **BACK!**
OUR SAVIOR!
EVEN **MORE** BEAUTIFUL THAN **BEFORE!**
QUEEN!
WE **LOVE** YOU!
TELL US **MORE!** TELL US **WISDOM**...!
QUEEN!
"...YOU'RE **EVERY-THING** TO US!"
SRP
S-STOP IT.
WHY, WHAT'RE YOU GONNA **DO,** YOU STUPID LITTLE **BUG?**
S-STOP, SHE'S GONNA BE **BACK** IN JUST A--

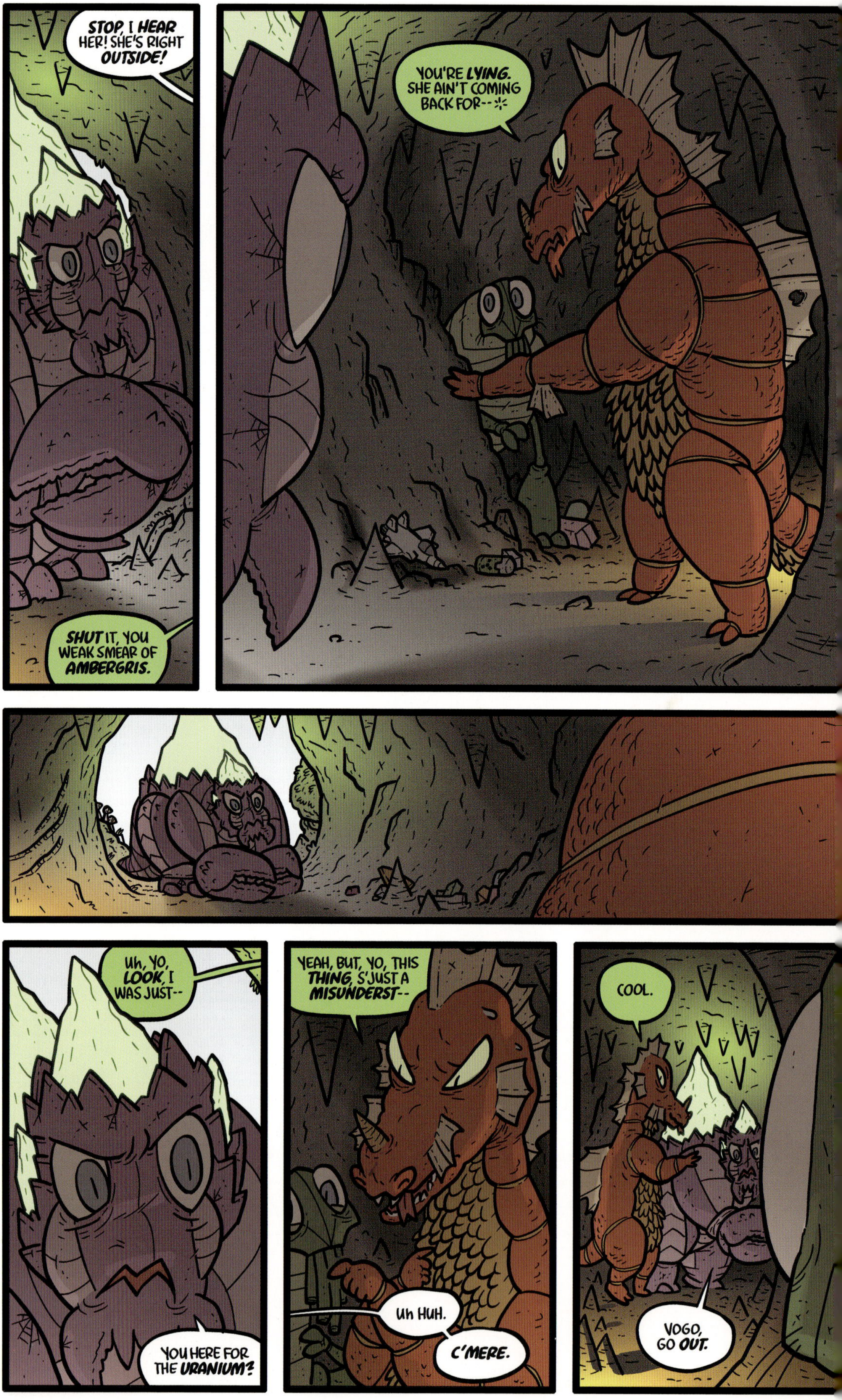
STOP, I HEAR HER! SHE'S RIGHT OUTSIDE!
SHUT IT, YOU WEAK SMEAR OF AMBERGRIS.
YOU'RE LYING. SHE AIN'T COMING BACK FOR--
UH, YO, LOOK, I WAS JUST--
YOU HERE FOR THE URANIUM?
YEAH, BUT, YO, THIS THING, S'JUST A MISUNDERST--
UH HUH.
C'MERE.
COOL.
VOGO, GO OUT.

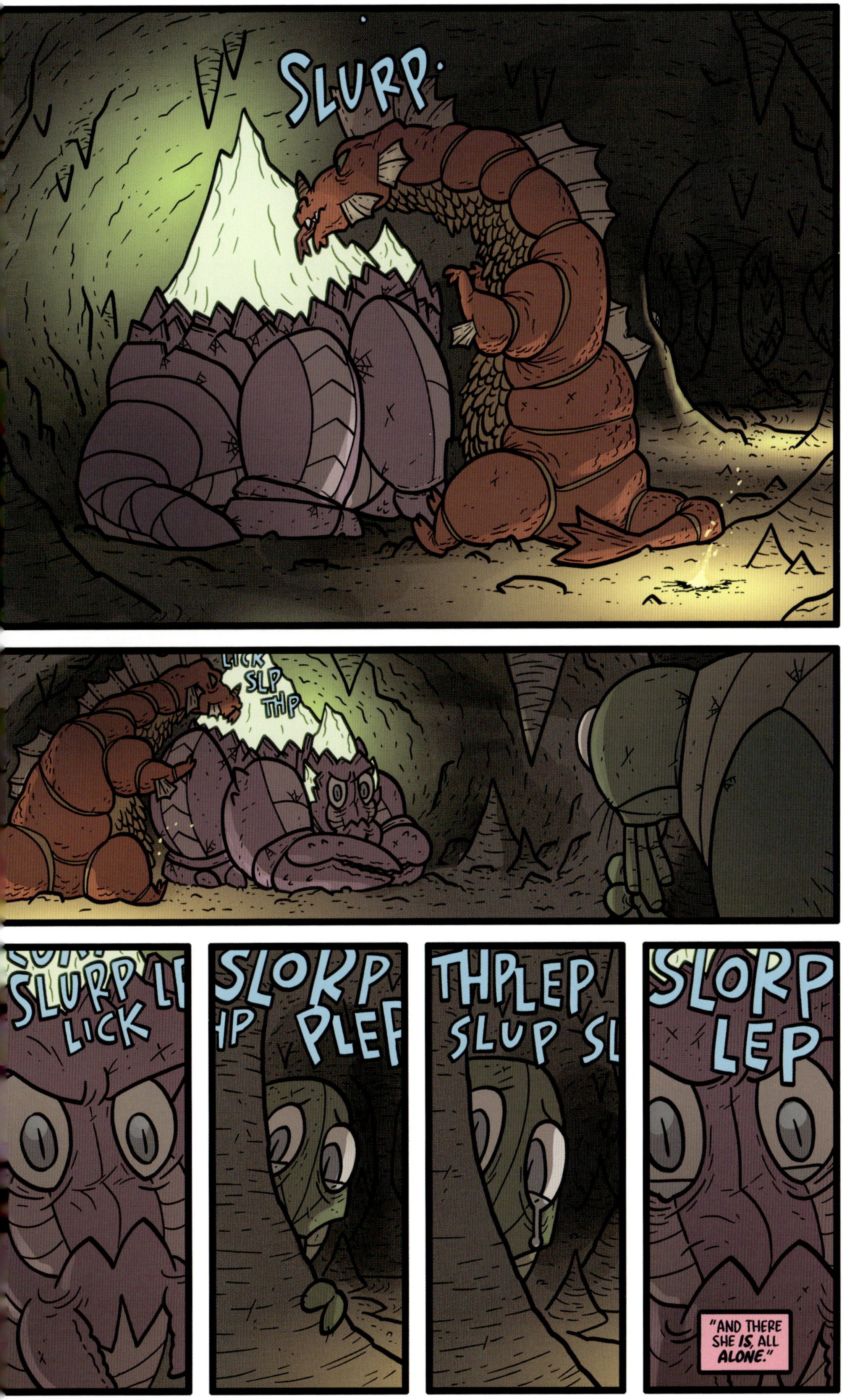
SLURP
LICK
SLP
THP
SLURP
LICK
SLORP
HP
PLEP
THPLEP
SLUP
SLORP
LEP
"AND THERE SHE *IS*, ALL *ALONE*."

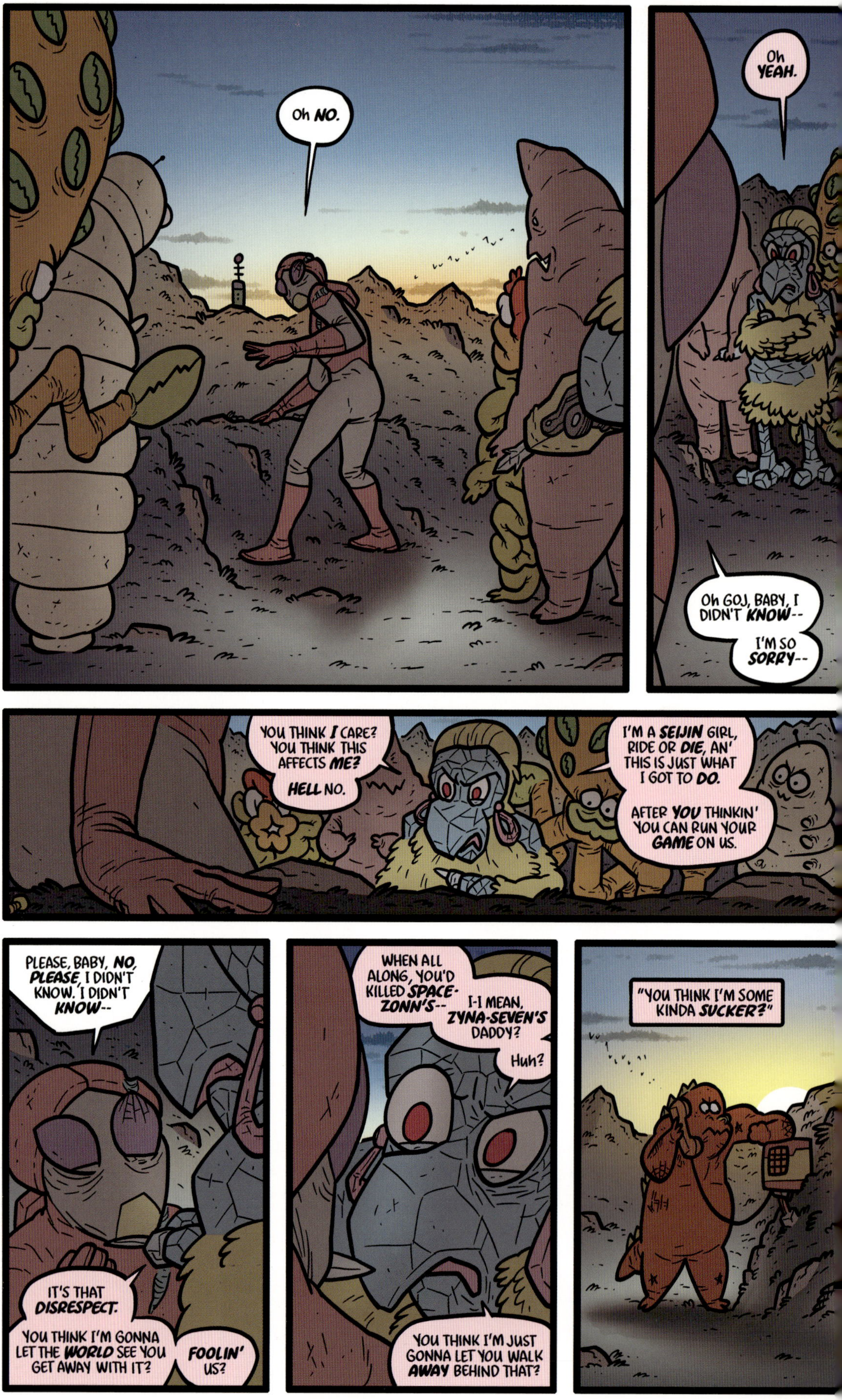
Oh NO.
Oh YEAH.
Oh GOJ, BABY, I DIDN'T KNOW--
I'M SO SORRY--
YOU THINK I CARE? YOU THINK THIS AFFECTS ME?
HELL NO.
I'M A SEIJIN GIRL, RIDE OR DIE, AN' THIS IS JUST WHAT I GOT TO DO.
AFTER YOU THINKIN' YOU CAN RUN YOUR GAME ON US.
PLEASE, BABY, NO, PLEASE, I DIDN'T KNOW. I DIDN'T KNOW--
IT'S THAT DISRESPECT.
YOU THINK I'M GONNA LET THE WORLD SEE YOU GET AWAY WITH IT?
FOOLIN' US?
WHEN ALL ALONG, YOU'D KILLED SPACE-ZONN'S--
I-I MEAN, ZYNA-SEVEN'S DADDY?
Huh?
YOU THINK I'M JUST GONNA LET YOU WALK AWAY BEHIND THAT?
"YOU THINK I'M SOME KINDA SUCKER?"

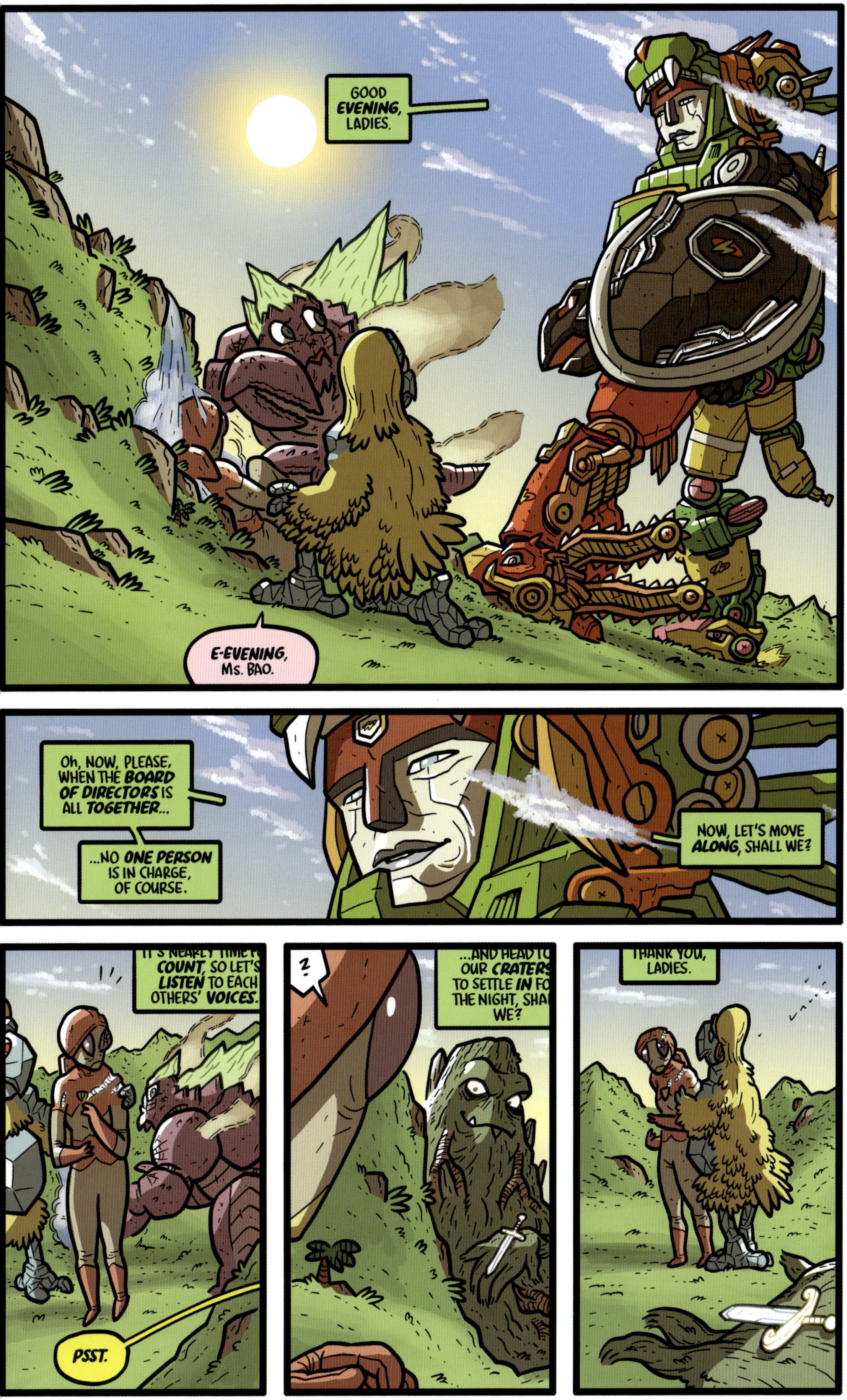

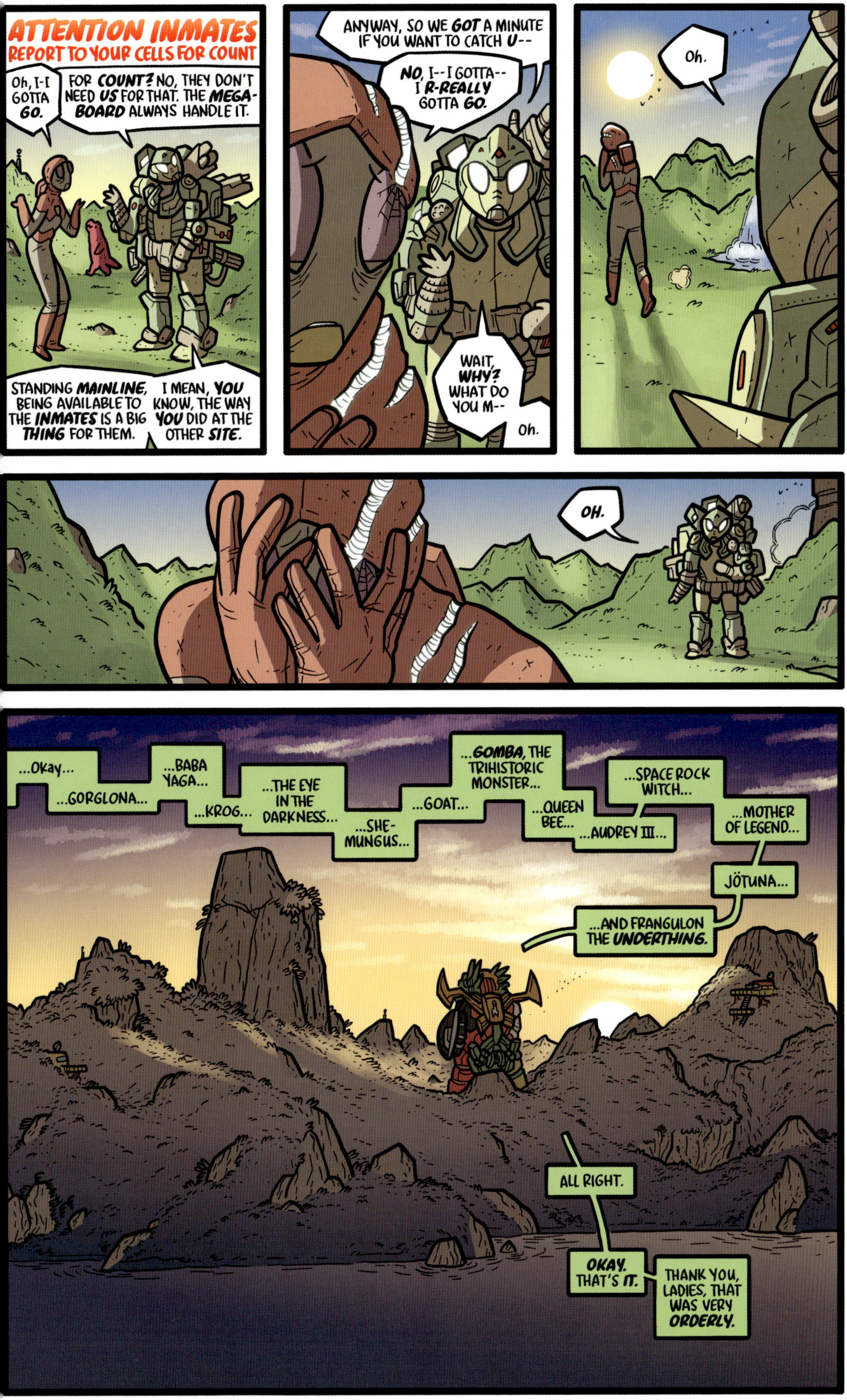

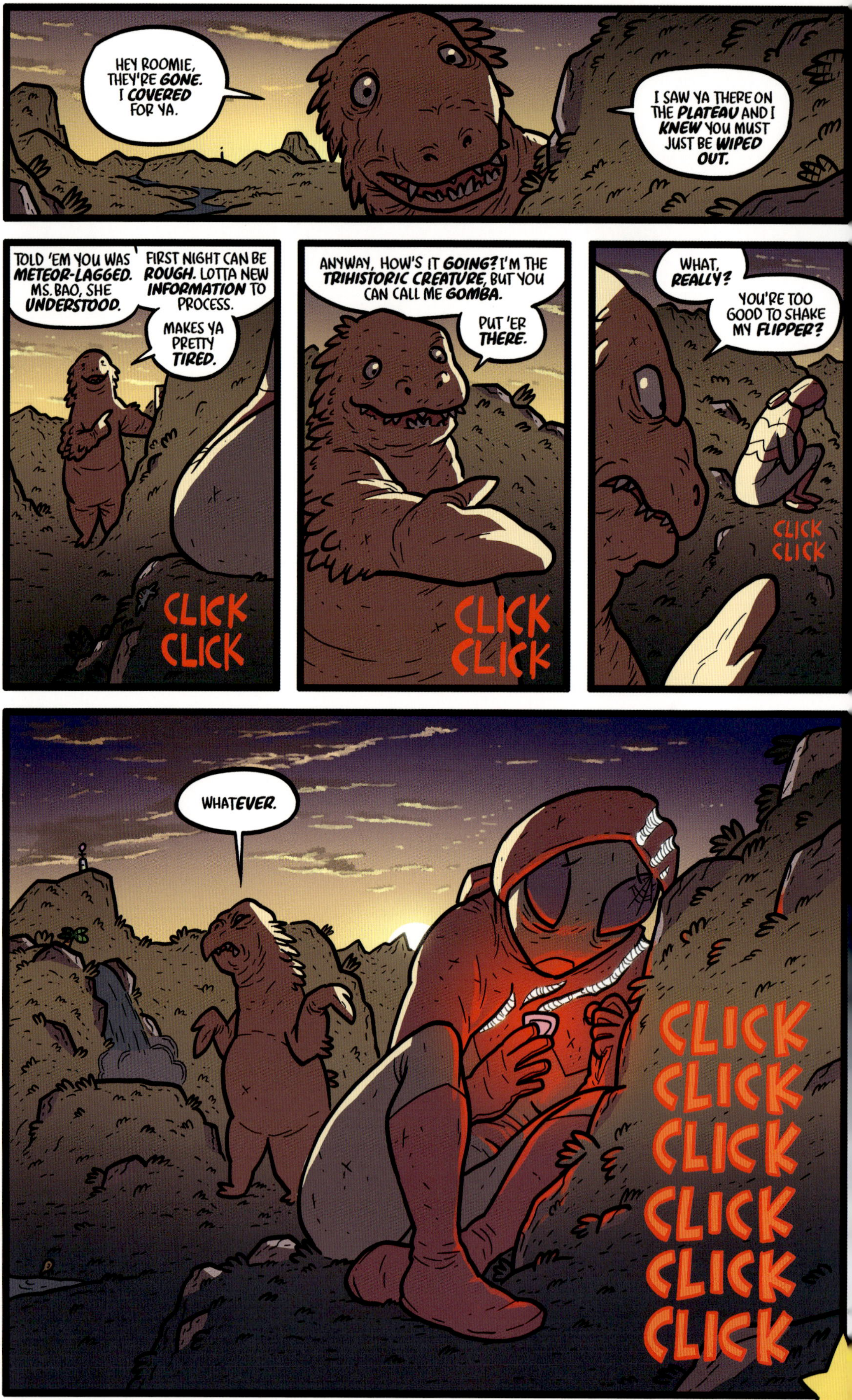

怪獣マックス

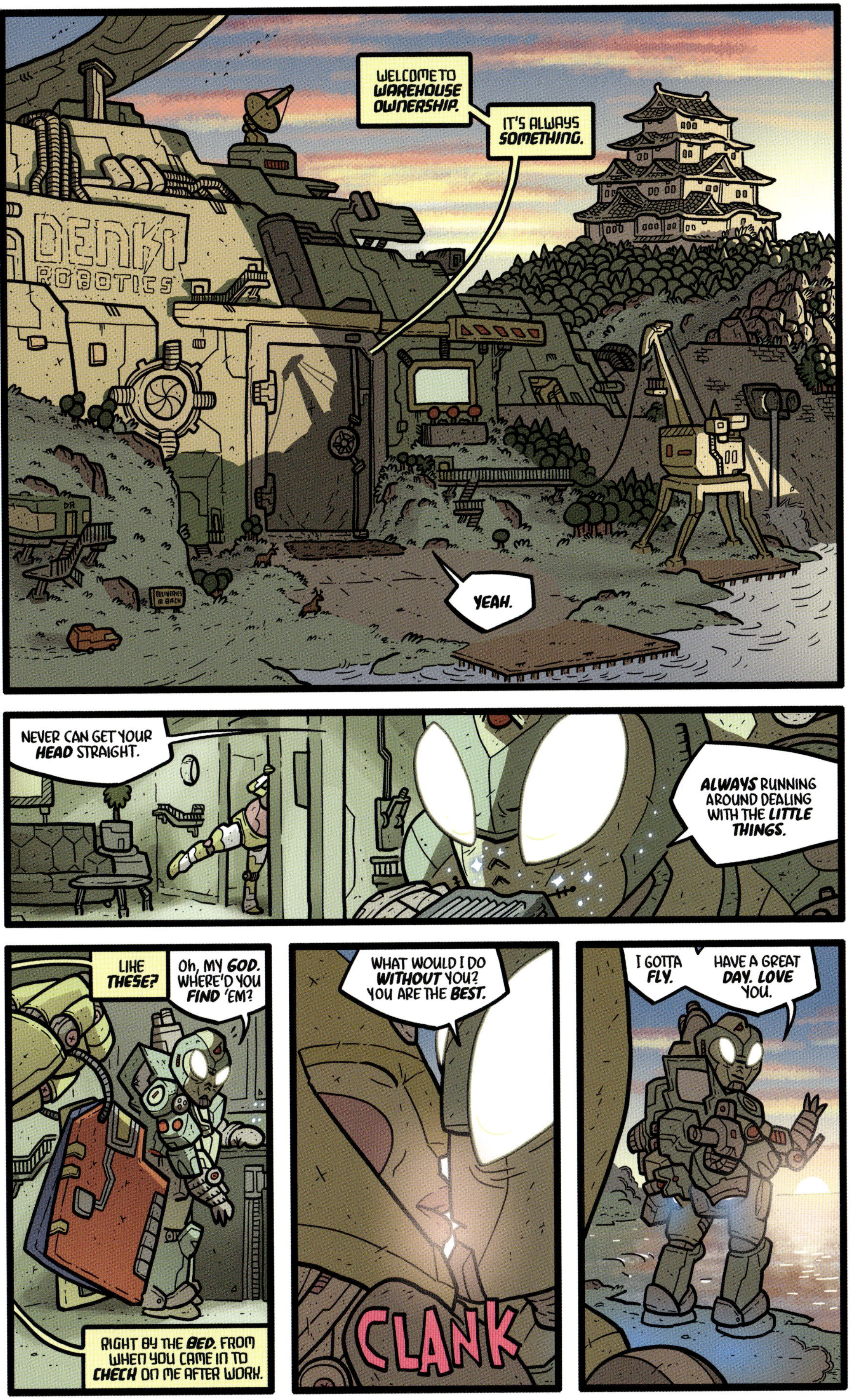

the BIG THINGS

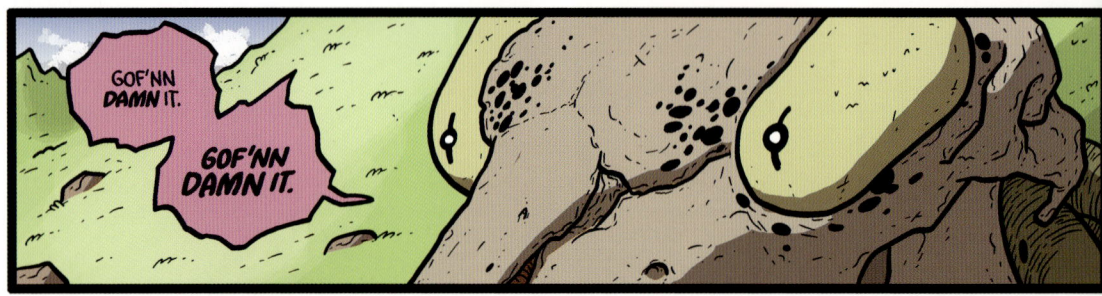

怪獣マックス

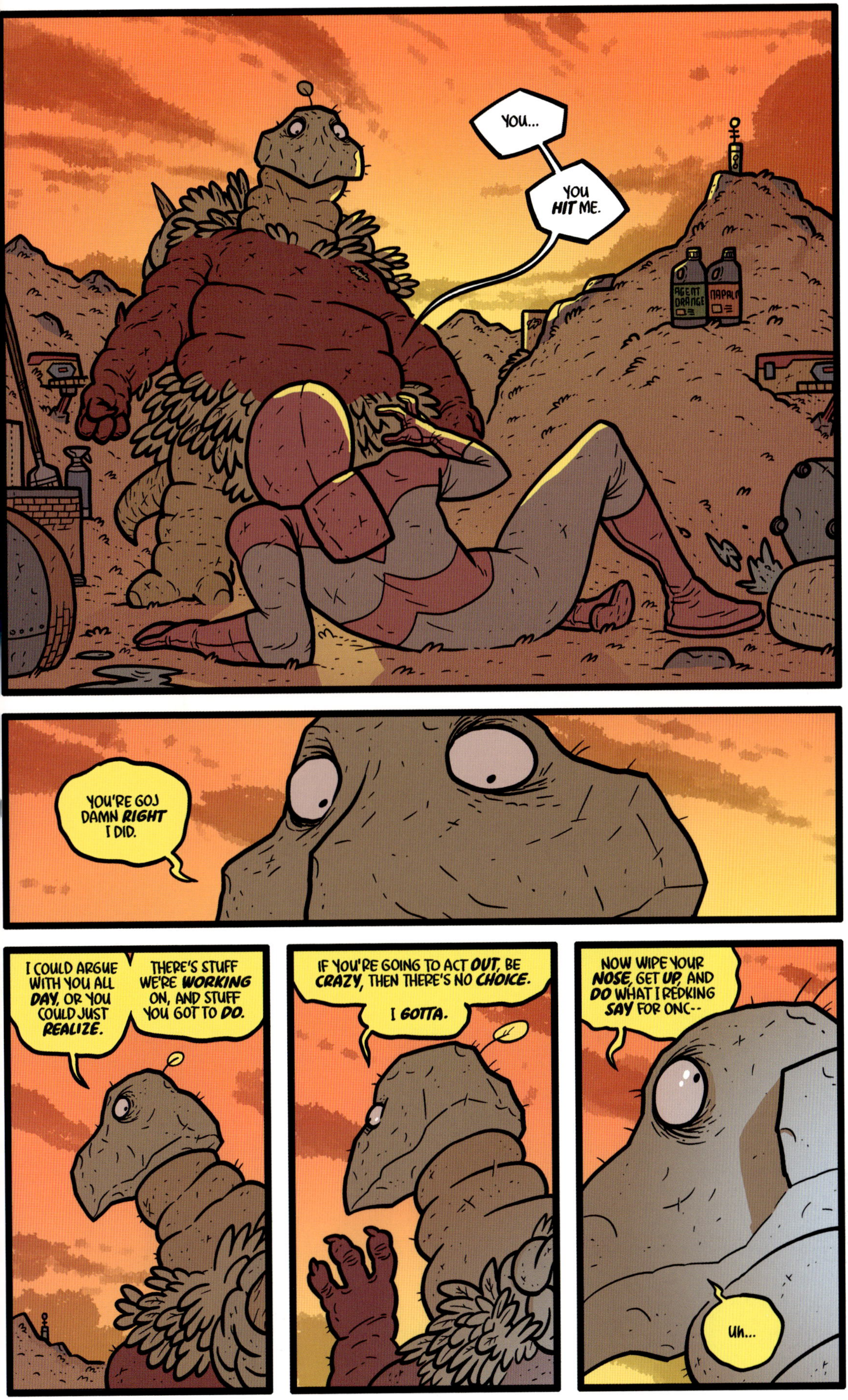

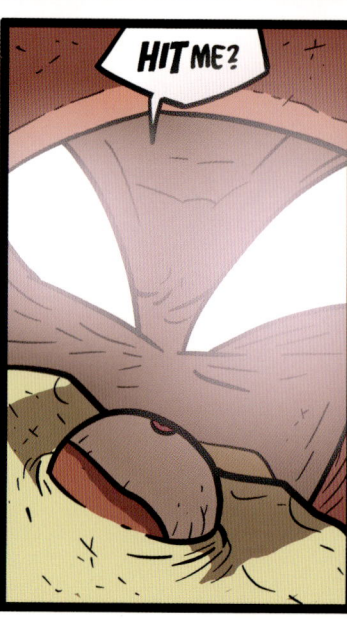

ONE FALSE MOVE

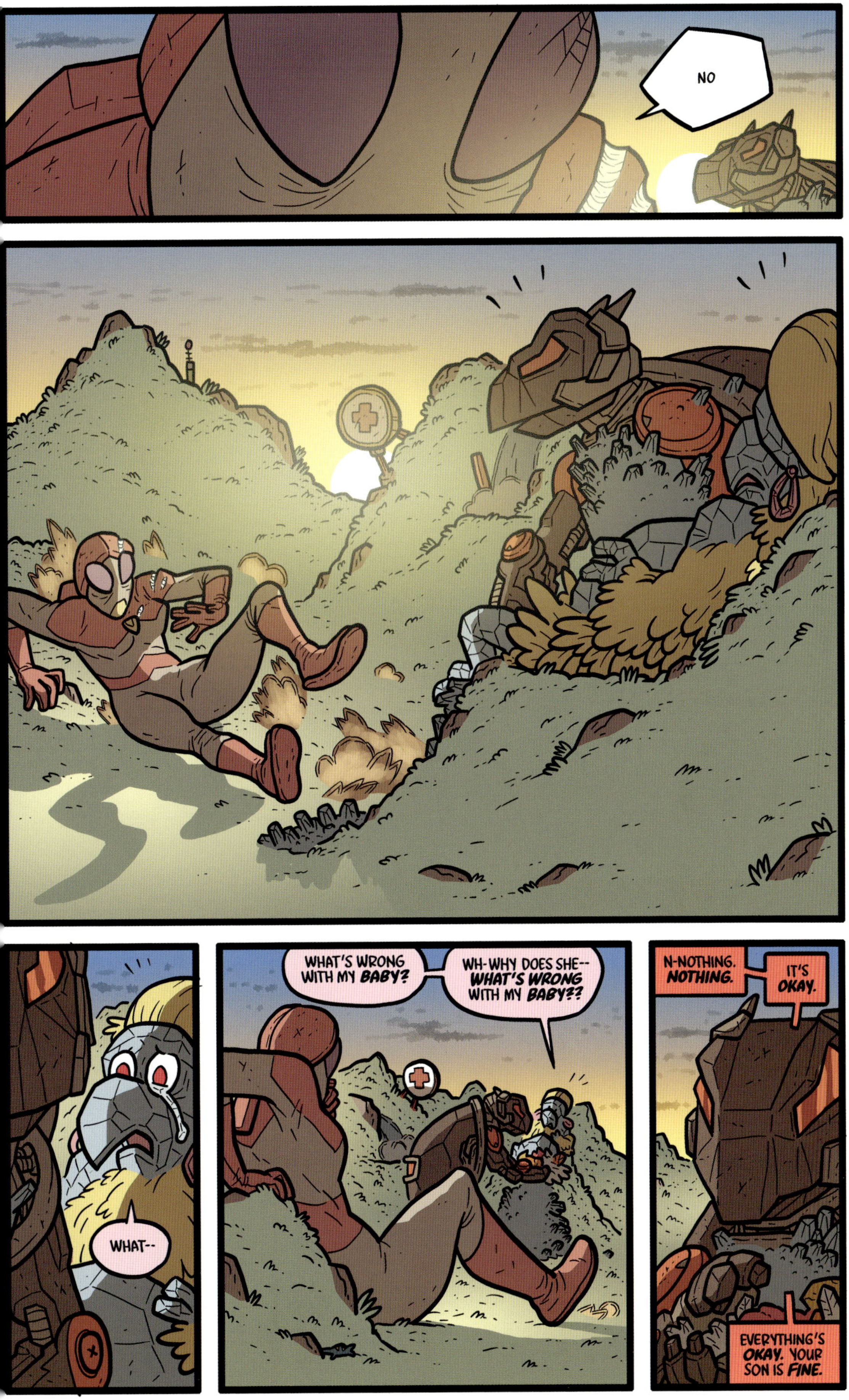

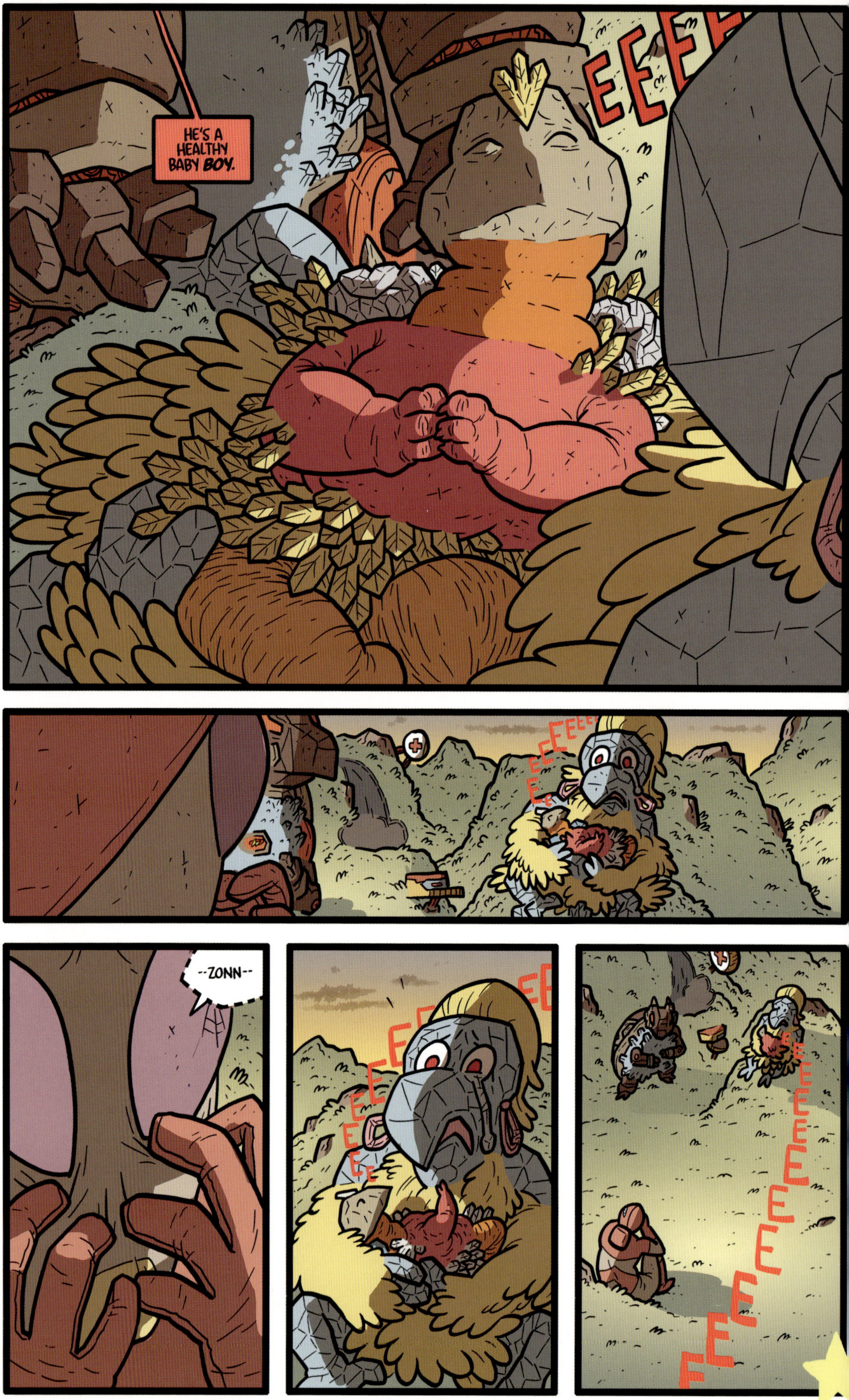
EEEE
HE'S A HEALTHY BABY BOY.
EEEEEEE
--ZONN--
EEEEEEE
EEEEEEEEEEEE

怪獣マックス

WHAT YOU GOTTA DO

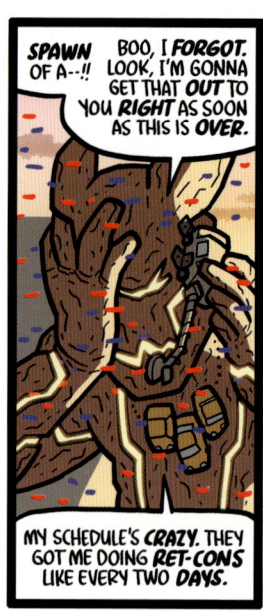

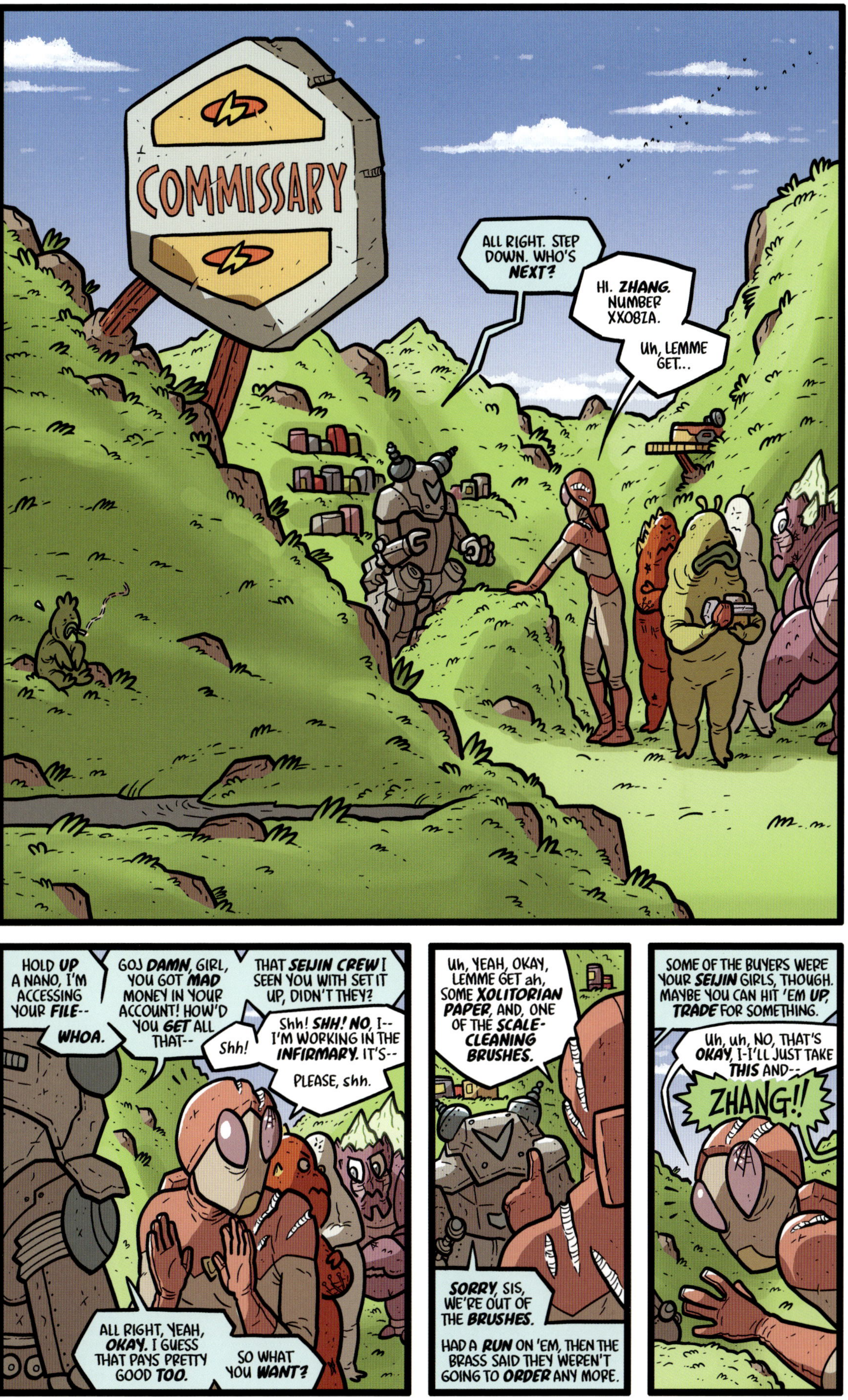
COMMISSARY
ALL RIGHT. STEP DOWN. WHO'S NEXT?
HI. ZHANG. NUMBER XX08ZA.
Uh, LEMME GET...
HOLD UP A NANO, I'M ACCESSING YOUR FILE--
WHOA.
GOJ DAMN, GIRL, YOU GOT MAD MONEY IN YOUR ACCOUNT! HOW'D YOU GET ALL THAT--
THAT SEIJIN CREW I SEEN YOU WITH SET IT UP, DIDN'T THEY?
Shh!
Shh! SHH! NO, I-- I'M WORKING IN THE INFIRMARY. IT'S--
PLEASE, shh.
ALL RIGHT, YEAH, OKAY. I GUESS THAT PAYS PRETTY GOOD TOO.
SO WHAT YOU WANT?
Uh, YEAH, OKAY, LEMME GET ah, SOME XOLITORIAN PAPER, AND, ONE OF THE SCALE-CLEANING BRUSHES.
SORRY, SIS, WE'RE OUT OF THE BRUSHES.
HAD A RUN ON 'EM, THEN THE BRASS SAID THEY WEREN'T GOING TO ORDER ANY MORE.
SOME OF THE BUYERS WERE YOUR SEIJIN GIRLS, THOUGH. MAYBE YOU CAN HIT 'EM UP, TRADE FOR SOMETHING.
Uh, uh, NO, THAT'S OKAY, I-I'LL JUST TAKE THIS AND--
ZHANG!!

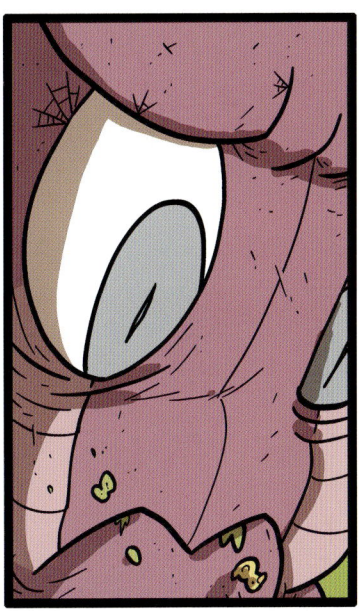

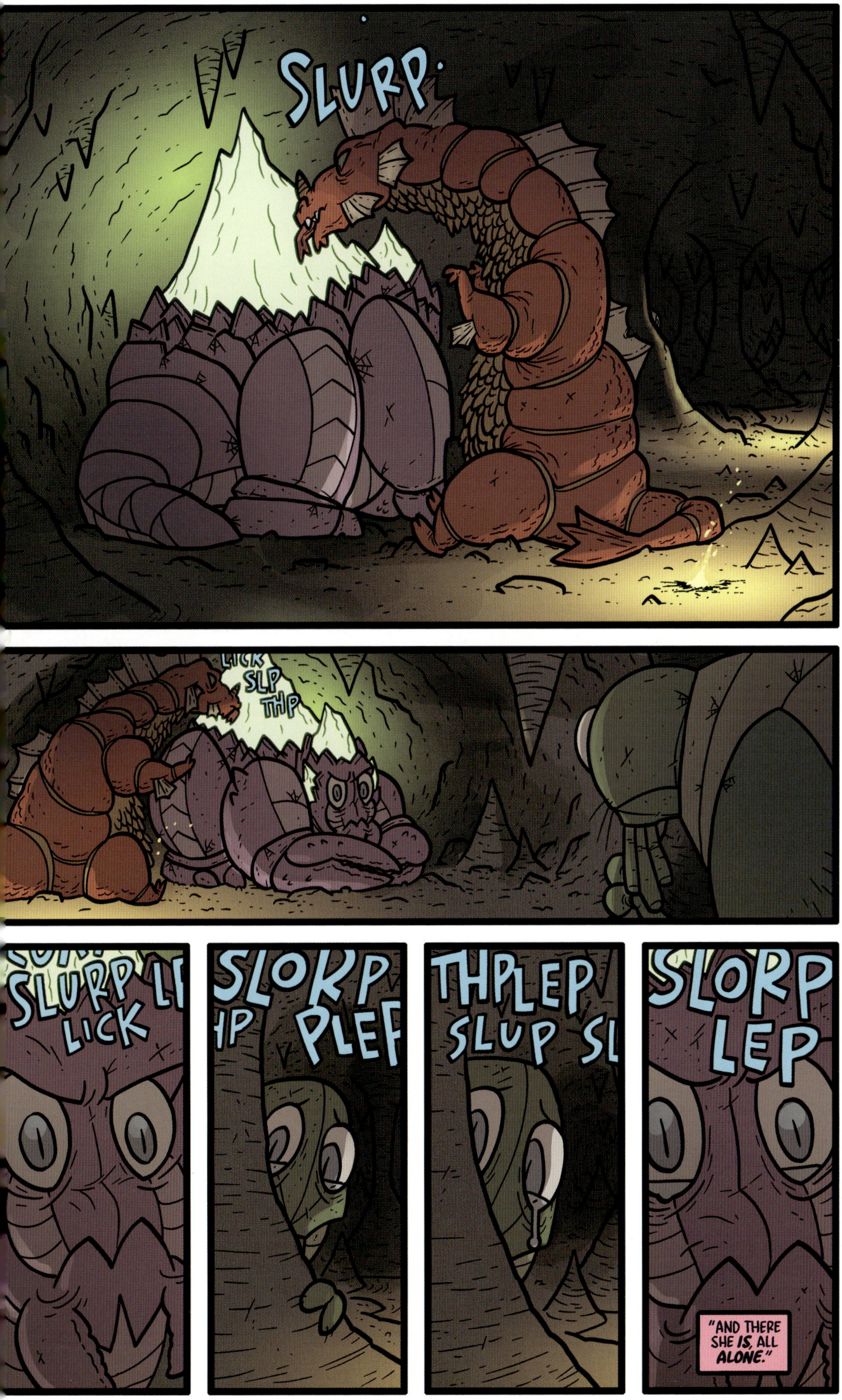
SLURP
LICK
SLP
THP
SLURP
LICK
SLORP
THPLEP
SLUP
SLORP
LEP
"AND THERE SHE *IS*, ALL *ALONE*."